TUGGA'S
MOB

Stephen Johnson

Clan Destine
PRESS

First published by Clan Destine Press in 2019

PO Box 121, Bittern
Victoria 3918 Australia

National Library of Australia Cataloguing-In-Publication data:

Johnson, Stephen

TUGGA'S MOB

ISBN: 978-0-6485567-7-0 (paperback)

      978-0-6485567-8-7 (eBook)

Cover Design © Willsin Rowe

Design & Typesetting: Clan Destine Press

www.clandestinepress.net

To my Cath
and our daughters
Rachael, Michelle and Natasha.

June 1 1986

Day One: *Judy Williams, from Waikato, New Zealand, is now officially in London. God, what a flight getting here: delays in Sydney and then Singapore, but we weren't allowed to leave the airport. Such a long haul from Auckland to Heathrow, but it's worth it to be in what I've always considered the coolest city in the world. There are millions of cars, people, and houses and the city noise is incredible. It's close to how I imagined it would be. All those English magazines and movies I've spent a fortune on over the past 10 years have prepared me well.*

No problems at Heathrow. My work visa was hunky dory for a friendly immigration officer, then it was off to find the Piccadilly Line to Earl's Court.

Smart girl, I followed the other backpackers who led me straight to the Tube. The energy in central London is amazing, so different from Te Awamutu where nothing happens outside the rugby season. There's nothing for Mum and Dad to worry about. I feel safer here than in Hamilton; there's a safety in numbers. Bizarre thinking? Maybe, but I'm surprised at how comfortable I am in one of the world's busiest cities a few days after leaving the farm.

It was disappointing Charlotte had to cancel her ticket at the last minute because of her mother's illness. Family comes first, always, but it's good not to have a chaperone who might inadvertently blab about any shenanigans – especially to Russell. He knew when we met in March how long I've been planning this trip, and how important it is. I'm glad he understands and we'll see what happens with that relationship when I get back to New Zealand.

The hotel in Hogarth Road was a hop, skip and jump from the tube station. It's grotty and there's a shared bathroom down the corridor where you pay 25p for a trickle from the shower. I'm sharing the room with two Aussie girls. They're not bad for Victorians who have never heard of the All Blacks. We're off to an evening session at the nearest pub, The Prince of Teck. It's a few yards up the road and there's no need for a black cab or a double decker bus. They're on tomorrow's must-do list, plus Buckingham Palace, the Tower of London, Big Ben, Camden Town markets and everything else I can squeeze in. I'm sure the Union Jack-waver in the family – Mum – would want me to stay longer to watch the Queen Trooping the Colour, or even hunt for Princess Di at some charity event. But I can't stay, Mum – Europe is calling. Maybe next year.

It feels like the centre of the universe in London with all these different cultures. I thought Earl's Court was supposed to be full of Kiwis, Aussies and South Africans but there are thousands of Arabs, Pakistanis and Indians. The aromas from their cafés and restaurants are tantalising and nothing like the takeaway shops at home. Reckon I'll pack on a few kilos before I even get on the bus on Saturday. Imagine – five days in London, then bonjour Paris?

Judy Williams you are going to have the time of your life!

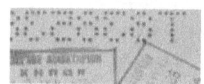

For a 30-year-old trip diary it was in remarkably good condition. The front and back covers were festooned with a montage of entrance tickets and holiday snaps of mid-20s travellers at Europe's most famous landmarks. They appeared to be Aussies and Kiwis judging by their scrappy T-shirts, battered shorts and thongs; or jandals, depending which side of the Tasman Sea they called home. Droopy moustaches were the fashion for the men who lounged on the greenery of the Champ De Mars in front of the Eiffel Tower. Most of the women wore summer dresses that would have seen them refused entry into Notre Dame, the Vatican or a host of other must-see European sights during the 1980s. New Zealanders called it the Big OE – overseas experience. Australians never bothered with such lofty titles for their backpacking days, although their aspirations were the same – to see the world and have fun. It was a rite of passage, a transition from the innocence of a carefree South Pacific adolescence to becoming citizens of the world.

In the pre-digital days of the 1960s, '70s and '80s, when Baby

Boomers swarmed into Europe like a plague of locusts every northern summer, the adventures were recorded on Kodak cameras and in trip diaries, such as the one currently held by shaky hands.

The images had faded slightly, but not nearly as much as might be expected, given the passage of time from the first excited scrawl in London to the latest perusal by the current reader, who wasn't the author. The pages were smudged here and there with fingermarks and the detritus from life on the road; pizza, sausage, calamari, beer, wine and chocolate. Antipodeans were out to taste everything and oft-handled possessions such as diaries would carry lifelong reminders of those tactile experiences.

It appeared though as if few people had read, or even handled, this diary in the years since that great adventure. Had this unique record of a golden summer in a young person's life been hidden away; pushed to the back of a drawer, or dumped at the bottom of a cupboard or trunk, out of sight and out of mind?

Did it contain memories that shouldn't be rekindled?

Chapter 1

The Great Ocean Road curls around coastal crags, twists in and out of gullies and occasionally hides beneath a canopy of Otway Ranges greenery on Victoria's south-west coast. Tugga Tancred couldn't count the number of times his battered utility had travelled the road that is dedicated to Australian soldiers killed during the First World War. Tugga didn't care either. It was black bitumen to him, a link between his weekday work around Geelong and the Bellarine Peninsula, and his second home near Apollo Bay.

Most of Tugga's clients gave him a quizzical look when he told them he was off to the *bach* for the weekend. Tugga was an ex-pat New Zealander and some words never slipped from his vocabulary. He would shrug and explain – his beach house. A nod and half smile was also the standard response from the clients, who no doubt thought their under-the-table cash was going to fund a luxurious palace with floor to ceiling panoramic windows framing Bass Strait in all seasons. The reality wasn't that grand: Tugga's weekender wasn't much better than a shack. The timber walls and corrugated iron roof framed a combined kitchen, bedroom and living area. Heat was provided by a potbelly stove and the long drop toilet was 20 metres from the back door.

It might have been basic, but it was Tugga's haven, and had been for 26 years. He bought the land cheaply in 1990 as the region struggled to climb out of the economic slump brought about by the 1987 stock market crash. Tugga was in the right place at the right time when the elderly land owner needed a few thousand dollars to pay local council bills. *Fuckin' council rates? Do I ever see a fuckin' garbage truck up here? Miserable thievin' bastards.* It was mostly wasted land for the farmer anyway; steeply sloped and tucked into the ranges a few kilometres from town. Tugga didn't tell the old man that he should have looked at *herbal* options.

The privacy was perfect for Tugga with few people venturing up the track to say hello or share his retreat. It left him free to indulge in his favourite pastime: cultivating grass – the smoking kind. He didn't have a big marijuana operation as police helicopters made regular sweeps of the Otway Ranges looking for plantations. Tugga kept his crops small, hiding them in fern-covered gullies. He grew enough to provide weekend bliss and to sell to regular contacts when he was back in Geelong. Victoria's drug laws meant Tugga had to keep his weekend activities discreet, so enjoying a toke but flying below the radar was his approach. Under the radar was also how Tugga liked to run much of his weekday business. Customers willing to pay cash were rewarded with generous discounts. Who cared if the tax man never found out about the backyard transactions? None of his Apollo Bay neighbours had cottoned on either. There had been no evidence of pilfering from his crops in quarter of a century. Tugga always assumed they were growing tonnes of their own dope in the Otways. Most of the surfies were permanently stoned whenever he saw them at the pub.

Tugga also appreciated the irony of his patch of heaven. He was surrounded by gum trees, ferns and other native trees that would never bear the mark of his axe or chainsaw. But he spent his weekdays chopping down trees and grinding up the waste. His business was called TSG – Tugga's Stump Grinding – and he happily charged a hefty price to suburbanites who didn't want to risk a splinter or two when landscaping their gardens.

Regardless of the month or weather, every Friday afternoon found Tugga on the Great Ocean Road heading for his bach. His internal GPS knew every curve, rise and descent of the road all the way to the seaside town with the golden sand. And being a bachelor of great height and expanding girth – even at 54 Tugga still preferred to describe himself as "six foot six of pure muscle and gristle" – his thirst was well known in all the pubs between Geelong and Apollo Bay. His first drink stop was always at Grovedale, originally named Germantown after Lutheran settlers. These days it was part of the urban sprawl of Geelong.

"Just a wee jug for the road," was Tugga's standard request after a hard week turning trees into sawdust. That was his same *rule* at the Torquay, Anglesea, Aireys Inlet and Lorne pubs. Tugga's reasoning was that he sweated the alcohol from his system on the drive between the pubs, that sticking to a jug per pub was just right for a big man. Further proof for Tugga's theory was the fact that he never had an issue on the road in more than two decades of commuting to the bach. How that theory ever survived, and Tugga for that matter, was a mystery as the jug rule was often ignored, usually by the time he reached the official start of the Great Ocean Road at Torquay. The local pub was often buzzing on warm Friday afternoons from spring until late autumn. Bikini-clad girls were a powerful stimulus for Tugga to linger until the babes vacated the beer garden.

It was anyone's guess how much beer Tugga had already consumed by the time he reached the pub at Aireys Inlet, just past eight o'clock on the last Friday in October. It was obvious that he was too pissed to drive and too pissed to be given more alcohol; the pub could lose its licence. That wasn't Tugga's concern as he fumbled through pockets in search of cash, expecting the staff to read his mind. *Beer. Now!*

At a table near the kitchen, duty manager, Davy Allpress, closed his eyes and sighed as he watched Tugga stumble into the bar. 'Ah shit. Here's trouble.'

His companions, 25-year-old twins Roxanna and Sophia from Melbourne, had their backs to the bar.

'What's wrong, Davy? You've gone pale,' Roxanna asked.

'Tugga Tancred's walked in and he's had a skinful. I've got to get rid of him without getting the pub destroyed.'

The women turned to the bar and gasped. Sophia whispered, 'Oh my god! He's a giant, Davy. What are you going to do?'

Allpress stood up. 'Pray – and hope I think of a plan by the time I reach the bar.'

The duty manager knew Tugga well enough to chat about the weather and other innocuous topics. Allpress would avoid the local religion – Aussies Rules football – as Tugga called it "aerial pingpong". Beer was a mutual interest and therefore safer ground for conversation. Tugga claimed to be a connoisseur as he had sampled Europe's best offerings many years before. He wasn't impressed: real ales were overrated and Dutch and German beers were for pansies. Rugby Union was Tugga's real passion. Allpress heard the big fella had broken the nose of a Lorne drinker who dared to call the sport bum-sniffing.

A drunk, two-metre tall ex pat with a reputation for violence when slighted wasn't good for business. Allpress watched his customers shuffle past him towards the beer garden and the rear of the pub. No need to crowd the big fella.

The duty manager believed he had two options to defuse a confrontation: diplomacy or getting physical. Allpress could handle himself in a bar scrap, but giving 20 cm away to Tugga, even when the Kiwi was pissed, wouldn't be a smart move. The gift of the gab that had charmed the Melbourne twins until Tugga's arrival might save him.

There were no other drinkers within cooee of the bar by the time Allpress reached Tugga. 'Jesus, Tugga, are you trying to get us closed down?' Allpress waited just outside of punching range, or so he hoped, while a befuddled Tugga made sense of that question.

'I just want a jug, Davy. What's the problem with that? I've only had a couple.'

Apart from a slight slurring, Tugga sounded coherent. It was the upper body sway while his feet did the sideways shuffle that betrayed him. Undeterred, Allpress played his ace.

'We got word the pub inspectors are doing the coast tonight, you know, looking for under-age drinkers and people who, ah…might have over-indulged.'

Tugga shrugged. Why should that concern him?

'I just heard from the guys at the Torquay pub. The inspectors have finished there and are heading for us.' Allpress allowed that to filter through to Tugga. 'And someone's dobbed you in, mate. Someone said there's a big Kiwi who shouldn't be drinking any more. If they find you in here, even if we don't serve you, we're busted mate. We'd be the pub with no beer, possibly for up to 12 months.'

That was the slam dunk. The king hit. No Australian town wants to suffer that indignity. It was bullshit, but Allpress hoped his bluff might get Tugga out the door.

The only noise came from the traffic hurtling past, unaware that the wheels of cogitation were grinding for Tugga.

'Fucking bastards. They hate us Kiwis. Think we can't handle this cat-piss Aussie beer.'

Allpress held his breath. Was that acceptance or belligerence? He edged around Tugga to place himself between the big fella and the bar. He took a gamble on acceptance and put a hand on Tugga's shoulder.

'Yeah, I know, mate. You guys are renowned for holding your piss and being good sports. I'll never serve any of the Chappell brothers if they set foot in here, you know that. It's the bloody bureaucrats, mate. They're always looking for scalps, you know? They have to ping someone with a huge fine or close down a pub to justify their junkets.'

Allpress steered Tugga towards the door. 'Look mate, give me your car keys. I'll shift your ute around the back and out of sight of the inspectors. It's not going to rain, so you can crash out in the back until morning. You'll be in Apollo Bay for breakfast, no problems.'

Tugga grunted and left. Five minutes later Allpress returned to find patrons eager for refills, happy that a messy showdown had been averted. *God, the crap I deal with to keep the peace.*

One of the locals called out to Allpress as he slipped behind the counter to help his staff. 'Well done, Davy. He's a big bastard all right but you know we had your back if he got out of hand, don't you?'

'Yeah, right,' Allpress muttered as he poured a pot of beer. He knew the ringside supporter and panicked mob would have trampled him if Tugga had taken the belligerence option.

In the carpark, Tugga sat in the tray of his ute with a travel rug wrapped around his shoulders. It smelled of sawdust and beer. He'd spilled his last roadie while rolling a cigarette. He managed to save half the VB stubby, but that disappeared in two swallows. He threw the bottle into the darkness and sniggered when it shattered. 'Fuck you, Davy!'

Tugga had no idea if the bottle hit a car or a tree as Allpress had backed his ute into a corner near the cricket practice net. He finished the cigarette and considered staying awake until the hotel inspectors arrived.

'I'll fucking teach them not to pick on a Kiwi.'

He slithered onto his back and wrapped the blanket tighter as he searched the sky for The Southern Cross. He found the constellation, but couldn't retain his focus. A minute later he was asleep.

Tugga's snoring drifted across the car park. The only person who could hear was in the cab of a battered Ford ute parked 20 metres away. The observer was slouched behind the steering wheel, a New York baseball cap pulled low. It wasn't important to keep Tugga in view, it would be obvious when he awoke. The dry horrors or early morning chill were bound to wake sleeping beauty in a few hours. If Tugga was true to form, he would piss against a car and resume his journey. The observer was relieved Tugga didn't cause trouble in the pub. It would have ruined carefully laid plans.

Chapter 2

The Melbourne television office for the fourth-highest rating news service – they were still beating the ABC and SBS – was all but empty by 1.30 on Saturday afternoon, which was usually a good sign. It meant the four reporters and camera operators on duty were gainfully employed on stories for the six o'clock bulletin, and that satisfied the weekend chief of staff, Ciaran O'Malley. He might at least keep his job for another week.

O'Malley was born in Ireland but showed few traces of his origins. He'd arrived as a toddler almost 40 years before. He was waiting for the weekend producer to return with their standard Saturday lunch: two meat pies each and a brace of caramel slices to top it off. He would atone for the heart disease risk by consuming lunch with a healthy green tea and a twist of lemon. A balanced diet in O'Malley's view, even if half the tea was never consumed.

The absence of annoying phone calls from reporters, camera crews or PR companies seeking publicity for their clients gave him a few minutes to trawl through online news sources to see if he had missed anything important. A grimace suggestive of a heart attack contorted his 43-year-old features when he spotted the lead story on the most popular news site, then a prolonged expletive bounced off the four monitors that streamed his opposition news channels.

'Fuck!'

Fatal Coast Road Plunge

Police believe alcohol was a factor in a car accident on the Great Ocean Road near Lorne this morning, which led to the death of the driver, a 54-year-old Geelong resident.

The utility was found upside down on rocks below a parking bay between Eastern View and the resort town. Police believe Kevin Tancred might have fallen asleep. They suspect the accident happened between 2am and 8.30am when the vehicle was found by a rock-walking group.

The Geelong landscaper was refused service at an Aireys Inlet pub last night after arriving intoxicated. The manager persuaded Tancred to spend the night in his utility beside the pub after surrendering his keys.

Police suspect Tancred, who owned a holiday home at Apollo Bay, had a spare key in the vehicle. It's believed Tancred, known as Tugga, attempted to drive home when he awoke during the night.

O'Malley ignored the rest of the story, the guts of it was in the first two paragraphs: fatal plunge off a famous tourist route, publican acting the Good Samaritan and the stupidity of drunk drivers. This was bread and butter material for a commercial television news service and he had no resources to deal with it.

'Fucking stupid arsehole,' O'Malley screamed at a picture of Tugga that accompanied the story. The anger wasn't frustration for a senseless accident, more a case of a missed story opportunity.

'You're an absolute tugger all right. Couldn't have done a high dive from somewhere more convenient? You wanker, how am I going to get a camera and reporter to Lorne and back before the news?'

Journalistic sympathies didn't extend far for those who juggled weekend news-gathering duties on limited budgets. Lower ratings meant fewer bodies to do the work. O'Malley's crews were committed for at least another hour or two, and the station's only news helicopter was 220 kms away at Echuca, on the Murray River. There was more chance of Hawthorn tumbling to the AFL wooden spoon next year than of O'Malley getting that chopper to Lorne in time for the news. It was career suicide to hire another chopper and send a stringer camera operator. The station, especially the news and current affairs departments, was on a cost clampdown. Every extra expense above $500 had to be approved by The Hatchet, as the financial controller Andrew Hackett was commonly known. He made the Federal Treasurer look like a philanthropist. It was at least a four-hour return trip from Melbourne by car, and that didn't factor in filming time at the scene and chasing interviews. The mobile broadcast truck wasn't an option either; it was in the garage to replace a blown head gasket.

O'Malley was still cursing Tugga Tancred when the news producer, Alan Deveraux, entered the room. Deveraux casually slung a plastic bag onto O'Malley's desk. 'What's happened?' His question unwittingly initiated a new tirade.

O'Malley took a deep breath. 'Some drunken landscaper has planted himself all over rocks beneath the Great Ocean Road near Lorne. A local publican tried to stop him from driving, but the pisshead managed to get another set of keys and tear off into the night. Naturally the tosser, who is aptly named Tugga, zigged when he should have zagged and did a *Thelma and Louise* off the road into the surf below. The only reason he wasn't fish bait is that his ute was so pancaked by the rocks they couldn't squeeze inside to nibble him.'

Deveraux reached into the food bag to retrieve a pie. He took a big bite. 'So, a good story for us, given we're post-footy season and we don't have rights to broadcast the Melbourne Cup on Tuesday?'

O'Malley nodded as he retrieved his own pie and scrabbled around on the desk looking for a sachet of tomato sauce. Deveraux was a bite ahead.

'I gather you don't have a camera, reporter or chopper within range to get to Lorne in time for the news?'

O'Malley nodded glumly, but continued to eat. Macabre scenes of mangled bodies on rocks could never put veteran newsmen off their tucker.

'No, the chopper's at Echuca for the wine story with Louise. Max, Liz and Dianne won't be back to the station for another two hours. I've got a casual camera operator I could call in, but getting a chopper, even at mate's rates, would cost me my left testicle. Well, that's what The Hatchet would take if I booked it without asking him.'

O'Malley let his producer digest that information. He knew Deveraux didn't like to upset station management. The Chief of Staff couldn't blame him as The Hatchet sent memos every month demanding all departments cut their expenses or face more retrenchments. O'Malley was divorced, but Deveraux had a wife, three teenage boys with bottomless stomachs, and a large mortgage. They needed the story, but O'Malley guessed Deveraux wouldn't jeopardise his job by bringing down the wrath of The Hatchet.

'Okay, we know The Hatchet will say no, but we have to go through the motions. Call him and see if he'll let the moths escape his wallet.'

O'Malley opened his mouth to protest about the futility of the gesture but was silenced by Deveraux's raised hand.

'We've got to cover our own butts as well, mate. If it blows up on Monday, and this guy turns out to be famous, we can say we tried to get another bird and camera to Lorne, but the skinflint said no.'

O'Malley nodded again as the last chunk of the second pie was demolished. He opened the treats bag and held up a chocolate brownie in bewilderment. 'What the? Where's the caramel slices?'

'Sorry mate, they were sold out.' Deveraux shrugged. 'Can this day get any worse?'

Seconds later, one of the opposition channels shoved his nose in the brownie, bursting on air with pictures of the Great Ocean Road from its news chopper. Deveraux dived for the remote on the COS desk and turned up the volume on the monitor. Naturally all four channels went to full noise. O'Malley snatched the remote back and muted the non-important channels, which were also getting a taste of the brown stuff.

The pictures showed a flattened vehicle upside down on the rocks with waves lapping nearby. Teams of police and rescuers loitered but no one seemed to be in a rush. The voice over for the pictures was more urgent, as if the reporter had dashed from the scene to the sound booth. She gave the same details as the online news source, although Tugga's status, while still dead, had now been elevated to "'famous' ex pat New Zealand landscaper" and his Apollo Bay abode had become "luxurious".

The cross lasted 30 seconds and promised more details of the horror crash at six o'clock.

Deveraux turned to his Chief of Staff. 'We've got a new lead story. Put in a call to The Hatchet and spell it out that you need approval for another helicopter, camera op and reporter ASAP. If he doesn't answer, as usual, leave it all on his voicemail.

'Next, call every cop, ambo, rescue service and rock-walking group between Torquay and Lorne to see if someone had a camera on site – I don't care if it's mobile phone footage. We need more on that flattened ute. If they sound like they have half a brain, get someone to record a FaceTime or Skype interview as well. Put a note on our Facebook page for any motorists who might have had a peek over the side of the cliff. And track down that publican.'

Deveraux saw an editor returning from his lunch break. 'Jacko! Make sure media ops recorded that news cross from the Richmond mob. If they did their jobs properly, grab the aerial shots of the crash site and work on a promo. I'll get stuck into a script shortly.'

O'Malley did a double take. He realised what Deveraux had noticed on the opposition's news promo, and what would ultimately save their day. The news footage wasn't branded, obviously missed in the rush to get the raw footage to air first. It was a cardinal sin in the cutthroat media business of Melbourne. You had to stamp your station's news logo over everything; with a swarm of news choppers around the crash site the pictures were bound to look similar. Who would know that their chopper didn't arrive until late in the day – or not at all?

O'Malley pointed at the monitor and lapsed into his Irish vernacular. 'Those boyos fucked up!' But when he slumped back into his chair to make a futile call to The Hatchet he uttered a silent prayer. *Please don't ruin my day and have that eejit turn out to be a former All Black, or someone important.*

Chapter 3

Four kilometres east of the excited newsroom an iPhone7 vibrated on a Tuscany-inspired desk. It was the South Yarra home office for Andrew Hackett, aka The Hatchet. Italian design features filled the villa that could have naturally blended into a hillside near Florence. Hackett loved to brag to visitors that it cost $4.3 million to build and furnish. Money was always in Hackett's thoughts and he had assigned an hour of his Saturday afternoon to work on station spreadsheets. After-hours work was necessary in his high-powered job, but also pleasurable. Hackett was a numbers man at heart and loved the symmetry when everything tallied, as it should.

Hackett saw it was work that wanted his attention and chose to ignore it. He assumed it was the news chief of staff wanting approval to hire more crews for a breaking story. He glanced over 10 seconds later and smiled when his assumption was confirmed. *Panic merchant!*

Hackett was mildly curious about what the latest request might involve: a plane, an extra camera? Did they want to pay for sensational footage, which the seller would pass on to the opposition for half the price? The smile broadened as he imagined O'Malley cursing him aloud while he waited for the call to be answered.

Should he pick it up for a change and catch the neurotic COS mid-tirade? That would be a laugh. Hackett was aware of the newsroom's nickname for him and it made him proud. *I've chopped a few of those news wastrels.*

Hackett had been employed three years earlier to turn around the financial state of the company. He had no experience in television production, but he was renowned in the business world for rescuing companies in dire financial straits. Hackett believed a television station shouldn't be different from other businesses he had saved. Squeeze the outgoings and income rises. His battle plan was consistent: slash staff numbers and operating costs. The strategy always worked and it had made the 55-year-old extremely wealthy.

The phone stopped ringing so O'Malley was left to beg on voice mail. Hackett would do the right thing and at least listen to it before departing with Marianne, his wife, for drinks with Ferdy Ackermann, his best friend. Hackett wasn't in the business of spending money unnecessarily. If he saved cash for the company it made more money for himself, thanks to a carefully crafted bonus scheme. Ironically, the company had improved from the dire predicament that had initiated his employment. Ratings and advertising rates were steady at his Melbourne operation, with an occasional boost when a reality show sparked online media outrage.

Significantly, Hackett's scorched earth policy was working. Staff had been culled and those who remained were too terrified to complain, even when the toilet paper ran out. *They still use their hands to wipe their arses in those oil-rich countries, don't they?*

The coffers were slowly filling again thanks to a raft of cheap reality TV shows, not that surviving staff would ever know that. International reality shows could be picked up for next to nothing, and back-to-back crime series kept viewers glued to their sets for hours on weeknights. Then there were the money machines; the programs that guaranteed audiences and advertising revenue.

Hackett knew the must-have programs in Victoria involved Aussie Rules football. Therefore, Hackett's savings were being squirrelled away in a private war chest to make a bid for the golden goose – rights to televise some of the AFL matches. The station had never been in the game for a slice of the live footy action before and Hackett knew he could never match the prices paid by big networks.

Under his guidance, the station was close to becoming a player. He wasn't after the whole goose, just a few golden eggs that would ensure the station's future and a significant boost to his own prestige and bank balance. Hackett also secretly fancied a seat in the AFL Chairman's hospitality box on Grand Final day.

That would be appropriate for my efforts!

Against that master plan, ad hoc payments for flights, reporters, cameras, news pictures and other petty requests didn't rate with Hackett. He decided to ignore the message and left the office.

I'll check it later, after drinks with Ferdy.

June 10, 1986

What a blur the last few days have been. It's Tuesday, I think, and the bus is on a four-lane motorway south of Paris with all the other traffic going about 150kms an hour. They're crazy drivers but they seem to know what they're doing as we haven't seen any accidents.

It was a fabulous and frantic three nights in the City of Lights, capped off by the Folies Bergere. They were cheap tickets – standing room at the back – but at least it gave us a taste of a real Parisian cabaret which I've always wanted to see since I first started dance classes. The dancers were stunning. They were tall, elegant and moved so gracefully. For most of the evening they were clad in feather boas, skimpy costumes, sequins and extravagant headdresses. The finale had the guys on our tour spellbound as there was a lot more flesh on show. We never saw anything as revealing in amateur cabaret productions back in Waikato! I think my lovely old dance teacher, Mrs Somerville, would have blushed at the risqué nature of the show. I can remember she almost had a heart attack when I organised an 'impromptu' performance of the Can-Can with the girls during an end of year recital. Mum laughed but still grounded me for a week for upsetting the dance teacher. Such are the ways of life in Waikato! Ha ha.

I'm still pinching myself to make sure this is all real. Saturday morning at 5am I was getting on a bus in London, that night the bus had taken us across the English Channel, driven down the Champs

Elysees, around the Arc de Triomphe eight times – what a madhouse – and stopped under the Eiffel Tower. And now we're heading for the Riviera and Monte Carlo. Amazing!

The Parisians weren't as rude or haughty as the English said they would be. A bonjour went a long way towards getting some courtesy in return, just like back home. We've tried much of the local foods, even escargot – snails! but they're too slimy and garlicky for my taste. I'm loving the baguettes, paté and cheeses though. Such variety and they're all scrumptious. Dad would be hard pressed to find a steak-and-three-veggies dinner anywhere in Paris. If he did, it would taste better than anything to come out of Gran's old cooking range at home. Apologies to Mum, it's just that the French know how to make the simplest food taste divine.

The weather has been pleasant for early summer and the city has been busy. There are dozens of coaches forever dumping or picking up us tourists — and all amidst such a babble of languages. It was crowded at the Louvre, Versailles and every other tourist site, but I still got close to the Mona Lisa (had to hip-and-shoulder a few Japanese gents out of the way) and I even touched a Rembrandt painting. Naughty me!

There are 35 of us on the tour: 16 Aussies, 15 Kiwis, three South Africans and one American. Most of them seem okay, but we're so rushed it's hard to get around everyone and say hello and have a natter about where they come from and what they do back home. That's one of the reasons I left Te Awamutu – I want to learn more about people and this big wide world.

At home, there were always plenty of customers in the pharmacy where I worked. I loved chatting to them although the conversations were starting to be too much the same: the family, farm life and rugby. Even in summer when there's no rugby they still like to look ahead to the next season.

I love Waikato, and rugby, but I know there is much more to discover out here. Speaking of discoveries, there are more boys than girls on the tour. Great, a couple of them are cute. One guy was quite attentive to me yesterday.

Dear Diary… should I share what happened after drinks at the camping ground bar? Perhaps another time!

The tour company seems amateurish. It was chaotic at the camp site getting meals ready and arranging tents.

Our driver and guide, Eddie Malone, is on his first trip by himself *and is struggling to cope with all his duties. I think he's getting around by following the other tour buses everywhere. A wally on a Contiki bus called us the Budget Bludgers after Eddie stuck to their rear bumper for the return trip from Versailles. We don't care as we're having fun. NB: fill in the blank dates while on the road!*

These early entries always brought a smile to the holder of the diary. The excitement and enthusiasm for the long-awaited adventure was infectious. The Judy Williams that Te Awamutu knew was always a glass-half-full person. She was blue-eyed, attractive and her engaging personality created many friendships across the community.

Her athletic physique was toned by summer tennis and winter netball. Dreams of a career with the Silver Ferns briefly flourished when Judy was selected for a Waikato junior squad as a Wing Attack. However, she stopped growing at 1.55 metres and the height and pace of the modern game left her behind. Judy's blonde ponytail would be seen bobbing up and down the court, leaping frantically for intercepts that her taller opponents picked off with ease. She never lost her passion for netball and usually played at least twice a week; occasionally in back-to-back matches if a team was missing a player.

Judy was never short of friends at school, or dates for the district's social events. She was briefly tempted by a Bachelor of Arts course at Auckland University, which could lead to a teaching qualification. A job at a primary school had some appeal. However, images of London and Europe had fuelled Judy's dreams from her mid teens. The only way to make them real was to save money, and to do that she had to work hard. And that she did, milking the dairy herd with her father in the mornings before a full shift on the counter at the pharmacy in Te Awamutu. All the customers, friends and family knew about Judy's dream trip — and that she earned it.

Chapter 4

Andrew Hackett found himself back in his home office at 5.50pm – earlier than he anticipated. Saturday afternoon drinks with Ferdy Ackermann and his latest beau Jacinta, hadn't gone well, at least not for the ladies. The men had been best mates since kindergarten and nothing could break their bond.

Hackett's wife was a supremely tolerant person, capable of making herself comfortable in any social gathering. She'd even left one former Prime Minister besotted with her charms at a Liberal Party fundraiser before the last election. But, two hours with Ferdy's latest conquest was too challenging even for Marianne.

The men had been engrossed in conversation – as per usual, leaving the ladies to entertain themselves – until the harsh scrape of a metal chair on concrete indicated things had gone awry. Hackett realised his wife was on her feet glaring at Jacinta.

'Andrew, take me home please before I do the world a favour and throttle this gold-digger.'

Marianne picked up her handbag and left their kerbside table across the road from the Botanical Gardens. As Ferdy's lady-friend was a regular face on the South Yarra social scene it ensured Marianne's parting zinger, heard by several tables of drinkers, would emerge on Twitter before Marianne reached the BMW.

'Jacinta clawed in cat-fight at the gardens!'

Hackett shrugged at Ferdy and hastily chased after his wife. He didn't feel any need to apologise to Jacinta, they hadn't said anything more than hello. His best mate had been squiring ladies of a similar ilk – tall, model-thin and many years his junior – ever since Ferdy accumulated the first of his many millions.

Hackett always compared Ferdy to the debonair British actor Sir Roger Moore in his prime. Unlike the James Bond heart-throb, Ferdy never endangered his playboy lifestyle by getting married. Most lady friends were accepted by Marianne for the duration of the romance which was usually weeks and, occasionally, a couple of months.

Hackett caught up with his furious wife at their car. He opened the passenger door and looked back to see Ferdy pouring more champagne. *Last drinks for Jacinta?* Marianne's only comment on the five-minute drive home was to declare that Jacinta was *never* to set foot in her house, and that Ferdy had some serious grovelling to make up for that social faux pas.

Hackett knew Marianne would eventually tell him the reason for her explosive exit. They had been few and far between in their 27-year marriage; or so he believed when he wasn't the cause of them. After storming around the home, tidying benches and rearranging cushions on sofas that didn't need attention, Marianne, still clutching a cushion, finally entered the office to release the pressure valve.

'Do you know what that silly cow said?'

'No, babe,' Hackett patiently replied, knowing it wouldn't have been wise to guess.

'After two hours of her twittering on about her social life and trying to get me to tell her how rich Ferdy is, she says she's off to Thailand for another boob and face job which, incidentally, she expects Ferdy to pay for. And then she *suggested* I might like to join her at the clinic. Get my boobs done. What a cheek! Does she want a group discount for Ferdy?'

'Ahhhh.' Hackett slowly nodded as the chair reclined, considering the best way to calm his wife. Marianne wasn't a vain or shallow woman. But turning 50 had made her a tad more conscious of her body which, in Hackett's opinion, was still sensational. Three sessions a week at the gym, regular squash matches, yoga, the occasional tennis game and annual visits to top-class spas ensured the attractive brunette could still turn heads in Toorak. However, Hackett knew that Marianne was sensitive about the size of her bust. For Jacinta to *suggest* Marianne should consider breast enhancement was more dangerous than playing with a hand grenade.

'What a stupid bitch.' Hackett assumed much of the steam had been vented. 'I don't know where Ferdy finds trash like that. Anyway, I'd never let those amateur-choppers touch your tits – I'd only send you to be the best Swiss surgical clinics. Maybe they could fill them with milk chocolate?'

Marianne's eyes widened and her nostrils flared after a sharp intake of breath. She held the indignant pose for several seconds, but it was a waste of time. She couldn't outplay her husband's poker face. She giggled and threw the cushion at him.

'You selfish bastard.' Marianne launched herself into Hackett's lap, almost tipping over the chair. 'Always thinking of your stomach. I'd make them put soy milk in. At least you might get something healthy for a change.'

Hackett playfully cupped a breast as they cuddled. 'You know I love you just the way you are, babe. Jacinta is held together by silicone. Give me the real thing any day – and chocolate milk?' They laughed. Hackett's gamble had worked and Marianne's insecurities were tucked away.

'I reckon Ferdy's already trawling through his date book for a new dinner companion. And speaking of food, I have a couple of things to check before I fire up the barbie for those steaks.'

That was Marianne's cue to exit and start dinner preparations. Cucumbers, courgettes, lettuce, broccoli and other healthy options would be chopped, cooked and served. Hackett would brush them aside, as usual. His wife had been trying to change his eating habits from rare steaks and potatoes ever since he turned 50. She would also regularly poke his middle-age paunch. The demands of the television job had restricted his gym visits to a couple of days a month, while the golf games were down to one a fortnight. Hackett believed he was still a healthy man and he would return to a stricter exercise regime once the AFL rights business was sorted.

He had a few minutes until the opening titles of the news, so Hackett listened to O'Malley's urgent voice mail. To be fair Hackett gave it due diligence, listing the salient points for himself – extra chopper, extra camera, possibly an extra reporter. That was several thousand dollars he saved the company by not answering the phone earlier. And what would be the result if he had granted their wishes? One minute and 20 seconds of breathless reporting by a young Communications Studies graduate on a story that would be forgotten by the first commercial break?

Hackett barely registered the story was about a car crash on the Great Ocean Road. His priority was the cost. Nevertheless, it was almost six o'clock, so he thought he would justify his decision by viewing whatever the news department had scrambled together.

I'll text O'Malley later, tell him it would've been wasted money anyway.

He reached for the remote and switched on the new Samsung 4K television that dominated the wall opposite his desk – paid for by the station, naturally. He swung the chair around and settled in for what he expected to be a few minutes of typical weekend news coverage: another horror road smash.

Hackett nudged up the volume. The first pictures looked like mobile phone video of a vehicle pancaked on rocks. *Why are they begging for extra choppers and cameras? Those pictures tell the story.*

Any minor pangs of conscience were forgotten as Hackett listened to the story unfold. An Aireys Inlet publican stopped a drunk from driving to his beach house, the idiot waited until the pub closed and used a spare key to resume the journey, but a few kms later drove over a cliff near Lorne. The story looked to be compiled mostly from a mobile phone, the pictures were wobbly and the sound was distorted. The aerials were the steadiest images and better illustrated the driver's death plunge from the layby. *Silly bastard.*

Hackett reached for the remote to switch the TV off when a photo of the victim appeared on screen. He froze.

Fuck me! Tugga?

Kevin Tancred. The victim's name at the top of the story did not ring any bells. Hackett probably never heard him called Kevin in the weeks they spent together all those years ago. He was simply known as Tugga. Hackett paused the TV on the driver's licence image. Three decades older than the last time Hackett had seen the big fella, and the face was more weathered and carrying heavy bags under the eyes, but there was no doubt: *that's definitely Tugga.*

When did you move here and why were you cliff-diving at Lorne?

A personal connection gave Hackett a reason to find out more about the story. He pressed rewind on the remote so that he could listen properly to the script. He learned that Tugga was an expat Kiwi landscaper who moved to Geelong in the late '80s. He built a thriving business, which enabled him to create a luxurious beach house at Apollo Bay where he spent most weekends. He was well known in most of the bars along the coast – a euphemism for being a heavy drinker – and was occasionally known to be belligerent.

Most of that stacked up with the Tugga that Hackett knew. He loved his booze and could be boisterous if he drank too much. The "famous landscaper" profession was a few steps up from when Tugga and his two mates left New Zealand for their Overseas Experience. Hackett remembered the big fella earned his travel money chopping trees in North Island forests.

Did you make it good Tugga, or is someone using journalistic licence?

Hackett paused the TV again on the photo of Tugga, mentally reconstructing the real-life Tugga that he once knew. Tugga was more than two metres tall, with muscular arms and legs, broad shoulders and a chest that could have stopped a bus. The massive frame was topped by thick dark hair and a drooping moustache which made Tugga Tancred hard to forget. Hackett recalled the man bragging he had been a promising rugby player, a prop, who lost any chance of being an All Black because of a youthful indiscretion. Hackett never learned what that sin was. He also recalled Tugga's dimples. When employed, they softened the physical impression of a bear in a man's clothing and helped Tugga portray a boyish charm that made most people comfortable in his presence. Or, at least, that they weren't going to be torn limb from limb as long as the big fella was smiling. Sadly, Hackett couldn't find any signs of the younger Tugga, or the dimples, in the photo on his TV.

He looks…haunted?

Hackett found himself, for the first time, wanting *more* from his station's news service. Tugga's demise was a surprise, naturally. He'd lost friends and family over the years to illness and accidents; had experienced all the emotions, or so he thought.

But Tugga's death was unsettling for some reason. They had known each other for seven weeks in the mid '80s, meeting as members of a tour group travelling through Europe on a coach/camping expedition. It was a fun and memorable adventure, literally sowing wild oats as most of the bus group partied from London to Istanbul, and back again.

Hackett had been 25 at the time, a few years out of university and yet to settle properly into an accountancy career. Ferdy, always more focused than Hackett at that age, had pulled out of the Europe tour at the last minute because of a business opportunity that came up in London before the trip began. Hackett had a thirst for excitement and girls, plus it didn't make sense to travel all the way to Europe and not see the most famous attractions. He met dozens of Aussies and Kiwis in London, mostly working in pubs, who never did more than travel to the running of the bulls in Spain and the Oktoberfest in Munich. Many couldn't afford much more, Hackett remembered. Pay rates in London were so low and the cost of living was astronomical. Although, even Hackett the fledgling accountant, thought some common sense and planning would have been beneficial for a lot of travellers in those days.

The news program continued, largely ignored now by Hackett as faces, cities and sights filtered through his memory. His eyes drifted from the television to what Marianne called his brag wall. It was filled with pictures of him with famous business people, politicians, sports stars, celebrities and the obligatory family photographs. Mostly the wall was full of people who would not have given him a second glance 30 years ago when he was a carefree tourist in Europe.

More personal mementos from his travels were tucked into a small alcove in the corner. From a distance, a white Major League baseball, signed by a Hall of Fame member, initially caught his attention.

Then there was the plastic cube containing a slim and dark piece of metal: a spent Turkish cartridge from Gallipoli. Hackett hadn't found it. One of the other passengers, Brian, returned to the camp site with his trophy after their day exploring the famous First World War battle sites: ANZAC Cove, Plugge's Plateau, Lone Pine, Chunuk Bair, Quinn's Post and many others.

They'd been nothing but names in school history books until that emotional experience of walking in the footsteps of the ANZACs 71 years later.

Hackett remembered Brian showing the dirt-filled 7.66 x 53 mm cartridge, with Arabic script and Islamic crescent at the base, to a hushed group. Everyone wondered if the business end had claimed an Australian or New Zealand life. Hackett offered Brian a six pack of Efes beer for the prized memento, but was rejected. A week later Hackett spotted it rolling around on the bus floor near Brian's gear, so he tucked it away in his own backpack.

Hackett's eyes rested upon another unframed picture at the back of the alcove, a group photo of young people wearing traditional Dutch costumes. It was taken in Volendam, a quaint fishing port north of Amsterdam. The visit and photo were a standard part of most tourist itineraries and was, in their case, in the final days of the journey. The tour started with a clog-making demonstration followed by cheese-tasting and small donuts with a sweet syrup. Then it was time to play dress-up with everyone in clogs, the girls in pointed bonnets, flowing dresses and long aprons. Most of the men donned dark jackets, trousers and caps, although there were always a few who swapped genders when a fun photo opportunity arose.

Hackett walked over to the alcove and picked up the photo. There he was frozen in time – 30 years younger with more hair and a Tom Selleck moustache that Marianne insisted he remove before their wedding a few years later.

Hackett was standing in the back row, one away from the now dead Tugga Tancred. In between was one of Tugga's New Zealand mates, Drew. On the other side was Gerry. Beside him, Helen, another Kiwi friend who followed the trio from Sydney to England for the Big OE. The photo brought so much back in a flash.

Tugga's Mob! That's what the other passengers on the trip called Tugga's mates. They were the biggest, loudest, booziest and, much of the time, most enjoyable group on the tour. They were the first into the campsite bars and usually the last to leave. Hackett had no natural connection with the Kiwis: no career, sporting, cultural or national affiliations. The only common ground was wanting to have a good time while seeing what Europe had to offer.

The Kiwis were big men, close to two metres, with Tugga still towering over everyone. Hackett was similar in height to Drew and Gerry but couldn't match their muscle mass, theirs being the product of several years felling trees. They had a shared interest in beer, and anything else alcoholic the Europeans could offer, and that was enough to bond them for seven weeks in 1986. So much so that, according to the other passengers, Hackett was one of Tugga's Mob for the duration of the tour.

Hackett's thoughts turned to the three surviving members of Tugga's Mob but were interrupted by Marianne, urging him to fire up the barbecue. He placed the Volendam picture face-down on his desk, saw the faded writing on the back and recalled how most passengers had written their names and addresses on that final group photo on the last day of the trip.

Hackett's curiosity about them and the other members of Tugga's Mob stirred for the first time in many years.

A Google search later might be interesting.

Hackett picked up his mobile and tapped out a text to O'Malley. He apologised for missing the earlier message, and told the COS they'd done a good job in the circumstances. Almost as an afterthought, he added that he knew the victim 30 years ago when travelling in Europe. Hackett wasn't sure why he mentioned his connection to Tugga to the news crew. He didn't think there'd be any more legs in the story; it looked like a straightforward case of drink-driving and falling asleep at the wheel. Was he trying to give himself more credibility with the lower ranks, show that he was more than The Hatchet? That he was human after all? The thought didn't linger. It was discarded along with the phone as he headed for the courtyard and a couple of marinated steaks.

Chapter 5

It was rare to find Ciaran O'Malley still working in the newsroom at 6.35pm on a Saturday. He had gone well beyond his rostered 12-hour shift, which started at 5am, even though no overtime had been approved at the station in this millennium. It was professionalism that kept him there, unpaid, to ensure the late-breaking Tugga Tancred story made it to air on time. Staff cuts meant Deveraux had the help of one junior producer to prepare the weekend news bulletins. O'Malley had therefore taken responsibility for the lead story himself, wrangling all the elements together to make the video package presentable.

They struck more good fortune after pinching the chopper pictures from the opposition channel. Curly Rogers, a senior producer with the station's current affairs show, was taking his wife to Lorne for a weekend without the kids. Mrs Rogers' holiday was delayed as Curly's news instincts kicked in when he encountered the emergency crews a few kms from Lorne. His biggest error was to call O'Malley and ask, 'Is everything under control?'

Ten minutes later a disgruntled Mrs Rogers was driving the family sedan on to the next layby to await Curly's summons for pick-up, as the crash site was packed with every police car, fire engine and tow truck on the coast.

Curly's on-screen news reporting days were long gone, like the thatch that once adorned his now shaven head. A certain "look" is required for commercial television reporters and Curly's chrome dome didn't suit the station's presentation requirements. Management still appreciated his journalism skills and encouraged Curly to try his hand at producing and directing. It was still television journalism. Curly loved telling stories with pictures and he successfully made the transition to production, earning himself several awards over the past decade.

But this night, equipped with nothing more than his mobile phone with video and sound apps, Curly launched into the story. He interviewed a senior sergeant, a paramedic and three people involved with the recovery operation, culling the dullest before emailing the files back one-by-one to the station.

Curly looked lean and fit enough to be part of the rescue crew heading down to the wreck. So, like a pro, the 43-year-old enthusiastic mountain biker and keen runner attached himself to the group that clambered down to the rock shelf where the flattened vehicle rested.

Earnest discussions were continuing about how to recover the body and vehicle before the next high tide. Curly picked up rough but pertinent dialogue and pictures. Then someone realised the dude without a fluorescent jacket pointing a mobile phone in every direction was part of the media. Curly didn't mind getting banished back to the road, as he had content the opposition channels didn't: exclusive sound-bites and close-up pictures of the mangled car.

Even better, he'd overheard a cop raise an alternative explanation for the crash. That angle would require time to check, and would better suit his current affairs show, *Melbourne Spotlight,* on Monday.

Curly emailed the last of the story elements through to the studio at 5.15pm The pictures and sound were barely broadcast quality, but in the news business that could be forgiven if you had no other option.

O'Malley, who'd written a script as the files arrived, hauled the newsreader back into the voice-over booth to record the final few paragraphs at 5.25pm. At 5.53pm O'Malley stood beside Deveraux in the cramped news edit suite to view the finished product.

'You've produced a bloody miracle, mate,' Deveraux smacked the chief of staff on the back. 'Tell Curly we'll shout him a few beers when he gets back to town.'

'Not sure if we'll see him again,' O'Malley laughed. 'His wife was so pissed off about spoiling their dirty weekend she left him to walk to Lorne. He'll probably have to hitch back to Melbourne too.'

Deveraux grinned as he headed to the studio. Teamwork, and a lot of luck, had produced a better news bulletin than they had contemplated before their lunchtime pies.

Therefore, post-program, O'Malley was feeling reasonably mellow. He looked forward to a cold beer on the way home, ignoring the fact he had to be back at the COS desk before dawn the next day.

That's when Hackett's reply text caught his attention. O'Malley sighed as he reached over and plucked the phone from the charger on his desk. He failed to notice the last reporter and camera operator making hasty exits from the newsroom in case the text involved a new story. They had Saturday nights in Melbourne to consider. Deveraux, however, continued to tidy his desk.

'You fucking wanker.' O'Malley exploded as he thumbed through the text.

Deveraux wasn't a mind reader, but guessed the expletives were directed at the station's financial controller, rather than himself. 'What does The Hatchet have to say about our request for another chopper? Sorry, got the message too late?'

'Yep. I reckon he has alarm bells on my caller ID on weekends. But get this: he knew the victim.'

Deveraux stopped binning the used news scripts. 'Is there a follow up? Was this landscaper more famous than we know? Some sort of modern Capability Brown? I can't imagine The Hatchet associating with the hoi polloi.'

'Nah, don't think so. Apparently, they travelled on the same tour bus 30 years ago. You know, those trips where you colonials drank and shagged your way around Europe for weeks on end? None of you could remember anything until you had your films developed six months later.'

Deveraux smiled and nodded. 'Ancient history now, mate. The BC days – before children.'

O'Malley laughed as he shut down his computer, ready for the pub. 'Yeah. I'm wondering if The Hatchet wants an update – any gossip that we picked up. Should I tell him Curly thinks there is something a bit whiffy about this accident? Well, at least according to one cop.'

'Nope,' Deveraux checked his wallet for enough cash for his round. 'If Curly can dig up some dirt, The Hatchet can watch it on Monday with the rest of us. Come on, two beers and then I'm out of there otherwise I'll be looking for new digs with Curly.'

June 21, 1986

Nine days in Italy – not enough! It is the most romantic country in the world. Sorry Te Awamutu, you're just not in the same league. The Italian men are gorgeous: dark eyes, long lashes, tight jeans and wandering hands. The other girls were complaining about getting their bums pinched. I loved it. (Dear diary – Make sure Mum never reads you!) We're just leaving Sorrento and on our way to Brindisi to catch an overnight boat to Corfu. Italy today, Greece tomorrow. If you had told me that 12 months ago I would have laughed.

I've wanted to travel here since I was 16 after watching a documentary series on England, France, Italy and Spain. It was the mixture of people, culture and hundreds of years of history that captured my heart. I made it a goal, working two jobs for years to make it happen, yet a little part of me wondered if it ever would.

Dating Derek for two years slowed things down but Europe always nagged at me. I tried to get him interested in joining me, but he never saved any money. He'll always be a rugby, racing and beer man which is like so many other guys in Te Awamutu.

My decision to cast off the shackles with him made me more determined to buy that plane ticket and now I'm living the dream, visiting places I've read about in books and magazines, or seen on TV. We went out to the Isle of Capri yesterday. It used to be home to one of the Roman emperors, or probably several of them. Eddie, our driver/guide, needs to do more research on his history spiels.

Anyway, we hired taxis which were old American convertibles. They were huge and we squeezed six people into each, so it was cheap for a few hours travel around the island. We went to Grotta Azzurra, the Blue Grotto, and took a boat inside. It was beautiful. I felt like diving over the side and wallowing in that clear, deep water. Might have been dangerous as there are so many boats trying to get in at the same time.

Then we took chairlifts to the top of a mountain near Anacapri (sorry, can't remember its name – so many!). Spectacular views but Tugga made a pig of himself. He was peeing from the chairlift. Gross! He's getting creepy. I caught him staring at me in the disco at the Rome camp site. He wouldn't take his eyes off me even though I was dancing with other guys. He's mostly okay during the day, in fact he and his mates can be funny and entertaining. But they start drinking heavily in the afternoons and Tugga's mood changes. There have been a couple of situations that could've turned nasty if Andreas and others hadn't stepped in to calm things down. Enough about Tugga.

It's Italy I love most: pizza, pasta, chianti, the history, the people – well, mostly the men – and the fashion. My God, the shops in Rome are stunning. I wish my savings would stretch to a Gucci handbag. The leather jackets and shoes are so stylish but also way beyond my budget.

It's such a funny country in a way. Everywhere you see the crumbling ruins of their great empire. And then you see the modern Italians; beautifully dressed and groomed and so nonchalant – as if the past has nothing to do with them. Such a pity.

Pompeii was fascinating (especially the brothels with the stone penises everywhere – or should that be penii?) The camp site in the olive grove at Sorrento has been one of my favourites. The fireflies dance through the olive grove at night and the smells of cooking from the camp site kitchens and local homes made me want to stay for a whole summer. Maybe one day in the future? It was very romantic.

We kept stumbling over bodies in the dark as we searched for a quiet patch of grass to watch the moon and stars. It was a giggle. Skinny dipping in the pool was a hoot as well. Enough about the naughty nights (and there have been a few – it's the Roman influence ha ha), I'm looking forward now to what Greece can offer. I'll be happy if it's half as good as Italy.

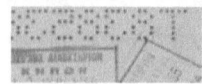

It was the line, *We kept stumbling...* in that entry that irked the diary holder. Who was *with* Judy on that hot summer's night 30 years ago in the Italian olive grove? There was no doubt she had been promiscuous. The number of trysts recorded in the diary was a shock. It was so out of character for the young woman who left Waikato. The other companions had been identified by collating references across several weeks and countries. They were one-night-stands that seemed irrelevant.

But not the Andreas mentioned in Sorrento. He appeared regularly in the diary as a bed companion for Judy. Yet it was difficult to properly identify and locate him, and that was extremely frustrating.

The diary holder took a deep breath and held it for the count of five, then exhaled to the same beat and repeated the stress relief exercise another four times. It eased the tension. Patience and diligence had brought results so far and was the right strategy to carry forward. The diary was closed, wrapped again in silk and returned to the small wooden box where it had been buried for three decades.

Chapter 6

It was mid-evening on Sunday before Hackett found time to indulge in more thoughts about his former travelling companions. The television news cycle was already moving on from Tugga's demise. The follow-up story was an interview with the bar manager in Aireys Inlet who confiscated Tugga's keys. Davy Allpress added a new subtext to the standard road safety theme of don't drink and drive – 'you can't help some idiots'.

Hackett made himself comfortable in the office chair with the Volendam picture and examined the faces in more detail. Not surprisingly, he struggled to match many of the names with the faces. It was 30 years since he had spoken to most of them. He had run into several at Antipodean parties and pubs in London over the following 16 months, before returning home with a new career focus. Even the people he met post-trip were hard to recall.

The Dutch costumes in the photograph weren't the most flattering either. The bonnets and blooming dresses almost time-shifted the girls back to another century. They covered the standard day wear of brief shorts, loose tops and summer tans. The smiles on many of the guys were more subdued than in other trip photos. It might have been from hangovers – they'd been on a brewery tour the day before, followed by the Red-Light District – or it could have been the 19th century studio backdrop that made them act more conservative than usual. Certainly, three of the girls that Hackett had known intimately on the trip looked demure in village costumes, compared to nights rolling around naked on tent floors and other impromptu shagging venues. He recalled their names more easily: *Judy, Denise and Helen.*

Helen had been the first and the easiest to lay. It was the second night in Paris after a fun session at the bar a few hundred metres from the camp site. Hackett noted on day one that she was attached to the big fella's group, but no one seemed to claim any proprietary rights to her – she was one of the gang.

Tugga, Drew and Gerry were casting eyes everywhere as well, sizing up who was willing to play on tour and when was the best time to strike. It was a different era and morality from Hackett's present-day life in Melbourne. Most passengers were away from home, work, families and friends for the first time and everything was a new adventure to be embraced. A tour guide from another company succinctly summarised the mood one evening in the Zombie Bar in Florence. He outlined the fundamentals that he believed applied to most trips: 'passengers hang up their coats, their brains and then their morals – for the duration.' The mantra for passengers and road crew was, 'What happens on tour, stays on tour'.

The moral ambiguity of sexual freedom while touring didn't suit everyone. A few settled into monogamous arrangements while others continued to play the field. Helen and Hackett fell into that second category. In between shagging each other when the mood suited them, they enjoyed the company of other passengers. That was how Judy, Denise and two other girls from different tour buses had ended up sharing a tent, or Hackett's spread-out sleeping bag, during the trip. It had been one of the most liberating times of Hackett's life, details of which had only ever been shared with Ferdy after returning to civilisation in London. His friend had been blasé. Ferdy's business venture had netted him £20,000 while Hackett spent £3000 living the *Playboy* lifestyle on a budget tour. Marianne had never budgeted anything in her life; her European visits were always five-star. Hackett, therefore, was cautious about sharing experiences from his first European adventure with his wife. He told her nothing.

Hackett looked more closely at the faces of Helen, Judy and Denise; his three Kiwi birds. Of the three, Judy was the stand-out: an attractive blonde with a fresh-faced country look and a megawatt smile. From a farming family, Judy was on the trip of her dreams. Hackett recalled that Judy fell in love with Europe via cultural documentaries and books as a teenager. Ancient castles, medieval abbeys and bustling cities were such a contrast to her rural life in New Zealand. She was determined to visit the most famous landmarks before marriage and children tied her to a farm existence in Waikato. Judy was supposed to travel with a girlfriend, but she'd cancelled just before the trip because of a family problem. Hackett remembered Judy saying after one intimate encounter that she was glad there was no one to report back to her boyfriend – or parents.

Raven-haired Helen was originally from Rotorua. That's where she met Tugga and the lads before moving to Sydney for better jobs and pay in the early '80s; along with tens of thousands of her contemporaries. She was still a Kiwi at heart, Hackett remembered, but was already being influenced by the darker side of Sydney. She always talked about getting stoned. He was surprised to learn that she was bisexual as well and had made attempts to bed other girls on the trip without any apparent success. Denise was another sweet mid-20s girl from Waikato. Hackett didn't consider Denise as cute as Judy, but she was a lot of fun and up for a bonk almost anywhere. *God knows how I ever found time for those American girls on the Contiki trip in Venice!*

Hackett looked at more faces and tried to match them with names. He would make a guess and then turn the picture over to see if he was correct. Not all the passengers put down their full names or home addresses. Many picked up tour nicknames for silly habits, stunts or mishaps. These trip monikers were more commonly used on the picture, although some had bracketed the nicknames with the ones assigned by their parents at birth. Tugga's name was there. It merely said: Tugga Tancred, NZ.

Hackett never learned the origins of Tugga's nickname or much more about his New Zealand life, apart from his early rugby prowess. That was reaffirmed by Drew and Gerry who'd watched Tugga smash scrums since high school. Tugga had always been their leader and he decided their daily agenda. If the itinerary didn't interest Tugga – '*not another crumbling church*' – he would locate a bar and settle in with Drew and Gerry to drink beer, schnapps, grappa or anything else alcoholic. They made sure the bar was close to where the bus was parked or the camp site. Hackett found himself regularly drawn to Tugga and his compatriots after his own excursions.

No wonder the other passengers considered me part of Tugga's Mob.

The Volendam picture made Hackett think about the end of the trip, when most of these details were written down. Hackett had to admit much of that final 24 hours in Amsterdam was fuzzy. He was wasted, like never before, or since, and considered himself lucky that Ferdy was in London to meet the returning bus, otherwise he wouldn't have found their flat again.

Hackett's last night on the trip in Amsterdam was spent enjoying copious amounts of space cake, a cannabis-fuelled high that obliterated several hours from his existence. He had no idea what happened. Like most of the passengers, Hackett was ignorant of the strengths of the cake offerings in cafés and the delayed hit from the cannabis. No buzz arrived after the first samplings, so they pressed on into La La Land. Luckily, eight of the tour group and the driver/guide abstained from the cake feast. They spent the rest of the night rounding up the new space cadets and herding them back to the camp site. Hackett had one recurring memory, when the dry horrors kicked in, of a female yelling that she couldn't breathe. Another passenger reassured the screamer she was still alive because the whole camp site could hear her.

Consequently, many of the space cadets were physically present on the last day to help pack up the tents, but mentally their brains were still in another galaxy. Hackett was earthbound, so firmly connected to the turf he couldn't rise from it. His limbs didn't have bones anymore; they had turned to jelly. He had preceded the space cake binge with a long booze session with Tugga's Mob in the camp bar. That left Hackett without energy to drag himself from his tent to assist with the packing duties. Occasionally a face would appear at the tent flap to rouse or motivate him, but to no avail. The packing continued around him until it came time for his tent to be folded and loaded into the bus. Suddenly he found himself tipped upside down into blinding light. He heard the laughter without any sympathy. *Bloody Aussies – can't hold their piss or their cake.*

Somehow Hackett scrambled together his possessions and shoved them into his backpack. Through bleary eyes he noticed his copy of the Volendam picture dumped beside his kit. A kind soul had obviously taken his picture to the group information exchange. That was appreciated. However, he noticed for his details they had merely written: *Andreas, Space Cadet, London or Melbourne*. He wondered if that was the same on all the other pictures.

It hadn't concerned him at the time, that no one on the trip probably knew his proper name. And it certainly wasn't a problem now; he didn't want any of those former companions turning up on the doorstep of his South Yarra villa wanting a bed for old time's sake. The nickname 'Andreas' stuck from day one when they were all introducing themselves on the bus microphone. Hackett revealed his birth name was Andreas, in honour of his family's German heritage, although he preferred to be called Andrew. Naturally, that was enough for a busload of Aussies and Kiwis to take the piss by calling him Andreas for the duration.

Hackett pulled over an A4 notebook and wrote down the names he considered worthy of a Google search for old time's sakes: Andrew (Drew) Harvey, Gerry Daly, Helen Franks – the other members of Tugga's Mob. He also wrote down Judy Williams and Denise Howard, the trip girlfriends. Luckily their surnames were included on the back of the picture because Hackett couldn't recall them. He didn't bother listing the Contiki girls from Venice, given he couldn't even remember their first names.

What a party place that Venice camp site was.

Hackett's first port of call when he researched someone prior to a business meeting was LinkedIn. Facebook was next on the list as it contained pictures and more personal details that often proved helpful. It would reveal families, friends, hobbies and interests – all good background information.

If Hackett ever wanted more leverage in negotiations he would turn to Google for the dirt. The most salacious stories sat higher in the pecking order because of the volume of hits.

Hackett remembered Drew's stocky build, thick brows and constant struggles with the values of the various European currencies. He believed LinkedIn wouldn't be much help on this occasion and went straight to Google.

A heartbeat after typing in the name, the world-wide search engine produced 6,430,000 results. At the top of the list were the Drew Harvey profiles on Facebook. Next were the Top 10 Drew Harvey profiles on LinkedIn. Then there was a personal website and a Wikipedia listing: definitely not Hackett's man.

He could speed up the search with a couple of keywords, but Hackett always liked the numbers that Google threw at him: 6,430,000 results with a Drew Harvey connection. Big numbers like that were exciting, especially when viewed online in his bank account. With a couple of deft taps, he refined the search to news pages and topics that might be more pertinent, starting with New Zealand sites.

Tugga's move to Australia had surprised Hackett, particularly after the big fella spent seven weeks singing the praises of the All Blacks. Tugga, along with Drew and Gerry, loathed rugby league and Australian Rules. *Games for sissies.* They all harped on about the Bledisloe Cup, an annual trans-Tasman battle, reports of which rarely migrated beyond Sydney and Brisbane. Hackett doubted that Drew had abandoned the All Blacks and crossed the ditch to set up residence in Australia. A few minutes later his assumption was close to confirmation, but the Google discovery was still a shock.

Hackett found a death notice for a Drew Harvey listed in an Auckland newspaper in September. The age of the deceased – 54, coincided with Hackett's memory. The guy in the online report was a family man and the obituary listed affectionate tributes from his wife, three children and work colleagues.

The Drew Harvey in Europe had been a rough diamond and didn't have much success with women on the trip. So much so he couldn't resist throwing a few snide and obviously envious remarks when he saw Hackett emerge from a tent with Judy, Helen or Denise in the mornings. If this was the same Drew in the obit, he might have eventually found a good, or desperate, woman to love him.

Hackett read that Drew died in a tragic accident on 31 August. He checked the online newspaper in case it featured a story. The accident rated a mention and a picture, which confirmed it was the same Drew Harvey he knew. Thirty years since Europe and his face was still identifiable as Tugga's first lieutenant. Drew had aged better than Tugga – laughter lines around his eyes instead of bags beneath – perhaps the benefits of a loving family. But they hadn't saved him from being turned into fish bait – like Tugga. Hackett focused on the news report.

Fisherman swept away at Muriwai

The search continues for a fisherman swept off rocks at Muriwai on Auckland's dangerous west coast. Police confirmed they are now treating it as a body-recovery exercise.

The fisherman, Drew Harvey, 54, a forestry worker, is believed to have been swept away at the notorious fishing spot late on Wednesday afternoon. Police believe it must have been a rogue wave as there wasn't a big swell at the time.

Harvey was the only person on the rock shelf, which has claimed many lives in recent years. By the time Harvey's absence was reported it was too dark to mount a search. His bait bin and other items were found wedged between rocks on Thursday morning.

Police have repeated their warnings about the dangers of fishing on wet rocks at Muriwai. They say fishers should wear life jackets, never turn their backs on the sea and that it's safer to cut a snagged line than attempt to free it.

The Harvey family were shocked by the tragedy. A family spokesman said Harvey had fished at Muriwai for 25 years and that he was safety conscious. 'He always wore a life jacket, even in calm conditions, and made sure his companions did as well,' the spokesman said.

Hackett couldn't comprehend such rotten luck: two mates dead within two months of each other. He knew that Tugga and Drew had grown up together in the North Island, and now both had died in accidents involving the ocean.

Different coastlines in different countries but freakily similar.

Given Tugga had moved to Australia nearly three decades ago, Hackett wondered how much contact he and Drew had over the closing years of their lives. Tugga seemed to have been a confirmed bachelor and Drew was a family man, so there probably weren't too many boys' reunion weekends. Tugga, Drew and Gerry were once a tight unit and now two of them were dead.

Hackett recalled Helen telling him one day, in Greece or Turkey or somewhere else that was humid, that she'd first met them when they moved from Palmerston North to work the forests around Rotorua. They liked the pub where she worked and they were big drinkers – at least four or five nights a week – and had been in a few scraps. However, Helen said, they always looked after her if there was any trouble. She had shagged them all at different times but by late 1983, when she took off for Sydney, they were more like brothers.

Hackett yawned as he pondered the fickle nature of life. The discovery of Tugga's death unsettled him, yet Drew's demise, while a surprise, didn't quite have the same impact. Probably because he remembered that Drew seemed to tolerate Hackett as part of Tugga's Mob, knowing it was only for the tour, not a genuine friendship.

Hackett wondered whether to start a new search for Helen Franks and Gerry Daly. He looked at the clock on the computer screen and decided at 10.29pm it might be wiser to call it a night. His first meeting in the morning was an early bird with the station manager. It was a key discussion about the state of the war chest and their strategy to snaffle a share of the AFL television rights. Those matters were best planned with few inquisitive staff around. Hackett knew, even after the staff cuts, you didn't find too many people around the office at 7am on Monday mornings.

Hackett shut down his computer and made a mental note to allocate time for another Google search on Monday night. He stood and stretched, then laughed quietly as a macabre thought entered his head: *Two of Tugga's Mob are dead – I don't want to find a third this weekend.*

Chapter 7

Monday morning found Curly Rogers choosing public transport instead of the usual 40-minute walk to work from his home in Middle Park. The same idea occurred to other foot-sloggers in the neighbourhood and, consequently, the tram was packed. They hadn't been able to squeeze another body aboard since Albert Street, outside the old South Melbourne football ground. Curly, wedged between three suits and a student who refused to remove his bulky daypack, could still count his blessings. They were at least moving forward while the car drivers, stalled in a Clarendon Street jam, should have turned off their engines and saved the planet.

Like most on the tram, Curly was tuned out from the awkward commuter silence. He was plugged in to his iPod instead and to the sounds of vintage Santana. It was 7.55am and he was unaware that Hackett's first meeting of the day was winding up in a ghost station. Curly's thoughts hadn't made the transition from weekend mode to work yet; he was contemplating the crayfish salad he shared with Janine at Erskine Falls on Sunday afternoon. It was a rare treat.

He had gilded the lily with the Chief of Staff about his wife leaving him stranded on the Great Ocean Road on Saturday. Curly had been married to Janine for 17 years and knew she understood the irregular demands of his job. She was a pragmatic woman. Curly was returning from the rock shelf where Tugga died when Janine texted him an update. The drama on the coast road attracted so many sightseers there weren't any car parks available before Lorne. Janine wisely drove to the accommodation that overlooked the surf beach and put the wine, beer and nibbles in the fridge. She offered to return when he finished the story. Curly read between the lines – Janine wanted him to find his own way into town. It was easy enough for a gabby journalist to scrounge a ride and Curly arrived to find Janine halfway through the first bottle of sauvignon blanc. He grabbed a chilled Crown Lager from the fridge and texted O'Malley about having to appease his 'grumpy' wife. Curly knew he would never get paid for the extra duties, but he was going to guilt-trip O'Malley into buying more than a couple of beers after. Curly knew he'd take the money out of petty cash anyway and hope The Hatchet didn't find out.

Santana had finished playing by the time Curly exited the tram at Park Street, so his thoughts drifted towards work. He had four stories lined up for the week, although the first wasn't due on air until Tuesday night. High productivity was another vital skill in broadcast journalism these days; get your stories on the television or get shown the door. His gut instinct told him there was more to the Tugga Tancred cliff-diving story, but he doubted he would get the luxury of time to investigate it.

Curly reached the television station and steadily weaved through a rabbit warren of hallways and adjoining buildings towards the current affairs office. It was a long way from the management domain, which was both good and bad. Journalists never like being close to bean counters, but out of sight means out of mind for those who paid the wage bills. *We keep getting time sheets from the south corner of the complex. Who lives down there?*

The studios and facilities were built to cope with Australia's first Olympic Games broadcast in 1956. No one had any idea what was required apart from walls, roofs, cameras and miles of electronic cables and other technical stuff. The original network expanded over several city blocks in the following decades before selling the premises and moving to bespoke facilities in Docklands. Curly's employers hadn't seen any need to mess with history. Why spend money upgrading studios, cameras, presentation suites, recording booths or news rooms? They were in the business of making money, not spending it. It was a miracle management agreed to dump the typewriters and install computers.

Curly was still 20 metres away from the office when he picked up the first sounds of battle – Jo. Another female voice – Kim. Then a male voice, the tone indicating he was under siege – Mac.

Bugger. Give up mate and just pay.

Curly slipped into the office and headed straight for his desk, hoping to fire up his terminal and take refuge from the combatants. The man under fire was David McKenzie, *Melbourne Spotlight's* program producer, who was better known throughout media circles as Mac. Even his grandmother called him Mac. She could never remember his home address, so her Christmas card would be posted to Mac, care of whatever channel she thought was employing him. It sometimes took a longer trek, but everyone in Melbourne television newsrooms knew Mac and the card always ended up in pride of place on his office desk, usually with a few extra good wishes or ribald comments penned on granny's envelope.

That industry respect wasn't helping Mac at that moment as he was bracketed at the main production desk. The protagonists were Jo Trescowthick, production assistant and gofer extraordinaire, and Kim Prescott, the office researcher who was desperate to become a reporter. A showdown with the program producer at 8.23am on a Monday probably wasn't going to help that career path. But there were principles at stake: the coffee and biscuit kitty had been raided, again.

It was an odd sight, Curly had to admit. Jo would make a hobbit look tall. Kim towered over her colleague by 20cm, but even she had to look up at Mac who was a tad under two metres. Yet his wavy red mane atop a 110kg frame that looked more suited to the movie set of *Braveheart* was not intimidating the wee inquisitors.

'Curly,' Mac implored, 'give me a hand here. These harridans are accusing me of raiding the kitty. Why would I do that?'

Curly weighed up the options. *Who can I afford to piss off here?* Mac ran the show, but Curly knew where the real power lay – behind the throne. Jo could provide reliable camera crews, creative editors and all the other important elements needed to get his stories to air in a timely fashion. And Kim could turn out to be a handy ally if he was going to get the Tugga Tancred story to develop. Pragmatism won the day.

'The pub probably declined your credit card again,' Curly said with an apologetic shrug and half smile to his boss and good mate. The ladies turned to Mac with triumphant smiles and rattled the tin kitty which contained a few coins.

'Oh, you Judas,' Mac wailed as if standing before Pontius Pilate. Tearing at his imaginary crown of thorns wouldn't do any good either; everyone knew Mac was guilty, although there would be no need for a crucifixion.

Kangaroo courts, with Jo and Kim as judge, jury and executioners, were becoming regular events after another of The Hatchet's cost-cutting measures – recalling all the executive credit cards. The tea, coffee and biscuit kitty had become Mac's alternative to the ATM when his plastic failed at the pub. Two ex-wives and three kids in private schools never left much beer money by Friday. Strictly speaking, Mac shouldn't have qualified for a company credit card as Richard Templeton held the title of executive producer. But Mac arrived at the station under a previous administration and it had taken The Hatchet almost two years to discover that oversight. Most times Mac managed to replace the cash before the guardians of the kitty went shopping. Jo and Kim had now sprung him three times in a month, and Curly thought he knew why.

'Did you back that nag the sports guys were tipping at Flemington on Saturday? Surely you checked the form, Mac. That horse hasn't won in two years.'

'I know that, but they said their mate was the trainer's cousin and he was setting times better than Phar Lap before the Cup,' Mac replied with a guilty look. He pulled out the lone $10 note in his wallet and promised to find the rest by lunch time. Mollified, the guardians departed for the nearest 7-Eleven for a caffeine fix as the tea, coffee and biscuit containers were nearly as empty as the kitty.

Fortunately, Mac's lack of horse sense didn't extend to his news judgement. He knew there was a reason Curly let the girls eviscerate him. 'So, what have you got up your sleeve that you need Jo and Kim's help with?'

Curly smiled. 'Did you see that news story on the landscaper who drove off the cliff near Lorne on the weekend, the one I scrambled together for the news guys?'

'Yeah, just a drunk falling asleep at the wheel, wasn't it?'

Curly baited the hook. 'Could be a bit more than that.'

Mac raised a bushy ginger eyebrow. 'Okay, I'm listening.'

'I managed to get right down to the wreck on the rocks,' Curly elaborated. 'Being out of a suit and not carrying a big camera can work in our favour at times. Anyway, I heard a cop questioning his sergeant about skid marks in the layby. It sounded like he'd spent time with one of those crash investigation units. He said another vehicle could have been involved.'

Mac absorbed the information for a moment before asking the pertinent question. 'Did the cop think it was accidental involvement, or deliberate?'

'Unfortunately, that's when your citizen reporter was rumbled and sent back up to the road with the other ne'er-do-wells,' Curly said, as he walked back to his desk to retrieve his mobile phone. He scrolled through to his picture gallery and presented it to Mac.

'I went back to have a look at the skid marks after the news boys left.' Curly tapped through several images. He then went back to the first of six pictures. 'Initially I didn't see anything strange. Looks like the drunk woke up as he started to drift towards the layby and braked to correct himself. You know, instinctive?'

Curly pointed at the first image which showed a short tyre mark. The next picture showed the angle of the skid in relation to the road. It seemed to support his hypothesis. Curly then moved through to another picture and another skid mark, this one on an angle away from the barrier and cliff. He then explained how he ensured he kept his alignment with the direction the car would have been travelling if the driver had woken up.

'He's braked twice,' Curly pointed out to Mac, who was now listening intently. 'Wouldn't you think someone – even a drunk – who's just woken to a nightmare on the Great Ocean Road would stand on the brakes once he realised he's headed for the cliff? There should have been a 40-metre-long trail of rubber there. Depending on his speed, he might even have slowed enough to be stopped by the barrier?'

Curly allowed his producer to mull that information for a moment before suggesting his possible scenario.

'I think he's been given a couple of nudges at speed.'

Still no response from the boss as he flicked back and forth between the pictures.

'My suspicion is that Tugga Tancred wasn't asleep when he was tapped the first time. See – that first skid mark is right at the entrance to the layby.'

Curly retrieved the appropriate picture on his phone to help them visualise the scene. He then progressed to the wide-angle photo of the second skid mark close to the cliff.

'From what I heard about this Tugga, he was a big guy, not likely to be pushed about. I think he jumped on the brakes when he felt the first whack at the start of the layby. Then the ego kicked in – you don't tangle with Tugga Tancred. He planted the foot on the accelerator to outrun the idiot causing him grief.

'That's when he was hit the second time. Tugga suddenly found himself heading straight for the cliff, he stood on the brakes again, but it was too late and he went flying into Bass Strait.'

Mac didn't say anything for another 20 seconds as he flipped back and forth between the pictures. Finally, he broke the silence as he heard more reporters and camera crews arrive for their first planning session. He handed back the phone. 'Interesting theory, mate, but it's thin.'

Curly was undeterred. Mac hadn't dismissed him outright. 'Well, there is more potential evidence.' He found another picture from his Saturday sequence and turned it around to show Mac. It revealed red brake light fragments on tar seal.

'See that? It was scattered around the first skid mark.'

'Yeah,' Mac sighed. 'But that could have been from any car – at any time.'

'Well, that cop who raised doubts about Tugga's flying act thought it was important.' Curly held up his final picture, a profile shot of the policeman with the glass in an evidence bag.

Mac rubbed a hand through hair that looked as if it would require shearer's clippers to cut. 'Did you get that cop's name?'

'Yep. I think he's based in Lorne but I'll get the Media Centre to confirm that.'

'How are you placed for your stories this week? You know we have to keep churning it out to justify our existence.'

Curly sensed he was winning the battle. 'Tuesday's story is almost in the can, I need a couple of finishing edits tomorrow. And Kim is helping line up interviews for the other stories. She could even do one or two of them if this takes off. So, I'm under control. I think it's worth digging into Tugga's story. If this is murder, not an accident, we'll have the jump on everyone.'

'Okay, you've got today to find something solid, otherwise you owe me another four and half minutes of scintillating television,' Mac said. He headed towards the conference room to get the meeting underway.

Curly did a little fist pump as he returned to his desk to retrieve a notebook for the production meeting. The elation was witnessed by Kim who had returned from the coffee run with Jo.

'What's got you so excited today?'

Curly knew there was no need to be circumspect about the story. It was time to share the information with his colleagues as he was going to need their help. He joined Kim and the crew as they shuffled their way into the small conference room. 'I have a new angle on that landscaper who plunged off the Great Ocean Road. I think there was a second car involved.'

News ears are highly tuned to random comments and several heads swivelled towards Curly; eyebrows raised in silent demands for more information. However, it was 35-year-old senior camera operator Dugal Cameron who sideswiped the discussion.

'Maybe it was The Hatchet,' Cameron suggested as he slung an armful of camera cables onto the table.

All conversation stopped for a moment. No doubt, for a few in the room, Dugal's comment fleetingly raised hopes the penny-pinching Hackett might be found guilty of murder and banished from their TV station, forever.

Curly was a realist and knew they could never be that lucky. *More chance of winning Tattslotto!*

But everyone was curious about The Hatchet's implied involvement in Curly's story. They all looked at Dugal and waited for him to back up his bombshell comment.

'I was chatting to Ciaran O'Malley on the way into work. He said The Hatchet knew the guy who parked on the rocks at Lorne. Maybe the guy owed him $10?' Dugal finished with a shrug.

A collective sigh of disappointment escaped the room. Several staff were secretly fantasising about The Hatchet taking up residence in Barwon Prison with an over-sexed 300-kilogram cellmate.

Mac snapped them back to the business of the day. 'Thanks for that, Dugal. I guess you don't want to tag along with Curly when he pops upstairs to inquire whether The H– um, whether Hackett, was driving to Lorne on Friday night?'

A quick shake of the head was Dugal's only response while Curly blanched.

'Fuck, Mac! Do I have to talk to him? I've got enough to work on. There's the cop, the skid marks and the brake-light glass. Plus, I've got a wife, kids, mortgage and tickets to next year's Grand Final to save for. He doesn't know I exist down here.'

Mac joined in the laughter as he took revenge for the lack of support during the coffee kitty kangaroo court. 'Yep, your idea mate, so you have to chase down any potential angles. No palming it off to Kim either. And I would suggest you don't start by asking him for overtime on the weekend.

'Right, people. How are we going to fill the gaps between those incredibly well-paid and important commercials tonight?'

June 30, 1986

Greece is boiling – and the locals say it's not even the hottest month of the year! If the temperature got to 25 degrees in Te Awamutu everyone would hop on their ponies and go chill in the river. Jump in the water in Greece and it's more like a bath. I guess us Kiwis don't handle the heat.

Athens is different from Corfu. Lots more crumblies, which is like Italy I suppose, but the locals are even more laid back.

The Acropolis is majestic as it towers over the city, but I can't understand how they let things get this way. Dad would have a fit at the lack of maintenance throughout Greece. Maybe it's the economy, or the oppressive heat. Either way, vast swathes of the country look like they need a change in farm management.

The Greeks were the centre of the civilised world and now they are history's backwater (okay, I admit I heard a tour guide say that bit).

Corfu was very touristy – Denise and I loved the B52 cocktails at Ipsos Beach – and our camp site was close to the water.

We were a bit jealous watching the Top Deck passengers cruising around on their yachts for four days. We still caught up with them at tavernas and restaurants thanks to rented scooters and bikes. There have been some excellent parties and I've developed a big appetite for calamari. It's so tender and tasty compared to the rubbery squid one of the Hamilton pubs used to dish up every Friday night. Send their chefs to Greece for training. The food's a positive for Greece, but there's not much else I would recommend about Athens to other backpackers.

The city beaches look shabby by comparison to Italy and the camp site pool is empty. It's not flash at all. No wonder the other tour companies aren't here. We're off to the sound-and-light show tonight at the base of the Acropolis, so we're hoping that will be special. I'm looking forward to seeing Gallipoli in a few days as well. I must take lots of pictures for Dad as Poppa fought there for several months. I still have the list of battle zones – somewhere.

Funny how I'm looking forward to getting out of Athens, whereas everywhere else I wanted more time. There's more history here but either it doesn't appeal to me or they haven't packaged it properly for young tourists. I guess most visitors just want to go to the islands and enjoy the sun, sea and sex.

Speaking of which, I have to be more careful. I've lost a packet of my pills and I have no idea how to get more. I might have to revert to my good convent girl habits again. Or be more careful.

Mind you, the Greek men don't get me as giddy as those Italians – or another lad closer to home, or rather, the bus.

Ha ha. God, I can never let anyone else ever read this! Well, maybe Charlotte when I get home in a couple of years. And only if she promises never to tell Russell.

The diary holder always felt angry when reading that entry. A potential problem was identified, yet Judy didn't treat it seriously. What happened to the sensible woman everyone loved at the pharmacy? Judy was so attentive to their prescriptions and requirements, yet a few weeks travelling made her careless about her own needs. The hands holding the diary trembled as a twinge of guilt swept through. Was it too harsh to judge from a distance, not being privy to the morality, influences and passions of those times? But all acts and oversights have consequences, the diary holder believed. The diary was once again laid to a silky rest for another time. The final pieces of the puzzle were coming together and new plans had to be finalised.

Chapter 8

Camera crews and reporters wandered out of the Spotlight office in dribs and drabs after the production meeting, while Curly procrastinated about The Hatchet. He wondered what pertinent information the financial executive could provide; after all, the last contact with Tugga Tancred was 30 years before. Curly doubted he would even get to speak to The Hatchet, who was notorious for ignoring requests from journalists. It wouldn't cost The Hatchet anything to share background information on Tugga. Phone calls to the financial caller were a waste of time, therefore Curly chose the cover-your-butt option – an email. That way there was proof he tried to establish contact.

Curly quickly bashed out a message to Hackett via the internal server, asking for a chat about his connection to Tugga. He briefly pondered whether to reveal the theory that a second vehicle might have been involved in the accident. That was the only reason for pursuing the story further, but Curly decided to keep that information to himself. He would share his suspicion that Tugga was pushed over the cliff if Hackett agreed to meet. He tapped the send button, then turned his attention to the cop who believed Tugga's ute might have been whacked from behind.

The Victoria Police Media Centre confirmed the officer – Jim Laidlaw – was a constable assigned to Lorne. It was a small station and they suggested the officer might be on a day off after working the weekend.

The Media Centre wasn't overly curious about Curly's inquiry, especially after he spun them a storyline about staying alert on the Great Ocean Road over summer. Curly embellished the pitch with his first-hand experience of being at the crash site, noting the grim but heroic work of the police and rescue staff. Curly wanted to help prevent other horrific scenes, he said.

The former newspaper journo on duty in the Media Centre thought it sounded like a good PR feature. His office was busy enough with matters in Melbourne, so no one wanted to drive all the way to Lorne and back to hold a constable's hand through a puff piece on road safety.

Curly decided to strike swiftly, in case the media office sent a message to the Lorne cop outlining the story they had approved. He dialled the Lorne station number and was rewarded with a prompt pick up.

'Lorne Police, Constable Laidlaw speaking.'

Bingo! Curly was in luck.

'G'day Constable Laidlaw, it's Curly Rogers here from *Spotlight*, you know, the Melbourne current affairs show?' Curly never used his real name – Christopher. Too many calls from outside contacts weren't passed through because his own colleagues never knew him as anything other than Curly. If they couldn't see a Christopher in the office, and the call didn't relate to any of their own stories, journalists were inclined to send it back to reception – or lose it.

'I remember you – the cheeky bugger with the mobile phone who scrambled down to the wreck on Saturday. The sergeant was spitting tacks when he saw the TV news that night.'

Curly was worried he might have blown this potential source already. He stayed silent, hoping it was only the sergeant who was angry about his rock visit and not Laidlaw.

'Lucky for you we said it must have been one of the search and rescue mob who sent you the pictures. Saved us getting our arses kicked for letting you get that close. So, what further trouble are you going to cause me, Mr Rogers?'

Curly quickly decided Jim Laidlaw was a good sort: no mug and not likely to create trouble for himself or Victoria Police, but also not likely to sweat the small stuff. He decided against trying to bluff the country cop and went straight to the point.

'Firstly, thanks for saving my butt with your boss and, secondly, hopefully, I won't be causing any problems, but...' and Curly paused a moment for the cop to digest his good intentions, 'I am checking up on a couple of unusual aspects I noticed about the Tugga Tancred crash.'

'Unusual?'

Curly didn't want Laidlaw to cop flak from his sergeant for initiating the 'second-vehicle theory,' so, in case the phone call was recorded, he wanted it on the record that it was the journalist's own diligence at the crash site that sparked the follow-up.

'Look, I noticed fresh tyre marks and some broken glass in the layby. It suggests to me that the victim may have been trying to brake.'

There was a pause before Laidlaw responded.

'And what do you think happened?'

Curly was encouraged. The cop wasn't trying to steer him away from the theory he was about to put on the record.

'I would've thought someone alert enough to realise they were heading for a cliff would throw out all the anchors. There would have been a continuous skid mark from the first to the second mark at least; if not all the way to the cliff-edge. And what reason would there be for broken glass at the start of the layby? Could another vehicle have been involved?'

The second-vehicle theory was now on the table and Curly waited for confirmation.

'You saw me collecting the glass, didn't you?'

'Yes, I got pictures of the glass and you scooping it up.'

The line went quiet for 10 seconds.

'Look, I won't bullshit you. Sure, there are thousands of cars and dumb tourists looking at the view rather than where they're parking – and anybody could have left the marks and glass. But we might need some help if we're going to find out what happened to Tugga.'

That surprised Curly and he took the risk of taking a momentary tangent. 'You knew him?'

'More by reputation, but I had seen him around. He was a big fella, hard to miss in a bar. Usually cunning enough to avoid any breathalyser patrols. I've only been here a few months, but yeah, I knew who he was.'

'And by saying you want to know what happened to Tugga, you also suspect another vehicle might have been involved – accidentally. Or deliberately?'

'Back up the bus on your *deliberately* theory. I don't want that out there – at the moment. But yes, I suspect another vehicle was involved.'

Curly contained his excitement, realising he had to get this information on the record. Again, time and distance were not going to help him, they needed to get the new angle on air that evening before one of the other stations or newspapers stumbled onto the story. Or, were they already ahead of him?

'Look Jim, do you mind telling me if there have been any calls from other media asking about a second vehicle being involved?'

'Not yet. I think most people took it at face value. You know, drunk driver falls asleep and drives off into oblivion. The final 15 minutes of fame for the big fella.'

Curly thought back to Constable Laidlaw at the crash site. He was about 30; too young to be so cynical about the public's news attention span.

You're too clever to be twiddling your thumbs in Lorne, mate.

'Okay, so you're investigating that angle, as in what caused him to brake, the two tyre marks and the glass?'

There was another pause before the country cop answered, as if weighing how much information he should be sharing with a journalist.

'Yes. And we're looking into what was found at his Apollo Bay property yesterday.'

Curly was momentarily stunned. 'Found? What did they find at his beach house?'

'To call it a beach house makes it sound grander than it is. It's rustic you might say, not much above a shack. The location is close enough to town but still reasonably isolated. Apparently, he didn't have many visitors. He would chat to everyone in the local bar, buy them drinks, but no one can recall visiting his place in the 20-odd years he lived there. The old farmer who sold him the land died soon after and the gullies weren't considered good for anything. But it seems Tugga found a way to make money.'

'Okay, you've got me on the hook. What did you find, not the old farmer's body I hope?'

Laidlaw laughed. 'No, the old boy's pushing up daisies in town. It turns out Tugga had quite the green thumb. He might've spent all week chopping down trees but he made up for it on weekends by growing stuff. Tugga's secret hobby was growing dope.'

Curly wanted to leap up and do a double fist pump. His hunch was correct, there was far more to this story and they needed to get to Lorne and Apollo Bay ASAP.

He waved to Mac and Jo and gave a thumbs-up. Curly then pointed at a reporter sitting at their terminal – a sure indication no story had been assigned to them yet – whirled his hand like a helicopter and mimed *Lorne*. That was enough to get Jo rolling. The chopper was a joint share between news and current affairs. As the *Spotlight* crew rarely worked on weekends they had first claim on the machine on Monday.

Curly turned his attention back to squeezing more information out of the extremely accommodating Lorne copper.

'How much dope are we talking about? Was he supplying?'

'I think he was small time, the local cops found 20 plants and two bags containing a kilo of grass ready for sale. He was clever enough to stay below our radar on the coast. Our guess is he was selling it back in Geelong. He had the perfect front for the operation. That ute was always full of vegetable matter and junk, no one would ever have suspected. Probably made more from dealing in the green stuff than grinding it up.'

'Okay, so we could describe him as a small-time grower and dealer?'

'Looks that way.'

'Is there a chance his death and the tap from the second car might be related, that it was drug related?'

Again, there was a pause on the phone, long enough for Curly to wonder again why this cop was providing so much detail. Usually pulling teeth was easier than extracting information from police.

'On the record, I'll say we can't make any assumptions like that. Off the record, it's one angle that we'll definitely look at.'

'You know I'm going to need what you can give me on the record, and to get some shots of Tugga's property and the dope you've found up there. I can get a crew there in about 90 minutes. You happy to front for an interview?'

The delay wasn't as long as Curly expected.

'Yep, I guess I've kicked over the beehive, so I should do the right thing and front up.'

'That's brilliant, Jim. I'll go brief my boss and get the reporter and chopper on the way. They'll check in when they land and confirm your location. No doubt we'll be talking more in the days ahead depending on how things go. Just a couple of final things before I go.'

'Yep, fire away.'

'Firstly, what made you curious about the tyre marks in the first place?'

'I moved here from the Major Collision Investigation Unit. I spent a few years dealing with accident scenes, solving mysteries became second nature to me I suppose, until my wife decided she wanted the coastal life.'

'And I guess that last comment might partly answer my next question. Why have you been so forward with information? Doesn't happen too often in our business.'

Laidlaw laughed, he understood it was a rare situation. 'Well, the dope angle would have surfaced in a day or two from one of the pubs down here. The surfies are pissed off they didn't know about Tugga's stash sitting up in the bush, otherwise they would have helped themselves to a few plants when he was back in Geelong.

But you're right, there's something about this accident that doesn't stack up, so I want answers, whichever way I can get them.'

Curly was fizzing at the bung after he hung up the phone. He quickly updated Mac on the new angle – the famous Kiwi landscaper was a coastal drug kingpin. And the local cop believed a second vehicle was involved. Mac wanted to go a step further and suggest the accident might have been a hit by a rival gang, but Curly knew that angle would risk losing his new best Victoria Police friend in Lorne.

They swiftly dispatched the reporter and camera operator to the chopper base with shot lists, questions, contact details and preferred locations for pieces to camera. It was agreed that Curly's time would be better spent at the station, to script, commission graphics and source supplementary vision for when the reporter returned in a panic late in the afternoon. The reporter's name and face would be on the story, but it would be Curly's production.

It was good old-fashioned journalism – a gut instinct proved correct – and both producers were chuffed.

Then Mac had another thought from left-field. 'Hey, do you know what would make this story even better?'

'What? We've got two fresh angles the other stations don't have. How greedy do we need to be Mac?'

'Just imagine if The Hatchet *is* involved in the drug operation? Is he the Melbourne Mr Big?'

Curly looked up from his terminal to see Mac with a broad smile; teasing. Or was he?

The reference to Hackett reminded him to check his email inbox. There were the usual half a dozen corporate messages and a few from mates commenting on his weekend story.

Crap quality on the pictures mate, but good on you for getting so close.

But the email that caught his attention was the briefest. It was from Hackett.

'Jeezus,' Curly called out to Mac. 'The Hatchet wants to talk to me – as soon as possible.'

Chapter 9

The view from Andrew Hackett's tenth floor office was impressive. South Melbourne, Port Melbourne, Albert Park, Middle Park, a slice of St Kilda and a big chunk of Port Philip Bay were framed by his corporate eyrie. Most days he allowed himself a few minutes to enjoy the panorama. It was confirmation of his success. Only the smart and wealthy made it to these heights to indulge themselves with these perks.

The morning haze had evaporated, although a few low clouds drifted past from the south west. Hackett's eyes were fixed on the horizon, but this morning they didn't register the changing weather. He should have been revelling in the success of his early meeting with the Chief Executive about the AFL broadcasting rights. The next step, a mere formality, was to get the TV station's board to approve the budget.

But it was not the great start to his business day that preoccupied Hackett. His mind was focused on the strange death of another member of Tugga's Mob.

Hackett turned back to the news article that had stunned him more than the first two deaths, or perhaps it was simply accumulated shock. Gerry Daly had been killed while cycling in New Zealand in September.

Tugga, Drew — and now Gerry.

Three of Tugga's Mob all accidentally killed within two months of each other. This was more than weird; it was creepy.

Tugga's Mob has been obliterated. Well almost.

He read the news story one more time, hoping it might provide something more illuminating. It was dated 20 September.

Cyclist killed on Coromandel Road

Police are continuing their search for the vehicle involved in an early morning hit-and-run accident that claimed the life of a Conservation Ranger on Monday.

Gerald Daly, 54, an enthusiastic cyclist, was found in bush on a steep incline about three km south of Kuaotunu.

Police say the driver would know they had struck the cyclist. The badly damaged bike was discovered some distance from the body. Police suspect the driver might have panicked and urged them to make contact as soon as possible.

Daly lived on a lifestyle block near Whitianga and was often seen cycling the roads around Coromandel by himself. A search started on Monday when he failed to report for work. A friend saw Daly cycling towards Kuaotunu at about 6am which helped narrow the search area.

Colleagues say Daly was a respected member of the community and that he was a safety conscious rider. They say Daly started his working life in forestry but turned to conservation work after returning from Europe in 1986.

Police are urging motorists who used Highway 25 on Monday morning to contact them.

There were several more stories over the following days, but the mystery driver never came forward. The case was still open and New Zealand police were treating it as an accident.

Hackett had already made his latest grim discovery when the email from Curly had arrived with a muted ping. His adrenalin spiked. The *Spotlight* team was proposing a follow-up story on Tugga's death and wanted some background information on the big fella.

Hackett didn't trust journalists. Finely tuned instincts, and a healthy dose of paranoia helped him survive more than three decades in the corporate world. Right now, his gut told him the news bastards had inside information from the cops about Tugga's demise – and he wanted to know. Hackett glanced briefly at the name of the journalist who sent the request for a chat. Curly Rogers didn't ring any bells with him. He noted from the automated signature that Rogers was a producer on *Spotlight*, so that might explain why he couldn't put a face to the name.

Too ugly for TV, or too old?

Hackett knew little about the structure of the news and current affairs departments; things like who wrote or reported or filmed or did what to whom at whatever time did not interest him. He did know they spent a fortune every day.

Perhaps this interaction with the staff might be doubly productive. Hackett could glean the latest information on Tugga's death and assess the smarts of this producer. Curly's name could be added to the next round of redundancies if he didn't impress.

He composed a terse reply and hit send, smiling at the thought that Curly was unaware the command to ascend to the top floor had more at stake than background information.

Hackett also considered how much he should share about the deaths of Drew and Gerry. His own shock had certainly turned to curiosity.

Three accidental deaths – what are the odds?

There was also a momentary flicker of apprehension that the deaths of his three friends from a lifetime ago should concern him; he was, after all, now the only surviving male from Tugga's Mob.

Will this producer knob think I'm just being paranoid?

Or, would Curly struggle to hide his glee that The Hatchet might be the next member of Tugga's Mob to suffer an *accident?*

That was the nub of the matter: three mates, three accidental deaths, all in a few weeks. How could it be coincidental?

From Hackett's experience, journalists were always willing to latch onto a conspiracy. They could milk the story for days, or weeks, until it ran out of steam with readers or viewers. They then quietly let them slide and moved on to the next drama that might sell newspapers or TV shows. Although some people loved their 15 minutes of fame, Hackett's ego didn't require that sort of stroking and, professionally, his corporate image could do without any potential dirt that might stick from Tugga's exit.

Hackett's next meeting was 45 minutes away, and he had no idea when Curly would find his way to the corporate suites, so he decided it was time to track down the other surviving member of Tugga's Mob – Helen Franks.

Casting his mind back to the end of the tour again, Hackett realised he couldn't remember the last time he'd seen Helen. He didn't recall her being part of the space cake buffet on the final evening in Amsterdam. And there weren't any memories of Helen around the camp site during the final pack up. Mind you, that wasn't a surprise given his near catatonic state from the cannabis binge.

Hackett turned to Google again to launch another search, this time hoping for a better result: another living member of Tugga's Mob apart from himself. Less than a second produced 933,000 results for Helen Franks. Once again, he ignored LinkedIn and Wikipedia as potential sources.

You were never that classy, Helen.

July 3, 1986

We've just experienced a couple of the most emotional yet amazing days of the tour – Gallipoli. I thought I knew the history from school and listening to dad after a couple of glasses of Tawny Port on a Sunday night, but being here and walking amongst the graves and seeing the ages of the soldiers made me cry, several times.

Many of the ANZACs were younger than me, and I'm only 25. They volunteered for king and country and honour and glory and all that stuff that sounds so silly to me now. But here they lie, buried half a world away from home, their Big OEs a few months of terror in sunbaked trenches with flies, atrocious food and unimaginable slaughter.

I can't help asking, was it worth it? The Ataturk message at the Ari Burnu Memorial made me cry the most. It was the first time I understood that we were invaders. Of course the Turks were going to defend their homes and families as fiercely as they could. I always thought the ANZACs were on a noble mission to end the First World War. That's what school told us, and even dad's potted history lessons followed the same themes.

The Turks must have wondered who these crazy Colonials were charging over their hills and trying to kill them. Yet the Ataturk message is so noble and forgiving, telling foreign mothers who lost sons on these shores that they now lie in peace, side by side with Turkish sons, sharing the soil of a friendly country. I wonder if we could ever be that kind to former enemies?

That might seem a bit maudlin but we were all glad to experience such important history. We spent an afternoon visiting the various battle sites and cemeteries. Brian found a Turkish cartridge which Andreas spent hours trying to swap. I laughed at his persistence and told him to go find his own, which didn't impress him.

I managed to walk Plugge's Plateau where Poppa scrambled across under fire on that first day. I even saw a black snake curled up on a track, soaking up the sun. It was interesting to see it – and give it a wide berth – as we were never taught anything about those Gallipoli dangers at school.

We finished the day by following a Top Deck bus south along the coast to a small Turkish camp site. It was right on the water and basic, but beautifully located. People were saying it was hard to imagine such a lovely camp site could be that close to a battlefield. One of the Turkish managers told us the entire peninsula was a battlefield. It wasn't just Aussies and Kiwis – there were French, Indian, British and even a contingent from Newfoundland fighting the Turks, Germans and Austrians. Our education was finally being brought up to date.

It was an amazing night, sitting under the stars drinking cold Turkish beer and sharing our lives with the locals and a few backpacking Germans and Danes. This is what I came to Europe to experience. I learned so much today and developed a greater understanding and affection for the Turks.

There was also a hilarious story from a Top Deck driver about a previous tour. A Malaysian passenger – a chef – wasn't interested in Gallipoli history, unlike the Kiwis and Aussies, so he stayed at the camp site while they toured around. When the passengers returned, they found the Malaysian chef had been industrious – scooping up mussels and other shellfish from the shallows and preparing a spicy dish. The passengers were happily wolfing down the seafood until someone pointed out what we had only recently learned: that the beach had seen battles during the war, and people had probably died in the sea here.

Tears rolled down the Top Deck driver's face as he described how half the passengers dashed off to the dunes to be sick. The other half – including driver and courier – finished the shellfish feast with a bemused Malaysian chef. It was one of many funny stories that were shared on the night.

Sadly, for me, there was an ugly moment and it was caused by Tugga. For a big man he's light on his feet and can creep up on you without warning. The toilet facilities were primitive – smelly starting blocks, as we call them – and we were going into the dunes for a pee. I had just finished when I stood up to find Tugga standing a few feet away with his trousers down, but not wanting to pee. I told him he was gross and to stay away from me. He called me a cock-teaser as I ran back to the beach gathering. He is getting seriously weird and I'll have to be careful I don't let him catch me like that again.

I didn't tell the others as there is a good vibe in the group. Us Kiwi girls don't like to create a fuss, unlike some of those Australian prima donnas!

We didn't get much sleep that night as we were up before dawn to go back to ANZAC Cove to experience the time of the landing. It was spooky in the half-light and then everyone freaked when a firework exploded. I'm sure it was Tugga, or one of his Mob, but it was hard to tell with tourists from three buses mingling around the headstones at Ari Burnu, and they never owned up.

We spent a few more hours there exploring other famous battle sites – significant for us Kiwis and Aussies – before hitting the road for Istanbul.

Breakfast was fresh Turkish bread. This van arrived out of nowhere and I think we cleaned him out of loaves in a few minutes. Bread, jam and sugary tea – a basic breakfast, but so much yummier compared to what Poppa and his mates ever got to eat at ANZAC Cove. I think word spreads quickly along the coast when Antipodeans land at Gallipoli – again! This time the meetings are much friendlier. We're all now looking forward to exotic Istanbul and shopping at the Grand Bazaar.

The diary-holder flicked back through several pages to the briefer entries made during the days in Greece. Such a contrast in experiences and impressions of two ancient cultures. It was what the Big OE was supposed to be all about; opening blinkered South Pacific minds to the wider world. Yet, there was always someone selfishly wanting to spoil things, to get their own way. The diary was returned to its safe place once again.

Chapter 10

The butterflies in Curly Rogers' stomach struggled to keep up with the lift as it ascended rapidly to the executive offices on the tenth floor. He had been a journalist for 21 years: 15 working in television and the last 10 with this station, but he had never reached these heights before.

Most newsroom employees summoned to the upper levels rarely returned to rejoin their workmates. The lucky were permitted to collect their personal possessions, arrange a wake at the nearest pub and then depart the building with some dignity to search for a new network. The unlucky were escorted from the premises by a security guard, or two, only stopping long enough to retrieve their briefcases from the newsroom. Sometimes it was handed to them outside the front door.

That was the standard early departure for heads of news, executive producers and senior producers who had outlived their usefulness. The occasional female presenter who survived long enough to reach her 50th birthday might be allowed a final broadcast if she promised not to cry on air.

The hoi poloi – producers, reporters, editors, directors, camera operators, technical staff, engineers, media ops, librarians and admin staff – didn't need to go to the top of the cliff to be pushed off. A senior manager would sweep into the newsroom to declare a new cull was imminent because of poor ratings, budget blowouts or dwindling advertising revenues.

Thanks for your efforts; TV is a tough business; good luck out there.

The unfortunates would find out their fate from Human Resources in a few days. That usually stifled newsroom protests as no one wanted to put their heads above the parapet: the bullet with their name on it might not be fired in that skirmish with management.

Curly noticed in recent years that the Human Resources department took on extra staff to handle these company purges, yet their temporary positions became permanent after the newsroom bodies were removed.

The lift doors opened to a corporate world of white opal walls, plush dark carpet, floor to ceiling windows that framed vast swathes of the city, a two-seater sofa and a solitary receptionist who looked like she was recruited straight from a fashion shoot. It was the amazing views of Port Phillip Bay that reassured Curly he hadn't emerged from the TARDIS into a multi-national headquarters in London, Paris or New York. He didn't have time to decide if the décor was meant to welcome visitors, or intimidate them, before the receptionist greeted him.

'Good morning, are you Mr Rogers from *Melbourne Spotlight?*' She emerged from behind a long rectangular desk. 'I'm Zara, the Executive Assistant to Mr Hackett.'

Zara didn't offer to shake hands, accurately summarising from Curly's story-gathering attire: Rodd & Gunn chinos and open-neck shirt and sneakers that he was indeed one of the station minions, and therefore didn't require the star treatment.

Zara was stunning, even with her corporate no-nonsense face, toned and tanned legs in heels that elevated her to least 180cm, blonde shoulder-length hair and all packaged in a mid-calf dark blue sheath dress.

Curly struggled not to be snippy with his response, though he let Zara's inquiry hang for a moment longer than necessary to remind her they were both part of the same company.

'Yes, indeed,' he finally acknowledged as his eyes made another slow sweep around the glamorous surroundings. 'You've never visited the *Spotlight* office? Such a shame, it's only a hundred metres as the crow flies – but you might need a GPS to find us down at the coalface.'

Confirmation of his bona fides was accompanied by a smile, and was received with the professional mien he expected. The haves and the have nots in the company had formed their battle lines.

And here I thought we were struggling to survive. The bosses clearly don't know the meaning of the word!

'Mr Hackett is expecting you. Follow me, please.'

Interesting that The Hatchet's EA is the gatekeeper.

Zara pivoted and strode down a central hallway. They passed half a dozen doors with nameplates for executives, and the board room. All the doors were closed although the murmur of voices could be heard. Zara approached a corner suite, knocked and entered all in one fluid movement.

As Curly was presented with another majestic view of Melbourne's seaside suburbs he struggled to keep his jaw from dropping. Journalists never want to reveal when they're impressed.

Hackett showed little courtesy as he sat at his desk and tidied spreadsheets. 'Rogers, is it?'

'Christopher Rogers, as chosen by my mother at birth, but these days I answer to Curly.'

Hackett lifted his eyes from the paperwork and noted the lack of any follicles to support that moniker. He snorted. 'Newsroom humour?' He waved Curly to a seat facing the desk as he swept the papers into a folder and pushed it to the side and moved onto the next topic.

'Right, thanks for popping up here, ah, Curly. Tugga Tancred – I have to admit his death is causing more surprises than I expected.'

Curly's radar immediately pinged on the word *surprises*. Surely Hackett didn't know about the second-vehicle theory yet, or the dope crop Tugga grew in Apollo Bay?

Curly had only talked to the Lorne cop half an hour ago and didn't think the station grapevine extended to this tower. *Do they bug our offices now?* Paranoia was a required survival skill in the television industry. He decided the best option was to draw out whatever information Hackett had before sharing his revelations.

'What do you mean by surprises? You do mean plural – as in more surprises than Tugga's death?'

Hackett paused to assess the journalist more closely, realising Curly was sharper than he expected. He was fishing for information and he was used to asking the questions.

'Yes, there have been a couple more surprises since Tugga drove off the cliff. I hadn't seen or heard anything about him – or anyone, in fact from that trip – since Europe in '86. You know, we just happened to book the same tour because it was the cheapest. We travelled around, saw Europe, had a great time and went our own ways. I saw a couple of passengers at pubs and parties in London over the following 12 months, but never set eyes on Tugga's Mob again.'

'Tugga's Mob?'

'That was a nickname that became popular on the bus. Tugga was big, loud and enjoyed a beer. He was always up for some fun. He naturally drew attention to himself and those around him.'

Hackett's chair tilted back as he relaxed into memories of a younger life of adventure.

'Groups used to form quickly on tours in those days. Most passengers were early 20s and away from home for the first time. It could be daunting with the different languages, new food, multiple currencies and new cultures every other day. Border guards could be intimidating and bureaucratic, and all the big cities had bloody gypsies hassling you for money while trying to pick your pockets; that sort of thing. Probably not politically correct to stereotype people like that these days, but that was the reality then.

'Some travellers needed security in numbers. Others aligned themselves with people of similar interests. You would get the culture vultures who wanted to visit every museum, art gallery, castle and the birthplaces of famous composers or writers. And then there were the party people who wanted to enjoy themselves while still seeing the best of Europe. Those who gravitated towards the big fella were known as Tugga's Mob.'

'And which group were you in?'

Hackett rested his elbows on the desk before he replied. 'Technically, the other passengers considered me part of Tugga's Mob. I had a good time, probably drank more than I should have, but still saw all the highlights. I enjoyed their company at times and I also associated with lots of other people from the bus – and different tour groups.'

Looking at the 50-something television executive in his designer suit and silk tie, Curly struggled to visualise The Hatchet as a party animal in the '80s. Hackett looked as if he was born in an office.

Curly shrugged. 'It was much the same in the '90s when I did my own tripping around Europe, so to speak.'

Hackett ignored any kindred traveller connections. 'Anyway, Tugga's Mob pre-dated the trip. He arrived in London with a couple of mates from New Zealand – from memory they all worked in forestry chopping down trees – and there was a girl, Helen Franks. She was a bar worker they knew in Rotorua who had moved to Sydney. Helen chucked the Sydney job in and joined them in England just before the trip. She was always looking for a new adventure. I enjoyed a few beers in those days and that's how, in theory, I became part of Tugga's Mob.'

'That was 30 years ago. You've had no contact with Tugga or other members of the Mob since, right?'

Hackett nodded.

'So, what other surprises has Tugga's plunge off the Great Ocean Road generated? Have the other *mob*sters emerged through Facebook or Twitter to express their condolences?'

Hackett squirmed, then looked Curly directly in the eyes for the first time. 'No, far from it in fact. Tugga isn't the only one to have met an accidental death. His two mates were both killed in accidents recently. A bit weird, don't you think?'

Curly sat silently for almost five seconds as he weighed these new nuggets of information. *Bloody gold!*

'Tugga *and* his two best mates are dead? From accidents? What time frame are we talking about: when, where and how?' Curly kept his expression neutral despite the intensity of the questions. His initial gut instinct from the weekend might turn into an absolute cracker of a story. *Where's this all going to lead?*

Hackett could sense the excitement that coursed through the journalist. Was there even more to these accidents?

'They're all quite recent,' he said. 'Although the other two – Drew Harvey and Gerry Daly – died in New Zealand. Drew drowned while rock fishing at the end of August and Gerry was knocked off his bicycle in September. And now Tugga on the weekend.'

Hackett explained how the news about Tugga naturally, and for the first time in years, brought back memories of the trip. And that consequently, prompted him to Google the other members of the tour party. He'd wondered if anyone had become famous, or successful in business like him? Instead he'd found out about Gerry's accident, and then the third death amongst that tight group. He admitted he was sitting in shock when Curly's request for background information had come through.

Curly spent a few more minutes milking information from Hackett about the New Zealand deaths.

But Hackett, having verbalised it for the first time, started to understand the journalist's obvious suspicions.

Accidents, coincidence – or something else?

Hackett decided he should share the news about Helen – or the lack of it. He reached into a drawer on the right-hand side of the desk and pulled out the group picture from Volendam. He pushed it across towards Curly before speaking again.

'That's a tour group photo at Volendam, in the Netherlands. You probably did something similar on your trip?'

Curly nodded and waited for Hackett to continue as he picked up the picture.

'You can see the big fella in the middle, at the back. Drew's on his right, with me beside him and Gerry on his left. Helen is beside Gerry.'

Curly peered at Tugga's Mob. The big and brawny Kiwis had assumed the traditional staunch rugby pose, with chins thrust forward, arms folded and no smiles. The 1980s version of Hackett, however, was a marked contrast to the grey corporate executive who sat across from him. Thick, unkempt hair sprouted from beneath his Dutch fishing hat. He sported a then-fashionable drooping moustache that couldn't hide a broad smile. He appeared to be having the time of his life – the deep bags under the eyes were familiar signs of late nights in camping ground bars and continental taverns.

Hackett, only a little shorter than Drew, couldn't match the Kiwis' bulk. Their muscles had been toned on rugby fields and in North Island forests. Hackett's youthful physique hadn't survived the climb up the corporate ladder. Neither had his facial hair.

Curly scanned the other faces, stopping at Helen. She was attractive enough though the Dutch costume wasn't flattering and made her look severe. He asked the most obvious question. 'What about Helen? What do you know about her?'

'Nothing. Not a mention anywhere on the Web that I can find so far. I guess that might be a good sign?'

'If you mean it's unlikely she's also met with a recent *accidental* death. Maybe.'

Hackett's eyes widened. 'Four accidental deaths would make it too damn freaky, wouldn't it?'

Curly nodded, pondering how much more there might be to drain from The Hatchet before revealing his own info about the police investigation into the second-car theory. That factual detail suddenly took on greater significance when thrown into the news blender with two other untimely deaths… and the possibly missing Helen.

But was she really missing? She probably married, possibly several times in 30 years, and Curly doubted The Hatchet had the investigative skills to do a proper search for his former friend.

Curly was about to throw that caution onto the pyre when The Hatchet's mobile phone demanded attention.

Hackett glanced at the caller ID expecting he would be able to let it go to voice mail; after all, this journalist hadn't revealed anything yet. The caller was Reg Bradley, the station chief executive and the only person Hackett couldn't ignore. His phone greeting was politer than the conversation with Curly.

'What the fuck do they want, Reg?' Hackett shouted into the mobile as he paced the room. 'I've given them all the data, the numbers all stack up, the timing is perfect. Why can't they make a fucking decision?'

It was on Hackett's second circuit of the office that he realised this was a conversation that Curly shouldn't be hearing. 'Where are you, Reg? Okay, I'll be there in a moment.'

Hackett slammed the mobile on the desk and reached for the door handle. The Board's failure to rubber stamp his AFL broadcasting rights coup was more critical than talking to a journalist about three dead travelling companions.

'Look, something important has come up. I'll have to catch you later.' Hackett said as he exited the office, crossed the hallway to the other corner suite and entered without knocking.

The meeting exceeded Curly's expectations. Journalists don't need much to inflame suspicious natures: three accidental deaths among the same group of friends in a matter of weeks, plus a possible 'missing' fourth person, was like throwing a can of petrol onto a bonfire for the *Spotlight* producer.

Mac's going to love this!

Curly knew The Hatchet was rattled by the news about his former travelling companions, but didn't want to suggest, yet, the deaths were more sinister than accidents. That change in tone on the phone and Hackett's subtle deferment didn't escape the current affairs producer. Curly surmised it must have been the boss as Hackett didn't even apologise for disrupting their meeting. He turned his eyes to appreciate the view again while absorbing the one-sided conversation. The Hatchet wasn't happy.

Curly could still hear The Hatchet venting as he returned to the reception area and waited for the lift. Zara didn't bother acknowledging his departure. If she had, she might have noticed Curly was leaving with something extra. The Volendam picture was overlapping Curly's notebook held against his thigh.

Chapter 11

Mac was feeling remarkably chipper for a Monday. The office was virtually empty which meant all the reporters and crews were doing their jobs: creating television stories. There was only the quiet burble of Jo and Kim's voices as they worked the phones. Mac managed to get his ATM card to spit out $40 mid-morning to replenish the funds *borrowed* from the caffeine-addicts kitty, thus avoiding another public kangaroo court. Where the money came from Mac had no idea. It wasn't there Friday night when he tried to use the card at the pub. Perhaps Denise, his personal Minister for Financial Affairs in the suburbs, had mistakenly transferred money to that account while juggling the domestic finances.

She's been nagging me to get a haircut for weeks, was it for that?

Mac wasn't silly enough to ask but was pondering these weighty matters when a man on a mission charged into the *Spotlight* office.

Curly headed straight for his computer to collate the information provided by The Hatchet. He barely noticed the empty office or the quizzical look from Mac.

'You're back, Mr Rogers,' Mac commented dryly. 'A journalist returning to their desk and continuing to work after a visit to the top floor verges on the miraculous.'

Curly continued to type. 'Yep, and you're going to love this, Mac,'

'Enlighten me, oh great survivor.'

Curly finished the sentence he was writing, then picked up the

Volendam picture, marched over to Mac's command post, and pointed out the faces in Dutch costume.

'I present to you the cohort known as Tugga's Mob. The photo was taken in the Netherlands in 1986. All the bus trips did it, it was part of the tourist kitsch.

'That bloke there is Tugga. Next to him is Drew Harvey. On the other side of Tugga is Gerry Daly. They were life-long mates – and they have all died in the last eight weeks – supposedly from accidents.'

Mac raised both eyebrows as he absorbed the information, while he studied the picture. 'Is that Hackett there, trying to look like *Magnum PI*?'

'Yes, it's Hackett, but what the hell is a Magnum PI?' Curly ducked as a right hand swung out to cuff his head.

'Cheeky bastard, you bloody know who Tom Selleck is.'

'Yeah but it's a wonder you old codgers remember anything beyond your last pub visit.'

Mac laughed, his good humour blossoming as he understood the significance of Curly's update. He had unearthed enough material to make this a lead story. 'Is Hackett suggesting there's anything suspicious about these accidental deaths – that they might be related? And what's with this Tugga's Mob?'

'I don't think all the pieces have gelled for him yet; and that maybe he should be worried that three of his old travelling companions died so very recently from 'accidents'. Curly air-quoted the last word. 'There's also that possibility that another member of Tugga's Mob,' Curly pointed at Helen, 'is missing. Although at the moment that's a stretch.'

'So, four of Tugga's Mob are dead or missing? Tell me,' Mac almost begged, 'that Hackett had a really close connection with this Mob. And that he's the only bloke still alive. '

'Yep. He was one of the five in Tugga's Mob during that bus tour.'

'Yes! Okay, and these other deaths, is there anything suspicious about them? Is there enough doubt about them that we can raise the possibility some nutter is out there?'

Curly smiled. 'I know we love a good conspiracy, but in this case I'm sure we'll find something in the other two deaths as well. Drew Harvey died alone while fishing from the favourite spot he'd been using for 25 years. Gerry Daly was bounced from his bicycle in a hit-and-run on a lonely country road in New Zealand. No witnesses – and no driver has been found.

'The Hatchett said he couldn't find Helen Franks, but she may have got married and changed her name. So I'd be cautious about her at this stage. But my gut is telling me we are on to something.'

Mac was starting to visualise the story they could put to air that evening. 'So, what did Hackett say about the possibility of a second car involved in Tugga's crash and the dope growing operation in Apollo Bay? Surely that must have got him interested?'

'I didn't get a chance to tell him. Reg Bradley rang and he raced off screaming about the board being a bunch of fuckwits. He said he'd talk to me later, but I'm not holding my breath. I don't think we could count on him for anything on tonight's show – or ever.'

Both journalists paused as they considered the subtext: their boss might be a target if there was someone wiping out Tugga's Mob. Was it related to the tour 30 years ago, or was it something more current, such as the dope plantation in the Otways? They knew they didn't have to provide answers in their first story. Three deaths were suspicious and their duty was to broadcast the story and see what happened.

Mac looked around the office for support staff. It was still just Jo and Kim, who, from the arm-waving and phones attached to their ears, seemed fully engaged. Nevertheless—

'Jo, Kim, drop whatever you're doing and circle the wagons around Curly. He's got the lead tonight and you have to help us get it together.'

He turned back to Curly. 'I'm going to have to talk to Templeton about this when I can find him, because it involves a station executive. I suspect he'll be a softcock and want to keep Hackett's name out until he talks to him.

'I think our best bet, to avoid them yanking it at the last minute, is to structure the story along the lines of shocking revelations from the Great Ocean Road fatality. A second car might have been involved, the dope growing activities and the suspicious deaths of two other mates of the victim. You know how to milk it. Lots of innuendo and questions but nothing that will make the top floor nervous tonight. Once it's out there the other vultures will sniff the Hackett connection and we can go to town with that.

'Well done, mate. This could be our biggest story of the year, so get cracking. I'm going to work on a promo that will make the other channels weep with envy.'

July 7, 1986

Farewell exotic Istanbul. It's the turnaround point on my trip of a lifetime and what an amazing place for reflection. East meets West in this vibrant and exciting city and I'm sad to say goodbye. Topkapi Palace, the Blue Mosque, Hagia Sophia, the Hippodrome, the Bosphorus, the spice market, the bath houses, the minarets and the seemingly never-ending calls to prayer – it will all stay in my memories forever.

The people are friendly and I'm sure my teeth are going to fall out after the gallons of apple tea and sugar we've consumed.

The hospitality seems genuine. Sure, they're trying to sell us carpets, leather jackets or gold jewellery, but even when we say we can't afford that stuff they love to sit and chat. They still want to understand why our grandfathers travelled half-way around the world to invade their homeland. Being here now, most of us are wondering the same thing. King, country and duty don't make a lot of sense when trying to defend the Gallipoli campaign to the Turks.

It was funny seeing the mix of traditional Turkey – women still covered head to toe – with modern Turkey where many of the women were much more stylish than us.

Granted we are backpacking the world, but our battered shorts, T-shirts and jandals look dowdy by comparison to their daily wear. It was a giggle having to wear long dresses and head scarves in the 90-degree heat to visit sacred sites, but afterwards I could see how important donning that cloak of respectability was for them. Pity some of our group didn't treat the Turks with the same respect.

Tugga's Mob were rude in the Blue Mosque – yelling out to each other how it was big enough to play a game of rugby inside. They've been hammering the local beer because it's cheap, and we're all getting sick of them. I also had another nasty encounter with Tugga and a couple of his boys. It was in the Grand Bazaar. I was loving the place – it's massive, the biggest shopping centre I've ever been in – and then Tugga spoiled it. I was looking at some silk as I wanted to make a blouse for Mum when I get back to London. She would love the colours and, I fancy, we could have many hours of fun haggling with the store keepers as Mum always loves to bargain.

I was shopping by myself for a few minutes, which is rare in the bazaar as they usually swoop on westerners immediately, when I felt a hand grab my breast. I pushed the hand away and turned around to demand an apology when I realised it was Tugga. Two of his mates were laughing, thinking it was a hoot. I slapped him hard and he pushed me back into the rolls of silk and walked away. It tarnished my time in one of the great bazaars of the world and I ran back to the bus to get away.

Eddie, the driver, was there. I told him what happened and demanded he kick Tugga off the trip. He's a pathetic and useless tour guide and driver. He said he would have to clear it with head office and that they would require an official police report, otherwise it was Tugga's word against mine. He wanted me to drop the matter. I let him talk me out of calling the London office myself when he promised to pull Tugga into line.

It must have been water off a duck's back because I saw Eddie and Tugga's Mob sharing a carton of beers after the so-called 'telling-off' last night. I was angry when I talked to the other girls and they sympathised, because several had similar experiences to relate about Tugga making crude comments. We've made a pact to look after each other when he's around. Fortunately Tugga's Mob sit at the back of the bus when we're travelling, so we can keep some distance. But enough of that beast.

We're on our way back to Greece for a barbecue at the beach and then overland to Yugoslavia and Dubrovnik. That walled city is one place I've been wanting to visit since I saw pictures at school. I just hope the waters of the Adriatic are as crystal clear as the tourist brochures indicate.

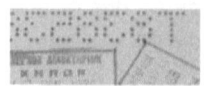

The 7 July diary entry always made the holder shake. Even with both hands on the diary the tremors couldn't be stifled and the anger coursed through their body. Tugga's sexual assault would earn him a court visit these days. But in the 1980s it was always easier to brush it under the carpet. Don't make waves: a very New Zealand approach to awkward matters.

The diary holder was frustrated that a more sensitive and pro-active approach to an ugly incident by the tour company could have prevented what was to follow. It might have saved lives.

Chapter 12

The door to Andrew Hackett's South Yarra Tuscan villa looked capable of withstanding an assault by several Roman centurions. Hackett, however, revealed its modern construction and frailty when he slammed it against the unyielding brickwork in the foyer. Three fractures appeared in the timber, not that Hackett noticed. His fury was focused on company business and the TV board which wouldn't support his AFL television rights coup.

Gutless bastards!

His brilliant day had turned to a pile of crap, made worse when a mid-afternoon text revealed Marianne wouldn't be home that night.

New drama with Juliette. I'll call later. Sorry darling.

Juliette was Marianne's twice-divorced younger sister with regular relationship problems. A hurried phone call from Marianne before Hackett left the TV station revealed the crisis was caused by Juliette catching her latest beau, Jeremy, shagging the massage therapist in the pool house. The boyfriend was banished from their Brighton abode and Marianne was summoned to provide a shoulder.

Hackett didn't care about Juliette's love life, but he was annoyed it meant he had to make his own dinner. He wasn't helpless in the kitchen but didn't fancy having to cook after a shitty day. He dumped his briefcase in the office doorway and went in search of a cold beer.

Hackett picked up the TV remote from the sideboard in the living room and flicked on the Samsung 82" 4K Smart TV. It was bigger than the set in the home office and cost almost $8000. It was also provided by his employers. Hackett watched the young female weather presenter finish her segment with a five-day temperature forecast.

Yeah right. If you weren't so cute, you'd be serving tables in Lygon Street.

Next would be a giggle session with the news anchor before he handed over to the *Melbourne Spotlight* frontman at the other end of the studio.

Curiosity welled in Hackett, as he hadn't managed to get back to Curly. And rather than getting information from the *Spotlight* producer, he realised he'd done all the talking.

But what else can they say about Tugga?

He grabbed a chilled Corona and a packet of salt-reduced potato chips, then settled into his favourite leather armchair. He filled his mouth with a comforting mix of carbohydrates.

And seconds later almost choked on the *Spotlight* presenter's introduction:

'Tonight on *Melbourne Spotlight*, shocking revelations from the weekend road fatality at Lorne. Was Tugga Tancred an innocent road victim, or was he murdered?

'An exclusive *Spotlight* investigation can reveal that a second car was probably involved in the Friday night accident which saw the Geelong-based businessman plunge to his death on rocks below the Great Ocean Road.

'We can also reveal the expat New Zealander led a sinister double life. By day he was a genial landscaper, while at the weekends he ran a sophisticated drug operation from his hillside property at Apollo Bay.

'Is there a connection between the crash and the marijuana he peddled up and down the Coast? We can tell you the police are taking a serious look at that angle.'

Hackett ignored the soggy chips splattered over his suit pants. *Murder? Drugs?* That was shocking enough. The camera then cut away from the presenter to a familiar photograph: it was his Volendam picture. The voice-over continued:

> 'Does this case have international connections as well? This photograph was taken on a bus tour in the Netherlands in 1986.'

The picture changed from the wide group shot into a close-up of Tugga, Drew and Gerry, all electronically circled for viewers. Hackett and Helen were mostly cropped, only parts of their arms and ears appeared in the close-up.

> 'That's the Lorne victim Tugga Tancred standing in the middle. Beside him are his two best mates from New Zealand.
>
> Tonight, *Spotlight* can reveal those other men – Drew Harvey and Gerry Daly – are also dead in mysterious circumstances. The timeframe? Just over eight weeks.
>
> We begin our exclusive and disturbing report from the Great Ocean Road–'

Hackett watched the report with raised eyebrows and without touching his beer or chips. The story introduction wasn't journalistic bluster. A Lorne cop confirmed he found pieces of the tail-light from Tugga's vehicle on the road. The implication was that Tugga's ute had been hit from behind. The camera and reporter followed the cop through the accident scene as he raised doubts about the first impression – that Tugga fell asleep and drove over the cliff.

The camera revealed two separate skid marks – one at the start of the layby where the tail-light glass was found, the second close to the repaired barrier. The cop was puzzled. He expected to find a continuous trail of rubber if Tugga was stomping on the brakes. The cop had credibility as an accident investigator. The reporter revealed Constable Laidlaw's service with the major collision investigation unit.

The report then segued into the drug allegations with pictures of marijuana plants found at Tugga's property in the Otways.

However, the cop refused to fuel speculation the drugs and the accident were connected.

Hackett noted the *Spotlight* crew didn't have much visual material to expand upon the deaths of Drew and Gerry. They returned to the Volendam picture again and website images of New Zealand news stories on their deaths.

Hackett had regarded the deaths of his former travelling companions as weirdly coincidental but just bad luck.

Spotlight made the accidents look sinister and suspicious. The report questioned the 'accidental nature' of Drew's death on a calm day at a fishing spot he'd frequented without any problems for a quarter of a century. On Gerry's death, they highlighted the fact the offending driver hadn't been found.

Hackett was annoyed the producer had taken the picture, but grateful the show didn't mention his name. Helen Franks was ignored as well, so he wondered if they'd discovered her living a life of suburban bliss far away from all this drama.

Anyway, why should Hackett be involved in this story any more than anyone else in the photograph? He hadn't seen those guys for 30 years. And no way was he involved in any drug syndicate with the Kiwis.

Hackett had ignored several messages from *Spotlight* executive producer, Richard Templeton, during the afternoon. Perhaps they intended including him in the story but the anxious Templeton vetoed it until speaking to him? Again, while Hackett couldn't see any valid or relevant connection to himself, he also couldn't explain the uneasy feeling that churned his stomach.

Hackett made a mental note to get Curly back into his office the next morning and, this time, get some answers. Did they have more information about the second car and drugs they weren't revealing? Did their news contacts in New Zealand know any more about the deaths of Drew and Gerry? He also wanted to give the producer a bollocking for using the Volendam picture without permission.

Decisions made, he felt better. He swept the crumbs from his lap – assuming the cleaner would pick them up the next day – and went in search of something tastier in the fridge.

Chapter 13

The Tugga Tancred story was a coup for the small Melbourne station. However, with a viewership far below Channels 7, 9 and 10 – but above the ABC and SBS – it didn't have the same immediate impact. *Spotlight* wasn't renowned for earth-shattering exclusives so the online services and newspapers paid it cursory attention. The station had no network affiliations, therefore it wasn't replayed in other evening current affairs programs outside Victoria. New Zealand television news services love sordid Australian stories, but they'd lost interest in their expat on Sunday. Besides, with the two-hour time difference, and being a Monday night, their journalists were almost into the land of nod after a hot Milo.

A station website is compulsory in the news business and it was there, several hours after the *Spotlight* story was broadcast, that a sub-editor on the *Melbourne Telegraph* took an interest. Tony Pascoe could see the story was heavily embellished, but the veteran noted enough facts to make it interesting for his readers. He looked around the newsroom for the junior reporter assigned to the graveyard shift.

Pascoe beckoned the recent University of Melbourne graduate towards his terminal. Anita Bentley tried to ignore the veteran newsman at first, worried she might be fanged for a few dollars for drinks at the pub. When Pascoe's arm-waving persisted, she finally trudged over to learn the summons involved a story and not a never-to-be-repaid loan. Anita's news instincts weren't on the same wavelength as the sub editor. She preferred to investigate stories with more substance than what *Spotlight* provided. Nevertheless, she was dispatched to verify the *Spotlight* facts and file a story for the *Melbourne Telegraph's* online news service.

Anita's first port of call, after watching a replay of the current affairs show, was to the Victoria Police media office. Did they have anything to add to Constable Laidlaw's comments about a second vehicle being involved? Could they firm up suspicions about it being a drug-related hit? Had a drug-gang war broken out on the coast? Would they work with New Zealand police to determine if there was a connection in the suspicious deaths of the three friends? Did it involve a new Mr Asia drug syndicate?

The reporter's call ruined a cosy Monday night for the former newspaperman on duty in the Police Media office. Andrew Houghton had recorded game five of the baseball world series, between the Cubs and the Indians on one of the many hard drives in the office. Nothing much happened on Monday nights and Houghton expected to watch one club rewrite the record books. Chicago hadn't won since 1908 and Cleveland's last world series title was in 1948. He was halfway through watching one of the great World Series comebacks when the phone rang.

Anita Bentley demanded answers about a story he knew little about. Houghton recalled the weekend fatality on the Great Ocean Road, but was baffled by Bentley's questions about drug gang wars and hit squads. There had been a follow-up email from the Lorne plods on Sunday about a small amount of marijuana found at the victim's beach.

Big deal. They all grow dope in the Otways!

But he had no answers to Bentley's questions about gang feuds and murder.

Houghton promised to make some calls and went straight for the *Spotlight* website. *Oh, shit!* The media minder realised someone should have been shepherding the Lorne cop when he fronted for *Spotlight.* If a spin doctor in Melbourne *was* aware of the story, then that minder was in for a serious arse-kicking; along with the garrulous constable. The *raison d'être* of the Police Media Office was to hose down speculation like this, not throw more petrol onto the bonfire. He resigned himself to putting the baseball on permanent pause for the night while trying to douse this blaze. Houghton didn't like his chances now that the mousy TV station found it could roar.

July 10, 1986

I'm writing this while sitting on the waterfront at Split in Yugoslavia. It's hot, the sea is full of sparkles and behind me is Diocletian's Palace – a former Roman emperor's retirement home that has become a World Heritage Site. It looks like he must have had a lot of relatives because the building is now infested with people living, or making a living, in every nook and cranny. It's a little disappointing as I thought it might be something grander since it's always touted as one of the most complete Roman architectural features on the Dalmatian Coast.

The coast itself is breathtakingly beautiful. We left Dubrovnik after an early breakfast and arrived in Split after winding around the hills for a few hours. We saw too many charming villages to count, hundreds of islands and inviting crystal clear water.

Everyone begged Eddie to stop for a swim, but he wouldn't. It's his first time through Yugoslavia and he was panicking about getting lost – so he followed the Top Deck bus everywhere. They didn't stop, so no swim for us!

It's interesting seeing a communist country for the first time. Life inland seems much tougher than on the coast since it was almost like going back to the early 20th century and a peasant existence. Farmers were using pitchforks to pile hand-cut hay into beehive shapes around large poles.

I couldn't imagine any of the Waikato boys doing that. If the tractor or baler doesn't work they'll go to the pub.

There were also little roadside stalls with meagre produce. We tried to buy fruit and eggs but the farmers wouldn't sell, even when we offered a stronger currency like the Deutsche Mark. Few people speak English. I don't think that was the problem though, I think they want to keep the food to trade with their neighbours.

Even in Dubrovnik the shops didn't offer much fresh produce. There were enough tourist items but nothing like you'd expect to find in a supermarket back in Waikato. And most things are inexpensive. A few dinar will buy you big meals, plus the beer is cheap. I can see Tugga's Mob loading up the back of the bus now with a couple of crates because they know how much it costs in Italy. That's where we're going next. We're only doing a short stop in Split and then it's on to Venice later tonight. Yugoslavia is a pretty country but still not prepared for an influx of western tourism. We're happy to have visited – especially Dubrovnik – but it will be good if the Yugoslav government can improve things. Who knows what another five years will do for this region? So many people are looking to explore new tourist destinations by road or by sea, so I hope they can develop a good base.

The diary holder didn't know whether to feel proud of Judy when reading that entry, or frustrated by her naivety. It was an honest evaluation of a communist nation, and Judy was positive about the future. But can any traveller understand the complexities of ethnic tensions during flying visits through the old world? Judy's optimism was shown to be premature as Yugoslavia was soon torn apart by civil conflict.

The diary holder sadly recalled watching television news reports in 1991 as artillery shells slammed into Dubrovnik, the city Judy once walked with other carefree tourists.

Chapter 14

There was plenty of noise in the *Spotlight* office on Tuesday morning. Some of it was good-natured banter about Melbourne Cup favourites later in the day, mostly the excited buzz was about scooping the higher-rating broadcasters. Mac wanted to capitalise on the enthusiasm now that *Spotlight* had revealed Tugga Tancred's death was more than a drunk driving off a cliff.

It was about ownership of the story. He wanted *Spotlight* to be first with the information flow for their audience. That meant being out in front for all breaking angles. Mac had his own ideas for the planning meeting, but he waited for Curly to finish his phone conversation before starting. He sat at the head of the conference table. Traditionally, it should have been Richard Templeton who kicked off proceedings, but the executive producer always wandered in towards the end of 'roll call.'

Curly finished on the phone and stormed into the room with a sour expression. 'Fucking police!' He slumped into a chair beside Kim. 'The bureaucrats have muzzled Laidlaw, our tame Lorne cop. He's not allowed to talk to journalists anymore without a spin doctor present. And none of those lazy bastards ever go past the last pub in Footscray.'

Mac shrugged. 'It was to be expected. Drop a bombshell in the provinces and the city boys are going to get covered in shit. What else could he have added today anyway?'

'Not much,' Curly conceded. 'But he would've been a valuable contact. Lorne's such a cushy job, he's not going to risk that for anyone in the media.'

'Okay, you knew that was likely. So, where does the second instalment of our Walkley Award-winning story take our viewers tonight? We have the inside running thanks to you – and we need to stay ahead of these other bastards for a few more days.'

Mac gave Curly a moment to calm down. He could feel the anticipation from the entire production crew. It wasn't often their program was treated as *serious* current affairs, and they were keen to stick it up the opposition for as long as possible. Mac waited patiently for Curly to articulate his new story ideas.

'We need the New Zealand deaths explored in greater detail. Drew and Gerry died in accidents without witnesses. Just like Tugga. To me, it's more suspicious than a tragic coincidence.'

Everyone nodded at that evaluation, and Mac encouraged his star producer to expand upon those thoughts. 'So, what next?'

Curly warmed to his task. 'We need to verify the facts. Drew could have been drunk or stoned when he cast a line from that rock. The same could be said for Gerry's accident. A bus or truck could have clipped him on those winding roads and not been aware of it. Who could blame a driver in that situation for not putting their hand up and possibly going to prison?'

Mac understood there was a lot of grey area in the New Zealand deaths. He decided Kim Prescott was the right person for a thorough investigation. Kim had arrived at *Spotlight* with a Bachelor of Communications a few weeks after finishing her studies at Deakin University. Her appointment would have raised eyebrows in most media organisations as it's rare for inexperienced journalists to be considered for current affairs jobs. However, it barely caused a ripple at *Spotlight*; not when everyone knew her father was on the TV station's board.

Fortunately, Kim turned out to be a talented and hard-working researcher. She swiftly quelled sniggers of nepotism with an instinctive journalistic nous. A warm and friendly personality also helped her blend seamlessly into the team, making Mac's job much easier. Everyone knew the 23-year-old was determined to clinch a role on the reporting staff.

Mac relied on Kim's empathy with people. She was an attractive, willowy brunette who could charm a head of state, or provide a shoulder to cry on for people who suffered life's misfortunes.

Mature beyond her years, that one.

Everyone felt comfortable talking to Kim, even on the phone. Mac knew her people skills would be critical as time pressures and the tight-fisted nature of the station meant they would never get approval to actually send her to New Zealand to talk to the families in person.

Well, not straight away. If the families were convinced foul play was involved, and they were prepared to talk on camera, they might have a chance of making the four-hour hop across the Tasman.

At this stage though, Mac knew the scales needed to tip more towards suspicious deaths rather than accidental. Three questionable accidents in eight weeks involving three mates was suspicious, but not yet a conspiracy.

Like most newsmen, Mac wasn't concerned if there was a plot to murder all Tugga's Mob. The longer the story dragged on, the better it was for *Spotlight's* ratings.

If there is a killer on the loose, please don't catch him too soon!

Mac dispatched Kim to call the Harvey and Daly families and then turned his attention back to Curly. The allegedly missing Helen Franks was high on Curly's list of story angles. They discussed whether that search should be allocated to another reporter or producer. It would leave Curly free to keep an overview of the story elements as they developed, or shut them down.

Mac delegated the task of finding Helen – dead or alive – to Pete Benson, a 30-year-old reporter with a reputation for being diligent and tenacious. Also, he begged for the story. Mac was pleased his team was eager to be involved. It boded well for the production that evening.

Benson made copies of both sides of the Volendam picture – the tourists and their personal information – and headed for his desk. He might get lucky and find some passengers were still in contact, or had found each other again through social media. Benson's first mission was to update the program's website, Facebook and Twitter pages – urging people who knew Tugga Tancred to get in touch.

There were other facts to verify and angles to explore, the most prominent being the drugs and the reason for nudging Tugga off the Great Ocean Road. Mac knew they were important, but he was ambivalent about finding the motive on day two of their investigations.

'Mystery is good,' he said. 'We don't want to do the cops' job for them and solve this too bloody quickly!'

Chapter 15

Melbourne Spotlight's executive producer arrived at work five minutes after the last assignment was allocated. The program countdown was always ticking for the production crew, but never for Richard Templeton.

'Everything under control, lads?' Templeton inquired without much enthusiasm. Given that Templeton, at 45, was a decade younger than Mac, the patronising term could have rankled him. But Mac hadn't survived a lifetime in commercial television news without knowing how to protect himself, most of the time, and when to ignore dumb questions from his boss. There was no need to show Templeton that he considered him a useless, lazy twat. The whole station knew the man didn't get the senior editorial role on *Spotlight* because of his ability; it came through a strategic liaison.

Templeton had traded his teaching job for journalism 10 years previously, his ambitions fuelled by dreams of dashing around foreign battlefields in a safari suit to rescue orphaned refugees. He was always perfectly groomed and coiffured during his reporting days, ready to step in front of the camera at a moment's notice. An endless collection of suits from Toorak's most expensive boutiques helped maintain the image required for his television duties. A modicum of journalistic talent might have seen Templeton's reporting career flourish.

But while Templeton looked and sounded like a television

reporter, he couldn't write or prepare a television news item to save his life. His stories had the facts, but lacked human interest and drama or, to be blunt, they were boring. Reporters who send the audience to sleep, or reaching for the remote control, don't last long.

Templeton's on-screen career had faced another handicap – Simon Glenny. The news anchor believed the younger and telegenic Templeton was a threat to his throne. Naturally, in keeping with the best television traditions, Glenny did everything possible to ridicule the newcomer, both on air and in private. He even suggested to a magazine that Templeton's year-round tan came from a bottle, rather than a naturally olive complexion. The white-anting tactic worked well enough to kneecap any hopes of Templeton progressing to the news anchor role.

But Templeton had a powerful supporter at the TV station: the chief executive, Reg Bradley. Rather than dump a face that looked good in front of the camera, Bradley demanded a producer be assigned to prepare every story for Templeton.

Most newsroom staff expected the humiliation would see Templeton slink back to academia – especially after Simon Glenny leaked the details to a gossip magazine.

Glenny never saw the irony in that revelation; after all, it was rare for news anchors to write their own introductions to the nightly bulletins. Glenny might tinker with a word or two, maybe debate the use of a phrase with a senior producer, or even make a grammatical correction. But most days he was content to arrive a few hours before the news bulletin, chat with veteran colleagues, flirt with the makeup lady for half an hour, pick up his scripts and confidently deliver the news of the day to his loving audience.

That was until it was announced that Templeton was marrying Clarissa: Clarissa Bradley, the chief executive's only daughter. On the eve of the nuptials it was revealed that Simon Glenny was returning to his boyhood home of Perth to pursue new journalistic opportunities. There was another bonus wedding present for Templeton – he was made executive producer of *Spotlight*.

The marriage and elevation from humble reporter to the most senior editorial role in the station was in 2013. Unfortunately for

Templeton, he had shown little aptitude for media management. His expectation of moving to an office beside his father-in-law in the executive suite failed to materialise. Reg Bradley loved his daughter, but he wasn't going to endanger the business by granting a modestly-talented son-in-law a free pass to the top floor.

Templeton had therefore been the bane of Mac's life for too many years. Fortunately, there were enough station meetings to keep him clear of the production area.

Jo was also enlisted in the mission to keep Templeton out of harm's way. Every invitation demanding media attendance for free publicity landed on her desk. The best invitations – movie premieres, restaurant openings, football tickets – were shuffled to a file to be shared by the crew. The 'important things' like Greenpeace, Amnesty International, Global Warming seminars, etc., were given to the boss.

Templeton's carefree office life, however, was about to change as Mac needed the executive producer to be the go-between with The Hatchet.

Mac knew Templeton's work ethic contrasted sharply with Hackett's. The latter started the business day early; as evidenced by The Hatchet's 7.07am text to Mac's phone. Curly had apparently received the same message two minutes earlier.

The Hatchet was angry they used the Volendam photo without permission. He wanted a meeting and an apology.

Mac had no qualms about using the picture; after all, The Hatchet handed it to Curly. It was relevant to their story and they *assumed* their TV executive would be happy for them to use it. They hadn't identified The Hatchet so, no harm done.

Mac couldn't tell from the text whether The Hatchet would try to stop *Spotlight* using the picture again. That wouldn't be a problem because Mac would ignore that commandment. The other TV channels, newspapers and news websites had already pinched the Volendam stills from Monday's program. No way was Mac going to drop a key pictorial element from their story that would appear in every other media across Melbourne.

The issue now was Andrew Hackett's role in the story. Mac knew the other news channels would follow the obvious story lines revealed by *Spotlight*. Bigger budgets, more crews, and having their pants pulled down the previous evening by the South Melbourne upstarts, would inspire their news and current affairs bosses to demand something better. It was Melbourne Cup day after all and there was only one other story in town that needed attention. The other news services had stronger network contacts with New Zealand media, so Kim was going to have to get lucky to break a new angle there.

Mac still had an ace to play: Tugga's Mob. The other networks didn't know about the five members, three of whom were dead, one was missing, and the other was in their building.

Should we paint a big target on the seventh floor?

Templeton had only learned about the story on Monday afternoon when he returned from a Feed the World luncheon. Mac provided a story précis and demanded *Spotlight* be allowed to use Hackett's connection to the story. The executive producer spent a fruitless three hours trying to get a meeting with the financial controller. Templeton even used his executive privilege to ascend to the top floor for a face-to-face meeting. Naturally he didn't make it past the gatekeeper. Zara politely ushered Templeton to the lift and reminded him that, 'Andrew is a very important and busy man.'

Templeton returned to the *Spotlight* office to deliver his disappointing executive decision that they should 'hold' the information on Andrew Hackett's tie-in with the three victims.

Mac showed as much disappointment as he could muster with 30 minutes until opening titles. No last-minute script or visual changes were necessary as Mac and Curly expected they wouldn't get approval to identify Hackett in the first story.

Plus, they felt they didn't need to play all their cards in the first hand. They had deliberately kept The Hatchet's involvement with Tugga's Mob, and the missing Helen Franks, for a fresh angle on Day Two of the story.

But they needed The Hatchet's co-operation, to some degree, and for that Mac knew his executive producer would have to earn his pay for a change.

Mac was surprised Templeton turned up on Melbourne Cup day. However, the executive producer's demeanour indicated it was a token appearance; he was already heading for the door and possibly Flemington.

'Hang on a sec, Richard.' Mac intercepted his departure. 'We're going to need your help again with the Tugga Tancred story. Everyone's onto it and we have to stay in the lead. We need you to get Hackett on board. Shall we step into your office for a moment to discuss some tactics?'

Chapter 16

The temperature was heading steadily for a pleasant 23 degrees on the New South Wales Central Coast. It was the first day of November, so there was nothing unusual about that.

Constable Duane Evans usually enjoyed any call-out to the coast at Terrigal on a fine spring day. The picture postcard setting of miles of golden beaches, blue seas, welcoming waves, lots of women exercising and a relaxed vibe was the reason he'd turned down the chance of a promotion to Sydney at the start of the year.

There was enough interesting police work on the Coast to keep Evans and his mates busy, without being depressing or messy like the crimes their city colleagues city usually dealt with. Until today, when an early morning walker made an ugly discovery on the beach.

Evans had been buried in the racing pages of the *Sydney Morning Herald*, looking for a likely winner of the Melbourne Cup, when the report of a body at the bottom of The Skillion came through.

The most prominent landmark in Terrigal, The Skillion was hands-down more attractive than any of the developer-built high-rises in town. The steep grassy promontory rose away from the sheltered main beach. Evans often took the invigorating walk to the lookout to take in the superb views, so he was grateful he'd skipped breakfast this morning as thoughts of a soft body meeting hard rocks below the famous headland conjured an image of ugly red porridge.

Evans and his partner, Sam Parker, left their patrol car in the car park that overlooked the beach, where the crowd, of about 20 people, indicated which side of The Skillion the body had fallen.

'Righto, Junior.' Evans grinned. He'd graduated from police college a whole six months ahead of Parker, so that gave him seniority in these cases 'Remember not to vomit in front of the taxpayers.'

'Nothing upsets this cast iron constitution. Want a bet on how far the eyeballs have bounced?'

'You're a twisted bastard.' He pointed. 'Looks like there's a few diligent citizens guarding the mess out by the point. Let's have a gander and see if it's one for the coroner, or if we have to drag the detectives away from watching the nags on telly at Flemington.'

The officers picked their way over the rocky beach preparing themselves for the unpleasantness to come. The five people close to the impact area parted to let them through.

'Should've taken that bet on the eyeballs,' Evans whispered to his partner, as they saw the victim wasn't in the state they'd expected.

The victim was a woman. And she hadn't jumped, fallen, tumbled or been pushed from the top of The Skillion. She'd clearly been alive right there at the base of the Terrigal formation, in a nook created by two rocks. On first impression, it looked as if she'd hunkered down to shelter from cooler night temperatures, above the high tide line. Her possessions were still beside her; a blanket to sit on, cigarettes, lighter, three full cans of a popular bourbon mixer and three empties. One can had been torn apart and contained a sticky residue. It looked like the victim had settled in for a late-night session while contemplating the South Pacific – and then checked out permanently.

Evans didn't think he was jumping to conclusions. The shoelace tied around her upper left arm and the business end of a syringe still jammed into the crook of her elbow told them everything. Except perhaps whether her death was suicide or accident.

He glanced at Parker, who nodded: drug overdose, probably heroin. They'd seen many similar incidents in their police careers; cases assessed and solved within 30 seconds of arriving on a scene.

Evans turned to the guardians who had retreated several metres from the body while the constables made their inspection.

'Who found the body?'

'I did,' an attractive 50-ish blonde woman responded. 'We were looking for fossils in the rock formations when I saw her feet sticking out. I thought she was looking at the sea – but when I walked below the rocks I could tell she was dead.'

Evans picked up an accent. 'You a Kiwi?'

'Yes, we're over from Auckland for a short holiday. Bit of a surprise to find a body instead of fossils.' The woman seemed to be taking the discovery of a drug overdose victim in her stride.

'You said we?' Evans asked as he looked around the other beachcombers.

'My husband's over there,' the woman pointed back towards the car park. 'He'd rather check out the female walkers than look for fossils – live women over dead ones.' The touch of Kiwi humour allowed everyone around the body to laugh.

'I don't blame him,' Evans said. 'Okay, Constable Parker here will gather names and addresses if you don't mind. Just confirming, no one touched anything on, or around the body?'

Five good citizens nodded confirmation. Being this close to the ugly side of the drug culture was enough for them. Parker pulled out his notepad and, starting with the New Zealander, began taking statements.

Evans meanwhile retrieved his own notebook and concentrated on the death scene in the rocks. It looked like a straightforward drug overdose. The victim was a slender, weathered woman somewhere in her 50s, or older. She had lived a hard life judging by her gaunt and heavily-lined face. She looked to Evans like the classic junkie who'd taken one hit too many.

Probably on the game to support her habit.

The victim's clothing, however, did not match the constable's assumptions. Expensive tapered jeans, a patterned blouse and leather sandals were much more fashionable than he expected a habitual drug user to wear. Spare cash usually went on the drugs, not on making fashion statements. Evans bent over the woman to inspect her arms more closely. He could see the scars of a long-term user, but not recent abuse; apart from the fatal dose.

Had she tried to clean up her act and then relapsed; the fresh hit too much to cope with?

Evans turned his attention to her drug kit. The torn-open bourbon can must have been used as the 'spoon' to heat the crap before she injected it. But there was no sign of any of the other usual stuff – no alcohol swabs, no water to mix and dilute the heroin, and no cotton or other filter to remove impurities. A long-term user never made it to this age without applying some standard practices. And, most curious of all, there was no bag or plastic wrapping for the heroin. It might have been blown away by the wind but, when weighed alongside the other missing pieces of kit, Evans realised the whole scenario was a little suspicious.

He knelt and looked more closely at the hypodermic in the woman's arm. There was still fluid in the syringe, but no blood. That was unusual. Evans knew junkies drew a little blood first to confirm they had the needle in a vein.

Instinct was telling him there was something wrong with this death. He couldn't escape the feeling the scene was staged; and that someone unfamiliar with junkie habits had injected the heroin.

He inspected the immediate area again, this time for signs of a second person; the someone else at this final beach party. Had they helped, badly, with the preparations and then scarpered when the woman died? Was it an accident – or deliberate? And if the latter, was it deliberate, as in assisted suicide? Or was it murder? All of these were questions for higher ranks than his own.

Evans rejoined his partner, who was taking his last statement.

'There definitely wasn't a body here yesterday morning when I took my regular walk to The Skillion,' the sprightly octogenarian declared. 'Shocking stuff. What will it do for tourism?'

Parker then filled Evans in from his list of 'no further helpful details'. The witnesses were simply walking along the rocky shoreline and encountered a body. End of story for them. No one saw anything suspicious.

'You took a long time checking the body,' Parker noted. 'Enjoy the whiff of a fresh cadaver on a hot morning, do you mate?'

'Better than napalm, Junior,' Evans grinned, upping the dark humour. 'But, I don't think our dead junkie overdosed. There's something suspicious—'

'Eh? She's out here on her own, a needle full of shit sticking out of her arm. How can that be suspicious?'

'I don't think she stuck herself, mate.' Evans tucked his notebook away and pulled out a mobile phone. 'We're going to disappoint those detectives who were expecting to get rich on the Melbourne Cup this afternoon.'

July 12, 1986

We have just spent our second day in beautiful Venice. Lots of tourists in such a small and cramped place, but I love it and all of Italy. The narrow canals and alleys are exciting to explore and then you emerge into the majesty of Piazza San Marco. There's fascinating history in every building in this city. I've got pictures of all the important sites like the Basilica, the Campanile, Rialto Bridge, Grand Canal, Doge's Palace and The Bridge of Sighs (no sign of Casanova but I did get my bum pinched again!) and we did the touristy things – gondola rides and a glass-blowing display. The glass-blowing was neater than I expected, but way too expensive to buy anything fancy. (Sorry Mum – maybe next time I'm back here I'll have more money to buy you something special.)

There are hundreds of churches dotted around the place, it's impossible to remember all the stories about them.

The camp site is a few kilometres across the lagoon from the heart of Venice. These massive ships float past just metres from our tents. Eddie has been dropping us at the entrance to Venice the last two days and we have been catching the ferry back to camp. It was good to have the freedom to wander as we pleased.

Some – Tugga's Mob – went straight for the bars. Others took in all the cultural highlights and the rest went back to camp after a few hours. I can't understand that. It might be their only chance to visit one of the great cities and they hardly give it any time because of the heat. Anyway, I've been enjoying it all. I spent a few hours this afternoon people-watching in St Mark's Square. I couldn't keep track of the different nationalities and tour groups drifting past.

Even after almost six weeks it's hard to tell the difference between a Spanish, Portuguese and Italian accent. You can always pick out the Americans — they're the loudest.

I had a sweet Italian waiter who didn't mind that I sat on an empty coffee cup for much of the time. I love the outdoor lifestyle here and want to visit again. The waiter showed me pictures of the piazza under water in the winter high tides. People were walking on trestles! I read about it, but it was hard to believe until you see the pictures. I must come back for Carnevale di Venezia! The masks look sensational and they sell them all year round. Such an exotic and mysterious city.

The camp site is full of Kiwis and Aussies and the bar is never empty. It's the last stop for the Top Deck overland trips coming from Kathmandu to London and they like to finish with a lot of fun. And all the European trips go through here. There's a barbecue most nights and it's our turn for a feast this evening. I'm looking forward to it as the camp meals our tour has organised have been hopeless.

I spent most of today by myself as I was annoyed with Andreas last night. We don't have anything exclusive going on, but after spending most of yesterday exploring Venice together I was hoping for another catch-up last night. He asked where my tent was before heading off for drinks with Tugga's Mob. I should have known. When he hadn't turned up two hours later I went and had a peek at the bar. He had his arms around two Contiki girls. That pissed me off. I know it shouldn't have, but a girl doesn't like to feel like she's second choice — or bloody third. Enough of the green-eyed monster. We're well into the home stretch now and there's still so much to enjoy and explore.

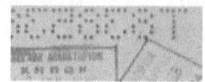

The diary holder was still pondering Andreas, aka Andrew, as the precious travel record was returned to its silken container. His identity had finally been confirmed. Andreas/Andrew had been a source of pleasure and pain for the writer throughout the trip. His immaturity might explain some of the inconsiderate behaviour. Or was he as deeply flawed and evil as the other members of Tugga's Mob? Either way, his fate was already decided.

Chapter 17

While Mac waited for Curly and Kim to provide updates on Tugga's Mob, he munched contentedly on the best hamburger in Melbourne. And not a mass-produced franchise thing with a dubious Scottish heritage. This was a real burger – a thick juicy meat pattie, runny egg, bacon, onions fried in butter, a lone lettuce leaf, and oozing rivers of tomato sauce between a toasted chunky white bun. And no beetroot. Mac's favourite burger bar at the South Melbourne taxi depot had learned over the years to never tarnish his twice-weekly lunch treat with bloody beetroot. Mac also judged the 15-minute trudge through traffic to the depot and back was enough to get rid of any fatty deposits.

Curly and Kim were still on their phones but Pete Benson had just concluded a call. Benson's obsessive nature was why he'd been tasked with finding Helen Franks and the other passengers. Mac waited half a minute to let Benson complete his notes.

'Pete, you had any luck chasing down the people in the photo?'

Benson swivelled his chair. 'Yeah Mac, seven so far. No luck with finding Helen Franks yet, but I *can* tell you about another death.'

Mac had just taken a bite of his burger, as he'd expected a lengthy reply. The news stopped him mid-chew. With his mouth full, all Mac could do was wave a hand frantically for Benson to continue.

Benson smiled. 'Sorry mate, the smell of that burger has been driving me crazy.'

Mac swallowed loudly. 'So, do we have another body or not?'

'Yep, although I don't think it has anything to do with Tugga's Mob. A New Zealand woman died a year after their big holiday. But one of the other passengers said she'd killed herself.'

Mac's excitement waned quickly, he picked up the burger again. 'Bugger, that doesn't fit in with the accidental deaths this spring. Okay, so what did the other passengers have to say about Tugga's Mob?'

'Tugga and his cronies weren't popular.' Benson flicked through his notes. 'Most described Tugga as an arsehole, a dickhead or a prick, and said his mates weren't any better. One guy, Matt Wilson from Benalla, was more generous. He said at the start of the tour they were tolerant of Tugga's Mob. They were young and excited about being in Europe for the first time. But Wilson said their patience ran out as the booze turned them from boisterous to boors. All seven passengers I spoke to said they tried to avoid Tugga's Mob after the first couple of weeks. They didn't want their adventures ruined by yobs.'

Mac nodded and swallowed the last of the burger before a fresh revelation could choke him. 'I guess we won't see them at Tugga's funeral then.'

'Nope. They won't be volunteering as pallbearers. They'd all kept their Volendam photos too; and several Australian passengers had a couple of reunions, but they never invited Tugga, or his mates. They didn't even realise the Kevin Tancred smeared over rocks at Lorne was their former travelling buddy.'

Mac drummed his fingers on the desk. 'That's all good background for our story I suppose. But it's a pity that fourth death was so long ago.'

'I have to admit I almost leapt out of my seat when Susan Paynter let that slip. I thought *yes,* we've got ourselves a serial killer. But then she said it happened in 1987; and that it was a suicide. That doesn't match our killer's modus operandi – if we really have one. I still got all the details of who she was and when and where it happened, just in case.'

'Good. Write them up and print a copy for Curly. He can sort out where it fits into his script. Go grab yourself some lunch and see if you can make some headway with finding Helen Franks. You've done a good job, Pete. I know you can find her.'

Mac almost felt guilty as Benson left the office with his wallet in hand. Benson didn't have time to get a burger from the taxi depot, and there wouldn't be much food left at the staff café.

The senior producer turned his attention to Kim Prescott as she chatted on the phone, her left ear red from the constant pressure of the electronic communication device that Alexander Graham Bell patented in 1876. Old journalists like Mac loved that sort of trivia. He idly wondered if Kim cared about footnotes in history, or whether she was more concerned with the results the modern device could provide from all over the world?

Curly was now perched beside Kim's desk, gleaning facts from the conversation and helping with questions. Egos are always in play in the media business as careers can be made or trashed on the scoops secured or lost. Mac was encouraged that his journalists worked as a team.

He recalled another era when a clash with a senior correspondent had forced him out of a larger news network. The reporter rejected Mac's advice on an international story and focused on the wrong angle. When challenged by the Head of News, the reporter blamed Mac and said he failed to pass on critical information. Mac lost the battle as management believed they could afford the embarrassment of losing a senior producer rather than the senior correspondent. The decision still rankled Mac 20 years later, although the five-figure *ex gratia* payment for long service eased some of the pain.

Mac learned well from that experience and prided himself on finding talented producers, researchers, reporters and camera crews who knew when to be team players. Unfortunately, he never had any say in who their bosses might be, or if they had any journalistic ability, but at least he could shape the working team.

Mac brought his focus back to the *Spotlight* office as Kim replaced the handset and stood up to stretch. Curly continued to scrawl away in his notepad. Mac gave them a few moments and called them over to his command post. They both looked harried, but pleased.

Mac kicked off by running through Benson's update. Their eyes widened with the news of the fourth death, then narrowed when they learned the suicide was 29 years ago.

'Pete will give you a copy of his notes soon. Now, what have you found in New Zealand? Are we on the right track?'

'Yep,' Curly said. 'We're sure the other deaths *are* suspicious. The families of Drew Harvey and Gerry Daly are certain their deaths weren't accidental.'

Mac smiled and waited for Curly to elaborate.

'The Harvey and Daly families are pissed off that no one has listened to them. Not the cops or the Kiwi media. No one before us. The Harveys said the investigation into Drew's death was half-arsed and that no way would he have been swept away by the surf.'

'How can they be so adamant? Who said the cops cocked up the investigation?'

'Joanne Harvey, the eldest daughter,' Kim replied. 'She said her Dad had been fishing at Muriwai for 25 years. He knew where rogue waves might strike and catch the unwary. Joanne said he never went to Muriwai when there was a chance of the weather cutting up rough.'

'This Muriwai is a dangerous place? Where is it exactly? And what sort of fishing do they do there? Rocks or surfcasting?'

'It's a black sand beach about 40 minutes drive from Auckland, on their west coast. There's a headland near the car park, with a rock platform at the base, and that's where the best fishing is done. The family admit the platform has a bad history and the waves can be dangerous. Dozens of fishers have been killed there over the years.'

'So, if it's a deadly fishing spot, how can the family be sure Drew wasn't another unlucky fisher? That he didn't turn his back on the biggest wave of the day?'

'Because it was calm that day and the tide was going out. We checked with the local weather bureau. Plus, Joanne said her Dad was wearing his life jacket, as always.'

Mac had to ask these questions to ensure his reporter and producer were being objective. He understood the Harveys would be devastated by such a tragedy. Would they continually defend the safety habits of the victim rather than admit that, just once, their loved one might have been too lax? Mac wanted his journalists to obtain facts rather than be swayed by emotion.

'What's so important about his life jacket?'

'I'll get to that in a moment, if you don't mind?' Kim waited for a nod from Mac. 'Okay, it wasn't ideal fishing conditions that day, but Joanne said Drew loved the tranquility of Muriwai, especially mid-week with few people about.

'Yet somehow a hypothetical and unlikely rogue wave on an outgoing tide sneaked up on a veteran fisher, swept him off the rocks – with his life jacket on – and sucked him out to sea where he drowned. They took four days to find his body and the fish had been having a feast. They were hungry, but I'm sure not even piranha could nibble their way through a modern life jacket – as in totally munch the whole thing. It's never been found.'

'You don't think he might have slipped it off to swim back to shore?'

'Not likely. They did an autopsy and they found that Drew had a skull fracture.'

Mac continued to play devil's advocate. 'He could have bashed his head when being swept off the rocks. We've seen that happen so many times over here as well. Knocked unconscious and gone before anyone notices.'

'Possible, but the family doesn't believe that's what happened. They say Drew was so careful he had adapted his jacket to fit a high-ridged neoprene flap at the back to protect against that sort of thing. You see little kids in similar jackets, so their heads don't tip under when they fall backwards in the water.

'Joanne said they can't rule out Drew being knocked unconscious, but they seriously doubt the wave would have caused a skull fracture because of the flap around his neck and head. Drew didn't care about looking silly, he wanted to be safe. But they can't get the local cops interested. The Kiwis have written it off as an accident and won't investigate further.'

Mac was pleased. There was enough doubt to confirm Drew

Harvey's place on the suspicious death list. The media could ask the questions. It was up to the authorities to answer them.

'This Joanne, is she prepared to talk on camera?'

'Yep, champing at the bit to get some attention. They have no clues on who might want to hurt their father, but they know he shouldn't have died like that.'

Mac turned to Curly with a raised eyebrow for the lowdown on the logistics of getting the angry family member on their program that night? Their show was broadcast in Melbourne and the interviewee was in New Zealand.

'Kim got to the Harvey family first, which is great news for us.' Curly looked down at a long list of notes. 'The other networks and local media were calling Joanne's mobile while we were talking on the landline.

'She's been the only family spokesperson so far, and is really pissed off that local reporters are only now taking an interest because of our story. So no favours for them. But to keep her clear from that lot, I've booked a family room at the casino and hotel in Auckland for the night. I told her it would provide better Skype reception for a live interview. She knew I was bullshitting her but was happy to play along. She told me the hotel is right across the road from Television New Zealand. Joanne's a cheeky one, she suggested we should say she's talking live from Skycity to send the network into a frenzy.'

Mac didn't balk at the expense, not even considering the cheaper option was actually to hire a TVNZ studio for an hour to interview Joanne. *Spotlight* had another exclusive story angle to protect and he would slap down the accounts department if they created a fuss.

'What about the other one – Gerry Daly? Any luck getting a family member to front?'

'Not really. He wasn't married and the closest relative is a brother, Patrick, who lives in Palmerston North. The brother is furious the driver who hit Gerry hasn't been found. Now that we're suggesting Tugga's death is suspicious, and that we have concerns about Harvey's death, he's ropable. He said New Zealand is so small, even professional French saboteurs couldn't escape detection when they bombed the *Rainbow Warrior*. Yet 30 years later, and with all the forensics at the disposal of police, he's angry they can't find one rogue driver on the Coromandel – wherever that might be.'

That made Mac even more excited. 'Well, that's great for us. Can't we get him on Skype too? Or anything else that will work in that part of New Zealand? Would he do that?'

Curly grimaced. 'I'm sure he would, but it wouldn't be a great performance – he has a bad stammer. We'd need an hour for his interview alone; that's if the audience could suffer through it.'

Mac shrugged. 'Bugger. But you've tapped him for family pictures?'

'Yep, and he's tech-savvy, which helps. He should be emailing pictures soon. And Joanne's shots are already here, including a picture of Harvey in the missing life jacket at the rocks. It looks strong enough to keep a sumo wrestler afloat for a month. We've got enough ingredients to make another good story – and I think we're still ahead of the chasing pack.'

The three *Spotlight* members sat quietly for a moment. They had strong story angles and fresh pictures. Now they had to work out how to best package them.

Curly would write the script and Mac and Kim would keep an eye on the editing to make sure the story made the deadline at the top of the program. Helen Franks was still an unknown element in the storyline, but they reasoned it was time to put her in the picture. More publicity might help locate her, if she were still alive.

It was Curly who finally addressed the issue of their own in-house member of Tugga's Mob.

'What about The Hatchet? How much do we reveal about his connection to Tugga's Mob tonight?'

Mac raised an eyebrow. He knew as well as his colleagues that two other unspoken questions went with that. Was Hackett a potential target for whoever was killing Tugga's Mob? And did he understand that yet?

Chapter 18

Richard Templeton usually enjoyed the views from the top floor of the station. He had been up there many times since marrying Reg Bradley's daughter. The view of the city skyline from his father-in-law's office was his favourite, taking in the Shrine of Remembrance and the gardens along the Yarra River. The conference-room view wasn't bad either. Templeton had spent more time in there, although seniority dictated who was treated to the better seats.

Currently though, he was taking in the panorama from Andrew Hackett's office. It was a first-time experience and it should have been impressive as the view was possibly even better than from Reg's office, yet Templeton wasn't comfortable.

He knew Hackett didn't like him. The unspoken accusations of nepotism always lurked behind regular inquisitions about current affairs expenditure and ratings. Those battlegrounds had been in the conference room and Templeton could generally rely on the cavalry – in the form of Bradley – coming to his rescue, after sufficient public blood-letting. Bradley was smart enough to let Hackett extract his pound of flesh, while hoping his son-in-law learned valuable lessons in financial management.

Templeton worried about the future when Bradley retired, as Hackett was considered the heir apparent to the chief executive's post. That was a scary thought. But right now, he was just annoyed, not that he'd ever let on. Sitting alone, twiddling his thumbs, in this swanky space, summoned by Hackett who hadn't bothered to turn up. Arrogant bastard. He'd been trying to pin Hackett down since Mac's morning briefing underlined the need to get Hackett's involvement. Supposedly the financial controller was keen to talk, but his gatekeeper insisted he was tied up with company business. Until the summons: 'Mr Hackett can spare you 10 minutes at 1.45pm.'

It was now 1.57pm and Templeton was worried the window of opportunity had been slammed shut. Zara had given him some Tim Tam biscuits and a flat white, but now the empty cup, plate and office were clearly indicative of how Hackett saw Templeton and *Spotlight*'.

Templeton tried to be fair. It was Melbourne Cup Day, a public holiday, yet all the senior executives were buzzing around the building instead of drinking champagne at Flemington. Templeton had been intending to spend the day with friends until his wife told him about the 'unusual activity' at the station. He didn't want to be the only executive missing in action and that's how he'd been cornered by Mac after the production meeting.

Hackett finally burst through the door at 2.11pm and was surprised to find Templeton.

'Oh, sorry to keep you waiting, Dickie.' Hackett's apology lacked sincerity. Templeton knew *Dickie* was intended as an insult. 'Been another frantic day getting things ready for the Board. You'd think they'd know it was Melbourne Cup Day, wouldn't you?'

'No problems, Andrew. I understand how busy management can be in the media business.'

Hackett settled in an armchair opposite Templeton, wondering if the newsman was taking the piss – if he even had the balls to – or was totally delusional.

'Yes. Well, I wasn't happy your boys used that Volendam picture last night. I don't see the relevance.'

'But you gave it to Curly, or so I'm told.'

'I did, but it was more to explain the connection to Tugga. We travelled on the same bus trip. He's dead and so are a couple of his mates. End of story. I was called away to another urgent meeting and didn't get the picture off whatever his name was. I want that picture back and it's not to be used again.' Hackett sat back and folded his arms. The boss had spoken.

'That won't be possible, I'm afraid. It seems the story is developing further than we expected,' Templeton countered. He watched Hackett's eyes widen, surprised by the defiant tone. Templeton so often felt like Hackett's punching bag during executive meetings, it felt good to take a jab at his tormentor.

'What do you mean? Even if you've learned more about Tugga's drug dealing or the other car, that — none of that — has anything to do with me and a bus trip from 30 years ago.'

Templeton smiled, grateful for Mac's update. 'There's nothing new on Tugga as that police source has been gagged. But the deaths of Drew Harvey and Gerry Daly are definitely looking dodgy. The families are screaming now they've heard about Tugga, and they want the New Zealand police to investigate the deaths as murders.'

Templeton watched the colour slowly drain from Hackett's face. He was really enjoying this whole 'knowledge is power' thing. He jabbed again. 'Three possible murders of three mates — all within a few weeks of each other. And still no sign of Helen Franks.'

Hackett blinked, then rallied. 'Murders? Okay, but I still don't get the connection to me? I didn't see any of them again after the trip.'

Templeton felt an adrenalin surge way bigger than the small smile he allowed himself. 'Well you see, Andrew, the trip *is* the connection. Apparently the three lads weren't life-long mates after all. Sure, they were thick as thieves when chopping down trees and drinking their way through Europe. But we've learned they *all* went their separate ways immediately after the trip. We don't know about the woman, Helen whatsherface, but we've been told the boys never saw each other again. Drew and Gerry returned to New Zealand, but took separate paths. There's a couple of years missing in Tugga's timeline before he ended up in Australia, but basically we believe they never kept in contact after Europe.'

Hackett sat quietly for a moment. 'So, what you're suggesting is that something happened on the trip 30 years ago, and that might be the reason for these deaths?'

Templeton nodded, looking suitably concerned while his inner glee was fairly bursting to rush home and share this with his wife.

'It looks that way. Helen, um–'

'Franks,' Hackett said. 'Helen Franks.'

'Yes. She is missing – or at least can't be found. Theoretically, Andrew, you might be the only surviving member of Tugga's Mob.'

The two men stared at each other for almost half a minute. Hackett was the first to break the contact as he shifted his gaze to the view towards St Kilda.

Templeton pursued him. 'What happened on the trip, Andrew? Do you know of anything that might have put a target on their backs? And maybe yours?'

July 16, 1986

Our first day in Munich and I'm having mixed feelings about the city and the people. The Second World War ended 41 years ago, but for Uncle Joey back in New Zealand it seems like last week. He still hates the Nazis after fighting at Monte Cassino in Italy.

We saw the rebuilt abbey as we travelled south from Rome to Pompeii and Sorrento. It was such a contrast from the pictures of the ruins after the battle that Uncle Joey used to pull out every ANZAC Day following the parade. I read that Munich is much the same – risen from the ashes after 90 per cent of its historic buildings were destroyed during bombing raids.

It looks like an impressive modern city, but I can't help thinking this is where Hitler began his rise to power. So much pain and misery started here with these people and their ancestors. I think we all felt a distance from the locals.

Austria and the Alps were beautiful to see the past few days, especially Salzburg, so maybe that is contributing to the quieter mood now we are back in a big city.

It was interesting to see the BMW museum and the 1972 Olympic complex. But even that was sombre as Eddie reminded us about the Munich massacre of the Israeli athletes 14 years ago.

Tugga made it worse for everyone, laughing about the attack and yelling that Dachau would show us how the Germans organised a 'proper massacre.' It was disgusting and disrespectful. Even Andreas paled after that.

I don't know what he enjoys about being part of Tugga's Mob. Drinking beer with obnoxious people is not a good way to see the world. At the start of the tour they seemed like a fun group, boozy but just like the rugby boys back home wanting to let off steam.

However, Tugga has shown there's a darker side to his personality and his Kiwi mates aren't much nicer. Even Andreas has shown himself to be selfish, cowardly and insensitive. He's university educated and comes from a good family, apparently, but I think he's allowed himself to be influenced too much by Tugga.

On a brighter note, we are staying at Campingplatz Thalkirchen on a canal off the Isar River. It's lush and tranquil by the water despite lots of Aussies and Kiwis around the camp site. A chance to sit on the side of the canal for a few minutes was almost like being on the banks of the Waipa River – one of the first times I've missed something from home.

This camp site is the Antipodean base during the Oktoberfest in September. I was curious why an October festival mostly takes place in September. One of the Top Deck couriers explained the history and how it started with the marriage of a couple of royals. He's been to five Oktoberfests and says Thalkirchen can be enormous fun or 'bloody messy'. He pointed out a dirt pad and said there would be 20 or more double decker buses parked side by side every night of the festival. And that is mostly the regular European tours passing through, not the special beer fest buses they organise. I've heard so much about it and I want to experience it. The courier said to keep an open mind. He usually avoids the main beer tents where the tourists *go and spends his nights in the traditional tents with the Germans. Sounds like a better plan if I do come back.*

I was talking to him about not warming to the German people because of the Second World War and the Nazis. He says he still struggles with the same feelings after more than a dozen trips to Munich. He says it's best not to blame the new generations for the sins of the past, which is probably the right approach. I'll try to be more open-minded tomorrow – even after visiting Dachau.

Such a sensitive soul. The diary holder acknowledged Judy's first brushes with the evil side of human nature had left her feeling uneasy. But greater inner strength is necessary to cope with the shit that life can throw at you. Death is a fact of life – the sands of time slipping away until the human organs are corrupted, or fate dealt you a crueller hand.

The diary holder knew that darker days awaited the writer – and she didn't have the coping mechanisms in place to deal with it. The diary was wrapped once again and returned to its safe place. New plans had to be prepared.

Chapter 19

The *Spotlight* crew weren't the only people working earnestly that day to learn more about Tugga Tancred and whether his worldly departure was an accident, or the work of a rival gang. Drug-related deaths were too low on the totem pole to call them assassinations. The word sounded sinister during broadcasts and looked great in headlines, but it wasn't good form to declare an assassination – unless a rival did it first, and then it was open season.

Most of the people doing the story-chasing at rival networks weren't happy about their assignment. It was Melbourne Cup Day – the climax of the Spring Racing Carnival and the final episode of a four-day binge. Half the city was at Flemington Racecourse for the festivities, the other half was doing the same at backyard parties all over town. Most made their once-a-year visit to the TAB to back the favourite, popped into the supermarket for the barbecue essentials and then emptied the local drive-through bottle shops of anything alcoholic. It was a Melbourne tradition.

Journalists were used to working public holidays, yet Melbourne Cup Day meant missing the biggest day-off party of the year. It was a waste of time catching up with friends after the celebrations. The mates who'd gone to the races, and who could still find their way back to the trains, were usually a gibbering mess. Those who couldn't locate the trains often found a cosy police cell for a few hours' rest.

The duty of bailing the latter out of the drunk tank on Melbourne Cup night wasn't a pleasant experience. The odour tended to linger for days.

Normally on the first Tuesday in November there was no other story in town. It was always about the dramas surrounding the lucky jockey, trainer, owner, the punters and the fashions on the field. The television scripts on the race virtually wrote themselves – you just had to change the names each year. When Makybe Diva won the Cup three years in a row from 2003 the TV journalists were ecstatic – they didn't have to change anything apart from the pictures.

To have the nobodies at *Spotlight* rub their noses in horse shit with a cracker current affairs story on Cup Eve was bad enough. Worse was knowing the bastards were going to chase the story harder on day two, despite the public holiday. All journalists assigned to catch up on the story suspected *Spotlight* had more revelations to come, and that peeved them even more. They'd have to bust their guts to get their stories underway, but expected to be dazzled by *Spotlight* again that night.

The Police Media office was also busy, but perhaps not as frantic as a normal Tuesday. The suburban parties were relatively calm as the extended nature of the race day kept people focused on their televisions. There were the supporting races, the colour of the fashions – good and bad – and the yobs on the grass. An office sweep circulated on what time the crowds turned feral. It was a Kiwi woman who won the title for the day's most embarrassing picture – caught on camera riding a wheelie bin.

Those shenanigans were always a part of Melbourne Cup Day so weren't serious enough to concern Police Media. They were occupied instead with inquiries from eager reporters about the hit squad that took out Tugga Tancred. The news cycle on some websites and radio networks ran faster than an Olympic 100 metres champion. They craved fresh information, anything. Media releases would be read out verbatim if they filled a two-minute gap at the top of the hour.

Something more salacious, like an alleged drug-related murder, had them in a lather.

The hacks on duty repeatedly cursed the Lorne cop who initiated the frenzy. He had been put in his place that morning with a severe arse-kicking, verbally delivered over the phone because no one wanted to drive two hours down the coast to do it in person.

Constable Laidlaw, however, let the media office vent its spleen and went back to work. He expected the knee-jerk reaction from the spin doctors after his *Spotlight* appearance. Laidlaw had achieved his goal. Doubts about the *accident* were in a public forum and resources would have to be allocated to investigate it properly. That would never have happened if he followed the usual procedures.

Chapter 20

All work on the Tugga's Mob story came to a halt just before 3pm. It wasn't a lack of initiative, resources, energy or an executive decree: it was Cup time. Tradition declared it to be the only race to stop a nation; or two, if you count New Zealand whose thoroughbreds have enjoyed great success in the world-famous 3200 metre race.

For 10 minutes, the *Spotlight* crew members in the South Melbourne office were a microcosm of Australia, and their neighbours across the Tasman, as they settled into chairs to watch the race. The winning racehorse usually took about three minutes twenty seconds to circle Flemington. The minutes before the barriers opened were just as important, as everyone argued about the favourites. Melbourne Cup sweeps circulated throughout the station for much of the day. As soon as one sweep filled up, Cup Day entrepreneurs started another. There was never a shortage of takers for $5, $10 and the occasional $20 shots at glory and small riches.

Mac felt extra lucky – he had drawn the favourite, Hartnell, in the cheapest and the richest sweeps. The rule is cash-up-front for one of the 24 horses in each sweep. The cashless Mac fanged Curly for the $5 sweep and Dugal Cameron for the $20 horse, assuring them payback that day from the winnings. If the impossible should happen, and Hartnell failed to win, Mac guaranteed his ATM card was 100 percent operational. The racing omens were extra good.

Hartnell was one of five Godolphin horses in the race. The owner, Emirates Airlines founder and race sponsor, Sheikh Mohammed bin Rashid Al Maktoum, had spent an estimated one billion dollars over two decades trying to win the race. Plus, New Zealand jockey, James McDonald was in the saddle for Hartnell. Surely the young genius would pilot his mount to glory that day – and provide Mac with beer money for the next week.

The office crew cheered along with the massive crowd at Flemington as the field swept past the grandstands from the starting barrier. The next time around it would be more frenetic, everyone screaming for their horse. Two minutes into the race, and about 1200 metres to go, there were four unfancied horses in front.

Mac was edgy, but still confident that Hartnell was well placed for a good run in the straight. It was a fiercely contested race and 40 seconds later the leaders turned for home, and that's when the Kiwi urged his mount forward. Mac leapt to his feet and the on-course commentary was temporarily superfluous. Mac's race call faltered at the 300 metre mark as Almandin and Heartbreak City zoomed up to the favourite. A hundred metres later race caller Greg Miles could be heard again as it was reduced to a two-horse race – and Hartnell wasn't one of them.

The two late chargers provided a classic Melbourne Cup finish, one of the closest in the race's 156-year history. Almandin claimed the victory by a neck over the aptly named Heartbreak City. Mac slumped into his chair as Hartnell crossed for a distant third. His expenditure on the race was a long way short of the Sheik's, but his disappointment was probably greater. There was prize money in the two sweeps for third place but not quite the beer budget boost Mac had anticipated 30 seconds earlier.

The sweep winners quickly converged on the sweep organisers to claim their winnings, the losers soaked up the Cup Day atmosphere for a few more minutes.

Live at Flemington Almandin's owner, businessman Lloyd Williams, had made a rare trip to the race track to witness his record fifth Melbourne Cup winner. Mac silently berated himself as he watched the interview with Williams, a man whose passion for Australia's biggest race had endured for more than 70 years.

'If I knew Lloyd was going to be there I would have backed his bloody nag!'

By the time the trophies were presented to the owner, trainer and jockey, Mac had emerged from his depression.

'Hartnell is younger than Almandin, so he's a certainty for next year's cup!'

When there was no response, Mac looked around to see all his staff had drifted back to work. Only Jo was seated at her station a metre away, the phone once again pressed to her left ear. The Cup had been run and won. For the workers, it was business as usual.

Chapter 21

Approximately nine hours and 40 minutes driving time north of Mac's command post, two police officers exited their vehicle in Wamberal, on the New South Wales Central Coast. They had motored over to the coast from the station in Gosford 12km away but stopped a few metres short of their destination. Their bastard sergeant had ordered them out of the office half an hour before the Cup was run, so they backed off the speed limit by a few km an hour, so they could sit in their car and listen to the race call on the radio.

Now they would tackle their most unpleasant job.

Constables George Papadopolis and Pete Turner had been assigned death duty: notifying the next-of-kin of the woman found at the bottom of The Skillion.

Turner straightened his cap. 'Why the fuck couldn't Evans and Parker do the death knock?'

Death notifications were the toughest part of being a police officer. It was an emotionally and physically draining experience for everyone. How did you find the right words to deal with family trauma? It never got easier and the message bearers and families usually retained permanent psychological scars from the experience.

'For the last time, you prat, they were on early shift,' Papadopolis responded. 'They're long gone. Cooked up a case for the detectives and raced to the pub in time for several beers while watching the Cup. The one we just lost a hundred bucks on.'

Turner made growling noises, reflecting his mood on losing money and the task at hand. He and Papadopolis were used to each other's idiosyncrasies after 18 months working the Coast together. Turner loved to bitch about everything while his third-generation Greek-Australian compatriot loved to slap him down with comments about his English heritage. The banter helped fill the hours on quiet patrols.

With their uniforms all correct and tidy, they turned to the house before them.

'It doesn't look like the sort of place an old junkie would live, does it?' Turner said

'No mate, can't say I've seen a junkie palace looking this flash.'

They stared at an elevated sandstone home with large windows and wide verandahs which provided impressive views of the South Pacific. It had to be worth several million dollars in the current market. Papadopolis estimated it would increase in value by another $10,000 by Christmas.

'I guess we can't judge a book by its cover – or a body by their home.' Papadopolis pushed a button beside the front door.

It was answered by a short man probably in his mid 70s, who looked as if he had already heard the news the police officers were about to deliver. Watery, red-rimmed eyes sagged over fleshy cheeks.

'Nooo,' he wailed as he stumbled back from the doorway, both hands pressed to his face. Fresh tears poured forth. 'Ohh, I knew it would be something terrible. Tell me – please. How bad is it?'

Turner deferred to his partner in these situations, preferring to play the strong silent constable while his university-educated colleague found the right words to deliver the fatal news.

'Perhaps it might be easier, sir, if you sit down,' Papadopolis took the man by an elbow and guided him to a couch in a living room off the foyer. Once settled, Papadopolis went through his prepared notification procedure, confirming the man was indeed the owner, Edward Morrow, and that he shared the home with Helen Morrow. Once confirmed, there was no more holding back.

'I'm sorry to have to tell you, sir, that Mrs Morrow was found dead this morning in Terrigal.'

Papadopolis paused as Morrow bent forward and keened into clenched hands; not loudly, as the death sentence had sucked much of the energy from his tired frame. He looked around the elegantly furnished home as Morrow dealt with his emotions, noting that The Skillion could be seen from the living room.

Morrow gathered enough of his wits and strength to ask: 'Where was the accident? Was there another car involved?'

'Accident, sir?' Papadopolis was confused. 'It wasn't a vehicle crash. Mrs Morrow was found at the base of The Skillion. It looks like a fatal heroin overdose.'

Morrow reared back as if he'd been slapped. His eyes suddenly regained some spark.

'Overdose?' he shouted. 'No, that's not possible, not possible. She's been clean for years. Totally, no relapses. It bloody near killed her to break it, but she did. That girl had courage – no way would she ever slip back into its grip again.'

Papadopolis grimaced. A death notification took much longer than necessary when a family member went into immediate denial. Before he could try a new tack, Morrow spoke again.

'And she wasn't my wife. We never married, but we found it easier for Helen to use my name when she escaped Kings Cross. She kicked drugs and prostitution, but not quite the booze. She still loved her bourbon, although that was under control.'

Morrow dried his eyes, energised by a need to protect the victim's reputation. 'Her real name is Helen Franks. So, tell me – what is this rubbish about her overdosing on heroin?'

July 19, 1986

We've just come back from our train trip up to the Jungfrau from Lauterbrunnen in Switzerland. It was brilliant! Even the few snobby Kiwis who have been blasé about the Swiss Alps, saying they were just like the Southern Alps at home, were impressed. The cog railway inside the mountain was fascinating and the viewing stations couldn't be beaten. I've been to Queenstown on a skiing holiday and Cardrona and the Remarkables are spectacular, but there was something special about looking out over the snow-clad Swiss mountains which made home feel so insignificant. Maybe, I'm becoming a bit of a Euro snob – but it's hard not to be impressed with the infrastructure they have in place and the long history of alpine tourism.

I keep seeing so many places I want to return to (with lots of money) and so little time on a two-year visa. I might have to spend the rest of my life playing catch-up with the new dreams. We were lucky to get such a clear and sunny day. It was expensive – almost 100 Swiss Francs, so I'm glad we didn't get to the top to find it covered in clouds.

The Lauterbrunnen camp site is beautiful as well. The valley runs for about six km with chocolate-box houses dotted along the roads and village, sheer rock walls and lots of waterfalls. They freeze in winter and one of the tour guides said they make an almighty clatter when the ice breaks off. I must come back here for some skiing if I can save the money in London.

Our Kiwi dollar doesn't go far in Europe and my savings are dwindling faster than I expected. Luckily a few of the lads are always keen to buy me a drink! We're up to day 43 now and not long to go, which means I have to think about a place to live and work.

I'm still loving the trip and mostly don't want it to end as Europe is everything I hoped it would be. I loved the Disneyland castle at Neuschwanstein, the Sound of Music house in Salzburg and the lake and timber bridge with frescoes in Lucerne were beautiful. I think I'm running out of superlatives for what Europe has offered. Call me a romantic but Europe is delivering everything I wanted from a scenic and cultural point of view.

I'm on to the tenth roll of film and I'm keen to find somewhere cheap to get them developed back in England. They will be wonderful mementos. Denise had a roll developed at a one-hour shop in Germany. It cost a small fortune but she gave me a couple to decorate my diary. I've used receipts as a visual reminder that I have been to places like the Eiffel Tower and the Sistine Chapel.

The only downside has been Tugga. Some of the other girls are being helpful and making sure one of them stays with me as much as possible when we are off the bus. Yet, Tugga seems to know the moments when I'm alone. Even up the Jungfrau. I was walking out of

*the loo and Tugga was standing there holding his crotch. Gross –
again! Eddie has been a waste of time in keeping Tugga in line. I
complained to Andreas that Tugga and the others were behaving
badly and he just shrugged it off, saying it was my word against
Tugga's and he denies doing anything wrong. Bastard – he didn't
want any confrontation with his drinking buddy. I was hoping to keep
in touch with him in London as he is cute, but not anymore.*

*Enough of that gloomy talk. We have another day here to explore
the mountains, eat lots of chocolate and I think we're booked in for a
fondue and schnitzel dinner tomorrow night. The clothes are feeling
tighter and Switzerland will add more pressure on the waistline. No
wonder a few of the girls are wearing their tracksuits everywhere. I'm
not at that stage – yet.*

The diary holder thought about those ten rolls of film as the trip
journal was returned to its safe place. In fact, there were 11 rolls of
film by the end of the tour and none were developed in 1986.

That had been done almost 30 years later and after some effort,
and not through a commercial developer. They were all processed
in private, old skills having to be learned afresh. Google provided
the research required for the chemicals, paper, environment and
techniques necessary to bring to light 35mm memories. It was a
trial and error process. Each roll contained up to 24 pictures, some
of which were obviously reflex snaps that produced blurred images.
The photography had improved throughout the trip with more
precision on composition for famous landmarks and monuments,
and greater clarity on fellow tourists and group shots. All up, the
films produced 257 clear photographs. The majority were exciting
snapshots of a thrilling chapter in a young woman's life. London,
Paris, Rome, Istanbul, Gallipoli, Switzerland, showing lots of young
people having fun. They would have been wonderful reminders, if
the photographer had developed them at the time. It was the final
pictures on the 11th roll that were disturbing. They were brutal,
sadistic and depressing – and possibly the reason why none of these
films saw the light of day until 2016.

Chapter 22

Andrew Hackett wished he was in Italy, rather than driving to a Tuscan-inspired replica home in South Yarra. He was an hour later than expected and that meant Marianne and Ferdy were probably on to their third gin and tonics, or through the first bottle of Marlborough sauvignon blanc. Hackett was annoyed. He was pissed off at the station board for dragging the chain over the footy rights bid, pissed off it required him to work on Cup Day and pissed off with the *Spotlight* crew for pursuing the Tugga Tancred story

Templeton had unexpectedly grown a set of balls and had obviously enjoyed his probing questions about the tour connections to the deaths of his one-time mates. Templeton showed a keener mind than Hackett ever witnessed in corporate meetings. Granted, those meetings were always on his turf and terms. But Templeton the reporter came out today, implying that Tugga, and the Mob by association, must have done something horrendous to warrant such calculated retaliation. But if so, this dish had been left to go stone cold before revenge was tasted.

And of course there was the unstated implication that he was part of that wrongdoing. Hackett wished he'd told Templeton to bugger off, that he hadn't done anything wrong, and had no idea why anyone would want to target Tugga's Mob.

But he didn't. That would make him look suspicious...

We're talking about bloody journalists after all!

But more importantly his own underlying curiosity wanted the probing to continue. Hackett was in no way convinced Tugga, Drew and Gerry had been murdered, but their deaths were disturbing.

Perhaps something might shake loose in the investigations and that would be good, to resolve this one way or the other.

Hackett admitted to Templeton that Tugga had been an arsehole on a few occasions, from what he had heard. He finally revealed that one female passenger, Judy Williams, complained that Tugga pestered her, was crude and allegedly tried to touch her.

No one else had witnessed the incidents and the driver didn't take them seriously. Hackett explained it was a different era and some men behaved *inappropriately* at times after a few drinks. Generally, any drunken antics or excesses were laughed away the next day and everyone looked forward to the next adventure.

Hackett did not reveal he'd shagged Judy a couple of times – well, quite a few times. Why should he? It was just a trip arrangement for Hackett, nothing serious and was never meant to be long term. It was the same for Judy. She was aloof with Hackett after Switzerland and he couldn't recall saying goodbye to her at the end of the trip. He wasn't going to reveal that he'd shagged Helen Franks several times as well. That was too much information to share with a gabby journalist.

Templeton was interested in the Tugga and Judy connection, even going so far as to term it *stalking*. He made copious notes on A4 paper lifted from Hackett's printer; and then rubbed salt into the wound by ending the meeting. He wanted to get the notes back to the reporter and producer in time to prepare the story.

Templeton declared *Spotlight* would name Hackett as one of the passengers with close links to Tugga's Mob on the tour. He'd deflected Hackett's protests that there was no need for him to be mentioned, by raising the bogey of other news networks getting it first.

His new balls were shiny indeed.

'How would it look if Channels 7, 9 or 10 revealed your involvement – even the ABC – and we didn't?'

Hackett shrugged. He couldn't control the editorial side of the business. However, Hackett refused to yield any ground about being interviewed. No way was he going to appear on camera to talk about Tugga's Mob. But that didn't stop him making script *suggestions*.

'Make sure they emphasise I did nothing wrong on the tour, saw nothing bad happen and that I've had no contacts with Tugga, Drew, Gerry – or any other passengers – in the past 30 years.'

Hackett recalled Templeton simply acknowledged that with a smile before dashing back to the current affairs dungeon.

Chapter 23

On the Central Coast, Constables Papadopolis and Turner had finally cleared the death notification scene in Wamberal and reported back to the station. It took longer than expected, and was likely to create more work for the detectives assigned to the case after the suspicions already raised by Constable Evans.

Edward Morrow's description of the two days before his partner's death had Papadopolis and his partner agreeing there might be something whiffy about the case.

The former company director and widower talked about the challenging but good 15 years he'd spent with Helen Franks. He admitted that details of her life before they met were murky; but guessed it was probably much the same as when he'd met her in a brothel near Kings Cross.

Morrow wasn't at all embarrassed to admit he fell in love with a sex worker. It was loneliness that had drawn him to the Cross but he made a genuine connection with the raven-haired drug-addicted hooker 20 years younger than himself.

Morrow said his persistence and support eventually helped Helen escape the drugs, prostitution and Sydney. They'd moved to the Central Coast 10 years ago and Morrow insisted Helen had been clean ever since. They were the Odd Couple to neighbours, but it was an arrangement that worked for them. The Coast helped heal

Helen from the demons that tormented her city life, and Morrow was grateful to have someone to care for again.

Helen had even grown strong enough to help others escape the sordid life of drugs, participating in local programs to prove there was light at the end of the rehabilitation tunnel.

Papadopolis had heard similar stories of recovery before; and too many more that included sly detours back into old habits. But, unless Morrow was completely deluded, it seemed like Helen Franks had beaten the drugs. How then had she ended up on the rocks with a needle in her arm?

Morrow said Helen had received a call for help on Sunday afternoon. It was literally a call, on her mobile phone, and it had rattled her.

Normally, she would share details with Morrow about pleas for help from former friends – most of whom were working girls still on the game – and together they would discuss a strategy.

Sometimes it worked, mostly it didn't. The couple were savvy enough to know when people were trying to tap Morrow for drug money, and Helen had never gone down that road – even for a really good friend. But if there was a chance of saving a tortured soul, Morrow was more than willing to provide the funds and Helen the benefit of her experience.

There was something different about Sunday's call though. Morrow said Helen announced she was going to catch a train alone to Sydney the next day to help someone she knew a long time ago. She wouldn't say who, or what their connection was.

Morrow assumed it was drugs, or prostitution related, and that Helen was trying to protect him from possible illegal activities. Mostly they travelled together for these 'rescues', but on the rare occasions when Helen went to a meeting alone she always returned by nightfall. She hated Sydney after dark now and never stayed in the city. It had been the source of her pain and she avoided it at all costs.

Morrow said Helen was agitated when she left Monday afternoon. and he was worried when she failed to return that evening. All his calls to her mobile phone went straight to voicemail.

Such was the trust in his soulmate, Morrow never considered that she might have slipped into old habits. He just hoped the rescue was proving more demanding than usual, or, at worst, she might have been involved in an accident.

He called all the major hospitals but found no answers. Those had come with the visit by the two constables.

Papadopolis duly passed along the information which, by itself, didn't mean much. The victim, after all, had been a long-time junkie and was found with a needle of heroin sticking out of her arm.

But his report, added to questions raised by Constable Evans, might help the detectives.

The only clue to just who might have called Helen Franks on Sunday was the name Morrow heard her mutter when she answered the phone: *Judy.*

Chapter 24

The opening titles for *Melbourne Spotlight* rolled across Andrew Hackett's family television. He had already quaffed a large G and T – more gin than tonic – and had a second in hand. He was partly trying to catch up with Marianne and Ferdy but mostly preparing himself for the latest episode of the Tugga Tancred saga. The opening voiceover did nothing to ease his feelings of dread:

> 'Tonight – fresh revelations about the deaths of a Kiwi drug baron and his former best friends. Were they murdered, and does it relate to a bus tour in Europe 30 years ago when they were known as Tugga's Mob?'

Hackett groaned and tipped his head back against the padded armchair, his eyes searching for a guardian angel to save him from journalistic excess. Marianne and Ferdy stared at him, unaware the drama on the television screen directly involved a husband and best mate. They turned back to the television with more interest as *Spotlight* presenter Todd Waterman continued in earnest tones.

> 'Last night we revealed exclusively how drug grower and supplier Tugga Tancred was probably shunted off the Great Ocean Road by another vehicle. Our investigations also revealed that his two best mates died recently in New Zealand in mysterious circumstances.
>
> 'Tonight, we have further proof those deaths are more than suspicious. The families of the victims, having learned

about the hit on Tugga Tancred, are even more certain their loved ones were targeted as well. They are convinced their deaths, in so-called accidents, were staged – and that the men were murdered.

'The connection now appears to be a bus tour through Europe in 1986.

'We begin the first of our exclusive reports with an interview about the first victim of what could be shaping up to be a triple murder.

'Joanne Harvey, daughter of Drew Harvey who supposedly drowned while fishing from rocks in August, joins us live from Auckland.'

Hackett, Marianne and Ferdy watched as the Skype interview unfolded. Joanne Harvey was convincing in her assertion that her father was not swept away by a rogue wave. She was articulate as she explained Drew's safety precautions and held a replica of the life jacket he wore. It was a compelling interview.

The studio then broadcast an older photograph of Drew in the jacket on the rock platform. Joanne spoke about the facts that aroused *Spotlight's* suspicions – the missing jacket and the skull fracture. The family hoped the other deaths would give them traction to get a proper homicide inquiry underway.

In Chez Hackett, the drinks remained untouched while Todd Waterman wrapped up the interview then summarised the story for viewers who had switched on late. He promised more revelations after the commercial break. Hackett drained much of the gin and tonic in his glass before Marianne spoke.

'What is that all about – and why does it have you so agitated?'

Ferdy watched him with equal interest.

Hackett sighed. 'I knew them.'

Marianne was shocked. 'Pardon? My Australian TV executive husband knew three New Zealand murder victims?'

Hackett knew this sort of drama happened – on television, in newspapers, in books and to other people – but not to them, not to comfortable and affluent South Yarra residents with impeccable standing in the community. He guessed Marianne was worried about the furtive looks that would be directed her way at the gym, now her husband was *associated* with drug dealers and suspicious deaths.

Marianne shuddered. Hackett continued to watch the television, so she prompted him again. Her tone was sharper.

'What do you – or did you – have to do with those three men?'

Hackett looked across at his wife, irritated by the question. 'Bugger all,' he fired back. 'I knew them 30 years ago, on a bus tour of Europe – for a few weeks.'

Husband and wife glared at each other until Ferdy intervened with more drinks. Hackett accepted the glass and turned back to the TV, silently berating himself for not telling Marianne about this before the show aired. He blamed the sister-in-law's turbulent love life for absorbing his wife's attention all of Monday and half of Cup Day. The silly cow rebounded quickly with a late call-up from a girlfriend to chase men in the corporate hospitality tents at Flemington.

Spotlight continued after the break with a report on Gerry Daly's death. The brother provided pictures of Daly on the tour in Europe and others of his life as a ranger on the Coromandel Peninsula. There was also a shot of Gerry, Drew and Tugga in a forest, posing for the camera with chainsaws.

The story segued to another Skype interview between their own Kim Prescott and a chatty policeman in Whitianga, the town closest to where Daly died. The case was a straightforward hit-and-run according to the local cop. He said it was tragic for Gerry Daly and police were 'rigorously pursuing inquires to find the driver.'

The cop's smile waned, however, as Kim outlined details about Drew Harvey's death, and that Tugga's death plunge in Australia was being investigated as a probable murder. By the end of the interview the friendly cop looked like a terrified possum about to be slammed by a truck. He finally conceded he would 'broaden inquiries'.

Hackett was perspiring profusely by the time Todd Waterman reappeared on camera. He assumed his connection to the case was about to become public; and tried to ignore the curious glances Marianne and Ferdy were throwing his way.

'New Zealand police seem to finally understand there is something more sinister in these deaths of the three mates. *Melbourne Spotlight* will update you on any developments as the pressure mounts for a Trans-Tasman Task Force to work on the case.'

The presenter's image on the television was then replaced by a full frame photo of Helen Franks. It was lifted from the Volendam picture and enhanced with computer graphics software to make her face clearer.

'Helen Franks was the only woman known to be part of Tugga's Mob on that 80s bus tour, having met the three New Zealand men before the trip.

'If anyone knows of her whereabouts, please contact our producers on the website you can see on your screens now.'

Waterman then glanced down at his script, a news anchor's subtle way of changing gear as everything he needed to know was on the autocue in front of the camera.

'Tonight, we can reveal that there was another member of Tugga's Mob on the European tour – an Australian named Andrew Hackett.

'Some of you may know he is the Financial Controller for this television station.'

A corporate still of a suitably serious Andrew Hackett filled the television screen. Waterman continued.

'Mr Hackett says he's upset to hear about the deaths as he had close ties to Tugga's Mob, as they were called by other tour members.

'However, he knows of no reasons which might explain why his former travelling companions have been targeted. Mr Hackett says he saw nothing untoward happen back in 1986. He said they were a group of mainly Australians and Kiwis enjoying the trip of a lifetime over a European summer. He says he had no contact with any passengers after the tour.'

The camera returned to Waterman, which allowed Hackett to take a breath. And another drink.

Well that could have been worse.

His mobile phone vibrated once, then twice. He looked at the message senders, before their content: Reg Bradley, and Bartholomew Fitzherbert, the chairman of the board.

Brilliant!

Hackett responded to Bradley first. Fitzherbert was old-school Melbourne and would require more finesse. Those blue bloods still wept about the end of the Imperial Honours system, and the loss of their potential Knighthoods. Any hint of scandal had that mob sniffing with disgust.

July 24, 1986

Amsterdam, the last city on our amazing journey around Europe. It's sad to think it's ending after seven weeks, but I'm happy to have seen all the magnificent places I've been reading and dreaming about all these years.

I picked up a letter from Charlotte at Post Restante in the city centre. She says her mother is still unwell and that she won't be able make London this year. I'm sad for her as I know what she has missed. Maybe her mother's health will improve by the next European summer and we can get a cheap Kombi van to tour around in. I'll know all the must-see destinations now and we can easily find some travelling companions in London to share costs. If we get super lucky one of them might be a mechanic as most of the vans have been around the clock a few times. Funny how I'm already thinking of future travel plans – and I haven't even finished my first tour yet!

Yesterday we did a trip around the canals and went to the Anne Frank house. It wasn't as depressing as Dachau, but still quite emotional to know Anne and her family were forced to live in a room behind a bookcase to escape the Nazis.

We had free time in the city to visit the museums and galleries. I'm no expert on paintings, but the Night Watch by Rembrandt at the Rijksmuseum was captivating. I can't say the same for Van Gogh's works. They hardly sold while he was alive – yet people now pay millions for them. Go figure.

Today was a trip to the country for a clog-making demonstration, cheese tasting, donut sampling and a group photograph in traditional Dutch costume at a seaside village called Volendam.

I made sure Tugga was at the other end of the studio as I didn't want him sneakily trying to touch me again. Mind you, it would've been difficult through those thick and heavy Dutch dresses. I really won't be sorry to see the end of Tugga's Mob, including Andreas.

The highlights for me were Paris, Rome, Florence, Venice, Pompeii, Sorrento, Corfu, Gallipoli, Istanbul, Salzburg, the Disneyland castle, Lauterbrunnen and now Amsterdam. That covers just about everything on the itinerary and in between. Ha ha. The sights have been fantastic and most of the camp sites were cool as well (loved the disco and pool in Rome) but I can't say the same for the tour company. Eddie was useless – disorganised most of the time, lost some of the time when he couldn't follow another tour bus and a sleaze the rest of the time. That's a minor grumble as I'm happy to have started my OE.

Now that I know there is much more to see and enjoy here in Europe, I want to save money in London and get back as soon as possible. Other travellers keep telling us how exciting Berlin is and the Russia-Scandinavia tours sound fantastic. I might make that my target for 1987. Maybe the Kombi van will have to wait.

Enough dreaming, dear diary. We have one more night to enjoy the hedonistic delights of Amsterdam before a final pack up and drive to Zeebrugge for the ferry to England. No doubt we will be heading back to the Red Light District and it sounds like space cakes will be on the menu for many. It could be an interesting experience. Do I dare have a nibble? Ha ha!

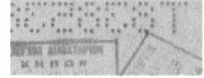

The diary holder always choked back tears at that entry. It marked the end of the innocence of a South Pacific upbringing. Two drops moistened the silk as the diary was returned to its haven.

Chapter 25

A few kilometres south of Hackett's abode, high-fives were exchanged around the *Spotlight* office. Chuffed, delighted, stoked, joyful – you would need a bag of synonyms to define the glee at the program post mortem on Tuesday night. Slam-dunking their media rivals for a second day in a row was rare for *Spotlight* – rare, as in never. The giddy high it created for the hard-working crew was addictive and they wanted another rush tomorrow. Mac and Curly knew they could deliver the buzz once again and, surprisingly, it was thanks to Templeton's good work that afternoon.

The executive producer returned from grilling Hackett at 4.55pm with a source of conflict on the tour. 'Tugga Tancred was stalking a passenger.'

Pete Benson was sitting at his terminal nearby when Templeton named the woman. 'Hang on,' he spun his chair to face the trio of producers. 'Did you say Judy Williams?'

'Yep, according to The Hatchet.' Templeton shared a wry smile with his team. 'She complained about being harassed by Tugga throughout the latter part of the trip. The Hatchet said no other passengers saw anything, so it wasn't taken seriously by the tour guide.'

'Well,' Benson retrieved his own notepad, filled with a day of researching passengers on the 1986 tour. 'Apparently, Judy Williams is dead as well.'

Mac was the first to respond. 'Fuck me. Is that the woman who died a year after the tour?'

Benson nodded. 'Yeah, she drowned in New Zealand. A place called Te Awamutu. Apparently, a coroner returned an open verdict, a kindness to the family, rather than declaring it a suicide, which was suspected.'

Benson felt embarrassed as Templeton's update on the tour sunk in. 'I got that info from a woman in Gippsland. I was chasing Helen Franks and didn't get time to follow up.'

Mac raised his hand. 'Hey mate, we've all been flat out and her death only becomes relevant now we've got this stuff from Richard's session with Hackett. Teamwork will bring it all together.'

Mac turned to call for Jo and almost tripped over the PA as her chair was parked behind the trio. Jo had overheard the breakthrough in the story and guessed her services would be required.

'Jeezus, Jo,' Mac spluttered as he regained his balance. 'Your radar freaks me out at times. Right, I want two tickets to New Zealand tonight for Pete and Dugal. I don't care how you do it but get them there ready to hit the ground running tomorrow morning in Te Awamutu, wherever the fuck that is.'

Mac turned to Templeton for acknowledgment of the expenditure. The current affairs boss nodded without even considering running the expense past The Hatchet. Jo was already on the computer website for one of the Trans-Tasman airlines.

'You're going to have do a Jack Reacher, Pete. No time for anything but a passport and toothbrush. Jo will update you with an airline when you get to the airport.'

Senior camera operator Dugal Cameron heard Mac talk about flights and drifted towards the centre of the action.

'Dugal, you're off to the Shaky Isles – now. No time to organise the usual customs documents, so you're going to have to travel light – grab the smallest camera and sound kit we've got, give Pete the laptop and try to wing it through customs as tourists. We'll hook up with a Kiwi network for more technical support if the story takes off.'

Mac took a gamble that both men kept their passports at the

station like many veteran news crews. It was a punt that paid off; Benson and Cameron left the building for the airport 10 minutes later. They were barely out of the crew car park and debating how best to avoid the race day traffic from Flemington when Jo texted Benson with an airline:

AirNZ. 18.45 flight – but running late. Will message hotel and rental car details later. My fee is a duty-free bottle of vodka! Jo xxx

Mac was excited that plans for Wednesday were underway and their Tuesday show hadn't reached the broadcast deadline yet. But Templeton's breakthrough created a conundrum: what to do with the information about the fourth death from the 1986 bus tour? Was Judy Williams' suicide related to the murders of Tugga, Drew and Gerry, and should they reveal the possible link now?

Mac could see the invigorated executive producer was gung-ho for getting every angle on air that evening. He listened carefully as Templeton warned that the other networks would be back to full strength post-Melbourne Cup. They had bigger budgets to throw at the story. 'We've had a good run for two days, but we could be swamped tomorrow.'

Mac gave Curly the same attention as he provided a counter argument. 'If we tip them off about Judy Williams tonight, it gives them a chance to use the Kiwi networks tomorrow to catch us. We're still ahead of the pack on that angle. I think we should wait and let Pete and Dugal provide more detail. My gut's telling me she could be the key to this whole thing – she was the one that Tugga was stalking.'

Mac nodded as he wrestled with the merits of each point of view. Secretly he was pleased that Templeton was finally showing some journalistic spark, and he didn't want to snuff that out too quickly. However, experience told him Curly's argument had more merit.

'I'm torn, Richard,' Mac said. 'Part of me wants to get as much information on the table as soon as possible. It shows we're setting the agenda on the story. But in doing that, it tips off the networks about the stalking victim. It would become a scramble tomorrow to get to the family first, and the Kiwi networks would be that much quicker than our boys in unfamiliar territory.'

Mac opted to hold the Judy Williams angle for the next day. With the decision made, and no ego irreparably damaged, the newsmen returned to the task of finishing the Tuesday program.

Chapter 26

Kim Prescott watched the huddle between Benson and the senior production members of *Spotlight* from her desk with a few pangs of envy. *She* was the researcher who spent an exhausting day on the phone to find crucial contacts and interviews in New Zealand, yet *he* gets the junket. A part of Kim hoped that Mac might have given her the nod to make the mad dash to the airport. Kim also had her passport in the office, just in case. Was it churlish to think that Benson had missed a critical angle early in the day, yet got to play foreign correspondent?

Yes, you're just a tired and grumpy 23-year-old.

That thought almost made Kim laugh out loud, not that anyone would have noticed, or cared. People talk to themselves all the time in newsrooms and they're not considered crazy. Usually they're sounding out scripts or rehearsing pieces to camera, so a laugh would have been lost in the usual cacophony. Kim had grown to love that aspect of the *Spotlight* office, especially as the program deadline approached. She felt bewildered and intimidated by the whirl of activity during her first few days. Now she thrived on the adrenalin buzz as scripts and stories came together for broadcast, sometimes only seconds before they were due to play. It helped recharge batteries that were nearly empty after hours of non-stop activity.

With Benson and Dugal on their way to New Zealand, Kim returned to the task of finding more pictures to illustrate developments in the Tugga's Mob story. She didn't even need to leave her desk as the digital library was at her fingertips. Deftly, she isolated the stills the editor required and transferred them to an online bin that he could access from the edit suite. Kim's production duties were many and varied, and were a hazy notion when she set her sights on a media career during her fifth year at secondary school.

She was fortunate enough to attend one of Melbourne's better private schools for 'young ladies'. It provided ample resources for career guidance, regular seminars by industry professionals and work experience weeks with suitable companies. Kim also had a big advantage over most other media aspirants: her father was on the board of a television station. Kim impressed the news crews with her knowledge, work ethic and desire to make a career in journalism during her few weeks in South Melbourne. It was no surprise to the survivors of The Hatchet's purges when Kim Prescott joined the staff of *Spotlight* a few years later.

Kim's interest in writing developed at secondary school where she entertained friends with short stories. It always thrilled her to read them out loud, keeping half an eye on her friends' reactions as the stories unfolded. Mostly they laughed when she expected them to, or provided suitable emotional responses which were valuable feedback for the next story. Kim's themes were everyday experiences for teenagers, with her own dramatic or quirky twist. If some of the teachers knew how rudely they were being pilloried, Kim might have found herself under closer adult scrutiny.

She flirted with dreams of being a novelist – famous, of course – until she started media studies. Kim believed she had ability as a writer, but questioned whether she had the dedication, flair and commitment for longer form writing. Her school stories were written overnight and presented to classmates the next day. A swift turnaround for an immediate response was Kim's motivation. Media studies helped crystallise ideas about writing and opened her eyes to opportunities provided by journalism. When the media studies course delved deeper into visual production Kim knew she had found her vocation – television journalism.

An intranet message came through from the editor for another picture of Drew Harvey, so Kim delved back into the library as she sipped on a lukewarm cup of coffee. Her eyes scanned the images from New Zealand while her mind multi-tasked. She pondered the confrontation with Mac about the coffee kitty on Monday morning. It was part fun, part serious. Was that a measure of how much her confidence had grown in the past two years? Probably. Although in Jo's case, she was scratchy from a hectic social weekend and a broken coffee machine at home – the office supremo needed someone to yell at. Mac just happened to be the first person in the office to give Jo cause to vent. Kim knew it was water off a duck's back to Mac. Pub gossip with the crew revealed her program producer had survived greater office crises than Jo's caffeine addiction and empty kitties.

She glanced over her terminal to where Mac stood at his command post, his large frame, confident air and Scottish ancestry a momentary distraction.

He looks like he should be fighting his way through a Highland glen.

Kim appreciated Mac's sharp mind and finely tuned instincts for current affairs stories. He also fostered a strong team spirit, well, when he wasn't raiding their coffee kitty for Friday drinks. Apart from that foible, as Mac preferred to call it, Kim knew she could learn a lot about television journalism from him.

Kim could see Curly at the computer beside Mac. She regarded him as a friend and another important mentor. He was dedicated to his profession but still managed to juggle work and a family life. Curly was a rarity. Kim was initially shocked to learn the number of divorces in the office. Mac was on his third marriage and most of the station staff over 40 had made return visits to the altar, or registry office, praying for better luck with their second nuptials. Kim hoped to avoid that occupational hazard. Currently single, she was well aware of the pressures the job placed on social lives.

Who has time to be social these days?

Kim didn't lack companionship however. She had Rex, or Sexy Rexy as she usually called him. His sharp features, gorgeous eyes and adorable nature made most women swoon. Sexy Rexy loved the attention. Indeed, he lapped it up. It never made Kim jealous when

Rex's admirers wanted to fuss and fawn over him. Kim knew that Sexy Rexy was a one-woman dog. To be precise, Sexy Rexy was a GAP dog – a former racer who passed through the Greyhound Adoption Program to take up permanent residence in Kim's Richmond apartment after she joined *Spotlight*. He made the perfect house pet for Kim – happy to sleep for up to 18 hours a day while she worked, ready to slobber her with love and affection when she returned home. The pair were a feature in Richmond and South Yarra on their late-night walks.

Her personal life might have been limited but Kim was pleased with the independence that both senior producers gave her these days. They regularly praised her research and were impressed by the development in her scripting and presentation skills. Age made no difference for Mac and Curly. Being able to do the job properly and efficiently were their priorities. And here she was, at 23, deeply involved in one of *Spotlight's* biggest stories. Who knew where the Tugga's Mob story might lead? Kim had learned that opportunities occur when you least expect them. It was a matter of being in the right place at the right time.

I missed out on New Zealand today – but my turn will come.

Chapter 27

Seventy-five kilometres south west of Melbourne, in Geelong, Eddie Malone soberly watched the *Spotlight* program. He'd missed the Monday bombshell about Tugga being helped over the cliff. Clear-headed was a rare condition for Eddie after a long weekend. Friday evening would be celebrated with a slab of beer and bongs produced from the Otway Ranges' finest cannabis, courtesy of Tugga. Eddie managed his supply to ensure he could drift off to dreamland for much of the weekend until Tugga returned from Apollo Bay with more grass every Monday.

But not anymore. Eddie smoked his entire stash on Saturday night after the news report about Tugga's death. Eddie was so shocked by the footage of Tugga's ute on the rocks at Lorne he puffed until there was nothing left.

Tugga dead? Fuck!

His brain was still befuddled on Sunday evening as he sought more information from the TV news. Eddie was disappointed to find Tugga reduced to a road fatality statistic – his death plunge part of the weekend road toll wrap-up.

By Monday afternoon, Eddie was back on planet Earth and trying to locate a new dope supplier. He was puzzled by Tugga's death. The big fella had driven that road thousands of times, in all weather conditions and usually half pissed, without any trouble. It was tough luck for Tugga, but Eddie's main concern was finding more dope.

A possible source popped into Eddie's head a few minutes before the Monday TV news. He was surprised he didn't think of it on Sunday, it was so obvious – Tugga's place. Not the Apollo Bay beach house to which Eddie had never been invited and wouldn't know where to look. No, Eddie thought about the big fella's Geelong residence. That's where he collected his weekly supply every Monday, or Tuesday, depending on Tugga's mood or work schedule.

Shit, Tugga probably has heaps of dope stashed there!

Eddie knew that Tugga didn't like visitors, so the chances of anyone being on the property on a Monday evening were extremely remote, as in zero. He could drive over and load the car. There might be five or six kilos of grass waiting to be smoked. *Sweet!*

Tugga's Geelong home wasn't much flasher than the coastal abode. When he bought the two-acre property, with a modest two-bedroom weatherboard house in 1988, Marshall marked the outer limits of Geelong. Next stop for motorists was the sand and surf at Barwon Heads or 13th Beach. The property suited Tugga perfectly: no close neighbours, the nearest pub was three minutes away in the ute and he had ample space to dump garden waste from the stump grinding business. Tugga usually convinced customers the wood chips were good mulch for their gardens. For those he failed to sway, Tugga added $50 to the bill to haul the chips back to Marshall.

Geelong's need for more homes in the decades after Tugga's arrival saw residential estates sprout like mushrooms. But Tugga wouldn't sell and property developers learned it wasn't wise to knock on his door. Tugga wasn't averse to money but he preferred his privacy more. The agents would be in a lather when they learned a prime piece of urban space could finally be on the market.

Thoughts of real estate potential didn't register for Eddie though, as he sat in his Ford station wagon, 80 metres from the entrance to Tugga's home at 6.37 on Monday evening. Normally Eddie drove straight onto the property as there were no locked gates or dogs to worry about. Eddie hated dogs, they always snarled at him, and he was grateful Tugga never felt the need for four-legged guardians.

However, there was a guard on duty that night. A police car was parked in the driveway and a cop sat behind the wheel. Eddie spotted the sentry as he approached the property, so he drove past and parked in front of a house close to Tugga's boundary fence. He could still see much of Tugga's home between two gum trees – along with two other police cars in front of the house and six cops milling around.

That motivated Eddie to engage drive and cruise back to his one-bedroom flat in Norlane, on the northern side of the city. New dope suppliers could be found, eventually, but not from inside prison. Initially Eddie was confused by the cops prowling around Tugga's home. Surely road accident victims didn't warrant that sort of attention. As Eddie crossed the Moorabool Street bridge over the Barwon River the penny finally dropped.

The cops found the dope at the beach house!

Eddie mourned the loss of a supplier rather than a travelling companion, as he browsed the internet late on Monday evening. He didn't have to worry about getting up early for work since his job at the Ford factory ended when the company closed its doors after more than 90 years. The irony that the announcement came on the eve of the Bathurst 1000, the greatest motorsport battleground for Ford and Holden V8 Supercars, escaped Eddie. He worked at the factory and marked its demise by going home and getting stoned. Eddie knew he needed a job soon as the redundancy wasn't going to keep him in dope, booze, food or rent beyond Christmas.

Eddie wasn't in the mood for browsing his favourite porn sites, so he made a rare visit to a news site. He was stunned to find a report that described Tugga as a coastal drug baron. It even suggested Tugga might have been shunted off the road. And Drew and Gerry had recently been killed. Three of the five members of Tugga's Mob were dead within a few weeks.

What's going on?

Sure, Tugga grew and sold dope, but Eddie didn't believe he was a drug kingpin.

Who the hell would want to kill him?

Tugga didn't deal in the quantities to make him a target. Eddie knew the crystal meth trade was dangerous – the gangs involved were scary, but everyone grew their own weed down on the coast. They didn't need to bump off rivals, surely?

The dregs of a bottle of Bundaberg rum and flat cola had been drained, along with the last can of beer in the flat. But Eddie was relatively sober as he read the online story several more times. Tugga goes off a cliff; he's fucked. The cops said it might be deliberate. They found Tugga's dope in Apollo Bay. They searched his Geelong home. Another stash?

Then a current affairs program reported that Drew and Gerry were dead. The New Zealand cops treated them as accidents, but the media claimed they were suspicious. And there's no mention of the other two members of Tugga's Mob – Helen and Andreas.

Is that good or bad?

Eddie trawled through other websites for information. It became obvious the online stories were all lifted from the *Spotlight* program. It was their website showing the Volendam picture that gave him another jolt.

How the fuck did they get that?

It was grainy, obviously digitally lifted from the television program. He was pleased to see that it was not the whole tour group, just Tugga, Drew and Gerry.

The dead ones. Surely it can't be related to Amsterdam?

A lot happened in the 30 years since that picture was taken, not much of which Eddie cared to remember. His career as a tour guide and driver hadn't even lasted a season – three trips in total. The seven-week debut with Tugga's Mob finished in late July 1986. It was a learning experience, to put it mildly. Eddie struggled with the bus, directions, languages, a tour budget and guiding young antipodeans through the highlights of European culture. He'd been swayed by a mate who worked with other tour companies in the early '80s; lured by stories that it was the 'easiest way to see the world, shag as many girls as you wanted – and get paid to do it.' How could you beat that?

Eddie found getting the bus job was easier than expected. All he needed was an endorsement on his Victorian car licence, which didn't even involve driving a bus. Eddie had to answer a handful of questions from an examiner and then do a short drive in a truck. He didn't even have to haul around the trailer, just the cabin was enough to get the endorsement. Eddie then sent an application to the Victorian Public Service for a bus licence and paid a fee. He was a legal bus driver within a few weeks without having driven a bus. The tour company was so desperate for road crew that anyone who turned up with a valid licence for Europe was hired on the spot.

Eddie's second trip hadn't been any better than escorting Tugga's Mob around the bars and tourist highlights. He ran out of food kitty money, the group was kicked out of two campsites because of fighting among his passengers and they all slammed him in their trip reports.

His final jaunt had been a Beer Fest flyer: London to Munich for the final five days of boozing and debauchery. The passengers were mainly English, Scottish and South African; the Aussies and Kiwis were smart enough to go with Top Deck because the double decker campers guaranteed accommodation.

Eddie had arrived at Campingplatz Thalkirchen in Munich and couldn't find a spare blade of grass to pitch a tent, let alone 20. The Scots were the most philosophical. They dumped their packs on the bus and went straight to the beer halls. They weren't seen again until the bus was ready to return to London. The English tourists had harangued Eddie to the point where he threw the bus keys at them, picked up his own pack and walked away.

He hadn't shagged a passenger in three months and had spent his own money to keep the trips on the road. It was little consolation when he returned to Australia at Christmas to learn the tour company had folded.

It was an unremarkable career as a tour guide and yet, if pushed, Eddie would have to concede it was the most interesting job he'd ever held in his 63 years. He had dropped out of school as soon as it was legally possible, but the lack of skills limited his employment prospects. Eddie had been a driver, cleaner, dishwasher, car groomer, fruit picker and storeman in between frequent bouts on the dole. His five years with Ford was the longest job.

A Queenslander by birth, Eddie had drifted up and down the east coast in search of dope and enough money to keep himself alive. A chance meeting in a pub in Norlane in 2011 provided an opportunity for work at Ford. The money and the conditions were good, although the long-term prospects for the company weren't. That wasn't such an issue for Eddie as he had held few jobs beyond six months.

It was another chance encounter in a pub in central Geelong soon after his arrival that ensured Eddie's stay in Victoria's second largest city would be longer than expected. Eddie had been trying to buy dope: doing the rounds of the pubs and chatting to smokers outside. He'd been told to find the tree fella: 'a big guy, you can't miss him. Usually in the pub down on the river on Tuesday nights. Good prices too'.

Eddie took the advice. It was easy to spot the dealer when he walked through the pub door. Even seated at a table in a corner, with his back against the wall, Eddie recognised the 'tree fella' straight away: it was Tugga Tancred.

It hadn't been a warm or boisterous reunion. Not much kept the big fella from his beer, but pub patrons were surprised that evening to see Tugga leave without draining his jug. They noted an earnest conversation with a scruffy guy in his 60s while the beer remained untouched. Tugga was the first to leave after 20 minutes of lowered heads and voices and well before his standard closing time.

Eddie asked the barman for a fresh glass and finished the jug with a contented smile.

That weekly deal for marijuana kept Eddie content for five years. Good dope at a reasonable price. The exchanges with Tugga were perfunctory, purely business, almost as if their previous association in Europe happened in another life. Eddie could see Tugga was a changed man.

In Europe, Tugga was full of the brashness and confidence of youth, backed up by a bulk that meant he felt no fear.

Who would be crazy enough to take on a man that big?

Eddie was no psychologist, but he could tell that Tugga was out of his depth with the languages, the currencies, the cultures and even the food. Once in Greece, Tugga thought he was ordering a hamburger when it turned out to be roast lamb dinners for the whole table, which was Tugga's Mob. They ate the meal and Tugga paid for everyone.

Rather than ask for help, Tugga's habit was to bluff his way through, making a joke of everything to perhaps cover his naivety. Drew and Gerry behaved the same way; they were a pack and there was safety in numbers. The three of them looked an intimidating sight when standing shoulder to shoulder, so few ever challenged any boisterous behaviour or ridiculed their mangled attempts at cultural interaction. Their French, Spanish, German, Italian, Greek or Turkish didn't extend beyond ordering three beers, or five if Tugga's Mob was in full session.

Eddie recalled that Tugga didn't have much of a clue geographically or politically about Europe. They were driving down an autostrada when Tugga ambled forward from the back seat to ask, 'Do we have to go through this Roma place to get to Rome?'

Tugga also caused a long delay for the tour on the Italian-Austrian border. A guard walked through the bus to check day packs for evidence of drugs while his companions trawled through gear stowed in the lockers below. Tugga's mistake was to snigger loudly when the guard sniffed a small film canister.

The guard showed no fear of Tugga's bulk as he had supreme powers in the days when Europe had borders. Everyone was ordered off the bus and all the tents, backpacks and kitchen gear were thrown onto the side of the road. They waited for two hours until a drug sniffer dog was driven to the mountainous border post. The border guards thought they won that power play, despite not finding anything to set their dog barking.

And Tugga had the last word as they departed Italian territory, 'Of course we don't have any drugs. We haven't been to Amsterdam yet!'

That episode didn't endear Tugga to the rest of the passengers as it had been a chilly afternoon in the mountains. Eddie later realised the majority tolerated Tugga's Mob, believing it unwise to provoke a giant and his big mates. There was a slightly more serious allegation against Tugga from one of the Kiwi women. Eddie managed to deflect her complaint of harassment as he didn't want to deal with head office, or tell Tugga to get off the bus.

The closest Eddie came to witnessing Tugga being *ugly* was in Monaco. The tour included a visit to the famous Monte Carlo Casino. The women got the wrinkles out of their best dresses and the men swapped thongs for shoes to hopefully rub shoulders with jet-setters. The absence of celebrities, and not being able to match the budgets of the high-rollers, saw most passengers end the evening in a bar that overlooked the Formula 1 circuit and port.

Eddie walked the streets of the Principality until midnight when he checked for stragglers in the bar. He was told the last group had just left for the elevator that would take them back to the bus park. Twenty metres from the bar Eddie noticed a late-model Mercedes with its driver's wing mirror smashed. He looked further down the hill and two cars away he could see more glass on the footpath. It was from the wing mirror of a BMW. There was more evidence of vandalism as Eddie approached the lift entrance; broken pottery, dirt and flowers littered the 30-metre tiled hallway.

Eddie was surprised as Monaco was renowned for its urban security in the 1980s, yet some clown seemed to be running amok. When Eddie made it back to the bus he found Tugga, Drew, Gerry and Helen giggling hysterically. The other passengers were on the bus and looked eager to get away.

Eddie decided it wouldn't be wise to challenge Tugga's Mob about the damage, even though it was obvious they were the culprits. Instead, he leapt into the driver's seat and raced back to camp. He had one eye on the road and the other on the rear-vision mirror to make sure there were no flashing blue lights.

Eddie wondered during the tour about Tugga's motivation for visiting Europe. Well, it was more a fleeting thought as he was so busy trying to keep the other passengers happy and not get lost. The Kiwis all talked about the Big OE. It was almost an obligatory visit to the Old World that had to be undertaken before settling down and starting a family.

Not that Tugga had done that. In fact, he had done the opposite. He never returned to New Zealand, never married and didn't father a family; as far as Eddie knew. The few times Eddie tried to engage Tugga in conversation about their European adventure the big fella's mood changed and the conversation dried up quickly. It was as if Tugga never wanted to be reminded that he'd ever been there.

The Tugga that Eddie met for his weekly drug deals was a sombre, older and greyer man. He still loved his beer, but the spark that was present in the company of Tugga's Mob was struggling for oxygen.

In Europe, even in his naivety, Tugga would laugh away his indiscretions and mistakes and call for more beer.

We're here for a good time, not a long time, was Tugga's mantra. Drew and Gerry dutifully parroted the phrase. Helen laughed at those moments, while Andreas smiled drunkenly. At the pubs around Geelong, Tugga drank alone as he plied his after-hours trade.

Tuesday evening found Eddie no closer to solving his problem of a new dope supplier. The Melbourne Cup had been a lonely affair with no workplace sweeps to enjoy the occasion.

He was in a morose mood by the time he tuned into *Spotlight*; the mob that seemed to be leading the pack on the story. The new information about Drew and Gerry – the family's convictions they were murdered – shocked him more than the first online report the previous evening.

Three deaths, all possible murders. Connected to the tour. Could it be that?

The report that Helen Franks had not been found was also unnerving, but possibly explained by a name change through marriage. He was surprised Andreas, aka Andrew Hackett, had done well for himself in the business world.

Pity there's no way to tap him for a few dollars!

Eddie might not be able to profit from that affluent ex-passenger, but he wondered if there could be a way to make some money.

Should he sell his story to the media? He heard that gossip magazines and TV stations paid thousands of dollars for exclusive interviews. Eddie knew all the victims in this case; surely that must be worth something? But then he had another thought; would putting his head above the trenches make him a target like Tugga, Drew and Gerry?

July 25, 1986

I think something happened last night, but I don't exactly know what. I'm sore all over and my head has been pounding for much of the day. I had a few drinks and tried some space cake, but not enough to make me feel this awful. I've got bruises on my arms and legs, but I don't remember falling over.

It was messy early in the night with half the tour group pissed before we left the camp site – especially Tugga's Mob. Andreas was stumbling about even then. I remember going to a café with everyone and trying a bit of cake. But nothing after that.

Most of the passengers looked like zombies this morning and those who tried the space cakes seem to be struggling to recall much of the evening. Just like me. I woke up naked in my tent. Alone, thank goodness, but without a clue how I got there.

Denise was just as wasted apparently. She says she lost track of me and everyone else around midnight, although we all made it back to the bus and the camp. Not a great way to end the tour.

It was a slow process cleaning the tents and camping gear before leaving for the ferry at Zeebrugge. It's a quiet bus now as we drive to Belgium.

Even Tugga's Mob; Drew, Gerry and Andreas are sleeping and Tugga is sitting at the back with a smug look on his face.

There's no sign of Helen. Eddie said she wanted to stay in Amsterdam for a few more weeks. I won't miss her on the ferry trip tonight – she was as creepy as the other Kiwi guys. I'm sure she was making a pass at me a couple of times on tour. She used to get too close when we were in bars, always draping her arm around my shoulder, supposedly just being 'friendly,' and wanting to dance with me in discos. She bragged about being bisexual but she must have known I'm only into men, after all, she walked in on Andreas and me at least twice.

I'll be glad to get rid of them in a few hours. I've loved Europe. Travelling through so many different cultures and landscapes every few days. My priority now is to get some accommodation in London, find a job and save enough money to come back and see more of this magical continent.

It was not to be. Silent teardrops fell from the diary holder as they imagined the events of that last evening on tour, and the growing anxiety of the following weeks. Seven weeks visiting the postcard sights of her childhood dreams provided the final episode of happiness for Judy Williams. For that, the diary holder was at least grateful.

It was so tragic that the achievement of a long-held dream should be followed by her death 12 months later.

Chapter 28

Curly Rogers contentedly sipped a second glass of tawny port. It was 11.30, Melbourne Cup night, and he wasn't tired despite two long days at work. There was plenty of adrenalin left to cope with one of the biggest stories of his career. The luxury of the second glass was afforded by the fact his wife, Janine, and the kids were in dreamland long before Curly left the office. Not even the squeaky front door of their brick 19th century terrace home could rouse them. Although it reminded Curly there was one more job on their expensive renovation project to complete.

He looked forward to a free afternoon when he could remove the door, replace the ancient hinges, strip the paint and apply a fresh coat. The renovations were a labour of love for Curly and Janine and, on occasions, their two adolescent boys. The terrace house had been in Janine's family since the 1940s and had fallen into disrepair. Middle Park was now part of a strict heritage-conservation area, and the Rogers were proudly doing their duty to restore the terrace to its former grandeur. It was solid, but needed lots of modernising, and costs dictated the duration of the project.

Curly had his laptop open to a sports website which was full of Melbourne Cup Day stories. News was never far from the view of a veteran journalist. His mellow mood was enhanced by the likelihood of a third exclusive story in a row. He knew it was a risky decision to hold the information about Judy Williams. Curly argued strongly to wait 24 hours because he knew they could present a better story. They would have pictures and interviews from Judy's family in New Zealand. If they alerted other networks about her connection to Tugga on Tuesday night it would have given them a chance to catch up.

He'd spent the extra hours in the office tracking down a family connection for Judy Williams in Waikato, or *the* Waikato, as New Zealanders seemed to call the province. Kim had made the breakthrough again by finding a phone number and farm address for Judy's sister near Te Awamutu. She also traced another Waikato member of the tour group who lived in Cambridge, which wasn't far from Te Awamutu. That final discovery had been at 10pm in Australia – midnight in New Zealand – so it was decided to let Pete Benson make the first calls in the morning.

It was also agreed the crew should start with the Williams family and work their way back to Auckland via Cambridge. They would be on the road for more than five hours, but at least the Trans-Tasman time difference worked in their favour. The contact details and suggested questions were emailed to the pair, along with other vital travel information. Their hotel was 50 metres from the Auckland airport arrival hall and the car rental company was a five-minute walk. The hotel had a strong internet connection which would be convenient for a live cross to Benson. Curly knew the pictures might be crap but it would be cheaper than hiring a local television studio or live-truck.

Curly flirted with the danger of a *third* glass of tawny, without his wife finding out, as he flicked through to a news website. The lead story made him forget the port; the headline almost turned the fortified wine in his stomach to vinegar:

Fourth passenger from '80s tour group dead

by Anita Bentley

A fourth member of a European tour group in 1986 has been found dead in suspicious circumstances.

New South Wales police have identified the body of a woman

who died from a suspected drug overdose at the base of a Central Coast cliff this morning, as Helen Franks.

Police are treating the death of New Zealand expat, Franks, as a homicide. A spokesman said there were some 'inconsistencies' with the evidence found beside the body. Franks is reported to be a recovering heroin addict, having lived for 10 years at Wamberal without reports of any relapses.

Franks is connected to a current headline story in Victoria and New Zealand; the deaths of a group which toured Europe in 1986. Three New Zealand men – Kevin 'Tugga' Tancred, Drew Harvey and Gerry Daly – all died within two months of each other and in suspicious circumstances.

The third victim was Tugga Tancred, whose vehicle ran off the road near Lorne on Friday night. Police believe another vehicle was involved in the incident.

Harvey drowned while fishing from a rock platform near Auckland. Daly was killed after being knocked off his bicycle on the Coromandel Peninsula. The driver hasn't been found.

Current affairs program, *Melbourne Spotlight*, claims the men were murdered and their deaths staged to look like accidents. The program says the connection is the European tour. Franks was also on that tour.

Spotlight says the friends were known as Tugga's Mob on the tour. It also revealed one of its station executives, Financial Controller Andrew Hackett, was on the tour and had close ties to Tugga's Mob. Hackett wasn't interviewed but is reported to have no explanation for the deaths. Hackett said he hasn't seen his fellow passengers since the tour.

Curly felt deflated as he read the rest of the report, much of it taken from their broadcast. The late-night scoop by a web reporter had stolen their lead on the story. It was bound to happen; Curly was sad that it had come so soon. He was magnanimous enough to salute whoever Anita Bentley was, and took some comfort from the thought she could never make the connection if Curly and *Spotlight* hadn't made the initial broadcast on Monday.

Curly had no idea it was blind luck that Bentley ever made that connection between the heroin overdose victim in New South Wales and Tugga's Mob. Bentley was trying to make an early exit – her boyfriend was nearly comatose in a South Yarra bar after a day at the Cup – when sub editor Tony Pascoe requested one more round of calls to Police Media centres in state capitals on the East coast.

Pascoe's justification was that he didn't trust the Sydney or Brisbane offices to do their jobs properly.

Bentley was so annoyed she almost missed the name the Sydney cop gave her for the body found at the base of The Skillion.

Where the hell is that?

Asked to repeat the name, the cop confirmed it was an expat Kiwi called Helen Franks. The drunken boyfriend was ignored as Bentley gathered the facts and, with the help of the senior sub, compiled her first national scoop.

Bentley's mention of Hackett in her story solved one thorny issue for Curly. It had been the final topic of conversation before Mac departed for the pub to spend his third-place earnings from the Cup.

Sneaky bugger didn't repay that fiver for the sweep!

Mac and Curly had debated whether to alert The Hatchet about Judy Williams' death. Curly argued their boss might demand police protection, or pay for security of his own. Mac's counter argument had been that Templeton could do the deed in the morning.

'Our Boss is growing a set of cojones at last. It will do him good to keep that advantage over The Hatchet.'

Chapter 29

Andrew Hackett had cause to rue Mac's decision at 7.21am on Wednesday as he reversed the BMW from the garage. He was in a foul mood after hours trying to explain to the station board and executives his connection to a dead drug dealer.

Mostly Hackett couldn't believe so many of the station's senior personnel watched *Spotlight* on Melbourne Cup night. Watched it at all, really.

The street was usually quiet in the morning, so Hackett wasn't concentrating on what was behind him. He became aware of a shape in his rear-view mirror as a loud voice startled him.

'Oi, oi – look out there!'

Hackett slammed on the brake and, with heart racing, turned to see if he had almost run down a neighbour. Instead, he stared straight into the lens of a news camera.

'What the fuck? What are you doing there?' Hackett demanded. 'Get out of my driveway.'

The camera operator moved a step to his right, but Hackett could see his exit was still blocked. His instinct was to rev the engine to make the cameraman jump. Before he could plant the foot on the accelerator a cordless microphone was thrust through the open driver window.

'Mr Hackett,' a reporter bellowed. 'What do you have to say about the murder of Helen Franks?'

'What do you mean? I haven't heard anything about that.'

Hackett's inexperience with veteran TV reporters prolonged the engagement. He should have wound the window up and driven away before the cameraman could join the reporter at his window. Instead, Hackett's shocked reaction gave the newsmen valuable footage.

'Helen Franks was killed by a lethal dose of heroin on Monday night, but the local cops don't believe she did it herself.'

Hackett didn't get a chance to respond as the reporter continued with his verbal assault.

'They think someone killed her. That's four victims in staged *accidents* in two countries in just over two months and you're the only surviving member of this notorious Tugga's Mob. Are you the final target?'

Hackett was too stunned to respond. He didn't know the reporter played loose with the facts, that it was only the media who'd decided the deaths were murders.

'What happened on that tour in 1986, Mr Hackett? And were you involved?'

Hackett's head snapped back as if he'd been slapped. These were the same questions Templeton had thrown at him the previous day. And now a cheeky bastard from Channel 9 was trying to drag him into the sordid business.

Hackett growled. 'No comment.' He took his foot off the brake and accelerated onto the road. There was a squeal of tyres as Hackett escaped his inquisitors.

I hate fucking journalists!

The confrontation in the driveway was an exclusive for the opposition TV channel. By the time Hackett reached his office it had already been broadcast on the station's breakfast news. The whole clip was uploaded to You Tube by morning tea and Hackett winced as he reviewed his miserable performance. It had attracted 1,105 views by lunchtime with 389 people giving it the thumbs up.

Chapter 30

The first few km on Auckland roads failed to live up to Pete Benson's expectations of Aotearoa. There was a brief green belt as they drove away from the airport, before Dugal Cameron turned their rental car onto the south-western motorway. It plunged them into an industrial suburb that didn't feature in the Tourism New Zealand videos on the plane the previous night. They showed pristine lakes, rafting trips, kayaking, mountain climbing, bungy jumping, wine tasting, trail bike riding, jet boats, mud pools, volcanoes, whale watching and too many other adventures for Benson's tired brain to remember.

Instead, the Australian current affairs crew found themselves surrounded by factories. These blended into a shopping centre on the left of the motorway – which was under the flight path for the airport – and an amusement park, before they turned onto the main route out of Auckland, the Southern Motorway. That gave them the biggest shock: thousands of stationary cars.

Fortunately, the stalled traffic was on the other side of the motorway, so the journey south to Waikato proceeded at a steady clip. They were used to Melbourne's massive daily traffic movements especially on the M1, aka the Monash Carpark, and felt sympathy for the multiple lanes of commuters stuck in first gear. It was 6.30am and as the central city was another 25 km away, most would be lucky to reach Auckland before office hours started.

Within 20 minutes of leaving the airport the media crew was climbing the Bombay Hills with attractive lifestyle blocks nestled into the slopes. It's an unofficial boundary between the City of Sails and the rest of the country. JAFAs – a crude epithet that expands to Just Another Fucking Aucklander – is applied to everyone in Auckland by everyone outside of Auckland. They rated ahead of Australians in popularity, but only marginally.

Not that Benson was aware of these provincial rivalries as he yawned once again, still sleepy from their rushed trip and early start. He perked up when he saw an exit sign for Pukekohe. Technically it was still part of Auckland City, but that didn't concern Benson. He was excited by another sign that revealed the V8 Supercars were making their annual pilgrimage to New Zealand on the weekend. Benson was a racing-anything fan: cars, motor bikes, cycles, horses, people; anything going super-fast on two legs, four legs or with a high-powered engine.

'Hey, look at that Dugal – the V8s are going to be just down the road this weekend. If we get lucky, we might stay long enough for a day at the track on Sunday.'

Dugal was aware of his colleague's need for speed, but didn't share the same passion. Cameras, films, skiing, kayaking, rock-climbing and most outdoor adventure pursuits set Dugal's wheels spinning. Two years of working with Benson taught him how to puncture the reporter's enthusiasm. 'Oh joy. Can you imagine us turning up to a V8 Supercar race in this rental Corolla?'

Benson felt the painful barb and went quiet. It would be hugely embarrassing he conceded; having recorded numerous stories with V8 drivers and their teams he had built a few friendships. His pride could never take the hit if they saw him roll up to the track in a 1.5 litre four-cylinder rented Toyota.

Benson returned his attention to the countryside as provincial Waikato unfolded before him from the top of the Bombays. It was a pleasant sight, lush pastures stretched into the distance, divided by the country's longest waterway. The Waikato River would be their companion for much of their journey.

Benson wanted to study Kim's research notes on the two

interviewees they were meeting, yet for many km the reporter found himself distracted by the landscape. Sheep and cattle were scattered here and there, but not as many as he expected.

Don't they have 40 million sheep tucked away here somewhere?

Benson was from a rural background and wondered if farmers kept them away from the stresses and pollution of traffic.

'I can't believe how green this country is,' he said as they crossed the river north of Hamilton to avoid city traffic. 'It's only a few weeks away from summer and everything is still so lush. Dad's farm at Skipton is already browner than a dingo's bum.'

Dugal snorted. 'When did you last see a dingo in the Western District? Anyway, look at the drizzle mate, it never stops raining here. It's not just called the Shaky Isles. And Land of the Long White Cloud is more appropriate. Permanently wet.'

Benson nodded and glanced again at the copious notes in his lap from Kim's late-night email.

It was all new scenery to Benson, but his colleague had several ski trips to the South Island under his belt.

'It's a beautiful country I have to admit, especially the southern Alps. Switzerland in the South Seas is another description, but without the chocolate-box timber houses. Don't expect anything like an Australian summer here though. The Roaring Forties and all the crap from the Southern Ocean that bypasses us, smacks into New Zealand.'

Benson looked up from his notes. 'You going to audition for Kate's weather job on the news while she's on maternity leave?'

Dugal laughed. 'No mate, I don't look as sexy in a little black dress – or out of it.'

Benson chuckled as he estimated how far they were from their first destination, a farm west of Te Awamutu, towards the township of Pirongia. The background from Kim was invaluable, but Benson was unsure how productive the interview would be.

The contact Kim had discovered was Heather Langer, the only sibling of Judy Williams. Benson had waited until 7.30am to call. The sister was aloof, which Benson could understand.

Why would an Australian television program suddenly be

interested in Judy's death after almost three decades? Heather told Benson she hadn't watched any news reports since the weekend and wasn't aware of the deaths of Tugga's Mob, or their association with her sister.

Rather than spell out the full story over the mobile phone, and risk Heather refusing to talk, Benson said it would be better to explain in person. Heather reluctantly agreed to meet and confirmed directions to the farm. The only information she offered was that she hadn't been living in the region at the time of Judy's death. She had married a farmer and moved south to Manawatu.

As they drove through the gates Benson knew his father would have been envious of the Langer's dairy farm. There were undulating pastures, good fences and Mt Pirongia loomed to the west; a bucolic setting that was a sharp contrast to the dry plains around Skipton. The tidy, two-storey weatherboard farmhouse was surrounded by a garden full of spring flowers.

Lucky Dad never visited Waikato as a young man, or I'd be a Kiwi!

An attractive and slender, ash-blonde woman of about 60 emerged onto a large deck from the house and wiped her hands on a towel.

'Wow. She looks exactly like an older version of Judy Williams in that Volendam picture,' Benson noted.

Heather was, naturally, dressed in farm attire of jeans, a ragged sports jersey of red, yellow and black hoops and thick socks. Muddy gumboots stood near the door. If Benson had bothered to ask, he would have been told the jersey was the provincial rugby team. This was a no-nonsense and hard-working woman and Benson guessed she didn't want to waste time chatting to an Australian TV crew about ancient history. Benson switched on the reporter charm.

'Hello, Heather. I'm Pete Benson and this is Dugal Cameron from *Melbourne Spotlight*. Lovely property you have here, so fertile compared to my father's sheep farm back home.'

Heather nodded and glanced across to Dugal who had retrieved a small camera kit from the Corolla.

'Hello,' she finally responded. Benson was about to launch into more fulsome praise for the property when Heather cut straight to the reason for their visit.

'I did some research on Google after you rang. Looks like this Tugga's Mob are causing a fuss on both sides of the Tasman.'

'Yes,' Benson said, grateful he didn't have to make pleasantries. Dugal insisted on the flight over that the only thing New Zealanders cared about was rugby. Benson had never seen a game in his life and was silently panicking if the early conversation was steered in the direction of the performance of the Australian national team.

Are they the Wallabies or Kangaroos?

Benson was a Victorian and knowledge of other football codes wasn't required in Melbourne.

'Has the New Zealand media caught up with the latest death – Helen Franks?'

Heather nodded again, 'That makes four of them now, doesn't it? And just your boss left alive, from what I've been reading?'

Benson wanted to say that his own colleagues would've been happier if the killer had started in reverse order; but decided against it.

'That's right. We're still unsure of his connection to this mess. He denies any knowledge of serious problems on the tour that might've started a spate of revenge killings. It's a mystery to him – and us.'

Heather draped the towel over a wooden chair at an outdoor dinner table and placed her hands on her hips.

'Well, I don't care about him. However, I do wonder about the connection to our Judy. She wasn't one of that Tugga's Mob, as you lot are calling them, and she died in 1987.'

'Well, we think we might have found the connection,' Benson said as Dugal joined him. They looked up at the determined woman on the deck a metre above them.

'We learned late yesterday that Tugga sexually harassed your sister throughout the tour. We're not sure what happened, but The Hatch, um, Andrew Hackett, confirmed that Judy complained about being pestered by Tugga.

'*He* claimed he didn't see any incidents, but admitted she talked to him about it. We're investigating that angle as a possible motive for the current killings. And the police are likely to follow that up as well.'

Benson watched for a reaction from that bombshell. He was aware this could be a shock for the family, unless of course Judy had told her only sister about being stalked by Tugga. Did the events contribute to Judy's suspected suicide a year after the trip?

Heather remained still for several seconds and then, slowly, raised both hands to her face as tears rolled down her cheeks.

Dugal raised an eyebrow at his reporter. It wasn't an unfamiliar situation for Benson – an interviewee getting tearful. The television industry thrived on emotional responses and an experienced reporter generally knew how to marshal those forces: but the camera must be recording before the tears start.

The current affairs duo swiftly climbed the stairs and assumed their roles. Benson comforted a distraught Heather while Dugal surveyed the deck as a potential interview location. It was perfect. The drizzle had cleared, the table setting was modern and the hydrangeas and pastures would make a stunning backdrop. It was up to Benson to make her talk, and cry again, at the right time.

The two-hour head start on Australia was a bonus for them. However, they still had to drive to Cambridge, record a second interview, send the footage and then drive back to Auckland for a possible live cross during the program. Their interviews would be incorporated into the main story produced by Curly back at the station, which eased some of the pressure.

Benson knew he could afford a few minutes to calm Heather and convince her an interview would be worthwhile.

'Shall I put the kettle on for a cup of tea?' Benson spotted an electric kettle on a timber bench as he ushered Heather into the kitchen and picked it up. That helped stem the tears as it gave Heather a different focus. She reclaimed the kettle and set about being a courteous host.

The room had a golden hue from the light timbers of the walls, roof and cabinets. The feature was a granite-topped central island with a generous food preparation area, sink, tap and four stools. Benson was a fan of farmhouse kitchens and Heather's was a wonderful mixture of old and new materials.

'I love the wood you've used in here, it feels so warm. Is it all native timbers?'

'Yes. The walls are original kauri, but I had the cabinetry replaced five years ago. They're rimu.'

'My Mum would be so envious. She's been nagging Dad for years to build a new kitchen and to make it open-plan, like you have to the dining and living rooms. Dad almost has a heart attack at the thought of knocking down a wall through to his Grandad's old dining room.'

Heather laughed. 'I know what you mean. Farmers don't like change. My father was the third generation of the Williams clan to work this farm. We've mainly been into dairy herds, with room for a few hundred sheep when the lamb and wool prices were good. We've also had a couple of thoroughbreds over the years, but nothing that ever won any races outside of the Waikato.'

Benson's tactic worked. Heather relaxed as she talked about her family's life on the farm. He sat down with his cup of Earl Grey tea and listened. He soon steered Heather towards Judy and her dream trip.

'I wasn't here the last year before Judy went travelling. I married Bert and moved to the Manawatu. Judy and I were always close, so I was excited for her that she was finally going to live the dream. I couldn't quite understand her fascination with the old places in Europe, but I knew it was important for her.

'God, she used to chew my ear off about that Disneyland castle in Germany. Neuschwanstein I think it's called. She had to visit that, and the Eiffel Tower, and Rome. Just about every ancient city and monument in Europe appealed to her imagination.'

Benson noted details of Judy's European travels that would be pertinent for the interview, but didn't interrupt Heather. He kept an eye on the time as it was important to get her into the interview chair soon.

'We had started a family by the time Judy returned in mid '87. We had the farm and the baby to look after, so Judy and I never had much time to sit down and have a good natter about what she did over there.'

Benson realised Heather was on the verge of tears again and wanted to save some of that emotion for the camera. He steered Heather in what he thought would be a safer direction.

'What brought you back to the family farm from Manawatu?'

'The late 1980s and early '90s were bad years for us, unfortunately.'

Benson wanted to curse for not saving that question until the camera was recording. Heather continued to talk about the family's heartbreaking history.

'First it was Judy drowning in '87. That broke my parents' hearts. It didn't seem possible as she was relentlessly positive and happy before going to Europe. Two years later Mum and Dad were killed in a car accident coming back from an All Blacks test in Wellington. We don't know what happened, the car went off the Desert Road and rolled about six times. With no men in the family it meant Bert and I either had to sell this, or move back and work the property.'

Heather paused to sip her tea. Benson suspected there was more tragedy to come.

'Bert loved this farm. There was more land than what we had in the Manawatu and it was better soil, which meant we could milk more cows. They were thriving. But life kicks you in the balls just when you think everything is going great. Bert developed cancer in late '91 and he was gone before the start of the next rugby season.'

Benson winced. This family had gone through a rough patch, although it looked like the farm was flourishing.

'We, my son Jason and I, lost all our family in the space of four years yet, ironically, their deaths secured our financial future. Mum, Dad and Bert all had good insurance policies and we've never had to worry about mortgages on the farm or machinery since then. There was no stress finding school and college fees for Jason and I could afford farm workers until he was old enough to take over the management.'

'Is Jason out on the farm, or in town?' Benson asked.

'No, he's away travelling for a few days, so I've got a couple of the neighbour's lads to help me with the milking.'

Benson wanted to learn more about Heather's son, but she stood and placed the cup and saucer in the sink.

'I guess I had better make myself more presentable to your Australian television audience.'

Sixty-five minutes later, Benson had managed to get Heather to repeat the family dramas on camera along with a few appropriate teary moments. To learn that her sister was being stalked on tour, and that no one had done anything to stop the monster was the most distressing moment of the interview for Heather.

It was good background on Tugga's stalking victim, but Benson believed it didn't progress the investigative side of the story much, as Heather had little contact with Judy after her return. Benson explored reasons for her early return from London – Judy had a two-year working visa – but without luck. Heather did provide one gold nugget regarding Judy's death.

'Judy wasn't suicidal. I knew my sister and she wasn't the type. I accept she was out of sorts when she came home from Europe. *Everyone* said Judy wasn't her usual bubbly and energetic self, and they sniggered that she had packed on a few extra kilos. But I believe that was because of their diets in London. All the Kiwi girls who worked in pubs came home with extra baggage.

'But I will never believe that my sister killed herself in the river. I don't think we will ever know what happened there.'

Benson and Dugal were on their way to nearby Cambridge by 11am with one interview and 30 new pictures of Judy Williams on tape. They were typical travel photos of the '80s – Judy in front of famous landmarks, such as Neuschwantsein. Heather explained that was Judy's ultimate destination in Europe; her fairytale castle. Benson made sure they recorded other recognisable tourist spots like the Eiffel Tower, the leaning tower of Pisa and the Colosseum. Most were happy, smiling stills – lots of singles and doubles with other people on the tour and the occasional group shot – but not with any of Tugga's Mob. And none of The Hatchet, that Benson could see. There was a poignant shot of Judy at Gallipoli. It was a thoughtful pose at a place called Chunuk Bair, probably taken by a friend when Judy was unaware. Benson presumed the location held the same significance for Kiwis as Lone Pine did for Aussies and made sure Dugal included it. Surprisingly all the pictures were in remarkably good condition for their age. Perhaps Heather had them reprinted at some stage.

It was a good haul at the Williams homestead, although there was no tour diary to verify any problems Judy had with Tugga. Heather said she had never seen her sister with a diary and she couldn't provide an explanation for Judy's early return from London.

Benson felt Heather was evasive about Jason as she would only say he was on a working holiday.

If anyone has a motive to bump off Tugga's Mob it's this family, but why wait 30 years?

Benson shifted focus to their next interviewee. Denise Howard should be much better. She was on the tour, close to Judy at the time and could add more substance to the stalking claim. Denise would also be the first person from the tour to appear on camera.

Benson was pleased with their progress as he reached for his mobile phone to update Curly and Mac.

Dugal distracted him momentarily with some local history. 'Hey, did you know Tim and Neil Finn were born here?'

A blank stare was Benson's only reply.

'You know, the guys from *Split Enz* – and then Neil started Crowded House. I think they based a couple of songs on growing up around here.'

Benson nodded briefly and turned his attention back to the phone. 'I think my parents might have some of their records – or maybe they were CDs.'

Dugal looked across at his colleague, who was barely five years younger than him, and shook his head in dismay. 'You children have no sense of history, music or taste.'

Chapter 31

Heather Langer stared intently at the computer screen and read the message she composed minutes after the news crew left. It was written on an anonymous email account with *Petbe,* the Egyptian god of revenge, in the subject line. It wasn't sent; it would remain in the draft bin until the person it was intended for logged in. The message would be deleted after it was read, no trace of it passing through cyberspace as Petbe and Heather shared the same log in.

The hounds are on the scent. I've just had an Australian TV news crew here inquiring about Judy's connection to Tugga's Mob. They know that he was stalking her. I played ignorant, saying I had little contact with Judy after she went away. You might even see the interview tonight – a show called Melbourne Spotlight.

Have you arrived yet? Naturally they suspect revenge is a motive for the deaths, but I think they were convinced I had no idea, or connection. It seems the police here and in Australia are getting pressured to investigate. We knew it might happen but a bit more time to complete your tasks would have been better. It was unlucky someone made the connection so quickly with that bitch.

Let me know if you are proceeding according to plan or want to change. You have already achieved the main mission – the evil bastard and his friends are dead. I would be content to stop there if you believe the risk is too great. Your safe return is now my main concern.

Much love

Heather read the draft one more time before closing the account. She was proud of her performance with the Australian news crew. Her 'ignorance' of the details surrounding Judy had been easy to portray.

Heather's story stacked up: she lived 350 km away from Te Awamutu at the time of Judy's return and death, preoccupied with her own family and the farm. She was sure the Australians dismissed her as a farm wife, and that suited her perfectly.

She swung the chair away from the computer and rolled over to a shelf in the small study. Judy's diary was sitting there during the Australians' visit, albeit wrapped in silk and tucked away inside the box. The reporter had been smart enough to inquire if Judy left a tour diary, but Heather gambled he was fishing and denied any knowledge of one. Again, her excuse had been ignorance as she was in the Manawatu. That defence, technically, was accurate as well. Or, it had been for almost 30 years. The diary had been at the Williams family farm all along: the emotions too raw for anyone to open it, or develop the accompanying films.

It was a surprise visit that had changed everything.

Heather unwrapped the diary and debated whether to read another entry. There were only two more pages after the tour finished.

August 18, 1986

Ugh! London in August is becoming unbearable. It's muggy and stinky as everyone is sweaty. Our pub doesn't have air-conditioning. There's a slow-moving fan that does nothing to cool the main bar and the smell of sour beer and BO made me sick this morning – again. That's the second day in a row. It could be the food they serve here which is bland, fatty and stodgy. My taste buds must have been spoiled in Europe. God, that seems like ages ago now, although it's just a few weeks.

I've been so busy since getting the job here. The split trading hours don't leave me any time for exploring London. That's if I had the energy. By the time we boot the last of the lunch customers out and clean up, it's almost time to re-open again for the evening.

Some of the guys have been kicking on to clubs in Earls Court (Freddie Mercury goes to one just a hundred yards up the road!) but I've been too tired to join in. I might get more settled in a few weeks.

The accommodation isn't wonderful but at least I only have to share with one other girl, an Australian. And she doesn't sleep here very often. London is expensive and finding a pub job with food and accommodation is bit of a blessing, but it's not salubrious.

I can understand how some people get stuck in a rut in this place. Ron, the Kiwi head barman (who helped me get the job) has been here for almost two years but never been to Paris or Rome. He's been to the traditional stuff: the beer fest and the running of the bulls in Spain, but his visa runs out soon and he'll have to go home without seeing anything memorable. Such a waste.

But who am I to judge? I just have to make sure I don't get stuck here too long. Pub jobs are easy to pick up once you have some experience.

Ron understands that some of us want to see and experience Europe. They don't mind if we work for a few months, save some money and head off to explore again. There's always more Kiwis and Aussies coming through the door looking for work. My next goal is to go skiing after Christmas. Switzerland is too expensive for my budget so it will have to be Austria. It's not a bad option as Top Deck use a 400-year-old chalet that sounds wonderful. Passengers who stayed there during the summer season say the food is fantastic and most nights it's party time in the bar. That's where I should be – out the front having fun and not serving the drinks. Ha ha. Oh well, head down, Judy, and save quickly. I must also get those trip photos developed one day. Another expense to save for.

Heather stopped at that point, preferring to read one date at a time. Her thoughts would drift back to 1986 and imagine her sister at the time of writing. Judy was always vibrant, inquisitive, and more sociable than her older sister.

Heather didn't mind that as she was never likely to visit the same tourist destinations; learning from Judy's letters and postcards was enough for her. It was such a shame that evil in the form of Tugga and his mates had intruded.

But that misfortune was being remedied: four down.

Chapter 32

Benson's call to his senior producer arrived as the *Spotlight* daily conference finished. The entire production crew was focused on the Tugga's Mob story for Wednesday and duties had been swiftly assigned by Mac and Curly. The emotions were slightly mixed that morning. Many were gutted that another news organisation broke their stranglehold on the story with the website report about the fourth victim – Helen Franks. But Mac quickly urged them to look at the positives.

'We've been spot-on from the beginning. Curly's instincts told him there was something sinister about Tugga's death and it's escalated from there. And we've been miles ahead of the other wankers.'

The frowns changed to smiles, a few high-fives were exchanged and the reporters seated beside Curly patted him on the back. High praise indeed! Mac still held the floor.

'Four members of Tugga's Mob are dead, and the only survivor is up on the seventh floor shitting himself.' Mac pointed above their dungeon office and it brought a round of cheers.

Ken Withers, the acting senior camera operator in Dugal's absence, raised a valid point, prompting another raucous response. 'Should we mount a death-watch on The Hatchet? You know, like the Americans do with the President. They always have a camera crew and media around the president in case of an assassination attempt.'

The cheers faded as the production crew realised it was a serious topic. The Hatchet was the last member standing from Tugga's Mob. Would the killer have a go at him, even now that it was public knowledge the deaths were most likely murders?

And if yes, should they find a way to cover it?

Mac paused for several seconds as everyone considered the ramifications. 'I think that moral dilemma is one for the management.' He turned and raised a bushy eyebrow to Richard Templeton who nodded his agreement.

Mac resumed. 'Okay, Richard will take that up with Hackett and Reg Bradley first thing.'

He turned once again to his executive producer and, for the first time, felt pleased he was on the team.

'We'll also need you to break the news about Judy Williams to Hackett as well. It'll probably be another shock for him regardless of the timing. I'd love to get his reaction on camera, but I don't like our chances after Channel 9 door-stopped him.'

Everyone had enjoyed watching The Hatchet squirm on the breakfast news, even if it was an opposition channel. All eyes in the room turned to Templeton.

'I'll get him on camera. If he fronts for Channel 9 before breakfast, why can't he join us for dinner?'

Laughter peaked again, and applause greeted Templeton's rhetorical question. He let the joke run its course.

'I'll tell him about Judy Williams before we record. We need to be fair, but I'm sure he'll still be tighter than a footy at first bounce on Grand Final Day.'

Jo Trescowthick rolled in and out of the meeting room as she took calls and organised crews. It was a familiar sight: Jo's toes propelling her office chair back and forth. Everyone knew to steer clear of the first seat inside the door. The number of times Mac had his toes run over, or ankles clipped, depended on the length of the meeting and the urgency of Jo's communications. Her third return to the conference added to the general good mood as she finally tagged Mac in the shin.

'Jeezus, Jo,' Mac winced as he rubbed a bruised left leg. 'I'm going to remove all the chairs one day and make you bloody walk.'

'I'll borrow my Granny's mobility scooter. Anyway, stop your crying. There's a detective inspector at reception wanting a chat with the senior producer, and I've got Pete Benson on the phone from across the ditch.'

As Jo thrust the phone into Mac's hands and scooted back out the door, Mac said, 'She's a bloody menace on wheels. Any of you ever see her drive that rusty hatchback?'

The crew laughed at Mac as they followed the menace out the door. Enough jokes; they had their jobs and the clock was ticking towards that night's deadline.

Mac and Curly sat down again to hear what their new foreign correspondents had in the can. They had to wrangle all the elements of an evolving story into three coherent features. The station's news department also had to be considered. It was post-Melbourne Cup and non-racing news was back on the agenda. The news program would be broadcast before *Spotlight*, therefore they had to cover fresh angles on the story.

The old maxim in television programming was to catch the audience at the top of the news – give them a scintillating story and you had them hooked for the night. That might have been true in the days before television remotes. If the TV started on Channel 2 at 7pm, it stayed on Channel 2 – even if it was a test pattern. Now that people didn't have to get off their butts and walk across the living room to change the channel, surfing was the thing. Technology, and dozens of new channels, didn't improve the fitness of the average Australian viewer, but it did change their habits. So television stations needed new techniques and skills to hook viewers and keep them for the night.

Mac understood the station politics and told Curly they would have to collaborate with their news colleagues down the hallway.

They had to make sure the news story had enough information and pictures to pique the audience's curiosity, but enough to make them satisfied. It was a case of sharing enough crumbs to keep viewers following the trail and staying on-station to *Spotlight* and their revelations about the stalking of Judy Williams and her death. The best way to control the information flow was to produce all the stories themselves.

Mac griped at Curly. 'You and your bloody gut instincts!'

Chapter 33

'Shit, shit, shit,' Andrew Hackett shouted at the distant Tasmanian ferry docked in Port Melbourne. There was no danger of the captain, crew or passengers being offended by his tirade, Hackett was several km away from the dock. The ferry was an easy target for a dose of vitriol from his executive office as no one would answer back.

Hackett's temper had simmered since being cornered by the Channel 9 news crew in his own home turf. His performance under pressure had been far from executive-like. And that was the opinion of the boss himself, Reg Bradley. No doubt the board members would be tut-tutting as well.

Hackett didn't bother turning from the floor-to-ceiling view when he heard a tap on the door, he presumed it was Zara the gatekeeper with more dumb requests for information from the TV board about his AFL broadcast deal. Therefore, Hackett was startled when Richard Templeton spoke.

'It's such an incredible view, must be hard to tear yourself away.'

'Christ,' Hackett spluttered as he turned around to find the *Spotlight* executive producer approach *his* view with all the confidence of Donald Trump.

'What are you doing here?' Hackett blustered. 'Where's Zara? She should've told me first.'

Templeton shrugged. 'She must have gone AWOL.' He was never going to share his inside knowledge that Zara always prepared a pot of Earl Grey tea for Reg Bradley at 9.45am. The gates were temporarily left unguarded and Templeton had charged through.

He now confidently made himself comfortable on the sofa. 'There have been developments in the Tugga's Mob story and I thought I should brief you directly.'

'Fuck me.' Hackett groaned and turned back towards the Tasmanian ferry. 'I know about Helen Franks. She was a junkie. Okay, the timing's not great, but how suspicious is it when a junkie overdoses. She used to love getting high.'

Hackett regretted the words as soon as they left his mouth. He turned back to find Templeton with an arched right eyebrow.

'So, you do remember more detail about what happened on that tour?'

'No, not really. Helen loved to smoke dope and maybe more, I don't know. It wasn't like it was readily available on a tour bus in the '80s. We used to get guards and sniffer dogs at every border crossing. You would've been crazy to carry anything. The only time I saw her high was in Amsterdam. I mean, everyone could get it there if they wanted. Marijuana was legal – I think.'

Templeton appraised the station's money man; the controller of their budget. Accountants had ruled television for decades and it was nice to see this one flustered and under pressure.

'I think you'll find there's more to the Helen Franks story.' Templeton paused, and shifted slightly on the sofa to make sure he had Hackett's full attention. 'I'm afraid to say there is a fifth death from the tour.'

That rocked Hackett. 'Who?' he whispered.

'Judy – the woman Tugga was stalking on the tour.'

Hackett slumped against the vast window, his mouth open, one hand searching for a solid frame, the other dangled limply at his side.

Templeton eased forward, fearful about the safety codes for the local building industry.

'Judy,' Hackett mumbled. 'How, how did she die? Was it last night? How recent?'

Templeton was surprised by the impact of this death notice.

He assumed there must have been a stronger connection between Hackett and Judy on the tour.

'No, it wasn't. In fact, it wasn't recent at all. She died about a year after the tour. She drowned, back home in New Zealand.'

Hackett was bewildered. 'But how does her death relate to what is happening now?'

'That's probably best answered by the police, now they're taking more interest in these deaths.' Templeton allowed that to sink in for Hackett. The cops would want to talk to him.

'Judging by your reaction to Judy's death, I take it that you two were close on the tour?'

Hackett straightened and edged away from the window, eventually dropping into an armchair.

Templeton allowed him breathing space. He knew the tour was before Hackett met his wife; shagging and drinking was what carefree bachelors did in London and Europe in the '80s. That tourist image didn't match the modern facade of a dignified and successful businessman. That profile had been carefully cultivated over many years and Templeton understood why Hackett was reluctant to see it damaged.

Templeton was privy to executive gossip about Hackett. It was the Black Monday stock market crash of '87 that properly launched his career. Hackett found a niche for his accountancy skills working for an international company as business after business collapsed. The global financial crisis provided Hackett with a new focus and he cashed in. He returned to Melbourne mid-way through '88, wrangling a transfer with the company by identifying several lucrative opportunities. Hackett's 'international' credentials and renewed energy saw him rapidly climb the corporate ladder. The society wife, the luxury home, the coastal beach house, the right friends and all the associated bling made life comfortable for Andrew Hackett. Now it was under threat; not because of any business impropriety or lack of skill but from the whiff of a very old scandal.

Templeton waited patiently for Hackett to organise his thoughts, certain the reply about a relationship with Judy Williams was going to be an affirmative.

'Yeah,' Hackett ran both hands through his silver hair. 'Judy and I spent time together on the tour.'

Templeton nodded and waited for Hackett to fill the silence.

'It wasn't anything exclusive, you know? Just one of those trip things. She was attractive, had a bit of spark about her, and was keen to enjoy her trip of a lifetime. We would get together when the mood was right. You know?'

Hackett's gaze drifted to the wall beyond Templeton. It was blank, yet it seemed to stir more memories of hedonistic travels.

'We weren't the only ones. It was the '80s – the bright lights of Europe and all that, you know. Everything was so exotic and intoxicating for most of us. I was single so why shouldn't I enjoy myself?

'I think she had a boyfriend back home. He wanted to settle down, but Judy wanted to see the world before she ended up stuck on a dairy farm with a brood of kids. There were a few girls like that. They wanted to sow wild oats as much as the guys did. So, we had fun when we wanted. No big deal.'

Templeton shrugged. He wasn't a judge of moral standards. The admission from Hackett let more worms out of the can.

'Did everyone on the trip know that you and Judy were an item?' The real question was, what did Tugga think about a drinking buddy shagging the object of his obsession?

'I guess you mean, did Tugga mind?'

'Yes.'

'To be honest, I don't recall him ever saying anything about it. As I said, it wasn't exclusive between Judy and me.'

'By that you mean Judy, and you, had other partners on the tour?'

Hackett nodded. 'Judy was out to have fun. There were other tourists and she developed a taste for *Mediterranean* men, you know, the olive skinned, dark-haired lotharios with the tight jeans that seemed to flock around every tourist bar and camping ground. It didn't worry me as I knew we were never going to be long term.'

'And what about you? Did you chase the local talent as well?'

Hackett snorted. 'Tried to. The Spanish, Italian and Greek girls were hot, but they were out of bounds for non-locals. They flirted, but disappeared if their brothers or fathers started to take notice. Plus, we were only ever in one location for a day or two, so it was easier to chase backpackers and girls in tour groups.'

'Who else did you sleep with from your tour group?' Templeton's abrupt change of gear pulled Hackett out of his whimsical mood. 'Did you sleep with Helen Franks or anyone else?'

Hackett's nostrils flared. 'Fuck off! What does *who* I slept with have anything to do with the deaths?'

'I don't care who you did or didn't shag on that tour, Andrew. But the police will want to know now that they are involved. I'm doing you a favour as these are the questions they'll ask. I can guarantee you they won't be as sympathetic or understanding as me. You're the only person left alive from Tugga's Mob, and you slept with the fifth member of the tour who turned up dead.'

Hackett was reluctant to admit Templeton's argument made sense.

'So, I take it from your silence that Helen Franks was an *occasional* bedmate as well?'

A slight nod was Hackett's only response.

'Was Tugga upset about that? Or Drew and Gerry?'

'No. She was a free spirit and they knew that. I think Tugga might have shagged her, but if she did Drew or Gerry, I never saw that.'

'Anyone else?' Templeton had to bite his tongue lest he added *left alive* to the question.

Hackett looked to the office door. Would Zara redeem herself by announcing an urgent meeting for him?

'There was another Kiwi girl on the tour. Denise, Denise Howard, I think. She was nice, but it was all the same for everyone, casual.'

Templeton threw Hackett a bone. 'You were a popular lad in those days!'

Hackett gratefully accepted the token of macho envy and added some gravy. 'You wouldn't believe what it was like in those days, Dickie. Take Venice for example. The camp site was always buzzing, and I don't mean the bloody mozzies which were everywhere. There was a couple of girls from a Contiki camping trip whose names I don't think I ever found out.'

Hackett didn't notice both of Templeton's eyebrows rise in response to that admission.

'Okay, Andrew, sorry if this all sounds prurient to you, but we're trying to find a reason for what started these killings so many years after the trip. And currently, Tugga's obsession with Judy Williams looks the most interesting.

'The cops might see it differently, but I doubt they'll share their investigations with *Spotlight*. Either way, we still have news and current affairs programs to broadcast. Like it or not, this is the biggest story of the moment, and we need to get your side of things on camera.'

That made Hackett refocus on Templeton. The current affairs wimp who used to be his corporate punching bag had turned into an assertive executive.

Templeton took Hackett's silence for acceptance and rubbed his hands together, eager to get back in front of the camera.

'I've got a couple of cameras on standby downstairs, so we can do this straight away. Curly Rogers will come up to supervise the interview and make sure we get all the important answers on tape before the cops get hold of you. They're talking to Mac now and said they'd come up here next.'

Hackett groaned. His work day was totally shot.

Templeton glanced at his watch. 'Don't worry, there is some good news. The crew in New Zealand should be recording their second interview. It's with Denise Howard – and she's still alive.'

Chapter 34

Pete Benson was delighted to discover that Denise Mitchell, née Howard, didn't need any encouragement to put the boot into Tugga Tancred's reputation.

'I never liked that bastard. He gave me a creepy feeling when I saw him at the tour pickup in London. You noticed his size first. He was about six and half feet tall with a stocky rugby player build. I've met many men like that – there are a *lot* of rugby players in New Zealand – but there was something about Tugga that instantly gave me goosebumps. It was his eyes, I'm sure, that made me wary.

'I'm a school teacher and a lifetime in the classroom teaches you how to read faces. With Tugga, his eyes were hard and calculating, always looking for an advantage. Make him angry and he looked like he could be your worst nightmare. Maybe my assessment was harsh as other passengers thought he had a roguish charm. But their opinions changed over the following seven weeks.

'Once Judy told me about her problem with Tugga I tried to look out for her, to make sure she wasn't alone. The tour driver, Eddie Malone, was totally useless, so Judy couldn't expect any help from him.'

'Denise, can you tell us more about what Tugga did to Judy? Did you ever see him sexually assault or harass her?'

'I didn't see Tugga touch her, although I was aware of his interest even before Judy talked to me. The women on the tour knew he had the hots for Judy. His eyes would follow her around the campsites, but we never saw him do anything to her.'

'What did Judy tell you about Tugga?'

'That Tugga grabbed her breast in Istanbul, exposed himself at the camp site in Gallipoli and made a rude gesture on the Jungfrau railway in Switzerland.'

'And you believed her?'

'Yes. I didn't witness the events, but I believed Judy was telling the truth.'

Denise was the perfect interviewee for Benson. She was articulate, had a good memory about the tour and needed few prompts along the way.

'What can you tell us about the group of passengers that you called Tugga's Mob?'

'There were five of them: Tugga, Drew, Gerry, Helen and Andreas – I mean, Andrew. That was Andrew Hackett's nickname.'

Denise smiled briefly and then continued. 'They were the loudest and booziest on the tour. Most of the time they kept it within bounds, but sometimes, they were obnoxious; swearing and making sexist or crude comments. They were the sort of comments and acts that were forgiven more easily in the '80s. But as for anything happening on tour that might be related to their deaths this year? I can't explain that.'

Benson noticed Denise's face when she mentioned Hackett.

Did she have a fling with The Hatchet?

He ignored that possible connection as the interview focus needed to stay on Tugga's Mob.

'Surely, Tugga's harassment of Judy Williams could be a likely and logical motive for the murders?'

'You might think that, but I can't really comment as I don't have all the facts.'

Benson milked as much information from Denise as he could before they finished the interview with an update on her life since the 1986 tour.

'I lost contact with Judy after we got back to London. I knew she was from Te Awamutu, which is about 20 minutes away from

Cambridge, and I expected we would catch up again at some stage. I briefly flirted with the idea of staying in London as it was so exciting, but it wasn't the right thing to do. The primary school where I taught granted me a leave of absence for the tour and they wanted me back at work by the end of August. I came home and soon met a handsome veterinarian who swept me off my feet. We were married within 12 months. By the time I thought about Judy again it was too late. She was dead.'

Benson knew the interview alone was enough to justify the expense of the trip to New Zealand. He was delighted with his temporary role as foreign correspondent. It was a rare opportunity at *Spotlight* as the travel borders for their stories were usually restricted to a two-hour chopper flight from Melbourne.

He had the base for a good story – Denise's answers – but he also needed vision for the editor to use during the interview. She gave Benson two photo albums from the European tour to look through while she prepared morning tea.

The pictures were priceless, Benson plucked out as many as he could find of Denise and Judy together. The 6 x 4 prints showed more signs of wear and age compared to the images provided by Heather Langer.

Denise must have looked at these many times since the tour.

He wasn't surprised there weren't any photographs of Tugga. There was one of The Hatchet with an arm around Judy Williams.

Friends, or more than that?

Benson put it on the pile for Dugal to record and settled down at an outdoor table where Denise had poured cups of Earl Grey laid out by a plate of Tim Tams. With the Tugga's Mob interview in the can he could turn his attention to a topic of special interest: racehorses. In the fields around Denise's home he counted six foals.

Which one of those is going to win a Melbourne Cup?

He tucked into the biscuits and started a new interrogation. 'How come you've managed to produce so many champion thoroughbreds in Waikato?'

'Look around you, Pete,' Denise gestured. 'Godzone, as we call it, is perfect for breeding. The climate is temperate, you can see how green and lush everything is and the horses can run all day in these big pastures.'

Benson nodded and plucked another biscuit from the plate. 'It looks ideal. Tell me, how close are we to Cambridge Stud? I always wanted to see where Sir Tristram made himself famous. What did he have – three Melbourne Cup winners? I've only seen videos of the place, but it looks magnificent; almost like England.'

'It's a few minutes north of here, the other side of town. You're right about Sir Tristram, he was a magnificent stallion, and incredibly feisty. I'm sure they were on tenterhooks when the Queen visited Cambridge towards the end of his career. But did you know there's another stud along the road from here that produced seven Melbourne Cup winners?'

That stopped Benson mid-reach for another Tim Tam.

'Seven? From the one stud? Which one?'

'Trelawney. They had seven winners between 1947 and 1971. Seton Otway, the stud master at the time, was recently inducted into the New Zealand Racing Hall of Fame for that effort.'

'I'm not surprised. I'm going to be doing a Google search on those winners tonight.'

Half the biscuits were gone, and Benson was on to his second cup of tea, when he turned the topic back to their reason for being in Cambridge: Tugga's Mob and Judy Williams.

'It's a pity Judy didn't keep a diary on the tour. It might have verified Tugga's stalking and provided more evidence for the police.'

Denise turned her gaze from a mare with a foal at foot in the nearby paddock. 'Oh, but she did have a diary. Most of us did on that tour. It was the standard thing in those days as we didn't have mobiles to record selfies.'

It was Benson's turn to look confused. 'But Judy's sister said she didn't keep a diary.'

Denise pondered for a moment. 'Her sister, Heather, right?'

'Yep.'

'Maybe she didn't know about it. You said she was living in Manawatu when Judy came back from London?' She continued after Benson nodded confirmation. 'Perhaps someone else sorted out Judy's possessions after she died. Maybe they threw it out.'

'Maybe.' Benson acknowledged. 'But you definitely saw her using a diary?'

Denise blushed. 'Look, it's hard to admit, but I *read* parts of it.'

The admission surprised Benson, yet he still laughed. A moment later Denise joined him.

'Okay, okay. It's not the nicest thing to admit, but it did happen. Normally people wrote in their diaries in the early evening, before dinner or going to the camp site bar. Occasionally they would *forget* to pack them away. Diaries were fair game for anyone to read if left on a table.'

Benson smiled and wondered how many tour secrets weren't so secret after all.

'And Judy happened to leave her diary out on one or more occasions?'

'Yes, she was a bit *loose* with her possessions. Too trusting, us Kiwi girls.' Denise laughed. 'We were both keen on the same guy – Andreas. I wasn't exactly comparing notes on his performance, you might say, just confirming he was with her when he claimed to be.'

'And was he?'

'Not always. He was a player and those camping grounds had lots of tents and loose Australian girls.'

Benson knew the slur on his nation's women was a joke, but he thought it wiser to move the conversation back to other elements of the diary.

'And did the diary detail Tugga's harassment?'

'Yes, everything I spoke about on camera was mentioned in the diary. I don't think Judy was a fantasist, so that's why I agreed to your interview. I believe it happened. How severe the stalking was is open to interpretation. Judy was usually a box of fluffies. The only time I saw her downcast was on the last day of the tour.'

Benson considered that for a moment. 'End of tour blues?'

'Possibly – or probably a hangover. It was a wild last night in Amsterdam. Most of us were debuting as space cadets. First-time consumers of cannabis cakes never get the quantities right. God only knows how we made it back to camp.'

Denise's eyes twinkled as she remembered those carefree days, or as much as she could of that last escapade.

'Mrs Mitchell, you wicked woman. What would your students think?' Benson chortled. They were still chuckling a minute later as Dugal joined them for a cuppa and the last of the Tim Tams.

Chapter 35

At 5.55 on Wednesday afternoon, Mac was sipping a hot cup of tea as he demolished four fingers of Kit Kat. The chocolate-coated wafer biscuits had to be consumed swiftly in Australian conditions to avoid fingers being coated in the sticky residue. It was marketed as the perfect afternoon break; something Mac noted that Curly intended to enjoy 64 minutes earlier when he bought it from a vending machine. Curly never had a chance to even taste it.

There was also a time limit on how long a Kit Kat could remain untouched on a work desk. He licked the last chocolate from his thumb as Curly reached for the lost treat.

'You bloody ginger-headed tea-leaf. I was about to eat that.'

Mac continued to lick his thumb, long after the last chocolate molecule had been removed. 'Kit Kat rules mate. You can't abandon chocolate in an office environment for more than an hour.' Mac raised his left wrist with an exaggerated flourish and checked the time. 'According to my expensive Swiss chronometer, your responsibilities for that four-fingered delight expired five minutes ago.'

Curly and Mac often engaged in nonsensical debates, usually on extremely slow news days. November 2 was not one of those days, so Curly promised there would be revenge when Mac made his next vending machine purchase. It might be next year before that happened, but Curly vowed to have his vengeance.

Mac drained his tea cup. 'Okay, stop your whining and let me know how we're placed for another award-winning program.'

Curly grunted. 'I've sent the last bit of voiceover for Todd Waterman to record and that wraps up the main story.'

Mac was pleased. 'It's looking good then, mate. I'm sure we've got much more than the opposition.'

He counted the winning story elements on his fingers. 'We've got the fifth death, which no one else knows about, we've got an interview with the victim's sister, we've got a female friend on the tour who confirms Judy was being stalked by Tugga, and we've got our own inside man from the tour. Not brilliant, but at least The Hatchet won't be talking to other news crews, unless they're in his garage, and we've got footage of the cops being told by *moi* how to do their jobs.'

Mac paused a moment for Curly to pour praise on his elder statesman for being a modern-day *Poirot*. Curly grunted again, not prepared to inflate his colleague's ego.

Miffed that Curly wouldn't play the game, Mac finished his state-of-play analysis. 'Okay, you're sure everything is in editing?'

'Yep, the opening scene-setter on Judy's death and Tugga's stalking will be ready once the editor gets that last voice from Todd. We have a variety of pictures of Judy at European landmarks. She looked happy and excited. The graphics guys have had a play with the pictures of Tugga; made him look menacing.

'The interview with Heather Langer went into Judy's story, along with some snippets from The Hatchet. The stand-alone interview with Denise in the middle segment reinforces the stalking angle from the diary. I've asked the editor to drop in a few more tourist pics from 1986 as overlay.

'The third segment kicks off with voiceover of your starring role with the cops, followed by them going upstairs to talk to The Hatchet. Todd will then introduce Templeton's full interview with the only surviving member of Tugga's Mob.

'By the way,' Curly looked at Templeton in his office. 'He did a masterly job with that interview. Properly briefed and focused, he could be a real asset again. He brings a certain maturity and gravitas to interviews that the younger reporters can't match.'

Mac nodded and changed tack. 'You still agree that we make the cops and Hackett the final segment in the show? The other channels will lead their programs with the police investigation.'

'No doubts at all. We've got an exclusive point of difference that's going to piss them off yet again.'

Curly picked up a TV remote and pointed at the monitors above their desk. 'Let's see what the opposition news channels have discovered about Tugga's Mob.'

Chapter 36

Music from Hackett's favourite band, The Eagles, filled the BMW X6 as it carried him home. But *Peaceful Easy Feeling* was far from Hackett's state of mind. His nerves were frazzled after a day of unexpected and tense meetings.

The television interview with Templeton for *Spotlight* was more combative than Hackett expected. The current affairs boss wouldn't allow Hackett wriggle room as he searched for a motive for the deaths of Tugga's Mob. Hackett was relieved when the camera and lights were switched off.

The respite was brief as Reg Bradley barged into the office minutes after the TV crew packed up.

'This is embarrassing, Andrew. We've never had a senior executive caught up with drug dealers and murder, or should I say murders. How many are dead now? What are our advertisers going to think? I've already had three calls from long-time clients asking if you are involved.'

Hackett was stunned; Bradley had never talked to him so harshly. 'What can I do about that, Reg? I keep telling everyone I have no clue what Tugga and those other idiots did to cause this shit. I haven't seen any of them for 30 years. Why should I be blamed? And it's only those bastards down in *Spotlight* who claim they're murders. The deaths have happened all over Australia and New Zealand.'

Hackett's passionate defence didn't mollify Bradley who showed his concern was solely the PR impact on the station's advertising revenue.

'You know advertisers are skittish. Any sign of negative publicity and they take their business elsewhere. Find a way to distance yourself from this mess.'

Bradley slammed Hackett's door as he departed, which must have almost hit Zara, who opened it seconds later to announce there were two police detectives who wanted to talk to him.

'Fuck! No, Zara. Tell them I'm too busy – I do have a TV station to look after. Organise something for tomorrow, or the day after. Better still, tell them I'm fucking booked up till next week.'

Zara shrugged as the door opened fully and the detectives brushed past her. One was about 40, the other a few years older. They were fit and intimidating in dark suits as they stood eye to eye with Hackett.

'That doesn't suit us, Mr Hackett,' said the older detective. 'We understand you're the only surviving member from a 1986 European tour group known as Tugga's Mob. The Mob's deaths have raised questions and we want them answered, Mr Hackett. Not next week; now, please.'

Hackett hoped he could get rid of the detectives within a few minutes. There was nothing he could add to the Tugga's Mob story. Hackett's mistake was in assuming the cops knew about Judy's death.

'Pardon? asked Gerard Cottrell, the senior detective. 'Are you saying there's been a fifth death?'

Fuck. Me and my big mouth!

'I thought you guys knew about Judy Williams? She died a year after the tour. But she wasn't a part of Tugga's Mob. And she was a suicide, or so the journos down in *Spotlight* told me. I never heard from her again after the tour.'

Hackett saw an opportunity to deflect the cops' attention. 'You probably need to go talk to the *Spotlight* guys again.'

And get out of my face.

The tactic worked as the detectives soon strode out the door to resume discussions with Mac.

Unfortunately, that left an opening for the New Zealand cops. They rang soon after the Victorians exited and *convinced* an exasperated Hackett that a Skype conversation would help their inquiries. Hackett was engaged in that camera call when Detective Cottrill and his colleague returned, without a warning from Zara. And they weren't happy.

'Don't you think you should have told us that Judy Williams was being stalked by Tugga Tancred all around Europe – and that you were having a sexual relationship with her?'

Hackett spent the next few hours being grilled by a Trans-Tasman police tag team. It was an unfamiliar experience for everyone and, Hackett believed, couldn't possibly advance their investigation. The interviews left him little time to concentrate on company business.

And then Reg Bradley capped his day from hell by calling to say the Board had deferred a decision about the AFL TV rights.

The Eagles hadn't mellowed Hackett by the time his car approached the driveway where Channel 9 had ambushed him before breakfast. Hackett didn't expect a repeat performance from a rival network as they didn't know about Judy Williams, or his connection. Yet!

Distracted, by everything including his mood, Hackett entered his driveway faster than normal. He squealed to a halt and faced another source of irritation: the garage doors he couldn't open because he'd misplaced the remote.

Shit!

A movement to his left drew Hackett's eyes and froze him to the driver's seat. A stranger was standing outside the entrance to his home. He was early 40s, athletic, with short dark hair and dressed in jeans and a polo shirt. It was enough to warrant attention. What was more attention-grabbing was the stranger staring at Hackett, had his right hand resting on a pistol in a hip holster.

Fuck me!

For a moment Hackett feared the Tugga's Mob drama was going to cost him his life.

Why me? What the fuck have I done?

The stand-off was broken when Marianne emerged from the house and spoke to the gun-toting stranger who nodded and took his hand away from the gun.

Hackett was too stunned to move or speak, Marianne walked over to the car window.

'I'm sorry about that, darling. You gave us a scare by braking so heavily in the driveway. I forgot you lost the remote.'

'*You* were scared?' Hackett exploded. 'I arrive home and find a man with a gun ready to blow my head off and *you* were fucking scared?'

'No need to be crude, darling,' Marianne responded icily. 'Come inside and I'll explain why *I* decided *we* needed proper security.'

Hackett snatched his briefcase from the front seat and eased out of the car. He wasn't going to be easily placated. 'A gunman guarding our door; are you serious?'

The couple bickered as they moved along a garden path, through the entrance and into the heart of the home. The security guard stepped out of their way, waited a few moments to give them some privacy then followed them into the house where he closed and locked the front door.

If the encounter had lasted a few more seconds one of them might have noticed a blue Holden Commodore drive down the Hacketts' cul-de-sac. It was the second pass by the vehicle. For the driver it had been unavoidable: the turnaround bay was four houses past the Hackett residence. The driver had to quickly decide whether to make the turn or pretend to be a visitor to another residence. Both were dangerous options.

The driver was as surprised as Hackett to see an armed guard outside his home. The driver chose the turn-around: it was better than a neighbour remembering a stranger who had the wrong address. The driver exited the cul-de-sac without a backward glance. Hackett's new security measures required a change of plans and schedule.

It was a mixture of bad luck and an uncharacteristic lapse in judgment that almost aroused suspicion. Everything had been below the radar, or so the driver believed. The driver hadn't listened or watched any news services since Monday, having driven from New South Wales via the coast. The scenic route through Eden and Lakes Entrance was a small indulgence, a time to reflect on a busy few days.

Four of Tugga's Mob were dead and, thanks to Helen Franks, the last member was finally identified: Andreas, aka Andrew Hackett.

It was a touch of euphoria that prompted a spur-of-the-moment decision to drive past Hackett's home. It was supposed to be a brief scouting mission. The driver hadn't followed Hackett from work. It was pure chance the next target stopped in the driveway during the drive-by. Spotting the security guard, who displayed the hallmarks of being a former soldier, was a bonus. It was time to withdraw and assess the situation. The Commodore cruised towards central Melbourne.

Hackett swallowed his first glass of gin with a splash of tonic in three gulps. It marginally improved his mood. He listened patiently to Marianne's explanation for hiring an armed guard. She had been inundated with messages from friends concerned about their safety.

More likely they were worried about her rather than me!

Marianne seized an opportunity when a yoga group member offered the services of a brother, a former member of Australia's Special Air Service Regiment. Mitch Stevens was between contracts in Iraq and had a town house in nearby Prahran.

As *Spotlight's* opening titles rolled, Hackett was comfortable with the notion of a former special forces soldier under their roof. By the end of the first two segments, which covered the death of Judy Williams, the stalking by Tugga and sexual relationships on the tour, Hackett was grateful the new house guest carried a 9mm semi-automatic pistol. He couldn't look at Marianne as he knew the interview with Templeton would be next.

The final segment was much worse than he feared. It wasn't the content alone that embarrassed him. Hackett was surprised how poorly he presented himself on camera. His body language and evasive answers failed to portray the man he believed himself to be: a powerful business leader.

'So, Mr Hackett, you can understand why police in Australia and New Zealand have now upgraded their inquiries into the four homicides?'

'Yes, but I don't know why Tugga, Drew, Gerry or Helen might have been targeted.'

'Do you believe the death of Judy Williams, with whom you were – um, well acquainted, should be included in that investigation?'

'I don't know. I really don't. I can't see any connection between the recent deaths and her sui– ah, death, 29 years ago. I can't explain anything.'

'And do you see yourself as a natural target now, as the only survivor of Tugga's Mob?'

'No, I don't think so. I didn't do anything to anybody 30 years ago to warrant anything like this. Nor did any of the others, as far as I know.'

'You say that even though you, supposedly, haven't had contact in that time?'

Hackett squirmed in his armchair as he suffered the verbal jabs from Templeton for a second time.

What are Bradley and the TV Board going to think about me?

He soon learned his concerns should have been closer to home. The extended examination of Hackett's sexual playmates on tour, and the liberal attitudes of the 1980s, coincided with Marianne's exit from the room.

Chapter 37

It was hump day, but the program debrief in the *Spotlight* office on Wednesday night was more like an end-of-week celebration. Templeton had slipped away during the news to buy two slabs of beer and six bottles of wine on his own credit card, which enhanced his stocks with the production team.

The Judy Williams connection to Tugga would've hit rival newsrooms like a bombshell. They'd no doubt felt confident of being back on par with *Spotlight* after police in Australia and New Zealand confirmed they were treating all the deaths of Tugga's Mob as suspicious.

But *Spotlight* aced them again and Mac could take some of the credit. He'd had to share the revelation with the Victorian police earlier in the day. But he had negotiated a deal with the detectives to withhold the information on Judy's death and Tugga's stalking from other media until 6.30pm; a move that denied the opposition a run at the story.

The production crew noisily discussed fresh story ideas for the next day as they passed drinks around the room. The clinking of beer bottles almost drowned out Pete Benson on Mac's speakerphone. Curly, Templeton, Jo and Kim huddled around the desk, all eager to contribute.

'Pete, well done, mate,' Mac boomed. 'You and Dugal blitzed the other bastards. They're crying in their chardonnays as we speak.'

'Thanks, Mac. It feels a bit strange to be so far away from the mothership, but good to know we're getting what you need.'

'That you are. And don't worry about us dropping the live cross to you tonight, we had so much content to squeeze in.'

'That's sweet, bro. Just learning some of the local lingo, in case you didn't notice. Anyway, I've sent through an email with possible story angles for tomorrow. I think we need to get the New Zealand cops on camera, get better footage of the so-called accident sites, maybe updates from the families of Drew and Gerry.'

'Yeah, that sounds good, although I think you'd better check distances between shoots as the Shaky Isles aren't as small as you think.'

'Too true. We'll do that. There's a couple of elements I'm still not sure about.'

The *Spotlight* crew exchanged a range of glances before Mac prompted Benson to continue.

'What do you mean, mate?'

'The Langers for a start. Heather denied that Judy kept a diary. But Denise says she read it on the tour. One possibility is that someone else dealt with Judy's property after she died. Another worrying point, for me, is that Heather was evasive about her son, Jason. She almost *wouldn't* say where he was.'

'Right. So, reading between the lines, you're suggesting that if Tugga was stalking Judy, something bad happened that might've been recorded in the diary. Judy topped herself, the diary goes missing, but someone might have read it, and 30 years later, starts knocking off Tugga's Mob. And you see Heather and her son as the avenging angels?'

Mac knew Benson was making the *Spotlight* crew address a possible motive. Whoever was killing Tugga's Mob had to have a reason. For three days, Mac's reporters and producers had been scrambling to simply confirm the deaths as suspicious, while tracking the pictures and talent to support their theories and stories.

Mac had decided early in the week that finding the killer and proving why they did it was a job for the police. More to the point he knew, now the cops were finally motivated, they would slap down any media organisation that jeopardised their investigation and ultimate prosecution.

Benson's theory – however tenuous – was food for thought though, as they considered the next angles to pursue. Mac pointed them in the right direction.

'Okay. I think you should call Heather Langer in the morning, Pete. Say you've been talking to other passengers and they remembered Judy writing a diary. Make it an innocent inquiry. Was there a chance the diary was overlooked? Could it be sitting in a cupboard at the farm somewhere? Obviously, there were pictures from the trip, as we used them tonight, so is the diary in another box with them?'

'Sure thing, Mac. She's a farm woman, so they'll be up early. I'll have another stab at finding out where the son is too. It's almost 10pm here and wee Dugal needs some tucker and a good sleep after all that travelling. Send us an email when you decide what else you want tomorrow and we'll be underway before you lot see the first sparrows.'

The usual good-natured office insults flew back and forth across the Tasman for half a minute before Benson and Dugal tuned out to search for a late-night feast. The *Spotlight* crew drank on for another hour, consuming all of Templeton's alcohol before heading home with dreams of leading the media pack for another day.

Chapter 38

The smell of petrol and smoke drifted over a 44-gallon drum behind the two-car garage. It was mid-morning and the spring breeze had freshened, taking the fumes and smoke away from the house. Heather had waited until the neighbour's lads finished their duties and went home for brunch. Jason, when he was home, could consume enough for half a rugby team at any meal, and the Rankin boys could eat enough to fuel the All Blacks. The ashes would be long gone before they returned.

Smoke over farm properties is never unusual, there's always rubbish to dispose and no city wheelie bins to park by the front gate. For this small fire, Heather wanted to ensure there were no leftovers, or witnesses. Tears flowed freely down her cheeks. It was a painful task to dispose of Judy's diary and a handful of pictures, but necessary after two early morning phone calls.

The first was from the Australian reporter.

Far too curious that one.

Pete Benson said he was following up a report that Judy had kept a diary during the '86 tour. Another passenger saw her writing regularly about trip highlights. Was there a chance the small diary was tucked away in an obscure place at the family farm?

Heather stayed calm, explaining it had been her difficult duty to tidy Judy's possessions as their mother was too upset. She tearfully told Benson she'd kept a few trinkets, as well as the trip photos. And that if there had been a diary of the happiest time in her sister's life, she would've kept it. She suggested it got lost during Judy's time in London after the trip around Europe. Judy had been living out of a backpack in a pub so it was obviously long gone, lost among a sea of travelling detritus.

Heather was pleased when Benson backed off, apparently not wanting to be insensitive. However, he tipped his hand again with another inquiry about Jason. Where exactly was he? The reporter finally signed off after Heather repeated Jason was away on a part-holiday, part-research trip in Australia.

The reporter seemed to accept her explanations, but Heather felt he had some doubts. And, understandably, now they were onto the story the journalists were trying to track down a motive for someone getting rid of Tugga's Mob.

It was the second phone call that increased Heather's anxiety and inspired the backyard burn. A detective in Hamilton wanted to arrange a time to drop in for a 'chat', following New Zealand and Australia media revelations over the past few days. He had been polite in confirming that police in both countries would collaborate on an investigation. It was a non-confrontational call, but both understood the Langer family would now come under scrutiny. Heather agreed to a farm visit at 3.30 that afternoon.

Was it foolish to burn the diary and the photos? Dangerous even?

No, Heather reasoned. The meagre ashes would soon be scattered over the nearby paddocks, the drum well and truly cold by the time the detective arrived, if anyone decided to check it. It was early November, the third month of spring, but cold winds still swept through Waikato and it would take a world-class forensic expert to find that anything other than farm rubbish was burned that day. That's if Heather gave them reason to even look. And she wouldn't.

There was nothing to connect her to Tugga's Mob, apart from

Judy, and the last shreds of relevant evidence in the family's possession had just gone up in smoke.

The tears continued as Heather walked to a nearby shed for a plastic bucket and pan. The final diary entry was still fresh in her mind.

August 30, 1986

Pregnant! I can't believe it, although I suppose I was taking a risk during the tour when I ran out of the pill. I got a supply when I arrived in London, not that I've needed them here, but here I am – 'with child'. It must have been those last weeks of the tour.

That means it's goodbye to the Big OE and the rest of my travels. No one else knows and that's the way I want to keep it, apart from telling Heather.

I'm ashamed to say I can't say for sure who the father is. Was it Andreas? Or that charming Italian I met in Lauterbrunnen. I was giving Andreas short shrift by then, so I can't really say as the nurse wasn't sure how pregnant I am.

And then there's that last night of the tour in Amsterdam. I woke up naked and sore around my genitals but without a clue as to what might have happened. Did Andreas woo me one last time?

I just don't know. I can't tell Mum and Dad, especially if I can't say who the father is. And Russell will be heartbroken. I know I left things in limbo with him before the flight. I guessed he'd probably wait for me. We'd only been going out a few months and he knew that my heart was already booked for Europe.

Russell said he thought I was special and that he understood I needed to explore the world and myself. That was sweet. He's a good, solid Waikato farmer who's never likely to venture further than an All Blacks test in Sydney. But I haven't written to him often enough and I'm sure his pride won't stand raising another man's child.

Termination is not an option for me. I can't do that to this wee thing growing inside me. But can I keep it and care for it? Certainly not here, as London is too expensive to live.

It's been a shocking week. Bloody Tugga Tancred wandered into my pub the other day. He leered at me all during the lunch session. I'm wondering if he's been searching for me because our regulars are mostly Londoners rather than Kiwis and Aussies.

I told a couple of the barmen how gross Tugga had been on tour and they said they'd look after me if he tried anything. He won't be a problem soon, once I leave London.

I guess Heather is the only one I can turn to now.

And that's the way it had been. Judy reached out to her sister who responded generously for her only sibling. They arranged for Judy to quietly return to New Zealand within a few weeks. The homecoming wasn't in Waikato. It didn't take much for Heather to convince Judy that it would be better to have the baby in Manawatu, to protect her from the stress and pressure of small-town morality.

They agreed to keep the pregnancy and Judy's return a secret from their parents, to provide a longer grace period while they decided about the future. A trusted friend of Heather's was enlisted to be part of a round-the-world correspondence trail, to maintain the charade that Judy was still in London. Fortunately, the Williams parents weren't the type to engage in long-distance toll calls.

The secret lasted the required duration: until Judy gave birth in mid-1987. Soon after, a pale and exhausted 'world traveller' returned to the family farm, 'heartily sick of dirty, noisy, costly and crowded London.'

A few months later Judy Williams was dead.

Chapter 39

Curly arrived in the *Spotlight* office on Thursday morning, later than normal, with a mobile phone pressed to his ear. He had been talking almost non-stop on the 40-minute walk from Middle Park. The calls were from radio stations around Australia and New Zealand – all seeking background on the story that was the post-Melbourne Cup obsession.

Something about the first week in November.

Talkback hosts couldn't find enough *experts* to fill the air waves with their theories, therefore Curly found himself inundated by stressed producers begging him to elaborate on *Spotlight's* investigation into Tugga's Mob. Snippets of Curly's guarded responses were clipped to fill the hourly news bulletins.

Normally, helping other media outlets fill their programs wouldn't be a priority for Curly. In this case though, the PR benefits of having *Spotlight's* name associated with the hottest story of the week were too important to ignore. The 'any publicity is good publicity' maxim would be a timely reminder to station management of the skills of their hard-working journalists. The recognition might last hours, or a couple of days, but it was better than being ignored in the dungeon.

Secretly, Curly had to admit there was a touch of ego involved as well. The Tugga's Mob stories would pad his CV and brag-tape for another 10 years. *At least.*

Curly sat at his desk and continued the seventh radio conversation about *Spotlight's* crusade. The phone interviewer was in Hamilton, New Zealand, so Curly mischievously embellished his rock-climbing skills for the exclusive view he'd had of Tugga's smashed ute at Lorne.

As he talked, he glanced through 20 or so Post-It notes, all colours of the rainbow, stuck to the front of his monitor by his colleagues who'd taken calls that morning. Half were from radio newsrooms or talkback programs. He was selective about which broadcasters he responded to. The New Zealand hosts were included to give Pete Benson some local contacts.

Quid pro quo, boys!

The *Spotlight* stories had prompted another four passengers from the '86 tour to make contact.

More fuel to the pyre to burn Tugga's Mob, no doubt.

Curly would urge Mac to give the job of finding the chattiest ex-tourists to Kim. He could tell by the handwriting that most of the notes were taken by Jo.

She's a bloody marvel.

He watched the pocket rocket as she peddled her chair on tiptoes between a computer and Mac's communication panel, an office phone to one ear and a mobile in her free hand.

Curly finished the radio interview and lifted a Post-It from the middle of his monitor. It was marked Anonymous, but still piqued his interest. Anonymous sources were never the most reliable and could potentially be a total waste of time.

 ANONYMOUS!
 Caller knows what happened to Judy.
 Scared, won't leave number. Email
 Wants money but won't front camera.
 Said Amsterdam was the key.

Curly waited to catch Jo between calls or mid-scoot, whichever came first. It took 90 seconds.

'Hey, Jo – time for a pit stop.'

The office Fangio pivoted on the spot, skirted Mac without

removing any chunks of flesh, navigated past several desks and parked in front of Curly a few seconds later. 'Coffee and four new casters please. You've got 30 seconds.'

Curly laughed. 'I can help you with the coffee in a moment, but those casters are good for another six months.'

'Nah, Mac's shins have ruined the alignment. Maybe I should take this down to the Bridgestone place on the corner? Okay, half your time has gone on pleasantries, you want to know why I prioritised that anonymous source?'

'Yep. What's so special about him? Was it a him?'

'Yeah and gut instinct. We've had a few callers saying similar things. But they sounded like the usual wankers. This guy said he knew all of Tugga's Mob and what they did and that it was worth some money. According to him Amsterdam is where some *bad shit* happened. The other callers weren't so specific.'

'But no phone number for a call back, just an email? That's anonymous as well I presume?'

'Yep. But it's a Hotmail account which would indicate he's had it a long time. He sounded like an older guy. A lot of those geriatrics over 40 can't keep up with the technology. He could've tweeted his inside knowledge and asked for the highest bidder from the media.'

Curly grimaced. 'Ouch! Millennials are so brutal to technophobes and old buggers like me.'

'If you feel the pain it means you're still alive, Curly,' Jo pivoted once again to race the chicane back to her desk. 'I think he's worth following up, but you get paid the big bucks to make the decisions.'

Curly looked at the email address while he contemplated if the message was genuine, and how much money the tipster wanted.

Spotlight and the news department didn't pay for stories any more. The Hatchet officially ended payments for amateur videos after an inexperienced reporter messed up a deal for pictures of a boat sinking. To 'save time', the amateur cameraman sent the *exclusive* video via a file-sharing server. That left the cameraman still holding the original tape. He then tried the same tactic with every other news service in Melbourne. The others were smart enough to demand the original tape before paying. The Hatchet almost had a coronary when he learned the scoop wasn't as exclusive as he believed.

Fortunately, *Spotlight's* stocks with management were on the rise. The whole station heard that Reg Bradley gave The Hatchet a bollocking for getting tangled up with the Tugga's Mob story. However, Curly also heard the Chief Executive changed his tone by afternoon tea on Wednesday when the advertising sales manager reported there were six new clients ready to kill to get their commercials on *Spotlight*. It seemed they didn't care at all that a station executive was caught up in the drama; they just knew people were watching the program.

Curly calculated that cash could be found if the anonymous caller had worthwhile information. He bent over the keyboard and composed an email. He didn't promise money, but indicated strong interest and urged the caller to contact him as soon as possible.

Curly then read the remaining Post-It notes. New requests for radio interviews were discarded as he had to focus on his own program. He was about to list *Spotlight's* priorities for the day when his mobile phone rang. He looked at the caller ID, not expecting it to be Mr Anonymous as that would have been freakishly quick. However, the caller was a surprise: Jim Laidlaw – the Lorne cop.

'Hey Jim, didn't think I'd hear from you again. Have you found that second car at Lorne?'

'No, I'm afraid not. Miraculous breakthroughs in cases only ever happen for TV cops.'

They laughed, the ice broken on what could have been a difficult resumption of their cop-media relationship.

'Look, I've been warned to stay away from the media. But I had to let you guys know that you're on the right track with Tugga.'

'Thanks, Jim. You helped kick things off by being generous with your information. Doesn't happen that often between our professions.'

'Well, we owe each other then, because I would never have got the technical support without your publicity.'

'We're a mutual admiration society now, long may it last, but

I sense you have more information which might need to be handled more – discreetly?'

'Spot on. And this has to be off the record.'

'Are we able to attribute it to another source? Is there another way we can get the information out there?'

'I think it's highly probable. Your sources have been good so far.'

'Okay, Jim, we're officially off the record for background information. Talk to me.'

'I have more information about Tugga's beach house, or whatever you want to call it. Or rather, what was found there.'

'I'm listening, Jim. We sent a camera and reporter there on Monday. Did we miss something?'

'Yes. Some pictures, which at the time, didn't mean that much – or so the first officers thought. They removed them before your mob arrived.'

'Go on.'

'Tugga had some old pictures on the wall. The old Kodak or Fuji type of prints. Glossy, but starting to darken with the years. I didn't know how old until last night.'

Curly made the connection.

'Can I make a guess that they were of Judy Williams? The woman who was being stalked by Tugga on the tour?'

'Yep. Bang on. But you can never use them.'

'Why not?' Curly asked.

A few seconds hesitation from Laidlaw gave him the likely answer. 'Oh. She's in a compromising situation?'

'Yes.' Again, there was another pause from Lorne; and a deep breath. 'The pictures are of Judy naked and having sex with what looks like Tugga, Drew Harvey, Gerry Daly – and probably Helen Franks.'

'Shit!' Curly's expletive was loud enough to catch the attention of half the office. Mac and Templeton drifted towards the intense phone conversation to learn more about the subject.

Curly's mind whirled. Judy having sex with the man who was stalking her, and *all* the rest of his mates?

He registered that no mention was made of The Hatchet.

But the situation didn't tally with everything they'd heard about Tugga and Judy.

'When you say the pictures show Judy Williams having sex with most of Tugga's Mob, does it look like a group scene, you know, an orgy?' Curly paused as his two immediate bosses did double-takes at that revelation.

'Or was it something more sinister? Was she being raped, as in a gang rape?'

More members of the *Spotlight* office tuned into the conversation, shocked by Curly's questions.

'That's a difficult thing for us to say,' Laidlaw eventually responded. 'First of all, it didn't seem to be an orgy.'

'Okay.' Curly was tempted to switch his mobile to speaker phone to include his colleagues. But he knew the acoustics would change and that could scare off Laidlaw. He decided to leave his workmates in limbo. 'So, if not a group scene, what did the pictures show? Was she a willing participant in the sex from what you can tell?'

'First impressions would indicate there's nothing wrong. The woman, Judy, isn't fighting them off or anything. She looks relaxed, her arms thrown back over her head and no sign of a struggle. These days, people take those pictures all the time and post them over the internet. It's almost like a status symbol.'

Curly nodded, absorbing the information and its implications but still unable to share.

Mac moved his head closer to pick up some of the conversation. Curly had already pencilled *Lorne cop* on his desk blotter.

'The first cops into the property from the Apollo Bay office thought they were old porn pictures – you know, selfies from the '80s, reminders of younger days. They took them down before your guys arrived and they ended up back here in Lorne. Theoretically it was part of our *wider* investigation. In reality, the detectives snaffled them from the local boys for a perve.'

Curly phrased his next question to update the listeners in his office.

'So, at first glance they looked like porn pictures. Then our stories last night about Tugga stalking Judy gave you another reason to look at them from a different perspective?'

'Yes. When I saw the pictures of Judy on your show I knew she looked familiar. I came back into the office to take another look at the prints we had.'

'And a second look confirmed it was Judy?' Curly said. 'And that she was being raped rather than in rapture?'

'They could be viewed that way, yes,' Laidlaw admitted. 'Judy's eyes are closed in every picture where she is identifiable. There are a couple where it's not totally clear who is underneath Tugga, because he's such a big guy, but it would be safe to assume she is the woman in each photo.

'One way to look at the pictures is to believe that Judy is enjoying the moment. You could also say that she appears comatose. Drunk, drugged or whatever. But after your revelations, I'm inclined to believe she was out of it and being raped by Tugga's Mob.'

Curly shifted in his chair and exhaled, conscious he was also trying to keep Mac and the rest of the crew informed. He repeated Laidlaw's bombshell.

'Judy was raped by Tugga's Mob, one by one.' A murmur broke out immediately and Curly quickly waved his arm to quieten them and to head off a lynch mob for The Hatchet.

'And the pictures show Tugga, Drew, Gerry and Helen. But not our boss, Andrew Hackett?'

'There's no sign of him in any of the pictures and there were about 24 on the wall. Probably a whole roll of film.'

Curly shook his head for the benefit of the crew. The Hatchet was an arsehole, but they were pleased in a small way that their low opinion of him wasn't about to go subterranean.

Curly blew out a breath and Laidlaw filled the silence.

'That's my interpretation of the pictures. And as you can tell from the first guys on the scene, without the background information that we now have, they can be viewed differently. If these pictures ever made it to court it would be difficult to say how they might be received. A prosecutor can present one scenario. A clever barrister might shred that opinion in a few minutes. With juries, it's often down to which of the legal jousters is the most eloquent.'

'Yep, I've seen that over the years – many times.' Curly wondered how to get this information into the public domain.

'You've still got the pictures there in Lorne, Jim?'

'Yes, I've already called Melbourne. They've got a team co-ordinating things with New South Wales and New Zealand. These pictures may provide a motive. I'm just a country cop, so it's out of my hands now. They'll be in the city by this afternoon.'

Laidlaw paused. 'You're trying to find a way to get this information on the record, aren't you? From another source, I hope.'

Curly laughed; already the ember of a possible source was flickering. 'You're too smart to be hidden down the coast, Jim. Yep. I'll come at it from another angle, without implicating you in any way.'

'I'd appreciate that. I know I've kicked another beehive, but this time I can't get caught in the middle. The detectives already know I made the connection between Tugga's photos and Judy Williams.

'I know you believed something bad happened on the tour, although maybe not as grim as what we've uncovered. If you've got good cop contacts in Melbourne they're all bound to leak like sieves once those pictures get to town.'

'Yes, we figured it must have been a shocking incident that started the revenge attacks. We did not envisage something as brutal as this. The other big question is why it's taken 30 years to come to light . I guess that's your job, or the detectives up here.'

The others drifted away from Curly's desk. They had the gist of what happened to Judy Williams. But he had one more question.

'Is there anything in the pictures that might indicate where the rape happened?'

'All the pictures were taken inside a tent, which doesn't help. It wasn't large, but a backpack can be seen shoved into a corner behind Judy. There was a travel guide in a couple of the shots.'

'That could be helpful. What was the guide book about?'

'Amsterdam.'

Chapter 40

Jockey Graham perched quietly on his favourite barstool at the *Commercial Hotel* in Te Awamutu. Beside a pint of beer on the counter was the racing form guide from a daily newspaper. The cord of a white earpiece snaked from a portable radio in Jockey's brown leather jacket. It was a familiar scene for pub patrons. The former hoop could be found in the same location whenever there was gallops racing. That was almost every day, thanks to broadcasts of race meetings in either New Zealand, Australia, America, Singapore or Hong Kong.

Jockey had just resumed his routine after a week at home with the flu, although the return might've been premature. He was deathly pale, all his joints ached, his nose felt raw and streamed constantly. The most obvious indicator of Jockey's health was the pint; it hadn't been touched in the 20 minutes since it was poured.

Tony Brown, the barman, was concerned. 'Are you sure you're okay to be out of bed, Jockey? You're sweating more than Phar Lap after winning the Cup – and you haven't drunk a drop. You're bad for business.'

Jockey jerked his rheumy eyes from the floor, laughed and tapped the earpiece. 'I'm sweet mate. I was concentrating. The *Radio Trackside* guys have some good tips for Flemington this afternoon.'

He took a sip of beer to reassure the barman. It worked as Brown shrugged and left him to it. Jockey, however, wasn't plugged into the racing station – he was listening to a talk-back channel.

The man was desperate for news rather racing tips. He'd been channel surfing since hearing about Judy Williams and Tugga's Mob on the 7am news. The paleness that Brown attributed to illness was shock. Jockey stared miserably at the pub floor as he listened to a replay of Curly Rogers' interview with the Hamilton radio host.

The ghosts of Jockey's past were screaming.

He knew Judy from primary school, but only by sight as they were never in the same classes. She was a year older and destined to be a stunner by the time she departed for high school. They moved in different circles in the following years. Their paths rarely crossed apart from Jockey's visits to the pharmacy, where Judy worked, for medication to ease the pain from race injuries. Judy was always friendly in the shop. She asked about his race wins and wished him good luck for the next meeting.

She was always so positive I'd win a big race one day.

Jockey, like half the men in Te Awamutu, had a secret crush on Judy. But those pleasant exchanges in the shop were a sharp contrast to the last time he saw Judy.

It was 1987, across the banks of the Waipa River – and he watched her being drowned by a giant.

Jockey picked up his pint and took a big swallow which brought a nod of approval from the barman. It tasted vile; nothing could wash away that awful memory. It was the darkest moment in a life that never reached beyond mediocre.

The racing world looked so promising when Jockey started his apprenticeship. He already had the nickname, courtesy of his primary school teacher. He stopped growing at 145 cm; a perfect size for a life in the saddle. A successful hoop, however, needed talent and horse sense, and Jockey didn't have much of either. He struggled to finish his apprenticeship with a handful of wins. And only a few more salutes to the judge followed as he failed to get rides beyond Waikato race tracks. A few trainers occasionally took pity on him and gave him rides on horses the best jockeys had spurned, knowing there wasn't likely to be a collect at the end of the race. Much of his earnings were derived from track work in the mornings and riding his luck with the tote.

Jockey was always on the lookout for extra cash. Petty pilfering from houses, farms and sheds in the region was his alternative source of income throughout his riding career. The goods were stored for a few weeks before a trip to a contact in Auckland to unload them. Jockey never kept the items at home, as he lived with other jockeys and stable hands. Instead, he created a hiding place by the river near Pirongia. And that's why Jockey was there, at his camouflaged cache, on the day Judy Williams was murdered.

It was Spring. Jockey was inside his lair when he spotted Judy strolling in the sunshine on the opposite bank. It made his heart flip. Partly it was delight at seeing her again but mostly the palpitations were caused by his predicament, surrounded as he was by items stolen from Te Awamutu.

Judy's fate tested more of Jockey's virtues than he expected. He cursed quietly as she settled on the grass to watch the river flow by. A few minutes later a huge man arrived. He towered over Judy.

To Jockey, he looked like a giant in a fairytale; an ogre who was a danger to the fair princess. That much was obvious to Jockey, as he could see and hear that Judy was furious. She shouted at the giant and the argument spiralled out of control. Within a few minutes the giant had drowned her.

To his everlasting shame Jockey did nothing to save her. He was half the size of the giant and couldn't swim. He stayed in his camouflaged hole and shed tears as he watched. After the giant stumbled away Jockey agonised for another hour about Judy's body. He couldn't risk a police search for Judy as it would uncover his secret hoard. Eventually Jockey used a nearby road bridge to walk to the murder site from where he towed Judy's body far enough away from his hide.

The only decent thing Jockey did that day was tell police he saw Judy's body in the river. Given the size difference between Jockey and Judy he was never considered to be a suspect in her death. No one was.

Jockey's cowardice haunted him from that day in 1987. He never saw the giant again and the town was ready enough to believe that Judy took her own life. Judy hadn't been her usual ebullient self since returning from London. She stayed on the farm and seemed reluctant to return to work in the pharmacy. There was gossip about the cause of her low spirits. The unkind suggested she considered herself too good for Waikato after the grand life in Europe. The more charitable considered depression was a factor in Judy ending her life in the waterway.

Jockey allowed that myth to become ingrained and never talked publicly about finding Judy's body, let alone what really happened. Her name soon disappeared from conversations, apart from when fresh calamities fell upon the Williams family.

It was only the previous year that Jockey's terrible secret was finally shared, and that was the cause of his current concern.

Jockey was drunk after celebrating a rare win that returned him $753 from the TAB. He was working his way through a bottle of single malt Scotch – Laphroaig, usually reserved for a Christmas treat – when Jason Langer walked into the bar. They had rarely spoken a greeting in the decade since Jason could legally enter the pub. Jockey preferred to keep his distance as Judy's nephew reminded him of his feckless behaviour.

Jockey's good mood soured that night as he observed Jason from his regular stool.

I should have been braver for your aunt. But I'm only four-foot nuthin' – and that bastard was a giant.

Jockey had finally tucked away what was left of his winnings and tottered for the door. The booze, an autumn chill and a high step almost proved fatal for wee Jockey as he saw the footpath rise to greet him. Strong hands gripped him before he face-planted the concrete. The good Samaritan's voice shocked Jockey almost as much as his unexpected stumble. It was Jason.

Judy's nephew saved me.

Jockey's conscience felt heavier than any lead that filled his saddle during the riding years. He felt a sudden, desperate need to unburden himself and so Jockey blurted out the story that had been the source of his long misery.

Jockey was never sure just how much he told Jason. He blathered and then vomited the expensive Laphroaig over the pub wall.

And Jason was gone when Jockey stopped heaving.

He didn't see him in the pub again for a month. Nothing was said and Jason didn't even look in Jockey's direction. It was as if nothing had happened. Did Jockey dream he'd shared the story about Judy and the giant? Maybe Jason didn't believe him; considered him a rambling old pisshead?

Whatever. Jockey made sure he was never that drunk again and kept his mouth shut about Judy Williams.

It was all safely contained, he thought, until he recovered enough from the flu to care about turning on the radio. The radio report this morning sent him racing to the breakfast television news for the first time in days.

And there, right there, Jockey was stunned to see the giant again. It was only a picture, yet he was certain. His name was Tugga Tancred and the media said he'd been obsessed with the lovely Judy during their European tour.

They don't know he killed her.

The only people who knew that were Jockey and Jason, or so he believed. Jockey's mind whirled. He told Jason that a giant killed his aunt. Now that giant – Tugga – was dead.

And not just Tugga; three of his mates were also dead in suspicious circumstances. Jockey was mortified to learn what his drunken confession might have unleashed.

What have I done? Oh jeezus, Jason, what have you done?

Chapter 41

Andrew Hackett's Thursday morning mood wasn't any better than his start to the previous day. Although at least Mitch had ensured there was no news crew lurking behind the garage door to ambush him. The security guard had taken a walk around the cul-de-sac before he returned to the garage and flicked the internal switch for the door.

The new source of tension was Mitch-related. There'd been a heated debate before Hackett found himself out-voted two to one by Marianne and Mitch.

Even then, Hackett had woken from a restless night with second thoughts about the armed protection. He conceded he could be at risk from a demented killer extracting revenge for unknown wrongs. He knew he could be the next target. But it was the overt nature of the protection plan that Hackett objected to.

Mitch wanted to stick with Hackett 24/7 until the killer was captured, or it was agreed the threat had passed. Naturally Mitch couldn't go without sleep for that amount of time. He wanted to draft in at least one — and preferably three — colleagues to provide around-the-clock protection.

The cost of the ex-SAS bodyguards wasn't the issue for Hackett; he could afford the fee. The awkward point for Hackett was being surrounded by a protection squad while trying to continue his business and social life. The entire station would know about his private army within five minutes of his arrival at work.

They'd think it was hilarious if an armed guard was inside my office.

It would be more embarrassing to make a booking at their favourite South Yarra restaurant, with an extra seat for the bodyguard. Would people laugh, or think the Hacketts were showing off their notoriety? Perhaps there would be a stampede for the door in case the killer took a more proactive approach to disposing of the final member of Tugga's Mob – like bursting in with guns blazing?

Ferdy had also chipped in with his opinions via the telephone before breakfast. He was concerned about the welfare of his mate but raised a valid point: would the killer dare to strike again after so much publicity? Ferdy said the killer's *modus operandi* was subterfuge. The deaths were staged to look like accidents to disguise the true motive. Would they risk trying the tactic again now that it had been exposed?

Foolishly, Hackett had used the speaker on his mobile phone to listen to Ferdy's views. Marianne caught enough of the conversation to shoot down Ferdy's theory. She was convinced the killer would try a more direct approach now their scheme was public.

Hackett lost the skirmish but won some concessions. Only one bodyguard would accompany Hackett in public and they were to be as discreet as possible. They would be allowed to accompany Hackett to the executive level but then had to return to the car park.

Hackett argued that access to the building required a security card and the TV channel employed six guards. Mitch told Hackett there were a hundred ways to get a security pass, but conceded that round. Hackett saw his new minder regretted that decision when the lift opened – and they were greeted by Zara.

Mitch suggested it might be safer if he stayed in reception. Hackett took great delight in banishing his private gunman to the basement car park – 10 levels away from his attractive executive assistant.

Hackett opened his computer and was surprised to find 39 emails cluttered his inbox. Many appeared to be from business associates and friends worried about his safety. Eight were from people who Hackett had clashed with professionally in the past; two said they would be happy to buy a full-page newspaper advertisement with directions to his office. A handful were from cranks who said all filthy capitalists were condemned to hell.

The important emails were internal: Reg Bradley wanted a *catch-up*, at his convenience; and Richard Templeton wanted to talk about new information the *Spotlight* crew had uncovered.

Oh joy – Templeton. Back to rub my nose in more shit!

Chapter 42

Seventy km away, Eddie Malone was reading a different email from a *Spotlight* staff member. It was Curly's response to his phone call. Eddie had been disingenuous about being too scared to leave a phone number. The truth was he had no number to leave; he'd lost another mobile phone, the third that year, and there was no landline in the flat. The mobiles were cheapies anyway, $15 at Harvey Norman's. If *Spotlight* came up with some cash, Eddie planned to splash out on a decent smart phone.

Maybe one with a chip or app, or something, in case I lose it.

The email didn't promise money. But the promptness of the reply and the request for Eddie to call ASAP was a good indication they might part with some dollars. He wrote down Curly Rogers' phone numbers – one for the office and the other a mobile – on a scrap of paper. The next mission was to find enough coins.

Eddie barely noticed the unkempt streets as he walked to the public phone box. He was lucky it hadn't been vandalised. The Ford factory closure wasn't the only industrial setback for the blue-collar suburb. People struggled financially, and there was no football to cheer their weekends for another four months. Houses needed paint, weeds choked gardens and cars minus wheels and other important body parts sat on blocks in driveways and front yards, their resurrection dependent on an improbable Tattslotto win.

Eddie kept a wary eye around him. He was 63, 167cm tall and

had never pushed the scales beyond 70kg. He knew he was unremarkable in his tattered denims, runners and grubby sweatshirt. Most people wouldn't give him a second glance, except the junkies willing to batter a mature citizen to secure a pittance for their next fix. The troubled ones were easy enough to spot and Eddie had learned that avoidance was the safest tactic: cross the street, turn around or run away – anything to avoid trouble.

A fast shuffle wasn't required today as no obvious threats were detected. A female walker in the distance posed no threat. Eddie reached the phone box, dropped in a handful of coins and dialed Curly Rogers at *Spotlight*.

Eddie decided $500 was a fair price to help *Spotlight*. But he knew it was better to remain anonymous, no matter what pressure the TV people applied.

Chapter 43

The *Spotlight* office emptied soon after the morning conference; reporters and camera operators drifted away to pursue assignments.

Templeton was tasked with telling Hackett about the rape of Judy Williams. Kim headed for an edit suite to complete Curly's backlog of feature stories which were sidelined by the focus on Tugga's Mob. Jo was temporarily missing in action, which left Mac and Curly debating the information from the Lorne cop.

They respected the convention of sources speaking off the record. Confidentiality for informants had to be protected, even under legal pressure from police and the courts. Every news organisation received off-the-record tips. Many faced a crisis of conscience on how to use that information if it turned out to be valuable, as was the case with Tugga's Mob.

Jim Laidlaw believed Tugga, Drew, Gerry and Helen raped Judy Williams, but couldn't make a formal allegation. The pictures were still a big breakthrough for the police investigation as they provided a potential motive. *Spotlight* could broadcast another exclusive that evening – if they could find a way to use the information.

Curly's instincts told him the anonymous phone caller could be their link. But he had to wait for a response to his email.

A part of his brain urged caution in case this was the killer playing games with them. It could be a deliberate attempt to lead them astray, as they had connected the dots far quicker than the police. It was unlikely, but Curly reminded himself to keep an open mind.

Imagine if we coughed up news tip-money to a serial killer.

The wait made the journalists irritable. Curly returned to the topic of the purloined Kit Kat from the previous evening.

'I need a chocolate fix. Get me another Kit Kat.'

'Can't do that mate. Chocolate rules applied,' was Mac's sanctimonious reply.

'Bullshit. You're skint again, aren't you?'

'Of course I bloody am. You demanded your Melbourne Cup sweep money.' Mac brightened. 'Speaking of which, what happened to that five bucks?' You can save the day.'

'I had to give that to Brandon for his school lunch.'

'Brilliant. Your offspring will survive the chocolate famine while we fade away.'

The bickering was interrupted when reception put through a call for Curly.

'*Spotlight.* Curly Rogers speaking.'

'Yeah, you sent me an email after I called this morning. It was about Tugga's Mob.'

Curly gave Mac the thumbs up. The fish was nibbling, now he had to land him – quickly.

'Yes, mate. We're interested in the information you might have. You've been watching our stories this week.'

'Yeah, most of 'em. I missed Monday's program. But caught up quick when you linked Drew, Gerry and Helen's deaths. Poor buggers.'

The familiarity with the names, and the sympathy, made Curly feel more comfortable. He couldn't rule out this was the killer on the phone, but leaned towards the caller at least being legitimate.

'You knew them all?'

'Yeah, Tugga and your boss too – Andreas as we called him.'

'So, you were on the trip. I'm getting the feeling you weren't a passenger though.'

'I'm not saying anything about that,' Eddie said with enough belligerence to worry Curly he might slip the hook.

'Okay, okay. We're just trying to establish your credibility. You're asking for money to tell us what happened on the tour. So, we need to ensure you're not trying to rip us off. We've had dozens of similar calls – all saying they know what happened. We need some proof, mate.'

Curly let the silence linger. The request for money hadn't been knocked back; it still dangled in front of the caller.

'Did any of them say anything about Amsterdam?'

That made Curly pause – Amsterdam was the new key word. He turned to Mac who was trying to follow the conversation. Curly mouthed 'Amsterdam' to his boss.

Mac nodded and cracked a big smile.

'What can you tell us about Amsterdam?'

'I know what happened there and I reckon it's got to be worth a lot of money.'

Curly waited for the caller to name a price.

He'll probably double it now he knows I'm interested.

'It was pretty risqué and kinky stuff, you know, even for those days. But sex sells in the media business, I know that, everyone does. I reckon what I know has got to be worth a couple of thousand bucks. You guys will get massive ratings and the advertisers will love it. Maybe what I got is worth five grand?'

Curly didn't like the caller – but needed him. He believed he was genuine and most likely was the tour leader and driver, Eddie Malone. Curly focused on being professional: he needed this guy to confirm the rape story. Yet, his stomach was squirming at the possibility Eddie had been a party to the assault or had done nothing to stop it.

'Risqué? Kinky? What do you mean by that?'

'Nope. I'm not telling you any more about that little party until we settle the money.'

The term 'party' made Curly pause again. Was this guy so sick that he viewed a gang rape as just another trip experience, or could it be that other interpretation the cops had assumed on first seeing the pictures on Tugga's wall?

That Judy Williams was a willing participant in an orgy?

Curly decided it was time to deflate some of the caller's cockiness.

'Look Eddie – I'm pretty sure now that's who you are; we already know about what happened in Amsterdam. There's pictures of Judy Williams being raped by Tugga's Mob.'

There was no immediate response from Eddie, only an expulsion of air. Curly waited and Eddie found his voice again.

'Raped? No, no, no. You guys got it all wrong. Judy wasn't raped, she was up for – she wanted a gang-bang.'

'A gang-bang? That's not what the pictures show us, Eddie.' Curly knew he was taking a punt, especially as they didn't have the pictures and were never likely to get them, but he wanted to keep the tour leader off balance and talking.

'Were you there, Eddie? Was that you behind the camera?'

'No,' was the sullen response.

'No, you weren't the photographer? Or no, you weren't there?'

Curly worried that Eddie might hang up. The danger for Eddie was being implicated in a rape.

'I wasn't there. But Tugga told me that's what it was!'

Curly noted the change of tone in Eddie's voice. The cockiness was gone; he sounded desperate.

'Tugga said she had been flirting with him throughout the tour, leading him on. It was all part of the fun. He assured me that's what it was.'

Curly let the silence hang and waited for Eddie to continue. It was a classic technique that worked once again.

'She wasn't a nun – Judy. I'd seen her shagging Andreas and a few other blokes during the tour. She was up for a good time. Loved them Italian blokes, the lucky buggers. And a few others from different tour groups. That's what it was like in those days. They were away from home and they all rooted like rabbits.'

Curly chipped in to puncture Eddie's self-justification. 'Be that as it may, we know that Judy approached you and complained about being stalked by Tugga. Why would a woman who was being sexually harassed suddenly turn around and engage in a group scene with him and his mates?'

'But Tugga said it was all part of the build-up.'

'Build-up?' Curly questioned. 'Was Tugga suggesting it was all part of some elaborate role play – the hard-to-get femme who suddenly swoons over his charms at the end of the trip? A bit fanciful don't you think?'

'No, not at all. That's what Tugga said it was. Her complaints were just an act. Tugga said Judy loved sex and that they cooked it up in London before they even left. It made sense, it really did – at the time.'

'So, you knew it was going to happen?'

'Not exactly, no. But I knew that's what they were up to that last night in Amsterdam. I could see the camera flashes in the tent and they were laughing. I didn't hear any complaints or screaming from Judy.'

Curly curtailed his anger at the ignorant fool on the line. He still needed Eddie. 'You didn't think to go check that was the case? That Judy was a willing participant?'

'No, I couldn't. I had my hands full with all the space cadets. Half of them went loopy that night when they tried space cakes for the first time. It fucking blew their minds. I had to run around the Red Light District rounding them up. Then I had to keep an eye on them at camp. Some went totally spazzo.'

'And was Judy Williams one of those who tried the space cakes? Was she as smashed as the others?'

Curly waited for Eddie to mull that implication.

Was Judy so drugged that she didn't understand what was happening in that tent?

Did Eddie understand that Tugga fed him a bullshit story?

He was surprised when Eddie's answer still had a touch of belligerence.

'Look, Judy tried the space cakes. Yeah, she was really high. But I know she wasn't raped. In fact, I'm certain.'

'How can you be so sure?' Curly interrupted. 'Judy complained to you about being sexually stalked by a member of the tour party. Yet you chose to accept the word of the *accused* that it was all part of an act. Then, when Judy is at her most vulnerable, you again accept Tugga's word that she was gagging for a gang bang?'

Curly had to cut himself off at that point lest he call Eddie a moron and risk losing him forever.

'No, no it wasn't like that. She seemed okay with it all.'

'How do you know?'

'I saw her.'

'How? Were you a peeping Tom as well?'

'No,' Eddie felt trapped by Curly's prosecutorial tone. 'I saw pictures of her with Tugga and Helen.'

That temporarily stalled Curly's hectoring tactic. If Eddie saw pictures of the scene in the tent, did he still have them? He needed this little prick more than ever now.

'You have pictures of that night? Did Tugga, or one of the others, give them to you?'

'Yeah, Tugga did.'

Curly wanted to do a fist pump but there was a more immediate priority. He had to play nice with Eddie Malone to get those pictures. Luckily he had the means to do that.

'Okay, Eddie. You say that you weren't a party to what police are now investigating as the gang rape of Judy Williams.'

'Oh god,' Eddie groaned. His greed for cash could possibly implicate him in a 30-year-old crime on the other side of the world.

'What can I do? You've gotta believe I had nothing to do with that. Do you have to tell the cops about me?'

Gotcha! Curly reeled in his prize catch.

'We can't avoid doing that, Eddie. We can't withhold information from the police that would help their investigation. We could end up in court as well.'

'Shit. I shouldn't go to court. I didn't do anything to anyone.'

Curly let Eddie wriggle some more before feeding him some line. 'There might be a way out for you, Eddie.'

'Yeah? I don't need this crap. What can I do?'

'Well, if we get your side of the story on camera first, you can explain how manipulative Tugga was. He lied to you about stalking

Judy and the gang rape. You were distracted by stoned passengers when Judy was at her most vulnerable. And all of it was orchestrated by a cunning brute – Tugga Tancred.'

It made Curly queasy to offer Eddie a lifeline. Curly was effectively telling him that the best way to protect himself was to go public. The former tour driver was being given a forum to squeal about being duped. The viewers and cops could decide if they believed him.

'Okay, I'll do it. Anything to distance myself from Tugga's Mob.'

Curly had landed his fish, but wanted more.

'We will need to verify your pictures of the attack on Judy.'

Curly was curious why Tugga would ever share a gang rape with Eddie, but that answer could wait for another time. He needed a sweetener in case Eddie realised that, although Curly knew about the pictures, he might not have copies.

'We might be able to give you a couple of hundred for the pictures. We probably filmed them at Tugga's bach, but best to make sure. Consider the money a facilitation fee for your assistance.'

'Yeah, okay.'

With the deal struck Curly wrapped up the call after obtaining Eddie's address in Norlane. All the reporters were assigned so it would have to be a job for Kim.

He told Eddie to expect her and a camera operator at one o'clock. Curly knew the suburb wasn't a photogenic location. He told Eddie the crew would take him to the waterfront at Rippleside for a more scenic backdrop for the interview

Curly had one final question before he handed the media gathering logistics over to Jo.

'Was Andrew Hackett part of that group with Judy on the final night?

'Not likely,' Eddie snorted. 'Andreas was so wasted he was like jelly. We had to carry him to the bus and pour him into his tent. The lazy bastard didn't move for another 12 hours.'

Eddie stepped away from the phone box and lit a cigarette, unsure whether to be grumpy or happy. A hot TV reporter would be knocking at his front door in about an hour and half – and he was going to get paid to talk to her. The *facilitation* fee wasn't as much as he hoped for, but it was better than nothing.

On the negative side was being conned back then by bloody Tugga, and having to go public to defend his reputation.

I don't need the cops crawling over me.

Eddie wasn't totally convinced by the *Spotlight* producer's interpretation of the scene with Judy. The pictures in his possession didn't look like a gang rape to him. But if the media was going to play it that way, he knew it was better to be on their side.

Eddie finished the cigarette and flicked it towards the gutter. It landed close to a woman in lycra leggings and top who was doing stretching exercises against a bus stop shelter. He wondered how long she had been there and how much of the phone conversation she might have heard?

It won't be a problem in a couple of hours. I'll be able to clear myself and blame Tugga for all this crap.

Chapter 44

Andrew Hackett struggled to recall a week as bad as this – ever – as he descended from the executive level accompanied by his new limpet; aka Mitch Stevens, personal gun for hire. It was just after midday, but Hackett was already on his way home. Not voluntarily, either. Reg Bradley suggested it would be better for Hackett to take some *gardening leave* until things settled down. Hackett knew it was the euphemism for getting rid of a troubled executive. Out of sight, out of mind.

In this case, a degree of panic was probably settling in among the station executives; there might be collateral damage if the Tugga's Mob investigation dragged on and the killer remained at large. Professionally the stigma of being associated with four murders could be damaging; personally, they didn't want to be nearby if the killer took extreme methods to dispose of one of their colleagues.

Hackett's foul mood wasn't tempered by a phone call to Marianne about the latest development. Her response was a curt, 'fine, see you at home.' Now he was in the downstairs car park and there was no sign of the BMW. A white Ford sedan was in his usual parking place.

'What's that heap of shit doing there?' Hackett demanded of Mitch who stood beside the vehicle. His eyes swept the executive park in case Mitch had shifted his car to a more discreet location. 'Where's the Beemer?'

'Tucked away safely for a while until the cops catch this killer.' Mitch dangled the keys to the Ford. 'I cleared it with Mrs Hackett while you were in those meetings.'

Hackett grunted and glared at the Ford. It looked common; there were thousands on the road every day. He hated losing his beloved BMW but understood the theory behind the change of vehicle. It was anonymous enough to keep any killer guessing; if indeed the killer even had him in their sights.

No car, no job – albeit temporarily for both – and a killer possibly stalking him made Hackett miserable. The latest visit from Templeton had also contributed to his growing depression.

Judy was raped by Tugga and the rest?

He wondered if that was the most awful revelation in a week of shocks. Templeton was convinced Judy had been raped, despite not seeing the pictures yet. He explained they'd spoken to bus driver Eddie Malone, who was about to provide some photographic evidence for *Spotlight*.

Hackett wasn't surprised that, if the rape pictures existed, Eddie would have copies.

Eddie was always a sleaze-bag.

Hackett remembered the driver lurked around the girls' tents as they changed into swimwear. Eddie used to say he was checking everything was okay, but everyone knew he was just a perve.

Hackett took consolation from one part of Templeton's news – Eddie had categorically confirmed that he, Hackett, wasn't part of the sexual assault on Judy.

But he was still disconcerted to learn that Eddie actually believed Tugga's story about Judy and the group sex.

Yeah right, Eddie!

Hackett knew that wasn't Judy. Sure, she was enjoying sexual adventures in Europe, but taking on Tugga's Mob – minus himself – was beyond belief.

Hackett made Mitch drive the Ford as he wasn't interested in a locally-made car. There was no comparison to the European models he'd been treating himself to for 25 years. He looked around the standard interior, grateful to find it had air conditioning.

'I don't suppose this chariot is bullet proof?' Hackett inquired.

Mitch ignored the sarcasm. 'Not this one, but I'm talking to a mate who has one coming free soon.'

'Shit,' Hackett shook his head. 'I was only joking, but I see you're not.'

'Nope. Not much time for humour in my business, Mr Hackett. Nothing funny about a principal getting a bullet in the head from a motorbike rider, or pillion passenger, while sitting at the traffic lights.'

Mitch knew that comment was cruel. As they waited for a green light on St Kilda Road, he noticed Hackett's face had paled and his darting eyes were sweeping the busy thoroughfare for black leather-clad assassins on high-powered two wheelers.

A bit of paranoia would be good for this subject, Mitch reasoned. He understood that Hackett was used to being in charge – the executive who delegated and demanded, who was rarely told what to do. Mitch wanted Hackett to feel fear, so that he would respond as directed in the event of an emergency.

The ex-SAS man was pleased Hackett's boss sent him home for a few days. Mitch never liked being separated from his client, even in a supposedly secure office. At least in South Yarra Mitch could make the home safe without turning it into a fortress. Mitch didn't care that the tour guide cleared Hackett of any involvement in the rape of Judy Williams. His concern was what the killer believed – and whether Hackett was still a target.

Chapter 45

Kim was elated when Curly and Mac dragged her from the edit suite for a briefing about one of the most important interviews of the Tugga's Mob saga. Eddie Malone had evidence of a horrible crime on the tour. It might provide a motive for the deaths, or it might not. Either way, Judy's traumatic night with Tugga's Mob was another revelation that would have the *Spotlight* audience riveted to their seats on Thursday night.

And Kim wanted to be a visual part of the story that had Melbourne, much of Australia and half of New Zealand captivated. She grabbed the address from Curly, snatched her handbag and sprinted to the camera car before another reporter could steal her prize.

Mac and Curly laughed, admiring her ambition and enthusiasm.

In Norlane, Eddie stood before a bathroom mirror trying to arrange thin grey hair into some semblance of order. He hadn't washed it for three days and even swiping water through it failed to improve the presentation. He couldn't avoid the vanity, but it wasn't every day a television reporter arrived on your doorstep.

Eddie hadn't ever seen Kim Prescott on the TV, but guessed there was some sort of production line that churned out hot chicks for the camera.

Eddie walked back into his open-plan living room and kitchen.

It was only half a dozen steps as the flat was only three rooms: bathroom, bedroom and living area. He picked up the pictures of Tugga, Judy and Helen and reappraised them for the fifth time since the phone call to *Spotlight*.

The two pictures were old and dog-eared from regular handling. The first showed Tugga with a shit-eating grin on his face while lying naked on top of Judy. Her face was partially obscured, so Eddie had always believed Tugga's story that she wanted the group scene. Judy's face was quite clear in the second picture, which showed her naked in Helen's arms.

The pictures had only come into Eddie's possession after his unexpected reunion with Tugga in Geelong. They were a separate arrangement to the dope deal and were, in fact, payment for a long overdue debt.

Eddie had caught Tugga trying to smuggle drugs from Amsterdam on the last day of the trip. The bag of marijuana fell out of Tugga's tent as it was being folded.

By rights, Eddie should have booted Tugga off the tour immediately. The bus would have been impounded and Eddie arrested if the drugs were found at a border crossing. It was the most important rule the tour company drummed repeatedly into Eddie during his one day of training: no drugs on the bus!

The quantity wasn't big – enough for half a dozen joints – and Tugga had used that to manipulate Eddie one final time. The big fella explained he'd forgotten to smoke the dope the previous evening. They were going to have a farewell session at the camp site, but Judy's lust had changed their plans. It made sense to Eddie – smoke a few joints or have a gang bang with Judy? Eddie knew what his decision would've been, if he'd been invited to join in.

The confrontation with Tugga was too much for Eddie at the time. He was knackered after his first tour-driving experience and didn't want any more hassles. Tugga saw the driver weaken and offered him a bribe – pictures of Judy's group performance with Tugga's Mob. That swayed Eddie, and Tugga returned to London with the tour.

It was a bad deal for Eddie as he didn't see Tugga again for 25 years. The former tour leader gently reminded Tugga of that Amsterdam debt at their riverside pub reunion, although Eddie was surprised when the big fella agreed to honour the promise. The following week Tugga handed over the two fading pictures; said the rest were lost in a fire years before.

It was a pity to miss seeing the whole collection, but overall, Eddie was pleased he'd run into Tugga again. He had a new source of cheap dope and hot pictures of a scene that had fuelled his fantasies for a quarter of a century.

Things were so different from the tour when the much younger Tugga could persuade or intimidate Eddie to do things his way.

Now, their association was over – permanently. But at least he was getting one final pay-off courtesy of Tugga: cash for the pictures. Eddie stared at them again, possibly for the last time.

Was Judy totally out of it that night? Did she know what Tugga and Helen were doing? Eddie always presumed Judy's face portrayed pleasure. Her eyes were closed, her lips slightly apart as she lay naked within Helen's arms. Surely Judy wouldn't have allowed Helen to play with her like that if she wasn't into chicks?

Well, that had always been Eddie's thinking until the journalist suggested another scenario.

I wonder what their photos show?

He now understood the tent pictures could be interpreted two ways and was smart enough to know he should support the media view.

Safest bet, Eddie boy!

He would tell the reporter that Tugga was always persuasive. The size of him scared most people. Eddie wasn't inside the tent in Amsterdam that night, so the public couldn't call him naïve or gullible. It was the reality presented to him by Tugga 30 years ago.

And Eddie had seen Judy with different guys all over Europe so a group scene wasn't beyond belief – for him. Eddie's confidence grew as he prepared answers for the TV chick. He wanted to deep rub the last of Tugga's reputation in it.

Eddie was still holding the photos when he heard a knock at the door.

That was quick!

The reporter and cameraman weren't expected for another 20 minutes. Eddie guessed they had a clear run out of Melbourne because it was middle of the day traffic – or they were eager to talk to him.

There was no window on that side of the flat. The entrance faced the carport where his rusty Ford station wagon was parked. Beyond that was the driveway and the 10-metre-high wall of an abandoned factory. Eddie's was the rear flat of four, which suited him. None of the neighbours ever ventured to his end of the property.

Eddie swung the door open and was pleased to find a tall, blonde and athletic woman. She held two letters out to him with her left hand.

'Hi, I found this mail addressed to you on the drive.'

'Oh, right. Thanks – that was kind of you,' Eddie said and instinctively reached for the mail.

The exchange was fluffed and the letters tumbled to the ground as Eddie touched them. He dropped to one knee to retrieve them and tried to cover what he thought was his clumsiness. 'Where's the camera guy?'

Instead of a reply, Eddie felt a piercing blow to his chest. It winded him and Eddie would have toppled to the ground if the woman hadn't grabbed his shirt collar over the left shoulder. He was trapped in place and the punches continued – sharp hits to his ribs, stomach, arm and shoulder. The pain was excruciating.

The woman's movements were so fast it took many blows before Eddie saw the knife.

I'm being stabbed?

Every thrust of the blade made it harder to breathe. Eddie panicked but couldn't find the energy to stop the frenzied attack. He was totally helpless in the hands of this crazy woman. He felt one final stab deep under his rib cage before he crumpled on the floor. The pictures of Judy Williams and Tugga fell from his left hand.

Why does this TV reporter want to kill me?

Chapter 46

Mac and Curly were feeling chuffed . The Hatchet had been banished because of fears about collateral damage should the killer decide to go ballistic. It was convenient for *Spotlight* – and the whole station – to have the financial boss scared shitless and cooped up at home.

Kim was about to record crucial pictures and an interview that could point towards a motive for the deaths.

And, once again, it was Mac and Curly's job to structure the content into another blockbuster program.

The interview with Eddie Malone about the rape would be their lead item. The pictures were the most important element of that piece. The two veteran producers hadn't seen them yet, but were positive technology could help them. A graphics operator would pixelate any genitals or X-rated components of the photos, but ensure there was still some flesh.

Mac instructed Kim to keep Eddie onside – at least until the photos were recorded on tape. Eddie could swear all he liked that he was duped by Tugga and had no idea what really happened in the tent. The viewers would make up their own minds about whether he was a scumbag, or a moron.

Spotlight once again had the best story of the day – or so they assumed – and that made Mac and Curly want to celebrate with a takeaway lunch from Clarendon Street in South Melbourne. They spent more time debating which establishment should be favoured with their business – Chinese, Thai, Vietnamese or the bakery – than they did on shaping the program. That was a no-brainer, while lunch was a split decision. Curly ended the debate by saying he would use his credit card to order if Mac drove to collect the Thai dishes. Mac caved, graciously, as his credit card strangely wasn't working – again.

Mac had just collected the keys for his seven-year-old Commodore – fortunately he still qualified for a station car park – when the direct line at the command post rang. Curly picked it up.

It was 1.02pm. It was Kim Prescott, and she was agitated; close to panicking. Curly signalled Mac to drop the keys as he switched the call to speaker phone.

'He's dead. I can't believe it. We're at Eddie's flat and there's blood everywhere. I think he's been stabbed,' Kim blurted.

She was clearly stressed, but she wasn't babbling incoherently.

'Where are you, Kim?' Curly was worried. 'The killer could still be around – are you still at the flat?'

'No, we're okay. We're back in the camera car. There's no one else about in the street or at the flats. It's a run-down area – but we can't see anyone dangerous.'

'Okay, that's good, Kim. You guys did the right thing.' Curly reassured his shocked colleague. 'And you're sure he's dead?'

Kim switched her mobile to speaker to include camera operator, Ken Withers.

'Yep, dead certain,' said the laconic camera op. 'No pun intended. He's been turned into a pin-cushion by some vicious bastard. His chest and stomach were slashed to pieces. I checked for a pulse – but he was gone. CPR would have been a waste of time.'

'You went into the flat, Ken?'

'Yeah, I had to – in case there was a chance he was still breathing. He was warm, but there was no blood pumping. Nothing was going to save him. He was on his back inside the door frame. It's a tiny flat – it was obvious that whoever sliced and diced him was gone.'

Mac and Curly knew they had minutes to form a plan that would enable them to broadcast the most incredible story of the week.

'Right, Mac here, guys. We know you have to report the murder to the cops ASAP. The trouble is, they're going to keep you occupied on the phone and then order you out of the crime scene until they arrive. They'll also tie you up for hours with questions – which could screw our chances for another exclusive tonight.'

'So, what should we do?' Kim was calmer now her mentors were on the case.

'Here's the plan.' Mac said. 'It's 1.05pm and you've just arrived – a few minutes later than expected – to interview Eddie Malone.

'Ken, grab the camera and record 10 quick shots of the body, blood, flat, Kim close to the doorway, and anything else that can help us with the story.

'Kim, you do the same with your mobile phone. Get a few stills and send them to us immediately. Then call the cops and report the murder. They'll tie you up forever after that, so we'll get another news crew down there asap to cover the rest of the circus.

'Ken, once you get those first shots, hide that disc in the back of the camera car with a label 'Curly's.' Then grab another disc and get as many shots as you can before the cops arrive and shut you down. If you can palm that off to the news guys – great; if the cops confiscate it, at least we're covered by Kim's shots and your first disc.'

Curly nodded, knowing the veteran TV newsman would rise to the occasion and get the footage. Mac was correct to assume the crew would be lost for the afternoon as the first responders and then detectives pored over the scene. It was the sixth death from the 1986 bus tour and was most likely the fifth murder. Kim's stills would give the news and current affairs teams a huge advantage over their opposition. The exclusive with the tour driver was lost but *Spotlight* was still in front of the game.

The producers didn't want to delay Kim. If a suspicious neighbour told police the camera car was parked near the flats for longer than the crew were going to concede, there could be serious trouble for Kim and Ken. However, there was still a crucial story element that needed to be explored, if possible: the rape pictures.

'Kim, Curly here again. One last thing until we can talk again. If you see the tent pictures with Judy Williams – get a couple of shots on the phone and send them. I don't care what quality they are, we'll look after that from this end.'

Mac chimed in one last time before they cut the call. 'Ken, leave the camera car unlocked. We'll take the risk the local lowlifes won't filch anything with half the Geelong police force on the street.

'When they get there, the news crew can say they need an extra battery or something, to get access to your disc.

'I will start negotiations with the Tugga's Mob task force here in Melbourne in 15 minutes. I'll tell them, regardless of the state of their investigation, *you* must be on camera for a live cross at the start of the program tonight. Okay, get cracking you two and stay cool.'

The call was disconnected and the newsmen raised their eyebrows.

'How much weirder can this story get?' Mac said. He picked up his keys again. 'It would still be a shame to let good Thai food go to waste. You brief the news boys.'

Curly nodded. It was going to be another manic few hours for the production crews – the sort of day news junkies craved – and the adrenalin was already flowing.

Chapter 47

In Norlane, Kim gritted her teeth and snapped several shots of Eddie Malone, the flat and the grim surroundings. There didn't appear to be residents home in the other flats. Or, if they were, they weren't curious, as Kim couldn't see any curtains twitch. What she did notice was the first flies circling the bloody wounds.

It was a gruesome challenge, but Kim knew this story could boost her chances of promotion to the frontline reporting staff.

Ken, armed with a new disc and full battery was less than a minute behind Kim in returning to Eddie's body. He was in his element: frame a shot, record, move.

With Ken fully operational, Kim sent her first half dozen shots of the crime scene to the station via her mobile. It was time to call the cops and report a suspicious death. She was not going to call it a murder over the phone, or say anything about Tugga's Mob. She knew that would tip off the opposition channels who monitored police radios. The longer opposition journalists took to react the better it would be for *Spotlight's* story.

Kim had taken her pictures from the doorway and all were focused on Eddie and the flat. As she stepped away she noticed two letters and two white cards on the concrete to the side of the entrance. She didn't care about the mail.

Can I get that lucky?

Kim knelt with her pen in hand – dozens of television crime

shows taught amateur sleuths to never use bare fingers – and flipped the first white card.

Oh My God!

It was a shot of Judy Williams. She was naked and in the arms of a woman that Kim presumed was Helen Franks. Kim quickly focused the camera on her phone and snapped several pictures. She then turned the other photo, more prepared for something equally confronting. It revealed Judy Williams, again naked, with Tugga Tancred.

Tugga's huge grin made her stomach churn. *Bastard!*

Kim fired the latest – and most important pictures – through to the *Spotlight* office. She then dialed 000 to report the death and began to prepare herself for a long afternoon of questions. Kim was ready to co-operate fully with the detectives but was annoyed it was going to take time.

Please get the cops to release me by show time, Mac. I really want that live cross!

Chapter 48

The *Melbourne Spotlight* production crew, and their compatriots in the newsroom down the corridor, were a clichéd hive of activity for the next five hours.

The murder of Eddie Malone changed everyone's plans. It was a scramble to re-write stories and record new interviews in the time available. A news van was dispatched to Geelong to send onsite footage and voiceovers for editing, and to set up live crosses with reporters for the news and *Spotlight*.

Mac was taken out of the play for much of the afternoon to ensure their ace – Kim's discovery of the body – could be used.

Pete Benson sent his latest offerings from New Zealand just after four o'clock AEDT; the two-hour time difference worked in the journalist's favour. Benson went to Muriwai in the morning to film the rock fishing platform where Drew Harvey died. It was a relatively mild day with a moderate swell, an occasional wave breaking around the ankles of a handful of fishers brave enough to cast their lines. Benson knew he would have to emphasise the surf was different on the day Harvey was killed.

With the beach footage on its way to Australia, Benson and Dugal were re-directed to Cambridge to confirm, on camera, Denise Mitchell's story about Judy Williams' diary. Privately, Benson was angry with himself that he hadn't done that the previous day.

Mac and Curly didn't criticise their reporter as they

understood Tugga's Mob was an evolving story. But they decided it could be important to have verification of the diary.

News of Eddie's murder broke late in the afternoon for New Zealand police and media. Benson and Dugal were ahead of the local contingent again, courtesy of Kim and Ken. They drove from Denise's property at Cambridge to police headquarters in nearby Hamilton to await the outcome of the detectives' chat with Heather Langer.

Four cups and saucers, a tea pot, sugar bowl, spoons and a plate filled with home-made biscuits rattled on a silver tray as Heather walked through the kitchen door onto the deck. She had no fears the two detectives seated comfortably at the table would interpret that as nerves.

'Geez, Heather,' said the younger detective. 'You've got enough there to feed the rugby team.'

'I've been trying to fill your huge stomach since you and Jason were in the Under 15s, Rory,' Heather laughed. 'I'm worried there still aren't enough biscuits here to get you through to dinner.'

Rory's colleague, Inspector Shane Flynn cut in. 'Detective Coleraine is on a diet after missing selection in the police team for being too fat.' He picked up two pieces of shortbread as Heather placed a cup in front of him and poured from the teapot. 'Therefore, I shall have to eat his share.' He took a bite from the first biscuit, sighed, and gave Heather a smile.

Heather ignored Flynn and pushed the plate towards Rory. 'I haven't seen your name in the team list, Shane, or the reserve bench for a few years. Maybe I should put these treats away for Christmas – give you an incentive to do some training.'

Their laughter was interrupted by Flynn's mobile. He retreated to the far end of the deck for more privacy.

Rory lowered his voice. 'Sorry we had to come out here and do this interview, Heather. It was orders from Auckland.'

Heather finished pouring the tea. 'Don't worry about it. We know you're just doing your duty. Ask us whatever you like when Shane gets back and hopefully we'll get it all sorted. I have to admit it's been a strange week. First there was that Australian TV crew – and now an official police interview. Judy's been gone almost 30 years and it's unsettling to think about such awful times again.'

'Don't worry, Heather. We've known you and Jason forever. You're not the kind of people to be involved in crap like this. It won't take long once Shane gets off the phone. By the way, where is that lazy sod, Jason?'

Before Heather could respond the Inspector returned to the table, a grim look on his face.

'What's up boss?'

'Would you believe they've found another body connected to Tugga's Mob?'

'Fuck me! Sorry Heather. That is a hell of shock. Who was it; that TV executive? He did come across as a bit of an arsehole.'

Flynn paused as Heather's tea cup clanged on the silver tray. She looked as shocked as the two detectives.

'No, it was the tour driver. A guy called Eddie Malone. A television crew found him dead on his own doorstep. They had arranged to record an interview with him about Tugga's Mob. When they arrived, they found he'd been stabbed to death only a few minutes earlier. The local cops say it's a really nasty crime scene.'

Heather couldn't say anything: she was horrified and elated at the same time. The timing of Eddie's death couldn't have been better. She worked hard to maintain the shocked expression, when she also desperately wanted to shout: *We got another one!*

Eddie was killed 2000 km away – and the Hamilton cops provided a perfect alibi. Not just for herself, for Jason as well. His quad bike thundered up the driveway and braked sharply at the entrance to the deck. Jason climbed off with a big grin.

'Spud, Flynny – I hope you haven't eaten all the bloody biscuits, I'm starving.' Jason couldn't miss the three shocked expressions. 'What's happened? You look as if you've found another body?'

'Not a good joke, mate.' Flynn responded. 'The Aussies *have* got another murder. The bus driver from your aunt's tour.'

Jason stopped at the top of deck stairs. 'Shit. I put my size 12 boots in that pile of poo. Sorry to be so flippant, guys.' He leaned against the railing and tugged at his muddy boots. 'But I guess that means your trip out here is a waste of time.'

The detectives nodded. If Eddie Malone was just killed in Australia, that put Jason and Heather in the clear.

'Yep. I hear you, Jase.' Flynn said. 'Looks like this shit belongs with the Australians. I'll give the Auckland squad a call to confirm you and Heather are with us. They might have a couple of questions, but I don't think you'll have to delay milking this afternoon.' He took his mobile to the other end of the deck.

Rory reached for another shortbread. 'I wondered what you were up to. Heather said you were just back from Aussie, which did raise some interest.'

'Yeah, Mum picked me up from the airport this morning. I had a few days in New South Wales. I did some farm visits – you know we're always trying to keep our milk production ahead of those sly Aussies.'

Rory nodded as he ate. Jason accepted a cup of tea from his mother and gave her a wink as he sat down. The conversation swiftly drifted away from Tugga's Mob to more important matters for the two rugby team mates: how much the All Blacks were going to beat Ireland by in Chicago that weekend.

Rory had no doubts. 'The Irish will put up a good fight for the first hour. But our fitness will be too good over the last 20 minutes – my money's on the All Blacks by 14 points.'

Heather left Jason and Rory to talk rugby as she returned to the kitchen for more tea. Out of sight, she felt she could emotionally regroup. It was wonderful to be free of police suspicion, because of the timing and location of Eddie Malone's death. But when Shane Flynn broke the news, it wasn't difficult for Heather to be shocked.

Stabbed to death?

That method of execution was never contemplated.

Pete Benson recorded a brief statement from Inspector Flynn outside the Hamilton police headquarters after his return from the Williams farm.

'We spoke with the only surviving family of the late Judy Williams this afternoon – soon after the latest death that has been connected to Tugga's Mob. Heather Langer and her son Jason were extremely co-operative, but couldn't offer anything to help the police investigation here, or in Australia. We will continue inquiries into the deaths of Drew Harvey and Gerry Daly, but we think the main focus of the investigation will stay in Australia.

All the news channels were across the latest murder by the time Benson's footage arrived at the *Spotlight* studio. They'd intensified their efforts once they learned the murder victim was discovered by a *Spotlight* reporter and camera operator.

The smart producers and news directors immediately made the connection to the Tugga's Mob story. That saw them pour more resources and crews into the story to find out about Eddie Malone and his connection to Tugga's Mob.

Two newsrooms even made cheeky requests to interview Kim Prescott and her camera operator once the police finished with them. Jo fielded those calls because everyone else was too busy. Short shrift would be the politest way to describe how those newsrooms were told by Jo to *fuck off!*

Everyone was so focused, including *Spotlight* executive producer Richard Templeton, that no one thought to alert Andrew Hackett.

The killer had changed tactics – and The Hatchet, and his bodyguard, didn't know.

Chapter 49

The gin distilleries were profiting from Andrew Hackett's current dramas, but not the tonic water companies. Three quarters of a bottle of Bombay Sapphire was consumed before the news bulletin on Thursday evening, much of it drunk by the television executive forced to endure an indefinite period of *gardening leave*.

Ferdy tried a small taster before moving onto a sauvignon blanc. Marianne helped Ferdy empty the bottle of Marlborough's best while she pottered around in the kitchen to prepare a meal for four. The fourth member of the household wasn't touching any alcohol.

Mitch regularly patrolled the large villa to check the doors and windows were secure. It was a warm evening and Hackett's complaints about a lack of fresh air were summarily dismissed by Marianne.

'Let Mitch do his job please, Andrew.'

Her tone irritated Hackett as he felt the implication: we need an armed guard to clean up *your* mess.

Hackett and Ferdy retreated to the home office. Ferdy was certain his mate would be back at work by Monday; or Tuesday at the latest.

'This is a one-week wonder in the news cycle, Andrew. Chin up. Your journalists will be bored by the end of the weekend and looking for fresh prey.'

'Wish I shared your confidence. I've never seen those current affairs guys so enthusiastic. Even their bloody boss has lost his wimpy nature. They're going to be pricks to get back under control.'

'Announce the station is considering a new round of redundancies – that'll make the reporters back off in a hurry.'

The thought cheered Hackett. 'Wish I thought of that yesterday!'

'I'm impressed with your gunman. Never seen those personal protection officers up close before. He looks tough, and efficient.'

Hackett snorted. 'Be my guest and hire him after I've kicked his arse out the door. Anyway, why would you need a bodyguard?'

'I was thinking of Jacinta – remember her?'

'It was only Saturday. I don't forget them as quickly as you. Is Jacinta giving you grief?'

'Yes, unfortunately. She's stalked a couple of my favourite restaurants and wine bars this week, asking if I've been in.'

Hackett laughed. Ferdy's love life was busy but never dangerous. 'You don't need Mitch to protect you. Marianne would shoot her for free.'

The friends emerged from the office a few minutes before the 6pm TV news. Hackett was reluctant to watch after his shitty day but Ferdy insisted they kept up to speed with the Tugga's Mob fallout.

'Forewarned is forearmed, Andrew. At least you'll know when to tell Mitch to use his gun.'

Hackett slumped into his usual armchair while Ferdy picked up the TV remote. Mitch sat on a stool close to the open plan kitchen-dining area. He kept everyone and the TV in view.

'What news service do you want?' Ferdy asked, as he settled into the sofa. 'Your lot – or one of the other channels for a change?'

Marianne emerged from the kitchen to top up his wine glass and then sat beside him. Exchanges between husband and wife were becoming terser.

'Stick with my wankers,' Hackett responded. 'Those jerks have been ahead of the pack since this mess began. If there's anything new, they'll have it.'

Hackett's dealings with the news and current affairs staff over the previous few days hadn't improved his jaundiced view. His bitterness would plumb new depths by the end of *Melbourne Spotlight*.

The news titles rolled across the screen then transitioned to recorded footage of the crime scene in Norlane. The voiceover smacked Hackett harder than three-quarters of a bottle of gin.

'A fifth murder in the Tugga's Mob saga – our news crew discover the victim in his home.'

Hackett sat open-mouthed. He hadn't really thought there'd be much left that could stun him this week. He looked hard at the screen.

The teaser for the main story featured footage of a doorway with a body on the floor. The pictures were taken from several angles, each shot lasting a few seconds. The victim was a male and there were ugly red splotches over his torso. The images were discreetly blurred to avoid making the scene too gruesome. News directors didn't want families barfing over their dinners.

But right now, the nuances of news production and filming were irrelevant. Someone else from the tour was dead.

Who the bloody hell is it?

Hackett glanced at the others. Ferdy was on the edge of his seat and Marianne had a hand over her mouth. Mitch alone showed no emotion.

The news anchor, Robert Cane, appeared on camera.

'Good evening. Another member of a controversial 1986 tour group in Europe has died – the fifth homicide associated with the tour in the past nine weeks.

'The latest victim was found stabbed to death on his doorstep in the Geelong suburb of Norlane.

'The grisly discovery was made by a crew from *Melbourne Spotlight* just after 1pm.

'Reporter Kim Prescott and cameraman Ken Withers had arranged to meet the victim who wanted to share important new information about the activities of Tugga's Mob.'

Hackett groaned as the newsreader kept the audience on tenterhooks while he summarised the Tugga's Mob 'story so far'.

Does he want everyone to think I'm the victim?

'I don't want a fucking summary. I want to know who's dead,' he shouted at the television.

'While police are baffled by this latest murder, two things stand out.

'The victim, 63-year-old Eddie Malone, *was* the tour guide and driver of that Euro-trip, but he was not part of Tugga's Mob.

'And this time there was no attempt by the killer to make his death look like an accident.'

'Eddie?' Hackett blurted out. 'He was a useless idiot – what does he have to do with this crap?'

'We can reveal exclusively tonight that Eddie Malone had pictorial evidence of a sexual assault on another passenger, Judy Williams, the passenger who drowned a year after the tour.

'In fact, Malone was about to confirm something far more serious – that assault was a gang rape in Amsterdam involving Tugga's Mob.'

'Fuck,' Hackett shouted. He looked at Marianne who had both hands to her cheeks, her eyes fixed to the horror show that was the six o' clock news.

'I swear I had nothing to do with that. I only found out about the allegations today.'

No one responded to Hackett's protestations of innocence.

The news presenter finally introduced a reporter who was live at the scene of the murder. The camera framed him at the entrance to a floodlit driveway where, over his shoulder, forensic officers were on their knees working around a carport. Detectives talked in a tight group a few metres away.

The reporter revealed Eddie Malone had been stabbed up to 15 times in the stomach and chest with a large knife. A policeman was given 10 seconds to say they believed Eddie died quickly. The reporter then followed up with information from a police source who suggested the attacker was out of control.

In the *Spotlight* office, Mac glowed with satisfaction as he watched the news reports on all channels.

We're killing the other bastards with content.

Richard Templeton had played an important role in that success. He was delegated the job of Solomon – deciding how the vision and story was to be shared between the news and current affairs departments. *Spotlight* was a major part of the story now – Kim had 'found' the latest victim and photos – yet, they couldn't hold all the good stuff for their broadcast.

This was where the news maxim of catching your viewers at the start of the evening worked. If viewers knew there was a big story brewing – and there were ample news promos across TV, radio, the station website and various social media – they expected to get the information at the top of the news.

If *Spotlight* played hardball, and kept all the juicy details for their program, there was a chance of losing that audience to another channel. The executives had to find a balance between providing good information during the news, while whetting the appetite for more on *Spotlight*. And here it was:

> 'We'd hoped to talk to *Spotlight* reporter Kim Prescott about her horrific discovery of the body here this afternoon. However, she has been assisting police with information on Eddie Malone and the pictures he was about to hand over.
>
> 'I can reveal that Kim has been told she'll be available to talk to *Spotlight* tonight. That exclusive story with the woman who discovered the body – and the pictures that could hold the key to this murder investigation – can be seen here in about 20 minutes.'

That was the best promo of the day for *Spotlight*. What viewer was going to switch to another channel once they had been promised almost an eyewitness account to murder – and pictures of a gang rape?

Now they had to deliver on that promise.

Chapter 50

The *Spotlight* office was calm. The scripts were laid out and allocated with just a couple of story durations to be pencilled in as the items were finished. Mac, Curly and Templeton sat at the command post as the clock over the desk nudged closer to their opening titles.

There was always a tingle of nerves beneath the surface, even for the longest-serving veterans. Sod's Law had tripped up many media productions when least expected.

'We all set with our reports, Curly?' Mac asked for the tenth time.

'Yep, Pete's story didn't need a lot of tidying up. I got the editor to insert some overlay and the Volendam picture to identify passengers. The backgrounder on Eddie Malone is almost done. The Melbourne cops are keen to calm fears about a frenzied knifeman chopping up former European tourists, so that's still a live cross.

'We've got the report with four still-living tour passengers and how they're shocked by it all. They're champing at the bit to say they always thought Tugga's Mob were a bunch of scumbags. 'Plus—'

Curly interrupted himself to check the desk monitor with a live feed from the murder scene. He was relieved to see Kim in front of the camera and adjusting her ear piece, as she prepared to do a sound check for the studio.

'Our new reporter is ready for her close-up, Mr DeMille.'

They chuckled. Everyone understood how important this cross was, for the program and Kim's career. Her appearance was the result of Mac's hard work – a mixture of years in the business, good police contacts and the ability to play hardball when necessary. The cops understood they could have requested her *assistance* far beyond the program deadline. However, they knew it wasn't worthwhile pissing off the media on the biggest scoop of their biggest story.

Curly waved a hand to indicate he was scooting up to the studio to offer some last-minute advice and encouragement for Kim.

Templeton leant in to make a confession. 'You know, Mac, in all of today's pandemonium, I forgot to do something.'

Mac grinned at him. 'Nothing too drastic I hope. Nothing to spoil our golden week?' He wasn't unduly worried; not even Templeton could ruin his evening. After all, they had the best story in town and it was a few minutes away from being broadcast.

'I don't think so. I think Hackett has to take some responsibility.'

Mac twigged instantly. 'Oh mate. You didn't get to tell him about Eddie's murder and that we got the rape pictures?'

'Nope. Hackett scarpered soon after Reg gave him his marching orders. That was embarrassing enough, but apparently there was another shock waiting for him in the garage. The body guard had switched cars. There was no fancy BMW to drive home, just an anonymous Ford to fool a potential assassin.'

A big smile spread across Mac's face. 'So, the Hatchet's sitting at home with his gun-happy Special Forces man learning about Eddie's murder for the first time?'

'I'm afraid so, Mac.' Templeton tried to look contrite while struggling to contain a grin.

Mac was a fair confessor. 'Well, your *mea culpa* is noted, boss, and your penance is a slab of beer and three bottles of red.'

Templeton had learned there was an expensive downside to being at the top of the current affairs hierarchy. But with Hackett out of action, and too scared to talk to anyone in the department, Templeton could at least claim the latest celebration on expenses.

'Mind you,' Mac said, as he stood up to make one final check in the edit suites, 'I wouldn't fancy being in Hackett's home right now. I reckon the missus might overpower the bodyguard to grab his gun and shoot Hackett in the gonads.'

Chapter 51

The Hackett's Tuscan villa wasn't a battleground with a bullet-riddled godfather – yet. Marianne found her voice after the news reporter signed off in Geelong with a promise of more startling revelations about Tugga's Mob.

'How could you do this to us, Andrew?' Marianne wailed. 'Our family name is being dragged through the mud – and all because of your philandering.'

Hackett was exasperated.

Does she care more about what her friends think than my life?

The killer was escalating, no longer trying to disguise his deeds as accidents. But was he still a target, anyway? The guy had gone after Eddie Malone for christsake; he wasn't even part of Tugga's Mob. Surely that might be good news for Hackett.

The media talked about a gang rape in Amsterdam – which didn't involve him. He was out for the count after that final night of drinking, partying and space cakes. He couldn't have performed – even at 25 – if his life depended on it.

Plus, Hackett knew he wasn't a rapist. He and Judy had been friends with benefits until the end of the tour.

Marianne wouldn't listen to his case so Hackett turned his attention to the silent jury of Ferdy and Mitch. The news and sport droned in the background as the countdown to the start of *Spotlight* ticked closer.

Ferdy dutifully listened to Hackett's argument about being spared by the killer, while Mitch was preoccupied with a call on his mobile.

'That sounds logical – to me. But I'm not the killer. He's the one working to his own plan. I don't know what to think after seeing your tour bus driver dead on his own doorstep.'

Hackett was crestfallen. *Does my best mate doubt my word as well?*

'I still believe in you,' Ferdy rushed to assure him. 'I know you're not the kind of man to rape a woman. The problem is, this killer has his own agenda – or hit list – and we don't know if you're on it. I think you need more protection than just Mitch.'

That stunned Hackett. Extra protection? It still wasn't the cost, it was the realisation that the changes to his life and business could be long-lasting. Could even perhaps threaten his marriage.

Mitch finished his phone call and stepped in front of the television. He demanded everyone's attention, as did the pistol now openly displayed in his shoulder holster.

'Ferdy's right on several points and possibly off the mark on another. Firstly, you do need extra protection. I have no doubt about that after the murder in Geelong today. The killer is out of control and, in my opinion, rushing to a conclusion.

'I can arrange more guards. I spoke to a few of my colleagues and they can be here within the next couple of hours – if you agree to our terms and price. It would be around-the-clock protection where you do what we say, when we say.

'If you don't want that, you can ask the police for protection. I don't know what the chances of that would be, or their level of commitment. It could be armed officers in the house with you, a car parked outside, or the occasional patrol car drive-by.'

Mitch knew he undersold the level of police commitment to protect endangered citizens. But *this* situation was his business and Mitch and his former special forces mates were experienced. They'd never lost a client – and didn't intend to. He had one more jolt for this client.

'I agree with Ferdy that the killer has their own agenda. But I disagree about his assumption of the killer's gender.'

Hackett nodded along with Mitch's sales pitch, almost ready to sign on any dotted line. Men with big guns sounded better than a lunatic with a big knife.

'What do you mean by gender? Surely the killer is a man. What woman would chop Eddie to pieces like that? It was so callous and vicious.'

Mitch gave Hackett a few seconds to ponder the shortcomings of his assumption.

'We never assume in our business and expect to stay alive, or protect our clients. If you eliminate one gender without proof, you remove a lot of potential suspects. You, and we, could let our guard down at the wrong time. And believe me, women are just as capable of wielding a knife. And they can hate and be psychotic.'

Mitch watched his client pale at that implication. Hackett would need to be careful of every stranger until the culprit was caught.

'I'm not saying this killer is a woman, but I'm warning you that you have to keep an open mind.'

Mitch turned to the television and noticed the weather segment at the end of the news was about to finish. *Melbourne Spotlight* was 30 seconds away.

'Look, let's see what *Spotlight* has to say and perhaps that might help your decision. My guys aren't far away and they're all good, experienced and dedicated blokes. I trust them with my life. We will all be here to help – if you want it.'

Hackett and Marianne sat down again, their glasses topped up with more alcohol by Ferdy, while Mitch sipped from a bottle of spring water. The newscast finished and the *Spotlight* titles transitioned through to the host, Todd Waterman, who looked grave and trustworthy.

'Thank you for joining us on what has been another shocking day of revelations in the Tugga's Mob saga.

'As you know, *Spotlight* broke the story by linking an increasing number of mysterious deaths to a bus tour of Europe in 1986. Each day we have brought you more exclusives as the jigsaw is slowly pieced together.

'Now there is a sixth victim, and this time the killer made no attempt to disguise the crime. It was a brutal death for Eddie Malone.

'You know from the news that it was our crew, Kim Prescott and Ken Withers, who found the body of the former tour driver.

'Eddie Malone was butchered – the killer stabbed him at least 15 times – and then left to die in a pool of blood on his own doorstep. We believe our crew missed the killer by just a few minutes – perhaps even seconds.

'Kim Prescott spent the afternoon with police helping them with their investigation into a killer who appears to be losing control. The first four murders were cold and calculating; the latest death was the result of a frenzied attack.

'This program will do everything it can to help police capture this dangerous killer before anyone else falls victim to a manic attack.'

Hackett glanced around at the other three viewers in his home and noticed that Marianne and Ferdy were nodding their heads. But the stern reassurance from the current affairs presenter didn't do much to ease Hackett's growing anxiety. His hand shook as he swallowed another healthy gulp of gin. It didn't calm him, as he expected the reporter was about to provide a chilling account of Eddie's last moments.

Chapter 52

Todd Waterman handed the baton to Kim Prescott, who stood nodding at the camera waiting to speak. She was poised and confident.

'Yes Todd, it was shocking to find Eddie Malone was stabbed to death just moments before we knocked on his door.'

Kim tilted her head slightly over her right shoulder, drawing attention to the same driveway view that was shown during the newscast. Kim's words had more impact for the ghoulish; she was, after all, the woman who walked into the grisly murder scene.

'Spotlight's first contact with Eddie came this morning when he rang to offer explosive new evidence about Tugga's Mob.
'We arranged to meet Eddie, here at his home, to record his story and verify that evidence. Barely 70 minutes later Eddie was stabbed to death.
'We have to ask how the killer knew that Eddie was about to talk to the media? And why was he silenced so brutally?'

Kim had no answers to those questions, but she did have what the audience wanted: a guided tour of a murder scene.

'There wasn't a soul around when camera operator, Ken Withers, and I walked down the driveway and under the carport to reach Eddie Malone's front door.'

That was the cue for the studio director to play Ken's first pictures from the scene, over Kim's narration. Mac's suggestion to hide the disc in the camera car had worked. The pictures were relayed to *Spotlight* three hours before police finished with the crew.

Ken used his experience to ensure the *Spotlight* footage was more dramatic than the news coverage. He recorded it from Kim's point of view as she approached the door. The vision of the body and stab wounds was blurred to conform to news ethics and standards. But the digital masking couldn't hide the savagery of a frenzied knife attack. The bloody wounds from the 15 thrusts filled television screens as Kim's story unfolded.

> 'You can probably imagine our shock after we eased through the narrow space around Eddie's 1988 Ford station wagon to find him butchered in the doorway.
>
> 'We admit our first instinct was to run. Had the murder happened just seconds ago? Were our own lives at risk? Was the killer lurking inside the door, ready to lash out if cornered?
>
> 'We knew this was connected to the Tugga's Mob story – but this time the killer didn't disguise their handiwork as an accident.
>
> 'We retreated to the driveway for a few moments to gather our wits.

In step with the narrative, the vision swung from Eddie Malone to the ground and became shaky as the camera operator and reporter ran from the murder scene.

Kim then reappeared on camera in the live shot.

> 'However, despite the obvious wounds, we thought there might be a chance to save Eddie Malone. We had to return and check.'

The camera once again moved slowly towards the doorway. This time it was the viewers' point of view: the living room and kitchen were small, untidy and empty. A turn to the left revealed a bedroom entrance... Was the killer hiding inside?

A peek around the door – a messy double bed, scattered clothes on the floor and no cupboards or anywhere else for a lurking murderer to hide. Viewers were taken to a tiny bathroom with a grimy shower and toilet. Nothing else. Then it was a careful backtrack to the body to avoid a pool of blood.

Then the 'appearance' of a hand reaching out to the victim's throat – checking for a pulse.

Kim's narration flowed seamlessly as she watched the vision on a monitor at her feet. It was professional and measured, not glorying in the fact that this was one of the most graphic crime reports broadcast by their channel.

> 'Eddie Malone was still warm to the touch but we established he was dead and no emergency treatment could revive him.'

Kim paused her commentary until the director cut away from the vision of Eddie and returned to her live shot.

> 'At that point, we knew we had to perform our duty and notify the authorities immediately – starting with the police.'

The production crew in the *Spotlight* office and studio watched Kim's star performance with admiration; her first live cross and she was nailing it. Mac and Curly had their fingers crossed the police never requested Kim's phone records to verify the timeline.

Kim had delivered on the first part of her performance, walking the audience through a real crime scene with a fresh body. Now it was time to change gears and introduce the rape evidence.

Earlier that afternoon the pictures caused a heated discussion between the news and current affairs production crews and their executive producers. Both teams knew they were ratings winners if suitably promoted.

However, Templeton – with Mac at his back – held firm: they belonged to *Spotlight*. News would be allowed to mention them and use them in future broadcasts, but not until after *Spotlight's* fourth exclusive in a row. The news crew grumbled but understood that possession was the law of the news jungle.

Back on screen, Kim segued to the spoils of that newsroom battle.

'Now, the reason we were going to interview Eddie Malone was because he claimed to have pictures from Tugga's Mob's final night on their European tour. He wanted to sell them to *Spotlight*.

'There are two pictures and both would normally be classified as pornographic. They show sexual activities between members of the tour group. There are three people in the pictures and they are all now dead – two of them killed in the past week.

'We don't know how they came into Eddie Malone's possession, as that was something we hoped to clarify this afternoon.

'We do believe the pictures could be crucial in the Tugga's Mob investigation and therefore, despite their graphic nature, our executives believe it is necessary to broadcast them to help viewers understand.'

The studio director inserted the picture of Tugga and Judy into the live feed. It was the moment much of Victoria was waiting for. But if they expected XXX rated porn, they were disappointed; standards had to be applied – along with judicious pixilation.

'You are looking at a digitally treated picture of Tugga Tancred and Judy Williams in Amsterdam in 1986. It is explicit and, until this morning, Eddie Malone said he believed it was a consensual act.

'We now know that interpretation was wrong – and that Judy Williams, who mysteriously drowned a year after the tour, was most likely the victim of a gang rape by Tugga's Mob.

'By *all* of Tugga's Mob.'

Mac knew Kim's incredible performance would swiftly elevate her to frontline reporting duties on any number of news channels. However, he felt a pang of guilt about the identification of Judy Williams as a rape victim.

The fact that she'd been dead for almost three decades had swung the decision in favour of showing her face. He had no qualms about letting the audience know that Tugga Tancred was a rapist. Mac tuned back in to Kim's monologue as the on-screen picture changed to the image of Judy and Helen, again suitably doctored for 6.30pm tastes and standards.

'It is the second picture that clearly reveals what is taking place. Judy Williams appears to be comatose. She was at the mercy of Tugga's Mob after a last tour party that involved her first use of cannabis-laced food, more commonly known as space cakes.

'Many of the passengers were in similar condition from a mixture of alcohol and drugs.

'Eddie Malone told *Spotlight* – while trying to negotiate the sale of these pictures – that Tugga Tancred assured him Judy Williams agreed to the group sex. Tugga claimed that Judy was a willing party to a gang bang.'

The camera cut back to Kim who showed no sign of tiring as she spelled out the case against Tugga's Mob.

'We found that hard to believe. Judy is known to have had intimate relations during the tour – on her terms. But on that final night, Judy Williams was incapable of deciding about consent.

'We have reported this week that Tugga Tancred was stalking Judy during the tour. Judy complained to the tour guide – Eddie Malone – about this sexual harassment. Yet, Eddie did nothing.

'And, on a night when most of his passengers were so drug-affected they had to be carried from Amsterdam's Red Light District to the bus, Eddie chose to believe Tugga Tancred's story about what happened.

'We were appalled by Eddie Malone's inaction, but to give him some credit he was prepared to verify these pictures and pass them to the police for their investigation. He most likely had them in hand when he answered the door to his killer this afternoon.

'We saw those pictures lying on the concrete and recorded them. We felt it would give the *Spotlight* audience a better insight into what happened on a cursed European trip in 1986.

'Back to you in the studio, Todd.'

It wouldn't have been good form to give Kim Prescott a round of applause for her compelling report about the death of Eddie Malone and the gang rape of Judy Williams, but there were several murmurings of 'well done.' That was high praise. Everyone on the news and *Spotlight* crews knew it would be the benchmark for the rest of Kim's career.

Mac exhaled a sigh of relief that their punt on an untested presenter paid off. He couldn't dwell too long on those feelings as *Spotlight's* frontman then introduced Pete Benson's report from New Zealand.

Mac injected some irony into that introduction; the people who had the motivation for revenge against Tugga's Mob had the best alibi in the world – the New Zealand police. Mac knew it was time to bring Benson and Dugal home from the Shaky Isles. The Langers were in the clear and the Harvey and Daly families would never talk to *Spotlight* again after the rape accusations.

They'll talk to everyone else – but not us.

Spotlight continued to play on the television in South Yarra, but Hackett was focused on other associated matters: calling in reinforcements.

'I don't care how many men you need, Mitch, or what it costs, make sure we're safe.'

Hackett turned to Marianne. 'I swear I had nothing to do with any of that. But some lunatic probably believes I did and we can't afford the risk, or I'll end up like Eddie Malone.'

Chapter 53

Amy Stewart massaged her right forearm as she watched *Spotlight's* final segment from an executive suite that overlooked Southern Cross Railway Station. Slender fingers rubbed anti-inflammatory cream into surprisingly tender muscles.

Who would have thought that stabbing someone could be so exhausting? It had felt effortless to plunge the knife repeatedly into Eddie Malone. He didn't fight back, merely stayed on his knees and mewled.

Amy had rammed the blade into Eddie's flesh until she could no longer hold him upright. She was panting from the exertion as she watched him gasp for breath; and it took almost two minutes for him to die. It was dangerous to wait, but she was too exultant to walk away until the job was finished.

Amy used a tissue to wipe the ointment from her fingers and reached for a cup of peppermint tea. *Spotlight* was ending with a summary of the six days since Tugga's death plunge off the Great Ocean Road. It was old news to Amy, even though it was the first night she had watched the current affairs program.

The 29-year-old was amused by Kim Prescott's story about almost walking into a murder. The reporter wasn't even close. Eddie was dead by 12.53pm and Amy was on the road to Melbourne by the time the media made their skittish entry.

It wasn't the first time that Amy had killed. She didn't feel guilty about any of her victims; they all deserved to die. If anything, Amy felt empowered with each act of retribution. Most had involved months of research and planning. The death sentences were carried out when there was little chance of the crime being detected. Ironically the first and most recent victims broke that pattern of careful preparation. The first was spontaneous, the second was instinctive – opportunities were presented, and Amy had acted.

Amy didn't realise she could take a life – and feel no remorse. She had punished six evil people and never felt a moment of shame or regret. The world was a better place without them.

Her transformation from respectable school teacher to killer began 16 months earlier. It was the most turbulent year in Amy's life.

A comfortable, affluent existence in one of Auckland's most prosperous and well-to-do suburbs couldn't prepare Amy for a series of traumatic events. It started with the loss of her elderly parents within a few months of each other. Beth and Mark Stewart were a loving and generous couple who were devoted to each other through 61 years of marriage. They adored and doted on Amy who they described as their 'surprise bundle of joy'.

'You were the little miracle I always prayed for, but never expected,' Beth told Amy at least once a month during her pre-teen years. Beth would even declare her love when Amy's friends were around.

'Mum! I know you and Dad love me – and I love you. But Rebecca and Erin think it's a bit weird that you keep telling me all the time.'

Beth had laughed and promised to make her future declarations more discreet.

Mark passed away first, aged 82. Dementia rapidly destroyed a powerful intellect while the end was caused by pneumonia. Beth pined for her soul mate from the day he was admitted to hospital, and died in her sleep from a heart attack in March 2015, two months later.

Amy barely coped with organising two funerals for the most important people in her life. Her parents had been her shield against life's calamities for almost three decades. Without their protection, the tears flowed frequently from one burial to the next, and beyond. It was a meeting with the family lawyer, however, that totally shattered Amy's world.

'Mark and Beth left this letter for you to read after *both* had passed away. It is separate from their wills, which have provided generously for your future. I have no idea what this letter contains. All I can tell you is that Mark gave it to me two years ago, not long after the first signs of his dementia became evident.'

The lawyer, who had looked after the Stewarts' affairs for almost 30 years, then left the room to allow Amy some privacy. That act filled Amy with dread. If their lawyer didn't know – or want to know – what on earth was in the letter; how bad could it be? Tentatively Amy opened it.

Dearest Amy
This is the hardest thing that Beth and I have ever had to do. First, please be assured that you were the most precious gift in our lives and that we loved you dearly. We cherished every day that we shared with you.

As you now know, my senior moments were much more than absentmindedness. Senility has been creeping up on me for a few years and, sadly, I will one day lose control of important faculties, such as speech.

It is that fear of incoherent ramblings which prompts this final message to you, our darling. Beth and I are both worried that I might inadvertently say something which would cause you great pain. Something that you would feel compelled to follow up.

Our great fear is that I might allude to a secret that Beth and I have kept for your entire life.

We love you more than any parents could – but we are not your natural parents. You were adopted. Please forgive us for not telling you sooner. We wanted to, but your adoption was not secured by the traditional process.

Our own efforts to start a family failed and we had long given up hope. Then an opportunity presented itself. A mother needed a good home for her infant – you. It was risky, but we jumped at the chance to care for a child; one who would finally make us a family.

As you grew, we worried if we told you about your adoption a slip of the tongue might cause legal problems. We didn't want to risk losing you. By the time you were in your teens we didn't have the heart to destroy your illusions, or ours. We were a family who loved each other dearly and we didn't want to jeopardise that.

If it comes to pass that both of us have died without the family secret being revealed, we can only apologise for any pain and anxiety this revelation causes. You have a right to know about your origins. Selfishly, we couldn't bring ourselves to tell you.

This has been a difficult letter to write and it feels awkward to say one final farewell. We loved you like our own flesh and blood and hope you swiftly get over the shock and enjoy a wonderful life.

All our love

Mum and Dad.

Amy shoved the letter into her handbag and fled the law firm without an explanation. Her red-rimmed eyes were the lawyer's only clue that the letter was devastating.

It was a revelation that Amy never contemplated. Life with Mum and Dad had been happy; there was no innate sense of difference to ever even consider they weren't her natural parents.

Physically there was enough similarity and personality traits with the older Stewarts to never question her birth. Beth had been blonde and so was Amy. Mark was a successful Auckland businessman who semi-retired while Amy was at primary school. He maintained a handful of company directorships to retain contacts with lifelong friends. It left him more time to help Beth look after Amy. They were always available for school events, sporting activities and holidays. Every school break would launch them on new excursions, initially around New Zealand and Australia.

As Amy progressed to secondary school the holidays took them further – to Europe, Asia, North America and other cultures that broadened the mind of an intelligent young woman. They were exciting and magnificent journeys that helped shape Amy's future as a school teacher. Her expertise was in physical education and outdoor recreation. However, a passion for art history – nurtured during trips to the Louvre in Paris and the Uffizi in Florence – encouraged Amy to teach optional classes to enthusiastic students at a prominent private school.

Mark's death and Beth's swift decline saw Amy take extended leave to look after the only woman she had called Mum. Amy moved from her waterside apartment in the city to the family's 120-year-old villa in Remuera. Yet, the close bond between mother and daughter couldn't stop nature, or grief, claiming the second important person in Amy's life.

The blows came too fast for Amy. Mark and Beth gone and then the real bombshell – they weren't her birth parents. Instead of returning to work, and the comfortable and familiar routines of school life, Amy extended her leave of absence. She was a valued member of staff, popular with students and colleagues, and the principal allowed her time to regain some equilibrium.

The Stewart family home sat high on the northern slopes of Remuera and was built to frame expansive views towards Rangitoto Island and the Hauraki Gulf. It was worth at least six million dollars on a booming Auckland property market, yet Amy couldn't contemplate its sale. It was an anchor to a settled and privileged life.

But her parents' parting revelation had caused great turmoil. Eternally grateful to have been loved and cared for by such wonderful people, Amy couldn't avoid a tinge of annoyance they hadn't overcome their fears to talk about the adoption.

Naturally Amy would have wanted to know more about her birth mother, but she would never have given up Mark and Beth. She just wished they had trusted her to weigh all the information and make a wise decision.

From an ordered existence, Amy's genteel life unravelled in a matter of months. Initially she struggled to deal with feelings of loss, until the adoption revelation shifted her brooding in other directions.

Who *was* her real mother? Was she anything like Amy?

Amy wasn't vain, but enough men had called her beautiful over the years to make her believe she was an attractive woman. But, did she get her looks from her mother, or her father? There was nothing in the letter to point Amy in the direction of either birth parent.

Why did both parents desert her? That made her angry. A big

rock had been dropped in her pond and there was no life-buoy, nothing to stabilise her emotions.

Amy decided a trip to the Coromandel Peninsula might ease some of the angst. The family spent several Christmas holidays in a rented bach at Opito Bay, one of the Coromandel's jewels. The long, sandy beach and turquoise water was always full of fizz boats, launches, game fishers, jet skis and families during January and early February. A steady stream of tractors hauled boats to and from the water's edge and kids perched on the towed vessels to avoid the hot sand or bitumen. Scallops and snapper were the staple fare when the fishing was good. Those were fun times for Amy who easily made friends with other children gathered on the swimming pontoon 100 metres from shore.

Amy was drawn back to Opito Bay as an adult, during breaks from university and her teaching career. The bay was a relaxed destination after a three-hour journey from the City of Sails. There was usually a mandatory stop at Kuaotunu – scrumptious wood-fired pizza and massive ice-cream cones – before the final dusty few kilometres into Opito Bay. Amy had added a 4.8 metre sea kayak to her sporting inventory while at university. She spent hours paddling around dozens of islands that were under Department of Conservation protection.

That was Amy's destination in April as she reduced speed in her Toyota Rav 4 near the Maramarua Golf Club on State Highway 2. It was a notorious accident black spot with impatient motorists causing carnage in their eagerness to get to, or from, coastal resorts. Amy had driven the road on dozens of occasions, her mind gradually casting off the cares of city-living as the green fields and hills worked their magic on her soul. It was while she glanced at those familiar paddocks that Amy registered a small white sign directly opposite the golf course. It had probably been there for years. But it was only recent events that made the message on the sign resonate with Amy: *Adopt. They'll live to thank you.*

Amy passed by too quickly to note if there was any link to an anti-abortion group, or a church. It didn't matter because it was the message alone that was important, and which made her shiver. Amy understood, for the first time, the difficult decision her birth mother had faced – adoption or termination. She reached a safe area to park the car before being overwhelmed. The tears flowed freely for more than half an hour, occasionally wiped away with a handful of tissues.

The mother she had never met had faced a momentous decision – life or death – and Amy was incredibly thankful about the choice that was made. It was cathartic. She would be forever grateful to Mark and Beth for raising her as their own child, bestowing more love, care and attention than she could ever have wished for. The feelings of abandonment and anger that had clogged her brain for weeks were brushed aside. And Amy felt an urgent need to find – and thank – her birth mother.

She was tempted to turn the car for home and start that quest immediately. Eventually she eased back onto the highway and rejoined the traffic heading to the Coromandel Peninsula. The road trip was already stimulating. A few more days in the peace of Opito Bay would provide more clarity. The soul-searching continued as Amy paddled her kayak and enjoyed fresh seafood. She returned to Auckland after four days with a new focus.

Chapter 54

In theory, there was nothing standing in Amy's way, but in practical terms, she didn't know how to find her birth mother. Amy tried her birth certificate, which was required for several passports over the years. Mark always handled that part of the family's business, so Amy had never seen the paperwork. Sadly, it provided no help when Amy found a copy, as the document listed Beth and Mark as her parents. Was it a real birth certificate – or fake?

She knew her father had extensive business contacts and wondered if he bribed someone to make the document. Their final letter via the lawyer hadn't provided any clues. There were no living relatives of Mark or Beth to approach either. They had both grown up as only children. Many of the family's elderly friends had also succumbed to illness and death over recent years so Amy couldn't expect any help from that direction.

The only clue was provided by her place of birth: Palmerston North. The family lived in Auckland. Mark and Beth said her birth in the lower North Island city was an unexpected *early* arrival during a business trip. Amy accepted that without question but now there were doubts. Was Palmerston North an excursion to collect a baby outside the adoption system?

That option looked increasingly likely and Amy realised she was out of her depth. A Google search revealed many private investigators who promised discreet services in the adoption sector.

They had the skills and experience and Amy had the money so it was logical to engage a professional firm. The results were delivered in a private meeting with the rather sombre investigator, Brian Phillips, in the middle of May.

'We have successfully completed our investigation, Ms Stewart,' Phillips pushed a folder towards Amy. 'Your birth mother was Judy Williams, from Te Awamutu. She was single. We haven't been able to identify your father.'

Amy ignored the private investigator and stared at the folder. Judy Williams. A name, something tangible at last! She pulled the report closer, eager to open it and read more about her mother's life. Good manners made her look at Phillips again. His expression was still grave. Amy's stomach clenched.

'What is it Mr Phillips? You don't look as thrilled as I feel. Is there something wrong with my mother? Is she in prison or something?' Amy had no idea where that notion suddenly sprang from. 'Or is it worse?'

'I'm afraid your birth mother is dead. She drowned in the local river in 1987.'

Amy went numb. The birth mother she'd only recently learned about had been dead since she was a baby. After the expectations and hopes of the previous weeks, the discovery was another crushing blow.

Amy's next question was barely more than a whisper. 'What can you tell me about her death? What happened?'

'I've read the coroner's report on her death and he ruled it an accidental drowning. There was a local newspaper report on her death. It quoted former friends who said Judy Williams had changed since returning from London. They said she was aloof and uncommunicative. Looking at the timeline for your birth, the adoption and her death – it could be argued that she was suffering from post-natal depression.

'There is some positive news. I've tracked down contact details for Judy's sister – your aunt. Heather Langer and her son, Jason, live at the old Williams homestead in Te Awamutu.'

Amy refused to cry. She already shed enough tears that year, and she was determined to reclaim her composure. She wrote a cheque, picked up the report and left the office with a polite, 'Thank you.'

The investigator's report was dumped in a desk at the Remuera villa. Not so easy to file were the questions that swirled through Amy's mind during the previous weeks. The negativity of abandonment at birth had given way to curiosity. Could Amy form a bond with her birth mother? Was her father still around? Would it be practical for her mother to move into the large Auckland villa – with her?

Hopes and dreams that were dashed and buried in Amy's antique roll-top desk, alongside Heather Langer's phone number. It was her birth mother Amy wanted to meet, not her aunt. That family reunion could wait.

Chapter 55

That latest disappointment was the catalyst for an out-of-character drinking bout, one with devastating consequences. She enjoyed a couple of wines with dinner and friends. A favourite treat was Mark's traditional summer brunch Bloody Mary; the tomato juice freshly crushed from his own vegetable patch. It was rare that Amy drank to excess. When colleagues from school over-indulged at end of term celebrations, it was Amy who made sure they made it safely home with sober drivers, or via taxi. Occasionally she would even hide car keys to protect innocent road users from the momentarily irresponsible.

The news about Judy's death sent Amy to the Auckland waterfront at Mission Bay. It was a popular destination for walkers as Tamaki Drive offered inspiring views of Waitemata Harbour. A late-afternoon power walk was her plan; she hoped the sea air would be a balm. Auckland's fickle weather, however, rained off that possibility, so Amy retreated to a bar overlooking the beachfront to sip a sauvignon blanc and wait for the sun. It didn't reappear. Instead, the drizzle turned into a downpour that emptied the beach and walkway. Despite the rain, Amy's mood improved as she was drawn into conversations with other refugees from the deluge.

Several hours drifted past with various people moving in and out of the loose circle of drinkers. A few packets of nuts and potato chips appeared on the table and were devoured ravenously. The mood was relaxed for a Thursday evening and Amy knew she was getting tipsy.

Why not? It's good to meet some new people.

One new friend was a handsome male in his mid-30s. James was keen to learn more about Amy. He was charming, well-mannered, witty and solicitous. James showed a lot of empathy for Amy's year of misfortune which emerged during more wines than Amy bothered to count. By nine o'clock Amy felt the effects. She found herself swaying on the way back from the ladies and knew the car would remain parked by the beach for the evening.

James courteously offered her a ride home, and Amy felt comfortable enough to accept as he'd already explained he lived on Remuera Road, close to her villa. It was only a few kilometres from the beach.

The sea air and the last drink, bought by James, slammed Amy like a rugby scrum as she left the bar. James had to carry her to his Audi A6, which was parked nearby. Amy was confused.

I've had more than I normally would, but I never get this legless.

The rest of the evening faded away. Her next conscious thought was waking in her bed the next morning. She was naked and felt disoriented and sore. A hot shower was always the best remedy for a muddled mind and she stumbled through to the bathroom.

Ten minutes later Amy was towelling her hair and realised she couldn't remember anything beyond reaching James' car. He was good looking and had been polite at the bar, but Amy would never invite a man to her bed within hours of meeting him. Yet, she couldn't escape the impression there had been a sexual encounter. There was no actual memory of it – and there was no sign of James; nothing that indicated he'd been inside her home.

The bed was a tangle, but that also wasn't unusual as Amy endured many restless nights.

Amy heard acquaintances describe similar experiences of waking up dazed and unable to remember events from the previous night. Two women believed they were assaulted while under the influence of the date-rape drug, Rohypnol. But they had no proof.

Shit! Is that what happened to me? Was I raped by James?

All doubts were eliminated when Amy retrieved her mobile phone. She noticed immediately it wasn't in the usual pocket inside her handbag. It was on top of all the usual paraphernalia, something Amy would never do. She smashed an iPhone the previous summer when her handbag contents spilled on to the road. Ever since then, Amy had been diligent about using the compartment.

Amy went straight to the picture gallery as a feeling of dread crept upon her. Her fears were confirmed.

No, no, no. Why did he do this?

Her phone contained 12 pictures of herself – all naked.

Amy's stomach lurched, but she fought the urge to run to the bathroom. In every picture Amy's eyes were closed. Anyone else would assume she was simply asleep; only two people knew that she was drugged.

James – you're a filthy fucking rapist!

Amy's anger grew like a Pacific cyclone, gathering strength with every hour as she sought something physical to vent that fury upon.

I was raped – and that animal thought he could have the last laugh.

She understood that controlling their victims was at the core of a rapist's psyche. The naked pictures were James' way of reminding Amy how easily she had been violated in her own home, her own bed.

Amy knew there was no proof to connect James to any crime. In her befuddled state she had unwittingly washed away all possible evidence that would identify her rapist. There was no housemate at the villa who could have seen James. The people at the bar were also strangers, drawn in by Auckland's stormy weather.

If I found them again, what would they say anyway; that I was happily chatting to a handsome guy?

Even the mobile phone wouldn't help. Amy had swiped through all the pictures taken by James. Her own prints would have smudged any evidence he might have left on the phone.

I bet you wiped every surface you touched as well, you bastard.

There was one thing Amy became certain of – she was not his first victim. James had done this before. He was too slick for this to have been his debut sexual assault. She recalled his attentive nature and the polite conversation that, in retrospect, hadn't revealed much about himself. He was generous, prepared to buy top-shelf wines or cocktails.

Easier to slip me a roofie – or whatever knockout drug you use?

Amy was furious that she'd fallen into a classic trap. There were extenuating circumstances: Amy was upset by a third death in her *family*, and a rapist exploited that vulnerability.

Bugger that.

She rechannelled her fury into the fact that there were men in the world like James.

She was determined the act would not go unpunished.

No tears this time. Amy Steward would have her revenge.

Chapter 56

Firstly, Amy had to find James, if indeed that was his real name. The clothing, the car, the smooth manner all indicated he was from a privileged and professional background. No doubt he lied about living in Remuera. Amy hadn't seen him in the cafes or shops around the upmarket village.

No, you wouldn't shit on your own doorstep.

Amy thought Mission Bay or the nearby suburbs of Kohimarama and St Heliers were more likely his home turf.

Amy didn't want her friends to know about the rape, so it became a personal crusade to find James. She began to frequent trendy bars she guessed might be his hunting ground, but drank only mineral water.

It was a simple plan to find him, but it was flawed. Amy was a tall, slender, attractive woman with shoulder-length blonde hair. She could never blend into the background. A constant stream of eager male suitors was given short shrift as she remained alert for her prey. Her amateur approach yielded no sign of James.

Her first stroke of luck came via a community newspaper. Amy usually discarded it after a quick flick through the first few pages. But in July it produced a breakthrough: a picture of real estate developers at a media conference to promote a new project in the Bays. There, in the middle of the group of five smiling men, was James, aka Jamie Baxter.

It took Amy no time to find more details about his business and family connections. Jamie was married to a leading interior designer.

A rapist and a cheating husband. You really are scum.

Jamie's company had a website which provided glowing references about his real estate projects and, most importantly, a mobile phone number.

Amy spent a day working on a plan. Her goal was to hurt Jamie and make sure he never raped another woman. That meant getting close to him. It would be repugnant, but necessary. Her tactic to blindside Jamie was to appeal to his vanity: the unsuspecting victim would offer herself to the rapist for a rematch.

That would be such an ego boost to a bastard like him.

Scheming was new to Amy; she'd certainly never plotted to ruin someone's life. But it was justified and that helped her prepare for the first part of the ploy – arranging a *date* with the rapist, she allegedly 'remembered' as a nice guy on a rainy day. Amy fidgeted with her mobile for 10 minutes before taking the plunge.

James answered after three rings. 'Jamie Baxter. How can I make your day?'

Amy's first challenge was to keep him talking. She didn't want him to hang up once she identified herself. One swipe of Jamie's thumb and the plan would be finished. She had to be courageous.

'Hi Jamie. I'm a sexy blonde who owes you an apology.'

Jamie laughed. 'I like the sound of that. Why would a lovely lady be saying sorry to my humble self?'

Careful not to grit her teeth, as that would make her voice tense, Amy tried for sultry instead. 'We met in May and went back to my Remuera villa for some sexy fun.'

It was a gamble to reveal the location so early, but she pressed on, hoping Jamie's curiosity and lust would keep him on the line. 'But I was so drunk that I can't recall much of the play. I looked like a zombie in those pictures that I posed for, so I'm hoping we both enjoyed it before I flaked out. I'd really love to find out how good you are in the sack. I'll promise to be sober this time.'

It took a few seconds for the response. 'Um, you're–?'

'Oh my God. Have you forgotten me already? Was I that bad?'

Jamie laughed. 'No, no. It's Amy, right? You really don't remember anything about that night?'

'Sadly, no, which is most unusual for *moi*. When I drag a hot male home the whole neighbourhood knows about it. Looks like I've blown my sexy minx reputation.'

'We'll have to do something about that,' he said. 'I've got a couple of nights free this week – shall we meet at your place?'

The location was another challenge for Amy. She didn't want a rapist to soil her home again. Jamie was married, so his house was out of the question. She gambled that Jamie had other options.

'I'd love to, but I have family over from Australia for a few weeks. I thought that, as you're a big real estate mogul, you might have a spare penthouse tucked away for discreet fun and games.'

'Not exactly, Amy. But I've got a mate who's away in Europe for a few months. He has a lovely apartment on Remuera Road which he allows me to use. We could meet there at eight o'clock tomorrow night. How does that suit you?'

Amy's hand tightened on the mobile. She kept her voice calm. 'Sounds super. I can promise you a night we'll both remember.'

The gambit worked. Jamie couldn't pass up an opportunity where the unwitting rape victim was begging him for more sex. He didn't even ask how Amy had tracked him down. She wanted to confirm the location and hang up, but there was still some groundwork to finish.

'Do you feel like being a bit adventurous for our second meeting? Are you into role play, Jamie?'

'I can be if it appeals – what do you have in mind?'

'I have an alter ego who can be even naughtier than me. You won't have to do much – just play along and expect the unexpected! Ciao Jamie.'

Jamie's love nest was 800 metres from Amy's home. It was an apartment on the seventh floor of a plush tower block. She had driven or walked past the building hundreds of times.

Amy's plan was straightforward: to publicly expose Jamie as a rapist. It would be the ultimate humiliation for a high-profile businessman. He might avoid a criminal conviction, but Jamie would forever be condemned in the court of public opinion. Amy intended to spike Jamie's drink, the same way he had incapacitated her.

While he was unconscious, she would strip him and use her lipstick to scrawl *Rapist* across every part of his body. Then, using his own mobile phone, she would take pictures and post them to all his contacts, followed by every social media website she could think of. She doubted Jamie would ever reveal who had beaten him at his own game.

The next day Amy approached the rendezvous on foot, although she left her villa 10 minutes earlier in her RAV 4. She'd undergone a transformation from blonde to brunette but didn't want to risk being recognised on busy Remuera Road as she entered the apartment building provocatively dressed. Nor did she want to alarm her elderly neighbours, who always noticed when she left the house. She was surprised how easily she adapted to the subterfuge and morphed from a respectable school teacher to a saucy femme fatale.

As she hadn't been able to obtain any Rohypnol she was resorting to the sleeping tablets prescribed following the deaths of her parents. Amy was aware she was winging it. She had to get the drugs into Jamie and then stay out of his reach until they took effect. One tablet usually knocked her out in 20 minutes; so she ground eight pills to dust and hoped they'd lay Jamie flat in half that time.

Jamie wasn't impressed to find a brunette at his doorstep.

'Amy? What happened to the blonde hair?'

'Hidden away for my little role play.' Amy had to get inside the apartment or her plan would be ruined. 'But I can get rid of the wig if it annoys you.'

'It might be a good idea.' Jamie swung the door wide and ushered Amy inside. He pointed along a hallway. 'There's a bathroom down there. Ditch the wig and tidy yourself up again. We'll have a drink and then get into it.'

Amy worked hard to hide her anger. There was no sign of charming Jamie from Mission Bay and this wasn't a romantic encounter for him, it was purely sexual. Jamie wanted to get straight to the dirty business. Amy barely took in details of the luxurious apartment as she rushed to the bathroom. It was going to be tougher than she anticipated.

She eased off the wig and squashed it into her handbag. But she couldn't find her hair brush. The dark granite tiles, the wide shower-head and the timber cabinetry under the stone vanity indicated it was a male's bathroom. She hoped his grooming habits extended to a spare hair brush. She pulled open a drawer and found shaving cream, razors, moisturiser and deodorant. She tried the next drawer and gasped. It held three boxes of condoms and a packet of Rohypnol.

Was it Jamie's supply? Or was his friend another scumbag?

Amy didn't waste time speculating. She retrieved four tablets and slipped them into the same container as her crushed sleeping pills.

Jamie was on the balcony when Amy reached the living room. She noticed, for the first time, that he was dressed in dark slacks and a white business shirt. The rest of the view was impressive. Lights from the North Shore and the east coast bays bookended the dark mass of Rangitoto Island and the harbour.

'There's some white wine in the fridge, help yourself. And get me another rum and coke while you're at it.'

Amy swallowed her bile, took Jamie's glass and walked to the kitchen.

'This is a fabulous apartment,' she said, as she prepared the requested drink and then dumped in all the drugs. She swirled the glass contents out of Jamie's sight and waited for the powder and tablets to dissolve.

'Did your company build it?' She added crushed ice from the freezer to hide the residue.

'No, unfortunately we couldn't get that deal. But we've done better stuff. This has the views, but our developments are classier – more glamorous than these old Remuera apartments.'

Amy wanted to keep Jamie's mind off sex for as long as possible. She returned to the balcony with the drinks.

'I think I need to catch up to you, Jamie. Bottoms up.' Amy drained her glass in one swallow, and smiled.

It was a challenge Jamie couldn't refuse. He downed the spirit and mixer just as quickly – and gasped. 'Christ Amy, you mix a mean drink. I don't want to be as legless as you were last time. How much did you put in?'

'A piddling amount.' Amy smiled again, more seductively. Her glass contained water, Jamie's was 70 per cent rum and sedatives.

'Come on big boy, you can keep up with me.' She reached for Jamie's glass, but he pulled it away.

'I'll make the next round. You enjoy the view for a few moments. We can take the drinks through to the bedroom. Forget about your idea of role play – I have to get home by 11, so let's not waste any more time.'

Amy tried not to panic as she watched Jamie replenish the drinks in the kitchen. His movements were steady, no sign of the Rohypnol or the other drugs kicking in.

'The guest bedroom's off the hallway. I'm going to the toilet, you bring the drinks with you.'

Jamie brushed the door frame as he left the kitchen.

Was that the first sign?

Her brain worked frantically for another delaying tactic. She stayed outside. A minute ticked by, then two. She heard Jamie slam the bathroom door. There was a thump in the hallway. Amy didn't dare investigate.

Jamie returned to the lounge a minute later looking woozy. His shirt was undone, his shoes were gone, his fly open. He looked at Amy and finally twigged something was amiss.

'You fucking bitch! You've spiked my drink.' He stumbled a few steps forwards.

'That's bloody rich coming from you. You're about to get a taste of your own medicine. You're nothing but a filthy rapist, Jamie Baxter – and I'm going to show the world.'

Jamie lunged towards Amy on the balcony. He had no co-ordination; his feet wouldn't go where he wanted. Amy easily stepped inside the lumbering charge and swung her right elbow into Jamie's temple. It felt really good.

Jamie was staggered by the blow and his upper body fell back against the railing, the fight draining from him. Amy's next move was instinctive. She swiftly bent down, lifted his legs and tipped him off the seventh-floor balcony.

It was so bloody easy.

Jamie's height and the low railing worked in her favour. His torso and flailing arms disappeared, then his legs and shoes. Jamie was so stunned he didn't even scream before he smashed head first onto the tennis court below.

Amy remembered every detail of that fatal plunge as if it were the previous night – not 16 months ago. She walked over to the sink of the Melbourne executive suite and washed the tea cup.

Amy Stewart hadn't intended to kill Jamie that night. The arrogant rapist put himself in a vulnerable position and she simply delivered the coup de grace.

How many innocent women did her actions save? Many, probably.

Did Amy have any regrets at the time, or since? Not one.

Jamie Baxter was wicked and had to be stopped from hurting other women.

To Amy it was logical – evil people had to be punished. And she was more than comfortable with her role as an avenging angel.

Chapter 57

The program debrief in the *Spotlight* office on Thursday night was like an AFL Grand Final celebration. The beer and wine fridge emptied rapidly as the production crew talked ten to the dozen about another amazing day in the Tugga's Mob saga.

A fifth murder, the rape pictures, the killer dropping all pretence of disguising the deaths as accidents: this was out of control, yet *Spotlight* had produced award-winning current affairs stories.

Everyone agreed Kim's on-air debut at the murder scene in Geelong was outstanding. Eddie Malone garnered little sympathy. The sleaze-bag wanted to profit from a rape victim he should have protected.

The noise level in the production area was boosted by journos and camera crews from the news department who had sniffed out the drinks session. The rowdiness forced Mac, Curly and Templeton to huddle around the phone in the executive producer's office to talk to Pete Benson. Jo lurked by the door, ready to pedal away to prepare new travel arrangements. Benson was disappointed about the early recall, but philosophical.

'It's a pity, guys. We wanted to get over to Coromandel tomorrow to get pictures of the site where Gerry Daly was shunted off his bicycle.'

Mac nodded. The pictures of the bush road would be handy, but the story had moved way beyond the Coromandel murder scene.

'I know, Pete, but we can't justify you enjoying the rain in the Shaky Isles while the killer is in our backyard.'

'Besides, the Harvey and Daly families are unlikely to talk to us,' Curly supported his senior producer's decision. 'Not after we've called their fathers rapists. We've already got a hysterical email from Drew's daughter. The other news crews are begging them for comment about our allegations.'

'Fair enough, guys. The foreign correspondent lifestyle was cool while it lasted. Get Jo to email us the flight details and try not to make it too early. '

'Enjoy it while you can, mate,' Mac cut in. 'Have a good meal and a few brews on us tonight. And remember to bring the receipts back.'

'Shall do, Mac. I can see Dugal has his eye on an expensive Otago pinot noir.'

They all laughed. Dugal Cameron considered anything over $10 for a bottle of wine extravagant.

Benson then brought the Melbourne bosses back to earth. 'So, where do you go with the story tomorrow?'

It was an open question to the three senior *Spotlight* men, but Mac nodded at Curly to respond.

'I was hoping to sleep on that, Pete. This story is moving so quickly. We started the day with the rape pictures as our lead story and a few hours later we get another murder.

'How often does a news crew find their interview talent dead on the doorstep? It's getting crazy.' Curly rubbed a hand over the stubble on his head.

'We've never encountered anything like this in our careers. Everyone responded superbly to make an incredible program, but it could be like this again tomorrow – especially if the killer is escalating.'

It was that statement which clarified *Spotlight's* focus for Friday. The killer was in Victoria, possibly in Melbourne. The last surviving member of Tugga's Mob was living a few km from the studio. Would the killer try to get Hackett as soon as possible, or would the intense scrutiny of police and the media scare them away?

Either way, Hackett was their next story – and it would be another exclusive. Was The Hatchet a hunted man; or a haunted man?

Eddie cleared him of involvement in the rape of Judy Williams. Would getting that message out to the killer spare his life? The Hatchet's innocence – albeit by the unconfirmed report from a dead man – would be *Spotlight's* leverage for getting the final target back on camera.

And Curly knew where that interview had to be.

'The Hatchet's the story now. He's the last man standing and he's *our* man.'

Mac and Templeton nodded at the assessment.

'And we must talk to him live, at home, surrounded by his hired guns. The desperate television executive trying to exonerate himself to a crazed killer.'

Mac broke into a sweat as he visualised their boss begging for his life under the glare of television lights in prime time. He looked at Templeton.

'Are you up for it, boss? You've had Hackett on the ropes for the last couple of days. If Reg gives his blessing, are you ready for the championship round tomorrow night?'

Templeton smiled broadly. 'Too bloody right I am, Mac. I'll call Reg now and get things underway. I think you can lock it in.'

Templeton picked up the phone and punched the speed dial for his father-in-law. No TV station chief executive could say no to a guaranteed ratings winner.

Mac and Curly left their executive producer to make the arrangements. They headed for the fridge in the vain hope some beer might have survived. It was Mac who voiced the thought that was on both their minds.

'Do you think this nutter – if he finds out Hackett is going live tomorrow night – do you reckon he might have a go at him? While we're on air?'

Chapter 58

If a crow flew nor' west from where Curly pondered Mac's dream/ nightmare scenario, in a matter of minutes it could land on the roof of the killer's apartment building.

Like most people following the story of Tugga's Mob, the *Spotlight* crew had made the wrong assumption about the killer's gender.

Amy Stewart had a takeaway meal of rice and beef with black bean sauce steaming on the granite bench in front of her. She nibbled at the meal in between tapping away on a laptop. It was opened to the email service she shared with her aunt, Heather Langer. The draft function was their *chat* connection, with each message followed by a reply. By avoiding the save or send key they believed no electronic record of their conversations would be kept if they deleted everything when logging out.

They weren't experts in electronic subterfuge, but hoped they never aroused enough suspicion to encourage computer forensics experts to delve deep enough to test their theory. They certainly didn't want police to learn the current conversation: the fate of Andreas, aka Andrew Hackett.

I drove past his house last night and spotted an armed guard.
Andreas reacted quickly to these media reports, so I went to plan B. I trailed Malone to a public telephone and overheard him talking to a Spotlight journalist. I had to act quickly as I didn't want him getting a

talent fee or revealing too much on camera. I didn't know anything about his pictures until I saw the show tonight. Hackett's likely to increase his protection now so I'm wondering what to do.

Amy took another bite from her meal and waited for Heather to reply. It came within a few minutes.

You have done a wonderful job so far. The police here don't suspect us anymore and you're not on anyone's radar. They still believe a man is responsible. I'm inclined to let Andreas stew for a while. He'll eventually reduce the security and probably dispense with them altogether. Our final dish will be colder, but it will still taste just as good. Come home and relax for a while. It will be good to talk again in person.

Amy put down her fork and replied to Heather's message. She had planned to return to Auckland late the following week: mission accomplished. But it made sense to postpone the final act of revenge. Hackett wasn't going to escape their wrath; his death would just be delayed.

I agree. I'll rearrange my flights and return this weekend. I'll let you know when I'm back and we can discuss the future. xxx

Amy cleared the draft page after five minutes then logged out of the email account. She resumed the meal, her appetite impervious to the bloody scene she caused at Eddie Malone's flat seven hours previously and the coverage it'd been given on the TV.

She'd scrubbed and dumped the gloves and clothing in rubbish bins across west Melbourne. Experience taught Amy how to prepare better for each new mission of revenge. The death toll stood at six: Jamie, Drew, Gerry, Tugga, Helen and Eddie. Only Andreas remained to be dealt with and that should be the end of her vendetta.

Amy sometimes wondered why the deaths didn't weigh on her conscience. A year ago she was a devoted school teacher who would never raise a hand to a troublemaker in class. It was abhorrent to even consider. Teenage girls liked to push her buttons, but she acknowledged it was part of being an adolescent. They were naughty, not cruel or evil like Jamie, Eddie and Tugga's Mob.

In their case, Amy was driven by an overwhelming compulsion for the kind of retribution that society could never deliver.

Her mind wasn't totally peaceful as she finished her meal in the Melbourne apartment. There was a niggle of concern that the media had linked the Tugga's Mob victims to her birth mother.

While it had already raised the question of motive for Judy's family, Eddie's murder in Geelong that afternoon provided the perfect cover for Heather and Jason, as they were on the other side of the Tasman.

Amy, however, had no alibi. Not that the police or those pesky reporters even knew of her existence; let alone her connection to Judy. Yet.

Only one other person, apart from the Langers, knew Judy was Amy's mother. Would the private investigator, Brian Phillips, who found Judy's details and the surviving sister, remember the names? She hoped he had so many similar cases the names all blurred together?

If he did make the connection between Amy and Judy, was there an ethical obligation not to volunteer client information? Amy didn't raise her concern about the investigator with Heather. If he became a risk, Amy would deal with him.

She opened the airline's web page to change her flight bookings to the next day. With that completed she sprawled on a chaise longue to consider her achievements over the past year.

Was it so wrong that each death filled her with pride?

She believed her bad luck had turned after the death of Jamie. She was never implicated in his fall from the balcony. It was dark, and no one saw her tip him over the edge. His body wasn't discovered until the next morning and Amy was careful to remove any signs of her presence in the apartment. Auckland police suspected he'd arranged a sexual liaison with a woman. However, there was no video evidence as – fortuitously – the security system in the foyer was broken that week. There was DNA from numerous people in the apartment. But police decided it would be too difficult to trace as the owner was a popular multi-millionaire bachelor. Jamie's family was aware of his philandering habits and wanted the matter dealt with discreetly. It was convenient for them to have the police decide that Jamie *fell* from the balcony while drinking alone.

Amy never experienced a moment's regret over Jamie's death. He was properly punished for being an evil bastard. Detectives put a lid on the case by the start of spring which boosted Amy's spirits. It encouraged her to address the other elephant in her room – Heather Langer – Judy's sister.

Chapter 59

Amy's first phone call to the Waikato home where her mother once lived was tentative. Heather was stunned to hear from Amy – the niece given away at birth – but she quickly overcame the shock and arranged a meeting. That family reunion was stressful as neither woman knew what to expect. Heather was the first to cry as she opened the farm house door.

'Oh, you look just like Judy!'

Tears rolled down Amy's cheeks too. She couldn't speak.

'You're taller than your mother, but your blonde hair, the blue eyes, and your smile – everything about you reminds me of Judy before she jetted off to explore the world.' Heather opened her arms. 'Welcome home, Amy.'

The pair embraced and cried for many minutes before entering the house. The stress evaporated as Heather revealed a family history Amy never suspected she was a part of. Heather fondly recalled Judy's long-held dream of touring Europe and working in the United Kingdom. Amy listened intently as Judy was brought back to life by her own sister. The pregnancy during – or after – the tour was a shock to both sisters. There was an embarrassing moment when Heather admitted that Judy couldn't identify the father. The sisters understood the pregnancy would be distressing for conservative farming parents. The stigma of a child born out of wedlock – and without a father – in rural New Zealand in the 1980s would be socially embarrassing. Therefore, they decided Judy should give birth in Palmerston North and put the infant up for adoption. Judy would then have two options: she would be free to resume her travels in Europe, or, if that no longer appealed, she could make an *early* return from London. The secret of the pregnancy would remain safe on Heather and Bert's property. Manawatu was only a few hours south of Waikato, but friends and family never made surprise visits.

Heather explained how she met Mark and Beth Stewart during the last weeks of Judy's pregnancy. The couple were passing through Palmerston North on holiday, destined for a fishing lodge in the Marlborough Sounds. Heather was in town with Jason for a scheduled visit with the Plunket nurse.

Was it serendipity that took Heather and her child into the same café as the Stewarts as rain poured down outside? Beth made a fuss of Jason and the ensuing conversation flowed into the biggest disappointment of their married life – the inability to have children.

Judy had yet to start formal preparations for the adoption process, but meeting the Stewart's gave Heather an idea. Could the friendly Auckland couple provide a better home for the newborn? Judy was anxious about handing her baby over to an unknown future in the state adoption system. Would a private adoption offer Judy some reassurance her baby would go to good parents?

Everything about the Stewarts was encouraging for Heather. They were an affluent and mature couple with a young outlook. They ticked all the boxes Heather would want to find in prospective adoptive parents. She took a gamble on her sister's behalf – did the Stewarts want a baby?

Mark and Beth were stunned by Heather's proposal. It was illegal, but they didn't say no. It was agreed the next step should be a meeting with Judy. That went perfectly as Judy was charmed by the potential parents. The soul-searching continued over the next week in Manawatu and the South Island until the Stewarts returned. A happy consensus was reached – Judy's baby would go to the them.

Mark said he could handle the paperwork. However, there was a condition: the Stewarts didn't want to risk further contact between baby and mother. They argued it was important for legal reasons as bribes would have to be paid to get the correct documentation. Mark had arranged a 12-month transfer to Wellington with his employer, to put distance between the two families. And as cover for Beth 'becoming a mother'.

Everything fell into place over the following weeks. Judy had a trouble-free home birth, in June 1987, supervised by a moonlighting midwife in need of extra cash. Five days later Beth and Mark Stewart arrived in the New Zealand capital with their daughter, Amy.

Grown-up Amy was relieved to hear the story about her adoption. Yes, she had been given away by her mother. But she hadn't been dumped without a care. Judy wanted to ensure her child would have good parents and a stable life. It was heart-warming to learn she loved her as much as Mark and Beth.

She was also convinced her mother would eventually have ignored the non-contact clause and searched for her daughter if cruel circumstances hadn't intervened.

What Amy yearned for were pictures of her mother. What did she look like? Did they really look so much alike, as Heather had claimed?

Heather retrieved two photo albums from a sideboard.

'These pictures were taken during the summer before Judy flew to Europe. She was 25 then, four years younger than you are now.' Heather pushed the first album towards Amy.

The front cover was headlined – *Judy 1986*. Amy eagerly flipped it over. She gasped. Judy, dressed in a white tennis skirt and posing with a trophy, smiled at her from the past.

Tears welled as she stared intently at her mother's face. It was almost like looking at herself: same blonde hair, although the styles were 30 years apart, same eyes, same cheekbones and chin. Because of her age in the photo, Judy could've been mistaken, by anyone comparing the two women now, for Amy's younger sister. They weren't doppelgängers, but were enough alike to prove they were mother and daughter.

There were four pictures on the first page, all taken at a tennis court. An action shot taken at the net indicated Judy was athletic and shorter than her daughter. Amy wondered if her height – 179 cms – came from her unknown father.

Amy lost track of time as she turned the pages in the album. Her mother had loved sport just like she did. The tennis photos were followed by ones at netball games, where Judy looked poised and determined – a tough competitor.

There were many group photos of Judy and her friends. The last dozen shots were farewell parties. Judy looked so full of life as she prepared for her biggest adventure.

Heather then pushed the second album across to Amy. 'These are of Judy when she was younger. There are photos from our school days, pony club, girl guides and dozens of other activities. We were always busy with the farm, but Mum and Dad made sure to take photos on important occasions.'

Amy smiled. 'No digital cameras or selfies in those days.'

Heather laughed and left Amy to examine the pictures as she prepared a fresh pot of tea.

Amy was pleased to see that her mother enjoyed a happy childhood, like her own. There were birthday parties and Christmas celebrations. Judy and Heather always smiled naturally in the photos which indicated they were comfortable as siblings.

What would it have been like to have shared a special occasion with her birth mother?

But something was missing from the photo collection.

'What about Judy's trip to Europe? I don't see any photos here. Surely she would have taken dozens of pictures of her big OE?'

Heather nodded, but her smile faded. 'By the time Judy reached our farm in Manawatu she didn't want to think or talk about Europe. Her focus was on the pregnancy and what we should do about the baby. She was exhausted after you were born. Then her emotions went haywire for a few weeks after you left with the Stewarts. She wanted to come back here to Waikato. I thought it was too soon, but she insisted. I never saw her again.'

The mood had turned sombre and Amy didn't know what to say. Heather left the room, returning a minute later with a small wooden box.

'Judy kept a diary of her trip.' Heather lifted it out, still wrapped in a silk cloth. Other objects rattled inside the box.

'She also took 11 rolls of film. I couldn't bring myself to have them developed.' Heather picked several numbered canisters from the box and placed them beside the diary.

Amy stared at them – a treasure trove of her mother's life – and then at Heather. 'You never read the diary either, did you? Why not?'

Heather's chin quivered. 'I just couldn't bring myself to do it. Judy tucked that box away as soon as she got home. *She* didn't want to be reminded of the adventures that had to be left behind in Europe. I had a feeling there might've been another reason why she never had them developed immediately. But Judy barely talked about her travels. She said the films could wait until after the baby was born. She believed they would help her decide whether to go back to London, or stick with life in Te Awamutu.'

'So, Judy brought these back to the homestead herself, but never did anything about them?'

'Yeah. I found them a few weeks after she died. Mum was too upset to tidy up Judy's room, so it became my job. I found the box in her cupboard but couldn't... Until now.'

Should Judy's diary remain untouched, unread? That was the dilemma that faced the two women. Amy assumed the temptation for Heather wasn't as strong, as the diary had been out of sight and mind for almost three decades.

Amy's desire was more compelling. Her mother's most intimate thoughts and adventures – in the lead up to getting pregnant with her – were sitting on the table in front of her. She desperately wanted to learn more. She settled the issue by unwrapping the silk to reveal the brightly decorated diary, for the first time in nearly 30 years.

She looked at Heather, who nodded and edged her chair closer.

They read the first 15 pages, thrilled by Judy's excited impressions of London, Paris and other European destinations. They learned the tour operator didn't live up to promises in their travel brochure, but Judy was having the time of her life regardless.

The first mention of the unwanted attention from a guy called Tugga Tancred, a fellow Kiwi, made Amy annoyed.

'What an arsehole. Bloody men, they're the same in any decade.'

The next couple of references to Tugga's 'mob' made Heather uneasy.

When a mantle clock chimed six o'clock, Amy was startled and surprised so much time had passed.

'Damn, I've got an engagement party for a friend in Auckland tonight. I don't want to stop reading, but I have to be there as I'm one of her bridesmaids. Could I take this with me?'

Heather covered her niece's hand with her own. 'Maybe not tonight, Amy. Now that I'm finally reading it, I don't want to stop either. Perhaps you can come back and visit.'

Chapter 60

Curiosity overtook trepidation. Heather was annoyed she had avoided the diary for so many years. She now couldn't rest until she read every page. The travel account revealed the momentous changes in her sister's life but also left Heather with many questions. The name of Amy's father wasn't identified which made Heather wonder, probably as her sister had, whether he was a fellow bus passenger or one of her casual local encounters.

The sketchy details of Tugga's stalking and the wild last night in Amsterdam made Heather feel queasy.

How did you get back to camp? Who looked after you, Judy?

She realised the undeveloped films might fill in the crucial gaps.

But could the pictures even be developed? They were so old. A Google search reassured Heather; there were five Waikato companies which dealt with *forgotten* moments in time.

But she didn't want to give the films to a local business to develop. Rural communities have too many connections. The last thing Heather wanted was for a member of the Bridge Club to ask why she was getting Judy's travel snaps processed after all these years.

It took three hours on the internet, a shopping trip to Auckland and handiwork with a hammer and timber to rig a temporary dark room. The first pictures of Judy's 1986 adventure enchanted Heather. The rolls number one to ten revealed the exotic icons and places Judy had so pined for during her teenage years: the Eiffel Tower, the Arc de Triomphe, Versailles, the Colosseum, Pompeii, the Parthenon, Neuschwanstein Castle and dozens more. In between were the fun snaps with Judy's travel companions – holding up the leaning tower of Pisa and parasailing on Corfu.

Heather's tears were of joy and absolute grief as she wished she'd shared this experience with her sister back in 1987.

After 245 prints Heather was kicking herself for being paranoid about what the diary hadn't said; and convinced the photos would explain things. Her instincts about what might have happened to Judy near the end on the tour must have been off kilter.

Then print number 246 went into the chemical bath. It chilled Heather.

Print 247 sickened her.

There were only a few more negatives to print, so she pressed on through tears of grief. When they were completed and hung to dry Heather stumbled from the dark room and vomited on the grass outside the shed.

Her sixth sense was correct. Heather had just developed evidence of a 29-year-old crime – the gang rape of her sister.

Jason returned to the farm to find his distraught mother on the ground. Heather was too numb to speak, so Jason fetched a cold towel from the house and a small medicinal brandy. When he went into the shed to get a chair he noticed the impromptu structure. He hesitantly pushed aside a heavy dark curtain and was confronted by the source of his mother's anguish – naked pictures of his Aunt Judy and four strangers having sex.

It was obvious to Jason that his aunt was not a willing participant. Judy looked comatose. And the man who figured in most of the pictures was massive, bigger than any All Black prop.

Heather filled her son in on what the diary had contained. She broke down in tears as she talked about the awful photos.

Jason cried too, knowing this agonising situation was about to get worse. He helped his mother inside where he finally shared Jockey Graham's pub confession.

'I didn't know what to think, Mum. I thought Jockey was just really pissed, and rambling after his big race win. Part of me believed him, because who the hell would make up a story like that? And why, after all these years? But I also thought maybe he didn't really know what he'd seen that day; or wasn't recalling it right. Years of drinking scrambles a man's memory. Either way, I didn't want to drop it on you, Mum, when I had this farm course coming up.'

The Langers understood the significance of Jockey's revelation. The conundrum for Heather and Jason was how much they should shared with Amy.

'We've just found her after almost 30 years, Jason. I don't want to lose her again by showing photos of her mother being raped by a bunch of animals. It would break her heart, like it's broken ours.

'I wish you'd been here to meet her the other day. She was thrilled to see the old pictures of Judy in the albums and to hear about the dream trip. Amy was learning to love a mother she lost at birth. It would be devastating to tell her we've discovered Judy was the victim of two shocking crimes.'

Jason usually had the calm, even temperament of his late father, but he struggled to keep his anger in check.

'The giant that Jockey Graham saw drowning Judy *must* be that big bastard in the pictures. Everything about her death makes sense now.'

'Tugga Tancred,' Heather snarled. 'That was the bastard's name.'

Jason pointed at the incriminating photos that were now lying on the dining table. 'We have evidence of the crime, Mum. Those arseholes wanted to humiliate Judy so much they used her own camera to taunt her. They must've thought they got away with it for all these years. There must be justice for Aunt Judy, Mum. And Amy should be included in any decision we make. Amy's our family and she's been kept in the dark for too long.'

Heather was swayed by Jason's reasoning and invited Amy to the farm again on Saturday. The initial reunion had been nerve-racking; this second visit would be awful.

Jason agreed to let Heather talk to Amy alone. He greeted his cousin warmly when she arrived, and said he'd back after tending to the cows.

Heather had brewed a pot of Earl Grey, made and put out scones, jam and cream but they went untouched as she stoically told her niece the things she'd learnt since they first met.

Heather clutched Amy's hands as she explained the terrible crimes committed against their beautiful Judy; that she had been drugged and raped by a mob led by Tugga Tancred.

'Then Jason came home and found me and told me the horrifying story from Jockey Graham. We knew then, *we bloody know*, that this Tugga also murdered her.'

Amy's tears were tears of anger. 'Let me get this straight. This brute sexually harassed Judy all trip and nothing was done about it. No one lifted a finger to protect her – not even Andreas, who was her closest male companion on the tour?'

Heather nodded.

Amy ran an index finger over the cover of her mother's gaily decorated diary. The action looked casual, affectionate, but when she spoke there was a new intensity in Amy's voice.

'Judy – my mother – never realised what really happened that last night of the trip. Then a few weeks later she finds out she's pregnant. The two of you arrange for my birth back here in New Zealand, and my adoption by Mark and Beth.

'Soon after that Judy drowns in the river you both swam in as kids, in an incident labelled an accident with the hint of possible suicide. But now we know she was drowned by a *giant;* most likely bloody Tugga Tancred.'

Amy pushed the diary away, scattering the photographs.

'Those animals have to be punished, Heather! Tugga and his mob committed awful crimes against my mother, your sister. They're fucking evil – and we have to make them pay for what they did.'

Heather was chilled by the iciness in Amy's eyes. She couldn't say anything.

'Are you and Jason prepared to help me get justice for Judy? Because if you are, I have something else to tell you.'

Chapter 61

Air New Zealand's business class meal arrived soon after Amy's flight departed Melbourne for Auckland. She barely tasted it. Plane trips made her reflective; strapped into an A320 seat at 36,000 feet left only the mind free to roam. Amy was disappointed the Australian mission was aborted, but content with what she had achieved.

The main target – Tugga Tancred – was dead. So were Helen Franks and Eddie Malone.

Andrew Hackett could sweat for a while longer. Until that week she wasn't sure if he was one of the rapists or not. Now she regarded him as guilty as Eddie; worse perhaps because Judy had trusted 'Andreas'. The two men had known about Tugga's sexual harassment and did nothing to stop what ultimately led to Judy being brutalised. Amy believed Eddie and Hackett deserved the same fate as the rapists.

Heather and Jason's support had been crucial to what unfolded in the 12 months since they'd all learned the truth. Amy had waited a few weeks before returning to the Waikato farm to outline her quest for revenge.

In between, she'd cut all ties to her teaching job. Avenging her mother would require total freedom. Amy wanted justice, but didn't want to spend the rest of her life in prison. The death of Jamie, the Auckland rapist, showed it was possible to avoid a murder charge. But Jamie had been a spontaneous decision. Amy knew she was lucky the circumstances that night made it possible for police to treat his death as an accident. She was confident that with time, money and preparation she could adapt the same modus operandi to her crusade against Tugga's Mob.

Her mother's rapists – and the two men who could have prevented it – escaped justice for almost 30 years. That wasn't right.

But was it right for Judy's family, and more specifically Amy, to pass a death sentence on each of the guilty?

Amy made it clear, from the moment she outlined her plan to her new-found and only living relatives, that she would be the avenger. She wanted their support, understanding and, most of all, silence but she would carry out the sentences.

Amy had waited another week for Heather to make a decision and commit to the vendetta. It came via a phone call as Amy watched the network TV news in Remuera.

'I'm in Amy. I'll do whatever you need to get Tugga's Mob.'

'I'm so grateful Heather. I know it wasn't an easy decision to make.'

'I have to admit there have been a few sleepless nights this week. I want justice for Judy as much as you do. But what we're considering is so foreign to me. I was fifty-fifty until I saw the news tonight.'

Amy instantly recalled the news item that would have tipped the scales for Heather. 'That story about the rapist and murderer?'

'Yes.'

Amy had watched the same item and felt it vindicated her plan. The story was about the family of a murder victim. The rapist and killer of their daughter had served his prison sentence and been released back into the community after the first parole hearing. Within weeks, he was arrested for assaulting a new girlfriend during a drink and drugs-fuelled binge. He never made it to court to face the charges – he was stabbed to death by another prisoner in the remand centre. The families of both female victims were ecstatic – the scum would never harm another person.

'We can't count on the police or courts for justice, Heather. It's been 30 years since the crimes against Judy; there's no guarantee the police would even investigate let alone prosecute Tugga's Mob. And there'd be an army of smarmy lawyers to defend them. If we want retribution – like those families on the news item – we're going to have to do it ourselves.'

It hadn't take a week to get Jason's support. He'd agreed by phone two days after Amy's appeal for help.

'I hate bullies, Amy. Always have and always will. Tugga's Mob were the worst kind.'

Amy knew Jason was almost two metres tall and physically strong from the farm work. She took a punt his attitude stemmed from childhood experience.

'Were you bullied at school, Jason?'

'Yeah. Primary school was fine, but I was still small and weedy by the time I went to High School. The fourth formers made my life hell until I had a growth spurt the second year.'

'And what happened then?'

'You could say their reign of terror ended. I taught them never to bully anyone again.'

Amy laughed. 'Have you always been a champion for the underdog?'

'I think looking out for people is in my DNA. It's part of life in a farming community – we help each other. I was young when Dad died, but he and Mum were good role models. And now you're back as part of the family, I want to help you get justice for Aunt Judy.'

Amy felt obliged to warn him her revenge was way more serious than kicking the butts of schoolyard bullies. 'You understand the consequences here Jason, don't you? It could be us that ends up in court – not Tugga's Mob.'

'That would be bloody cruel, but there's no alternative. Tugga's Mob have to be punished. The local cops wouldn't have the balls to take this case to court. It's been too long since Judy was killed, and Jockey would never make a reliable witness. The lawyers would crucify him in the witness box as a pisshead and petty criminal. Besides, I'd be worried what the defence lawyers would say about the photos. Those smartarses would claim she was a willing participant.

'No, Amy, if there's going to be justice for your mum, it's going to be rough justice.'

Chapter 62

The Air New Zealand flight continued its steady course towards Auckland as Amy remembered the day their mission gained momentum. It was the discovery of Judy's copy of the Volendam picture. Amy found by chance when she dropped the box that held the diary for so many years. The felt base in the bottom flipped out to reveal the hidden photo. Judy had been more meticulous than most tour members; she included full names and home towns.

Tugga's Mob was finally identified, except for one elusive member. Judy's info for Andreas merely said: *selfish bastard!*

Amy and Heather spent the following weeks tracing Tugga, Drew, Gerry, Helen and Eddie. Often it was a collaborative effort at the Waikato farm. When Amy returned to Auckland there were evening updates over the phone. She was surprised to find Tugga's Mob scattered so far and wide. She didn't know if they remained friends, but the geographical locations made it unlikely.

Tugga was the first and easiest to track down thanks to his unique nickname and his business. The global reach of the internet leapt across the Tasman Sea to Tugga's new home in seconds.

Drew and Gerry had returned to New Zealand soon after the trip. That information came via their regional newspaper's online archive, which featured local adventurers. It also provided new career details which were also easy enough to follow, thanks to Facebook.

Helen and Eddie had led more itinerant lives. Again, the internet came to Amy and Heather's rescue with tutorials on tracing distant relatives, old friends, and, more importantly, those who didn't want to be found.

By March, Amy had the information required to activate her mission. Jason's practical mind proved invaluable with ideas for 'fatal accidents'. It was agreed he would scout the New Zealand targets and Amy the three in Australia – Tugga, Helen and Eddie. Andreas was known to be an Australian, but they still had no proper name or home city. But Amy had no doubts they would find him.

The 'accidents' began in August. Amy selected Drew Harvey as the first target for logistical reasons – Muriwai was a 40-minute drive from Auckland. Drew was known to be a regular mid-week fisher, in all conditions.

It was the end of winter and still cool enough for Amy to wear a neutral coloured, well-padded jacket. She had hand-sewn a small pocket into the right sleeve to carry the heavy metal bar that was used to bash Drew's skull. Luck was with her that day as the fishing was poor and no one else ventured out to the rock shelf. There was no suspicion from Drew either as a pretty blonde wandered over to see if he had caught anything. They chatted for 15 minutes before Amy dropped her cheap mobile phone onto a lower ledge, just above the tide. Drew played the gallant male, putting his fishing rod carefully aside before clambering down to retrieve it. As he straightened up, Amy swung the metal bar with all her strength.

Amy didn't have to worry about the blow being deflected by Drew's modified life jacket. He had insisted Amy put it on, if she was going to watch him fish. The blow knocked Drew unconscious and sent him into the sea. A wave slapped against the base of the rocks and retreated, taking Drew with it.

Amy waited for six more waves, and when there was no sign of him, she wrapped his jacket in her own and left the rock platform.

Jason was waiting for Amy in a farm utility packed with fishing rods.

'How did it go?'

'Not a problem. He leant me his own jacket. It made it easier to belt him in the head.'

'And you're okay?'

'Yep, it felt good, really good. I thought of Mum as I lifted the metal bar and that made it easy.'

Amy didn't tell Jason that she wanted to hit Drew again, and again, but he went into the sea too quickly.

Jason returned Amy to her Remuera home and drove to Te Awamutu where he destroyed the life jacket in a bonfire.

Chapter 63

A male passenger in the row ahead of Amy was snoring loudly until a pocket of turbulence startled him. The businessman called the stewards for a glass of red wine. Amy's thoughts returned to her second victim: Gerry Daly.

His execution was equally clinical thanks to Jason's groundwork. Her cousin established that Tugga's old mate enjoyed early morning cycle rides between his home near Whitianga and Whangapoua. Much of the road was winding and narrow. It was almost as if Gerry had a death wish.

His 'accident' was the easiest of the four to arrange. Amy bought a rusty Holden station wagon with front mounted bull bars from a dealer in Great South Road, Takanini. It cost less than a thousand dollars and the proprietor wasn't fussed about paperwork, not even asking for proper identification. Cash in hand settled the transaction quickly.

It took two drives of the Coromandel road to identify the best location for Gerry's accident. By late September, she was sitting in the car reading a map on a straight stretch about five km south of Kuaotunu as Gerry rode past. He was mid-50s, reasonably fit and rode at a good clip. There was no other traffic and the sun's first rays were peeping over the horizon.

Amy engaged the old column shift into first gear and followed Gerry along the road. Three km from Kuaotunu, where the road descended sharply through scrubby bush, Amy drove into Gerry's pushbike with all the speed her rust bucket could muster. She watched him fly over two white-painted low railings which wouldn't have saved a pre-schooler on a tricycle. Gerry smashed head-first into a tree and dropped out of sight. Amy was certain he was killed instantly.

Her pulse was barely elevated as she continued down the road and prepared for the two-hour trip back to the Bombay Hills, south of Auckland, where Jason waited with the RAV 4.

'Any problems?'

'No. Even easier than Drew. I just planted the foot on the accelerator and – bang – he went straight into a tree. The road was deserted so it will take them a while to find his body.'

'I can't see any fresh dents on the wagon – that's good – what about Gerry's bike?'

'It went over the side with him. I didn't stop to check, but I'm sure it slipped into the bushes and can't be seen from the road.'

Jason smiled and handed Amy her car keys. The burned-out Holden was found two weeks later in an industrial area south of the Northland city of Whangarei. Local police wrote it off as the work of joy-riders.

Chapter 64

Amy called for a glass of mineral water and a warm blanket from the plane stewards. Her throat was dry from the air conditioning. The blanket wasn't to help her sleep; it was to make her comfortable as she continued the re-assessment of her Australian handiwork.

An exploratory trip in Winter to prepare for Tugga, Helen and Eddie's accidents confirmed that Jason's assistance would be required. Tugga's clockwork weekend trips to Apollo Bay suggested Amy could employ the same hit-and-run tactic that was used to kill Gerry. Most people would assume it was about time the big piss-head finally ran off a cliff – few questions would be asked.

Jason's help was needed to buy a vehicle. Amy wanted an old ute like Tugga's – bull bars, battered and nondescript – with enough grunt to shove Tugga off the road at the right time. There were thousands of old utes throughout Australia but Amy was worried an attractive blonde buying an old car might be remembered if police ever connected the vehicle with Tugga's death.

A farmer like Jason on the other hand barely raised an eyebrow when he bought the Ford ute in Ballarat on October 24. Cash again avoided the paperwork while a handshake and wave goodbye sealed the deal.

Jason then left the vehicle at the long-term car park at Tullamarine. The keys were hidden in the tray of the ute and the parking ticket was tucked under the sun visor. Jason could've left the keys in the ignition, and the doors unlocked, as it was the last vehicle anyone would want to steal. With the Melbourne logistics under control, Jason flew to Sydney to prepare the way for Amy's arrival on Saturday.

Tugga's stop at the pub in Aireys Inlet almost ruined Amy's plan. For a few minutes she was worried he wouldn't reach the layby near Lorne that night. If Tugga started a fight because the barman wouldn't sell him a beer he'd get arrested.

Thankfully the bastard accepted the manager's warning about the pub inspector – the whole pub heard it – and retreated to the ute where he drank the last of the stubbies and went to sleep.

Amy settled down to wait. She desperately wanted to walk over and bash Tugga's brains in with a lump of wood, or a rock. That would have felt good, just like it had with Drew. But it would draw too much attention: a murder instead of an accidental death.

At 3.31am Tugga woke, climbed out of the ute and pissed against a tree. He rummaged in his work bag, for a spare key as it turned out, and a minute later Tugga was in the driver's seat and turning the ute onto the Great Ocean Road. There were no other cars and in a few minutes Tugga would reach Amy's 'accident' zone.

To smash into the rear of another vehicle and expect it to plummet off the Great Ocean Road sounded straightforward, in theory. But Amy knew the reality would be more challenging. She'd only get one opportunity to smack Tugga and make it look like an accident.

Amy and Jason hadn't wanted to leave anything to chance. In the weeks after Drew and Gerry's deaths the cousins practiced the Tugga-nudge scenario with two old cars on the Waikato farm. They couldn't recreate the Great Ocean Road but, over several days, Amy learned the most effective way to control the direction and momentum of the forward vehicle.

One curious neighbour rang Jason to question the 'unusual' noises from the Langer farm. Jason explained he and a mate wanted to enter a speedway demolition derby in Auckland, and were practicing in the spare field. That satisfied the neighbour and nothing more was said.

Those practice runs proved invaluable, as Tugga did not react as expected when Amy first made contact just before 4am. Tugga braked but, either through desperation or machismo, decided he could outrun his pursuer.

Jason, however, had chosen their vehicle well. Amy floored the V8 and hit Tugga's ute again. This time it was too late for Tugga to brake and he had no room to swing back onto the road. His ute smashed through the barrier and out of sight. Amy swung her wheel to the right and quickly reduced speed, barely avoiding a similar flight path to Tugga. The crash on the rocks below was swallowed by the noise of the pounding surf.

Amy stopped briefly at the entrance to Lorne, fighting the urge to go back and make sure the bastard was dead. She climbed out of her ute to stretch her legs and make a casual check of the vehicle for fresh damage. Even before tonight it looked like it had starring roles in every Mad Max movie. The new and slight dent in the bull bar and a chipped indicator covering could've happened at any time in the last 20 years. It shouldn't even be enough to interest a highway patrol. If it did, Amy would have to rely on a smile and a promise to fix things to escape further inquiries. The two-hour trip back to the long-term park at Tullamarine was uneventful. Amy wiped her finger prints from the ute, locked it and walked to the domestic terminal. The car could sit there for weeks before anyone noticed.

Amy flew to Sydney to complete preparations for the death of Helen Frank. This one required more finesse.

Chapter 65

Amy felt the Air New Zealand plane's nose dip as it started the descent into Auckland International Airport. She knew it would be a long approach, which left her time to consider the retribution for Helen Franks.

The short duration between Tugga's last drive and Helen's final hit was all because of the required product: heroin. Amy and Jason knew nothing about scoring Class A drugs, or anything beyond paracetamol products for a headache. And Heather's internet searches yielded information on heroin use, but nothing on where it could be bought. Their best hope was for Jason to trawl the seedy bars around Kings Cross. He was still shaken by the experience when Amy caught up with him on the Saturday evening after Tugga's death.

'Shit Amy, I've heard about Sydney's underbelly but that was scarier than I ever expected. There are a lot of weird and dangerous people out there. I didn't know if I was going to get the heroin – or a knife in the guts. I hope your plan works because I can't do that again.'

'I'm so grateful Jason. I knew it would be tough, but I thought they would rather make a deal than cause trouble. That's why I needed your help; I could never have dealt with those people.'

'It's done now. Here's a syringe and a bag of what I hope is heroin and not icing sugar. If it's not heroin, I'm sure it will do the job anyway. The rest of the junkie kit you can gather before meeting Helen. The sooner we get rid of this stuff the happier I'll be.'

Amy tried to arrange the meeting with Helen for Sunday evening. The online research by Amy and Heather revealed that Helen was a recovering drug addict and former prostitute. There were news articles about her noble attempts to rehabilitate other junkies.

So Amy decided to play the guilt card: Judy Williams had a baby daughter nine-months after the space cake party in Amsterdam. There was possibly more truth in that statement than Amy ever wanted to admit, although it nearly made her vomit to call what happened a *party*.

Helen had been rattled by the call and Amy's tale of woe: years of misery and degradation caused by the early death of her only parent; finding her mother's diary and deciding to track down old friends from a time when she'd obviously been happy.

Guilt won the day, although Helen couldn't meet until the Monday afternoon. The delay was a risk, as news of Tugga's death might be covered by media services in New South Wales. Amy spent an anxious Sunday by herself as Jason visited dairy farms near Wollongong to create his alibi.

One look at Amy made Helen suspicious she was being conned. The fresh-faced woman seated at the King's Cross café bore none of the hallmarks of a junkie, or a life on the game. Helen approached Amy's table but didn't sit.

'What stunt are you trying on? You won't get money out of me.'

Amy saw that her intended victim could walk out the door and be gone in a few seconds. She grabbed Helen's wrist.

'I know all about the gang-rape of my mother in Amsterdam.'

Amy didn't bother to glance around to see if her comment caused a stir. She guessed it wasn't likely to in King's Cross.

'Who said it was rape? It was 30 years ago – why are you trying to cause trouble now?'

'Because I found the pictures – my mother being raped by you and the rest of Tugga's Mob.'

Amy felt Helen sag. She pulled out a chair and the older woman slumped into it.

'I always knew that was a mistake with the cameras.'

'Cameras? There are more pictures of what you all did?'

Helen rested her elbows on the table and rubbed her head. 'Tugga got Drew and Gerry to take pictures on his camera. Then Tugga told them to snap a few on Judy's camera, for a laugh. I was stoned but I knew it might cause trouble – one day.'

Amy wanted to lash out; to smash her coffee cup into the old junkie's face. She controlled the rage as there was a plan. 'Tell me what happened.'

'It was all Tugga's idea. He had the hots for Judy all trip, but she wouldn't give him the time of day. I admit I fancied her too, but she brushed me off a couple of times. At least I knew when to stop.

'That last night in Amsterdam most of us were wasted; we'd been drinking, smoking grass and eating space cakes for hours. It was a shambles trying to get everyone back to the bus – Andreas was like a blob of jelly.

'But not Judy. She was high and wobbly on her feet, but still mobile. I remember her slowly walking through the camping ground, making sure she didn't trip over any pegs. About 10 minutes later Tugga dragged me over to her tent. She was naked and sprawled on a sleeping bag. She was rambling but not making much sense. Tugga said she was ready for a group fuck.'

Amy sat still as Helen paused for half a minute.

'If I hadn't been so pissed and high I might've hesitated. I was younger and a lot wilder and didn't stop to think – I followed the boys into the tent. If it's any consolation, I'm sorry for what happened.'

Helen stopped and drank her coffee, she wouldn't look at Amy who drummed the fingers of her left hand on the table.

Stick to the plan!

'When you say the boys – do you mean all of Tugga's Mob?'

'No. Andreas didn't take part. He'd been fucking Judy most of the trip and Drew and Gerry didn't want him to join in the final party. He'd crashed out by that stage anyway. I saw Eddie and one of the other guys dragging him to a tent.'

'Who was Andreas? I know many of you used nicknames on the

tour, but I'm sure at some stage you learned his real name and where he was from.'

Helen didn't question why Amy wanted his identity.

'His name was Andrew Hackett. He's done well for himself since then, old Andreas. On the trip he was a fun-loving party animal like the rest of us. Now he's a high-powered television executive in Melbourne. I've seen his name and picture in a few newspapers over the years – hobnobbing with the rich and famous.'

Amy was satisfied. Hackett's business profile would make him easy to track. She didn't want to hear any more about Amsterdam. The next step was luring Helen to a place where she could deliver the heroin overdose. Amy had scouted a quiet section of park in Rushcutters Bay in September. She believed the best way to get Helen to follow her there was to get her drunk and talking. It wasn't difficult to get alcohol into Helen as she swallowed cans of bourbon and cola like water. More of Helen's troubled life was revealed with every swallow. As darkness approached Helen was getting twitchy.

'I've got to get back to Wamberal – I hate Sydney. The fucking Cross almost killed me. I need to get to the train.'

Amy drank sparingly and was well under the drink-drive alcohol limit.

'I can take you if you like. My car is close and it's only an hour to the Central Coast. We can grab a few drinks for the road and you can tell me more about your work with recovering addicts. I'm not happy about what happened to my mother – but I can understand now that was all Tugga's fault. You must be so proud to turn your life around.'

Helen drank steadily as they drove north. Amy used the time to trawl through her memory for a new location to kill her passenger. Wamberal was close to Terrigal, which Amy knew from a summer holiday with the Stewarts 15 years before. Helen was way beyond tipsy from the extra alcohol and lack of food by the time they arrived.

Amy guided her victim between the rocks at the base of The Skillion with promises of more bourbon. Once settled, Amy slipped sleeping tablets into a can and watched Helen drink. Within 20 minutes Helen was unconscious.

Amy waited another half hour as she watched the beach — there were no late-night walkers on that Melbourne Cup eve. She turned her attention to the heroin and prepared the syringe in near darkness. It was awkward, but somehow she managed to squeeze most of the drug into Helen's arm. Her only regret was that Helen died in her sleep; Amy wanted to look into the eyes of her mother's rapist as the lethal dose killed her.

Amy's reminiscences were interrupted by the flight crew preparing the cabin for landing. She could see the lights of Auckland from the window. By Sunday, Amy would be reunited with her aunt and cousin and together they could plan how to kill Andrew Hackett.

Chapter 66

Dugal Cameron's plane rolled towards the terminal at Melbourne Airport as he switched on his mobile phone. The first voice message was from Jo.

> Hey, Dugal. Sorry to say you're needed as second camera on live cross at The Hatchet's tonight. Ken has all the lights and we've roped in Simmo as the freelance soundie. Drop in my duty-free then head over to South Yarra. Pete can go home. Love your work, babe!

'What a bloody cheek,' Cameron groaned. 'She wants me to deliver her vodka and go straight out to work. Doesn't she know the working day is over in New Zealand?'

'There's your problem, Dugal.' Benson laughed. 'You're back on Jo time and if you're breathing and able to hold a camera, you should be working.'

Cameron shook his head as he started the crew car and searched for the airport parking ticket. 'Have I told you about the days when my old man was a camera op at the ABC?'

'Yes, a thousand times,' Benson sighed, knowing it wasn't going to stop the thousand and first description of the days when the job had fringe benefits.

'If they had to travel anywhere as far as we did, they would get a day off to recover. Plus, they would get per diems – meal allowances and proper breaks. And don't forget the overtime – back in those days they used to pay it.'

Dugal's rant about working conditions fizzled by Flemington. Most if it was wasted as he finally noticed that Benson had tucked in his Apple AirPods.

Kim Prescott felt jaded as she sat in the back of the *Spotlight* crew station wagon as they crawled through Friday afternoon traffic to the interview site at The Hatchet's home. She hadn't slept much the previous night after the emotional roller coaster that was Thursday. The low point was discovering a murder victim, the high point was nailing her professional debut as a reporter. Even a one hour walk along the Yarra River with her pet greyhound couldn't soothe jangled nerves. Sexy Rexy was ready for his bed when they returned to the apartment at close to midnight. But it was a few more hours before sleep shut out Kim's memories of the bloodied body of Eddie Malone.

Kim looked at Ken Withers who was driving. He was still excited, animatedly describing the whole experience for their freelance sound recordist, Robert Simpson, who sat in the front passenger seat.

'Mate, I've seen it all now. Have you ever turned up to record an interview and found the talent has been murdered a few minutes before you knocked on the door? Bloody amazing.'

Simpson laughed. 'You're one up on me there, Kenny, but I wouldn't mind if we found the same thing at The Hatchet's house. You two can be my alibi.'

They all laughed. Kim knew Simpson was forced to become a freelancer after Hackett retrenched all sound recordists in July.

'You won't take a pop at The Hatchet until after the interview, I hope? *If* we find him still standing'

'No need to worry, Kim. I can wait until the killer does the job. Mind you, I won't be held responsible if a light stand *accidentally* falls on his head.'

Kim playfully smacked the back of Simpson's head as Ken chortled. 'Did Jo know she was slipping an assassin past the bodyguards when she booked a freelancer for this job, Simmo?'

'I told her I'd do the job for free if the killer wasted him on camera. If he doesn't get shot or stabbed, I'll settle for a long, slow grilling under hot lights.'

The crew jokes boosted Kim's spirits as they approached Hackett's front door. Ken tugged on her elbow before she could reach for the knocker.

'You do the honours, Simmo. We're a bit gun shy after yesterday.'

Kim was puzzled, but stepped back. Simpson grasped the brass ring that was held in a lion's mouth and gave it two sharp raps. The door opened to reveal a bodyguard with a black pistol pointed at Simpson.

Ken popped his head around the sound recordist's shoulder.

'G'day. We're the camera crew from *Spotlight*. Here to do the live interview tonight. If you lower the gun, Simmo will promise not to piss himself and we'll get set up.'

Kim stifled a smile and stepped inside to find Hackett's security team had expanded to four men. They carried similar pistols as the doorman and they looked ready to use them. There was no sign of the target.

Mitch Stevens introduced himself. 'Are you the only three coming? Mr Hackett was expecting Richard Templeton to do the interview. Are you replacing him?'

'I'm the field producer. My job is to keep an eye on everything. There's no need for Templeton to be here until closer to broadcast, as the boys here set up the cameras, lights and microphones. Another cameraman will arrive about 5.30 and you can tell your guards that an outside broadcast van will here in a few minutes to provide the live link to the studio. I guess you'll want to look inside the truck to make sure there's no deranged killer hiding there.'

Mitch smirked and moved towards the doorman. Kim didn't want to tell him that Templeton's late arrival was a ploy to make The Hatchet nervous. Too much unnecessary chatter before the program might see Templeton lose the edge with his interviewee.

Kim turned her attention to Ken and Simmo who were rearranging furniture to create an impromptu studio. That's when Marianne walked into the room.

'What the hell are you doing? That's a $15,000 Italian sofa you're pushing around like a piece of driftwood at the beach. Why do you have to move anything?'

Ken and Simmo swiftly turned their attention to the cameras and lights, leaving it to Kim to pacify The Hatchet's disgruntled wife. Fortunately, she was saved by Hackett himself.

'It's standard practice Marianne when the crews are in the field. They have to create space for cameras and lights. I'm sure they will be extra careful.'

He turned to Kim. 'Everything will be returned to the same place, won't it?'

"Certainly. The guys have been doing this for years, Mrs Hackett, and they always treat people's property with respect.'

Ken gamely tried to add some reassurance. 'I've shifted so many lounge suites over the years I could start my own business, if I ever get the boot from *Spotlight*.'

The joke fell flat with Hackett, and Marianne wasn't satisfied.

'If it doesn't go back *exactly* the way it was, you might be making a career change sooner than you think.'

Ken shrugged and went back to moving sofas and chairs as Marianne stalked out.

Hackett watched the preparations. 'I expected Marianne to be grumpy. She yelled at me when I agreed to do the interview at home.'

He slumped into an armchair that had been shunted against the wall. 'The bodyguards were against it as well. Too many distractions and extra people they said.

'But I have to do the interview, don't I, especially now that Eddie Malone has given me an alibi for the stuff in Amsterdam. I'm not the kind of person who would rape a woman – if that's what this vendetta is all about.'

Kim didn't have to respond as Marianne returned to summon her husband to the courtyard. The doors remained open and television crew and bodyguards hear the full tirade.

'You're ruining us, Andrew. We're the laughing stock of South Yarra and Toorak – bodyguards and camera crews in our home – and all because of the awful companions you travelled with 30 years ago. I hate this.'

'But this is our best chance to stop it. Right here tonight. I can talk directly to the killer and tell them I wasn't involved in anything. Whatever Tugga's Mob did that has upset him – or her – I wasn't part of. That dropkick tour driver cleared me.'

Kim tuned out the bickering and checked the placement of the lights, cameras and chairs for the interview. She looked across at the senior bodyguard who watched the furious discussion under the replica Roman loggia.

Is he worried that Marianne will do the killer's job instead?

It was into that powder keg that Dugal Cameron arrived on schedule. Everything was in place which gave him a few minutes to catch up on work gossip with Kim.

'I leave the country for a couple of days and you two pick up some bad habits. Find any dead bodies today?'

'Not yet, but there's always hope Mac's promos might create some drama here. When I left the station, he was joking about putting an old air raid searchlight on the house for the killer. At least I think it was a joke.'

Dugal laughed and looked over at his camera colleague who was absorbed with his phone. 'What's Ken up to – telling all his Facebook girlfriends about his 'near-death' experience?'

'You guessed it. I looked over his shoulder a few minutes ago. The tape librarian was worried about him. Ken said *he* was totally safe as *he* had the SAS guarding him.'

Dugal grinned. 'What about Simmo, he looks a bit nervy.'

Kim looked at the sound recordist whose eyes followed the guards whenever they walked through the room. 'Ken played a trick on him by getting him to knock on the door. Simmo almost peed himself when it opened – and a gun was pointed at him. He swears that special forces soldiers drink blood every day.'

Kim's mobile rang which gave Dugal a chance to walk through the set and double check everything was ready. He returned when Kim hung up.

'Templeton's on his way.'

'Are you sure he's up for this? It's going to be the biggest interview of the week – the biggest ever for *Spotlight.*'

'Yep. You wouldn't believe the transformation in him these past two days. Templeton's developed journalistic nous at last. He's turned The Hatchet into his bitch.'

'Really?' Dugal laughed. 'He was always so disinterested in the past. I remember the days when I had to feed him the obvious question lines.'

'Well he's on his game now. Even Mac calls him Boss. Some of the interstate current affairs shows want extracts from the Hackett interview. Templeton is going to charge them $20,000 per 30 second grab – and only for use outside Victoria.'

'Wow! And Pete and I thought we were doing all the hard work in New Zealand.'

The doorbell rang and a minute later Richard Templeton strode in like a Hollywood news anchor.

Templeton kept his distance from Hackett until a few minutes before the six o'clock news. They were like two prize fighters waiting in the shadows for their cue to step into the ring. The news brought them both to the living room. Nothing had changed in the Tugga's Mob investigation since Templeton left the station.

Police in Australia and New Zealand had no suspect and they wouldn't – or couldn't – confirm if Amsterdam was the motive for the murders. From a media perspective the story looked to have stalled. Templeton watched with satisfaction as his news department colleagues played their ace: promoting *Spotlight's* live interview with the only survivor from Tugga's Mob.

At three minutes past six Templeton and Hackett sat in front of the cameras. The lapel microphones were attached by the sound man who then confirmed the audio feed with the station. It was thumbs up all round within a few seconds.

Templeton was relaxed as he listened to Kim's two-minute warning for the cross. This wasn't round one in the *Spotlight* stoush; it was the preliminary – another chance to promote the real encounter after the news program.

Hackett fidgeted as Kim gave the 30 second cue. There was a television monitor on the floor, but the sound was muted as there is a delay between studio broadcast and residential reception. Templeton had his own earpiece with a news feed and communications from the studio director.

Templeton listened and watched as news presenter, Graham Taylor, wrapped up the hunt for the killer of Eddie, Tugga, Drew, Gerry and Helen.

'That leaves just one member of Tugga's Mob from the 1986 tour of Europe. And that is this station's financial controller, Andrew Hackett.'

The camera shot revealed a glum Hackett.

'He is currently preparing to exclusively discuss the threat to his life with Spotlight Executive Producer, Richard Templeton.'

The camera cut to Templeton.

'That's right, Gray. Andrew Hackett is the only survivor from that ill-fated group known as Tugga's Mob. It was the trip of their dreams, yet 30 years later something has sparked a vicious trail of revenge against members of the group and their tour guide, Eddie Malone. As revealed exclusively on *Spotlight* last night we now suspect it has a connection to the gang rape of another passenger, Judy Williams.'

The studio director cut to a two-shot of Templeton and Hackett.

'Mr Hackett denies any involvement with the rape. On *Spotlight*, coming up straight after the news in about 20 minutes, he presents his side of the story. Will it be enough to convince the killer to spare him?'

Templeton held his flinty stare at the camera for 10 seconds until Kim confirmed they were off-air.

Hackett wasn't impressed with the promo. 'That was fucking melodramatic.'

Templeton unclipped the lapel microphone and stood up. 'Not at all, Andrew. You're a television executive and this is about ratings, which boost revenue for the station and your pocket. By the way a reminder about broadcasting basics. Please don't swear like that again when wearing a microphone – you never know when we're live and who might be listening.'

It was 15-love to Templeton. He caught a sour look on Hackett's face as he walked outside to await the next promo. Ten minutes later he resumed his seat for a solo promo during the second commercial break in the news. It was a snappy 15 second tease about a man about to be humbled on live television. Perfect fodder for the masses.

Templeton felt a tingle of excitement, not nerves, as Kim called out a five-minute warning for the program start. He had a copy of the rundown in hand: studio presenter, Todd Waterman, would open *Spotlight* and immediately introduce the protagonists at Hackett's home.

Templeton also had a copy of the questions he had scripted with Mac and Curly. It was a comfort to have them in hand, but Templeton was confident he wouldn't need to refer to them often. He felt well prepared and was ready to push Hackett hard. He was also reassured to know he had plenty of time to grill Hackett. Mac said he could drop another story if the interview was scintillating television. They even talked about spilling the interview into the second segment, a rare event for the show.

Templeton watched Ken and Dugal tinker with their camera settings; a tactic to avoid conversation with Hackett. The four bodyguards covered all the doors. They looked alert, although he noticed one former soldier glanced frequently at Kim.

Professional curiosity or something else?

There was still no sign of Hackett's wife. Kim told him Marianne had disappeared upstairs after throwing a tantrum when the crew arrived. She also said the senior bodyguard made two trips up the stairs – the first with a coffee, the second with a bottle of wine.

Templeton refocused on the job as he listened via the earpiece to the hot-seat changes in the studio's control room. He could tell from the voices that most of the *Spotlight* team were in place. He could still hear the news director call shots on the weather graphics. His final duty was to roll the *Spotlight* titles. He knew Grub would be opening his first beer in the newsroom within 20 seconds.

But for me – it's show time.

In South Yarra, the titles faded from view to reveal a muted Todd Watermann. Templeton nodded along to the introduction via the earpiece, ready and eager for the handover.

'Thanks, Todd. Yes, it's hard to believe what has happened in the week since an expatriate Kiwi landscaper set off from Geelong for his beach house at Apollo Bay, only to be smashed to death on rocks near Lorne.

'Thanks to the dedication and professionalism of the Spotlight current affairs team we now know Tugga Tancred's death was part of a much bigger story. It was an assassination, one of five that we know about.

'The connection is a 1986 European bus tour and the gang rape of a fellow passenger. The victim, Judy Williams, died in New Zealand in 1987.

'We know that rape was committed by Tugga Tancred and three of his friends, colloquially known on the tour as Tugga's Mob.

Tonight, we are about to talk to the only surviving member of Tugga's Mob – the last man standing, so to speak – Andrew Hackett, known to his fellow travellers as Andreas on the tour.'

Templeton turned to address his guest.

'Thanks for inviting us into your home tonight, Andrew. We appreciate your safety is paramount so naturally we won't reveal our location or your security arrangements. I think the first question is, do you feel lucky to be alive after what has happened?'

The director cut to a full frame of Hackett wincing at Templeton's hard-ball opener.

'Of course I'm bloody happy to be alive. I just don't understand why I should be a target for anyone.'

'You were a member of Tugga's Mob during the trip around Europe in 1986. All the others have been murdered. Can you understand why people are asking questions about your safety? Why they might believe you're next in line for termination?'

Templeton could see that Hackett was sweating. He wondered fleetingly if the camera crew positioned the lights to produce this effect.

'I never did anything to anybody to warrant this sort of treatment. I was loosely aligned to the group that was known as Tugga's Mob. We were young, travelling the world for the first time, enjoying ourselves – it's what every other Aussie and Kiwi traveller was doing.

'Like most, I might have drunk too much and been a bit loud during some parties, but I never hurt anyone or did anything criminal or illegal.'

'By criminal, I take it you are referring to what we now know about the gang rape of Judy Williams, who died a year after the tour when she was back in New Zealand.'

The director cut to a single shot of Hackett nodding agreement as Templeton built up to a question. Hackett appeared eager to talk, but Templeton was working to his own agenda.

'Before we get to that we need to establish your association with Judy. You were on intimate terms for much of the tour?'

It was a shirt-front by Templeton, deliberately aimed to knock Hackett off balance. He knew his subject was anxious to confirm his innocence. They would have time for that later.

'Yes, we were friends on the tour. She was a fun, good-looking and intelligent woman, so yeah, we were friends.'

'As in lovers?'

'Occasionally. You have to remember those were different times. Everyone was doing things like that – it was much more casual. You hooked up with people when the mood was right. We didn't have Tinder in those days, the buses and campsite bars were our meeting places. Judy and I knew it wasn't an exclusive arrangement. We both met other people along the way.'

Hackett smiled to draw empathy from Templeton and other men in the television audience. In spite of his best efforts to shrug it off, Hackett was likely being slammed in the Twitterverse. Templeton continued to probe his relationship with Judy.

'But Judy treated you as someone a bit more special than the others — someone she could confide in?'

'We got on well. Judy was easy to talk to and a good listener. She cared about other people. We were genuinely keen to see the famous landmarks and to explore as much of Europe as possible.

'Tugga, Drew, Gerry and Helen could take it or leave it depending on their mood and how far they had to walk to the tourist sites. Most times they went looking for the nearest bars whenever the bus stopped. Judy and I made sure we checked out all the sights.'

'So, she made her concerns known to you about Tugga — about his stalking?'

'Well, not in so many words. She said he was always looking at her. It was a small tour group. We were always around each other — it didn't seem anything was too wrong.'

'But Tugga did more than just look, didn't he?'

'I never saw Tugga do or say anything crude to Judy. Towards the end of the trip Judy said Tugga was annoying her. I told her to tell Eddie. I don't know whether she did, but I never saw anything that suggested Tugga was stalking her.'

'Eddie? This is Eddie Malone, the tour guide and driver who was found butchered on his own doorstep yesterday afternoon by our camera crew. Was Eddie doing a good job on his first tour?'

'Not really. He wasn't a great organiser and got lost several times. But I feel sure he would've done something if Judy complained to him about Tugga?'

'This is the same Eddie Malone who was found in possession of pictures depicting the rape of Judy Williams by two members of Tugga's Mob – Tugga himself and Helen Franks?
'That Eddie Malone?'

The studio makeup couldn't stem Hackett's perspiration and a drop fell from his brow.

'I don't know anything about those pictures or what happened in Amsterdam. The first I heard about it was this week – from you, in fact.'

'Tell us about that last night of the tour, which we now know concluded with the group rape of Judy? How was that possible? How could such a horrible crime occur in the middle of a campsite with hundreds of tourists around?'

'I keep saying I know nothing about the rape. I couldn't, I was out of it.'

'What do you mean by that?'

'It was the last night, so we hit the bar pretty hard at the campsite before Eddie drove us into the city. Many of the passengers wanted a special session on space cakes. It was legal to use marijuana in Amsterdam and space cakes were the big tourist items then. We were young, wanting to try all the experiences – that's the way things were.'

'So, you tried marijuana for the first time?'

'I tried the space cakes, yeah, for the first time.'

'And what happened?'

'Well, not much initially. They didn't seem to do much for us. I remember Tugga telling the café owner he didn't put enough of the good stuff in. We had some more and that's all I remember – until the next day when they tipped me out of my tent during the clean-up.'

'It was Tugga who said there wasn't enough of the active drug ingredient in the cakes?'

'Yes.'

'And was it Tugga who encouraged everyone to try more space cakes? Drugs and potentially other unknown products that were new to most of you?'

'I think so.'

Templeton let that admission sink in with the audience by referring to his notes for the next question. Everyone at home no doubt assumed the same thing: Tugga was getting everyone so stoned they wouldn't know what was happening.

'And you were unaware of how much alcohol or drugs you consumed that evening?'

'Yeah. The last thing I remember was the warm buzz of the café. It felt good, at the time.'

'How did you get back to camp?'

'On the bus, I presume.'

'How was that possible if everyone was in the same state of mind, as in stoned or drunk?'

'Not everyone wanted to try the space cakes, and Eddie was driving, so I guess some other passengers helped the rest of us back to camp.'

'And what about Judy Williams? Can you recall her trying the space cakes that night?'

'Yes. She did. She wasn't spending any time with me those last few days, but she was keen to be a cadet for the night. She was there somewhere.'

'But you don't recall what state of intoxication Judy was in before the tour group returned to camp?'

'No.'

'Or who she was with?'

'I think she might have been with Denise.'

'Who was also trying marijuana-laced cakes for the first time, presumably.'

'I guess so.'

'Which would have left both Judy and other female members of the tour party vulnerable?'

'Everyone was mates with each other, we all got along pretty well.'

'Until that last night, it would seem.'

Templeton had skilfully sliced away Hackett's dignity and reputation for acts committed as a younger man. He was in control, yet he felt there was still some fight left in Hackett.

'Look, I was a young man on an adventure. I over-indulged and flaked out. Am I embarrassed about that now? Yes. At the time it wasn't an issue, it's what young people do.

'But of anything beyond that I have no case to answer. I was not involved in what you're saying was a gang rape. I was asleep, not even able to move. And you know that.

'Eddie Malone told your reporters that before he was killed. Eddie confirmed I had nothing to do with what happened to Judy because I was a 'pile of jelly.' Wasn't that the term he used?'

'I didn't talk to Eddie Malone, but I believe he used a phrase along those lines.'

'So, if I wasn't involved like Tugga and the others apparently were, I shouldn't be a target for anyone. There's no reason to kill me if I didn't rape Judy. That crime is abhorrent to me. If I had known about it I would have supported Judy and gone to the Dutch police.'

Templeton felt Hackett's confidence rise.

'I had no idea Tugga, Drew, Gerry and Helen were so vile. They had a wild side, but it was more about partying. They showed no signs of ever doing something so awful. If someone has served their own form of justice, well, who am I to question that? It didn't involve me then and it shouldn't involve me now.

'My professional career and family life are being disrupted by this innuendo and speculation. I'm paying a bloody fortune for armed bodyguards and I shouldn't have to because there shouldn't be a target on my back. I didn't do anything wrong!'

Templeton could see the smugness surface again in Hackett. Curly, via the earpiece, suggested a new tangent to puncture that renewed confidence.

'So you say, Andrew. Of course, Eddie Malone is no longer with us to confirm that statement. However, his role in the crime is being investigated by police as well.

'Eddie had pictures of the rape; yet claimed he wasn't involved.

'If Eddie wasn't involved – and wasn't a member of Tugga's Mob – why did he end up murdered?

'Could it be the killer was angry with Eddie for not doing something about Tugga when Judy reported the harassment?

'And, on that basis, could the killer still see you as a legitimate target as you were also told about Tugga's stalking and, like Eddie, did nothing about it?'

Hackett blinked as he considered the best way to respond. Templeton seized the delay to tease the audience again.

'We'll come back to Mr Hackett's answer shortly. We'll take a short break and then continue our exclusive interview with the only surviving member of Tugga's Mob.'

Templeton held the camera pose for a few more seconds while raising a finger at Hackett, knowing the punching bag was about to unleash a few expletives.

Kim broke the tension first. 'We're clear. Back to us in two minutes thirty.'

'You fucking prick, Templeton. Are you trying to put a target on me? Why don't you give this fucking lunatic my address as well?'

'Don't tempt me, Andrew. And watch your mouth; the control room can hear you. And you're getting a chance to beg for your life.'

'And you're doing your best to kneecap me by implying anyone who knew Tugga was being a bastard to Judy should suffer the same fate.'

Templeton put his hand to his ear. 'Shut up for a moment, I'm listening to Mac and Curly. We'll be done in another five minutes.'

The South Melbourne studio was full of smiles. The interview was sizzling by current affairs standards: combative and belligerent adversaries going toe to toe. Mac and Curly didn't need Twitter updates to let the interview spill to the next segment. They could almost feel the envy pouring from the opposition current affairs shows. Their competitors were stuck with interviews with the Harvey and Daly families in New Zealand who were outraged that Drew and Gerry were now accused rapists. They all threatened legal action against *Spotlight* for defamation. Mac knew it would never happen under existing law as the dead couldn't be defamed.

The senior producers were prepping Templeton for the next part of the interview when the director's assistant gave the 30-second warning. They sat back with 20 seconds to go and watched him make himself comfortable, ready for the final round.

Both interviewer and guest were framed perfectly, and all was in readiness. The Director's Assistant started the 10-second countdown. The break sting was rolled – and that's when the orderly scene on the impromptu set in South Yarra turned to chaos.

A loud and terrifying explosion startled everyone in the control room and in South Yarra. The camera framed on Hackett showed he was petrified, but not bloodied. An instant later two bodyguards with pistols were at his side.

Mac screamed at the director. 'Cut to the live feed!'

The vision reached the *Spotlight* audience as the guards hoisted Hackett from his chair by the shoulders and dragged him from the room.

More explosions – louder than the first – boomed down the audio line from South Yarra.

Chapter 67

Templeton's delivery didn't falter as overlapping explosions reverberated through the house. Dugal Cameron scooted to the courtyard entrance to capture the necessary vision to explain the unfolding drama. They weren't under assault from a gun-toting maniac – the mayhem was caused by fireworks.

It was November 4, the day before Guy Fawkes Night which wasn't marked in most Australian backyards anymore after public fireworks were banned in the 1980s. Yet South Yarra was lit up by colourful rockets and other explosive items. The fireworks were being launched from the house next door, each new rocket greeted with loud cheers from the neighbours. Templeton won the gratitude of the bodyguards as he praised the professional way they removed their client from potential danger.

Templeton was restricted to the living room as his microphone was hard-wired to a central sound box. However, Dugal had a long cable on his camera and he edged further into the garden for a better shot of the fireworks.

Templeton's commentary segued into a potted history of Guy Fawkes and the failed Gunpowder Plot to blow up the English Parliament in 1605. He was filling time to give Hackett's bodyguards a chance to return him to the interview set.

He could hear encouraging comments from the control room as Curly kept the earpiece circuit open. Advice was coming from all quarters, but Templeton didn't need it; he felt strangely invincible.

The floor monitor showed fireworks as Mitch Stevens returned to the living room. Mac saw him on the second camera.

'Boss, grab the bodyguard and pull him to you for an update.'

Templeton understood what his producer wanted. There was no hand microphone – he had to get Mitch close for his answers to be picked up by the lapel mic.

> 'Joining me now off-camera because we need to protect his identity for security reasons is the leader of the team protecting Andrew Hackett. Sir, can you explain to our viewers what has been happening?'

Mitch understood he would *not* be seen, the television would remain on the fireworks. He played along.

> 'Our client's neighbour is new to Melbourne and didn't realise that backyard fireworks are banned. He's a New Zealander and they still allow them over there.'

> 'That sounds understandable, but Guy Fawkes is tomorrow night – and it's hardly dark outside.'

> 'They have grandchildren back home who always watch Pop's display. He set up Skype for the kids to watch them this year. It's almost 9pm over there and he wanted to let them off before the grandkids went to bed.'

> 'Any reason why he did it tonight?'

> 'Pop has another party tomorrow night – he brought Guy Fawkes forward.'

> 'And you're happy with the way your crew responded?'

> 'Yes, totally. It might seem like an over-reaction to some people at home, but we would rather be safe than sorry. I had better go check on my client, thank you.'

Mitch's exit was perfectly timed as the last of the fireworks faded into the smoky sky and the studio needed to bring Templeton back on camera. There was no sign of Hackett, so Templeton wrapped up and handed back to Todd in the studio. Templeton was delighted to see his colleague was underwhelmed.

Yes, Todd, there's a new threat to your presentation seat.

Mac and Curly guided the studio staff through the rest of the program. They had back-up stories, but Todd promised viewers they would return to South Yarra for any further developments.

Mac didn't care whether Hackett reappeared. He knew the man had been milked for the best content and the audience was hooked for the rest of the show by the fireworks fiasco.

It was a winning performance all round and a certain ratings record. There was no need for a program debrief. The production crew commandeered their favourite bar at the *Rising Sun Hotel* in South Melbourne and the drinks flowed freely. No one had any idea whose company plastic was going to pay for it. They all knew it wouldn't be wise to be the last person standing – or lying – in the bar when it closed.

Chapter 68

Saturday afternoon found Andrew Hackett at his desk in the home office, reading company emails. The information flow from the station had slowed appreciably in the last 36 hours as staff understood a wounded executive didn't need to be kept in the loop. The house was quiet; the bodyguards blended into the background. Hackett knew they were miffed because he gave them a bollocking for overreacting to the fireworks. He overheard two of the guards grumbling in the foyer.

'Does the prick want us to go inquire whether the next bang is a gunshot or a firework? Oh sorry, that man just blew your fucking head off.'

'If he had anything to do with what that Tugga's Mob did in Amsterdam, I'd be inclined to open the front door to the vigilante.'

Hackett understood he was meant to hear the comments. The professionals knew where their client was every second of the day. Secretly, Hackett had mixed feelings over the soldiers' response to the fireworks.

Initially he was impressed by their power and speed as they whisked him from the room and into the garage. He also hoped the next explosions were their colleagues blasting the killer to pieces.

His mood changed to anger when Mitch revealed the fuss was caused by the neighbour's badly-timed backyard display.

Texts from friends taking the piss about the hasty exit didn't help. He hadn't dared return to the interview set as the camera would have shown his agitation. Hackett's public reputation was still important, even when he was on *gardening* leave. He could only hope the killer heard his claim of innocence.

The rest of the house was still as Hackett searched for more business-related activities. Marianne had packed two bags that morning and left to stay with her sister in Brighton. Hackett didn't even object; he'd turned his back on her and stalked to the office. From the window he'd watched Mitch carry Marianne's bags to the car. The bodyguard was in the driver's seat when the car exited the garage and cul-de-sac.

I'm the target – and she gets the close personal protection?

Hackett found it hard to believe it was only a week ago that he was preparing for drinks with Ferdy, and the now ex-Jacinta. Life had been great then; the AFL deal was almost ready to ambush the pompous bastards who'd controlled the rights since the Prime Minister was in kindergarten.

Then came the call from the newsroom about Tugga's death plunge; not that he knew it involved Tugga at the time. Since then it felt like being caught in an avalanche; swept along until the ride came to an end. Hackett wondered when that would be.

His reverie was interrupted by one of the security guards.

'Your neighbour's at the door and wants a word.'

Flanked by the guard, Hackett sullenly shook hands with Bill Ridley.

'I'm sorry, mate. I brought those fireworks over in the container with the household stuff as we always celebrate Guy Fawkes in New Zealand. I would've warned you if I'd known about your security problems – and that we're living next door to the SAS!'

Hackett accepted the apology and tried to usher Ridley on his way. The neighbour was keen to see more ex-soldiers with guns.

'You know us blokes, we love blowing stuff up. Maybe I'll compare notes with your bodyguards one day?' Ridley departed with a hearty laugh.

Chapter 69

The setting for the Waikato post mortem on Sunday was a traditional roast lunch on the deck at the Langer farm. Amy was hungry, but couldn't match Jason for consumption as he tucked away half the leg of lamb, a dozen crispy skin potatoes, carrots, broccoli, peas and quarter of a jug of thick, rich gravy.

'I wish I'd been able to stop at Tugga's crash site, perhaps he didn't die immediately.'

Amy helped herself to more slices of pink lamb. Her appetite never waned during the mission. There were no nightmares or second thoughts. 'It would've been good to have told Tugga that I was Judy's daughter. To let him die knowing she was being avenged.'

Heather gave a faint smile while Jason nodded enthusiastically.

'I wish I'd been there as well. The more we learn about that bastard the more I think he got off lightly. Dragging him out to the middle of the desert and staking him to the ground would have suited me better.'

It was Amy's turn to nod agreement. The discussion turned to Amy's trip to Melbourne from Sydney. She explained how she'd almost been spotted by the bodyguard when she drove past Hackett's house.

'That *was* a bit risky,' Heather said.

'Yeah, but I guess my luck was running so well. It worked out in our favour. I was scouting to get a feel for location, and what might be arranged in Hackett's neighbourhood. I already scoped possibilities for Eddie on the previous visit. My original option was to do a hit-and-run with a vehicle as he returned from the local pub.'

Heather asked the question that had lurked since Thursday.

'Why did you break cover and stab him like that?'

Amy understood Heather wasn't admonishing her. Her aunt and cousin had a right to be wary as the plan was to make each death look like an accident. Eddie's murder removed any doubts the deaths were connected.

'I was doing a walk-past when I saw him scurry from his flat. He went to a public phone box, which was unusual as we know he's got a mobile. I followed him and did some stretches while I listened.

'It was obvious he was talking to someone at that TV station. He arranged to talk about Amsterdam. He wanted five grand. If the TV station paid he might have left town as he's still unemployed. I didn't want to spend a few months searching for him again.'

Heather and Jason nodded at her explanation.

'Besides, everyone knew Tugga's Mob was being targeted by then. Why go through the charade of trying to make it look like an accident?'

Heather wanted more details on Eddie's death.

'How did you get the knife? Surely you weren't walking around with that in your back pocket. The news reports said it was a military fighting knife.'

'It was a KA-BAR. I bought it at a hunting shop in Eden. It was just a backup, in case things went wrong and I was in danger. Don't worry about a record of the purchase. I paid cash and there weren't any security cameras. I said it was for my boyfriend's birthday.'

Heather dropped the Eddie inquiries at that point. Amy was glad as it would have been difficult to explain why she also carried rubber gloves.

The truth was Amy had loved the hands-on approach to killing Drew and Helen. It was a rush to bash Drew's head with the iron bar. She could strike back for Judy. She'd spent hours with Helen before plunging the syringe full of drugs into her arm. Their conversation hadn't brought Amy closer to Helen or cause her to waver. It strengthened her resolve to kill the bitch. Each minute took Helen closer to death and Amy controlled that timeline. It was more fulfilling than shunting Tugga off the cliff.

Amy had wanted the chance for another close kill – to look into someone's eyes as they died – and Eddie provided it. She didn't know how many times she stabbed Eddie until the news report that evening told her.

Would she have continued the attack if Eddie had stayed on his knees? Probably – the rage was strong. She also wanted to linger over his body longer, but the survival instinct kicked in. The job was done – it was time to leave the scene and get rid of the evidence.

Amy tuned back into the family conversation as Jason raised that point.

'And no one will ever find that knife – or any of your clothing?'

'Yeah, I'm sure. I rinsed my clothes at an isolated beach near Werribee and dumped them in different bins around Sunshine and Footscray. I'm sure they get regular rubbish collections. The knife went into the Yarra River near the Port. Who would want to swim in that brown muck?'

The knife story was a lie. Amy didn't want to throw it away. Instead, she made another trip to the long-term car park on her way out of the country on Friday. She hid the knife beneath the dashboard of the utility:

Andrew Hackett still had to be dealt with. It was dangerous to keep a murder weapon. She banked on the investigators never getting close to the ute or the KA-BAR.

Lunch was finished and so was the post mortem. Three targets were dispatched in the latest trip to Australia. The two New Zealand-based members of Tugga's Mob were already a pile of cremated ashes. That left one person. How and when was Hackett going to be murdered?

'You've got the main target, Amy. Tugga's gone and so are the other three who raped Judy. They've been punished. You can afford to bide your time with Hackett – or even let him go altogether.'

'No,' Amy shouted. 'They're all guilty.' She leapt out of her chair, her cheeks flushed, and strode to the railing that surrounded the deck. She gripped it until her knuckles turned white, finally inhaled deeply then turned back to face her aunt and cousin – who were clearly stunned by the outburst.

'Sorry. But they're equally culpable and they deserve the same punishment.,' she said calmly.

'Andreas and Eddie could've stopped Tugga any time before that night in Amsterdam. My mother went to them for help – they did nothing. I can't forgive them.'

Heather didn't respond. Jason brought them back to the practicalities of completing the job.

'We know you're committed, Amy. But I'm with Mum in saying you should wait a while before going after Hackett. He's got four or five bodyguards. Possibly more by now. And he's got deep pockets.'

Amy nodded reluctantly. 'But we don't have to be subtle with Hackett – just safe. There's no need to orchestrate an accident.'

'Yep, I agree but you're not likely to get close to him with a knife. Do you have any ideas?

'No,' Amy conceded. 'I haven't thought that far yet.'

'A gun would be the best way,' Jason continued. 'But have you ever fired one – and how do we get one in Australia? I suppose I could trawl the back streets of Kings Cross again. You've no idea the things I got offered last time. But it'd be way risky. A black-market gun would not be easy to buy, without raising alarms.'

Silence descended on the deck for several minutes before Heather smiled.

'What?' Amy asked.

'You've still got the utility parked at the airport in Melbourne. Why not try the hit-and-run method again? You could wait a couple of months until Hackett's bodyguards have been paid off. Surely, he would go walking in his neighbourhood sometimes. There must be plenty of places to run him down. You could use your time to assess the best place to catch him unaware.'

Amy bristled at the thought of waiting to dish out final justice to Andreas. It was a soft option, not as exhilarating as sticking a knife in his guts.

She wanted to see the pain in his eyes and hear Hackett scream as his life drained away at her feet. But, without a likely weapon or location to commit the final homicide, it would be wiser to spend time on research.

'Okay, I agree it's better to wait until the bodyguards leave – and he thinks his appeal for clemency on Friday night has worked.'

'Nothing's going to spare him, I guarantee you that. We'll just have to think harder about how we get to him.'

'Agreed,' Jason said. 'And I might have an idea that could work.'

'That's encouraging.' Amy returned to the table. 'Tell me more.'

'We want something that can be used at close range and still allows you time to escape undetected.'

Amy and Heather both nodded.

'I have a weapon that should do the job.'

Chapter 70

The first week of November had been the most hectic in *Spotlight's* history. For Mac, the second week felt like the Scenic Railway at St Kilda's Luna Park: chugging to the peak to begin another roller coaster ride.

The Tugga's Mob story stalled over the weekend as *Spotlight* and most of Melbourne's journalists enjoyed their days off. Monday found *Spotlight* back with the pack. With no exclusives to share with the world, they were left with the same story elements as the other channels: police media conferences, interviews with passengers from the ill-fated tour and updates from the crime scenes.

Detectives now controlled the investigation and, after a week of chasing multiple leads, mostly provided by *Spotlight*, they clamped the flow of inside information.

With no fresh bodies, the Tugga's Mob story withered on the news vine. Mac knew the news and current affairs business changed swiftly from feast to famine.

Spotlight's senior producer was surprised to find that the ratings boost generated by Tugga Week, as it became known around the office, was sustained all the way until their summer break at Christmas.

Spotlight's performance broke the trend of a ratings peak being followed by a trough as the hot story drifted from the news cycle. There was a dip in the ratings, but it was only slight. Mac believed viewers who turned to *Spotlight* during Tugga Week enjoyed the presentation – and kept coming back.

The production crew were energised by the experience. Mac encouraged his staff to think laterally, to avoid treating everyday stories as humdrum.

The viewers responded by 'Staying in the Spotlight', a cheesy phrase the station's marketing team coined to capitalise on the success. Twitter conversations buzzed around the city as people commented on the show's promos and stories.

Todd Waterman was told to take an early Christmas holiday so Richard Templeton could sit in as guest presenter. The marketing department polled viewers to find out who looked better in the main chair: Templeton or the incumbent.

But Waterman knew his days at *Spotlight* were numbered. The gossip columns reported that he had been approached by other media organisations. Photographs appeared online of Waterman dining in chic Toorak cafes and restaurants with opposition networks. Waterman would only say that he 'can't comment.' What Waterman neglected to say was that he'd paid for the meals, and there were no return invitations – or phone calls from his dinner guests.

Mac found more story ideas being emailed, posted and called in to the *Spotlight* office. Again, it reflected the performance during Tugga Week. Public relations companies were surprised by the quality stories the crew produced under stressful circumstances. They fed *Spotlight* exclusives as that's where the ratings were going.

Kim was promoted to the reporting staff and continued to shine with features from her contacts. She'd made a big impression during the night of the Eddie Malone coverage – poised and professional 'for one so young', were the oft-quoted words in newspaper reviews – and people wanted to be involved with her stories.

There were regular attempts to resurrect the Tugga's Mob story. By Christmas these efforts were down to weekly updates as the public grew tired of the same talking heads saying they were 'following good lines of inquiry but didn't have any suspects at this stage'.

Mac tried to arrange a story on Hackett's return from *gardening leave* on November 28.

'Fuck off,' was the reply to Mac's email request. Not even pressure from Reg Bradley could get Hackett to participate. Mac noted the financial controller was still accompanied by a bodyguard, the one Jo called a hunk. Mac's contacts told him Mrs Hackett *insisted* her husband retain Mitch Stevens for protection around the house.

Mitch drove Hackett to work and picked him up at night. Where he spent the time in between was everyone's guess.

Hackett launched himself back into the financial issues of the now thriving station. The news and current affairs ratings boost flowed through to other programs and advertising revenue; although it was too late to resurrect his master plan to snare an AFL broadcast deal.

Mac heard that Hackett worked up to 14 hours a day in the office, yet couldn't – or wouldn't – find time to provide *Spotlight* with any interviews about Tugga's Mob. Mac believed Hackett's declaration of innocence must have worked. Or, the killer had a heart after Hackett's humiliation.

By the Christmas party it was a happy station with gallons of booze, food and loud music – the three essential ingredients for media people to unwind.

Mac, a veteran of too many television parties to count, knew the bar was the wisest place to perch. Refills were close at hand, he could watch the shenanigans on the dance floor that spouses should never see, and it ensured *he* never had to apologise for bad conduct when everyone returned in the New Year.

Chapter 71

January 23 found the *Spotlight* staff in the office after several weeks enjoying the Victorian summer. Everyone was refreshed and ready to build on recent successes.

There was a change in personnel – Todd Waterman had departed to 'pursue new opportunities'. Apparently, he'd always dreamt of being Australia's David Attenborough, and planned to raise money for a wildlife documentary series in Tasmania.

Richard Templeton would be *Spotlight's* presenter and executive producer.

The first week back involved preparations and plans for the program's restart the following Monday. Mac kept the production meetings low key; no need for a gee-up until transmission day approached. However, he often reminded the crew about the story that turned around their fortunes: Tugga's Mob. Mac wanted something fresh on the Mob to kick-start the season.

By Wednesday, Mac was even *keener* for a result.

'Curly, any chance of doing a Lazarus with the story for next week?'

'I'm trying, Mac.' Curly flicked through messages on his phone. 'I'm looking for the Lorne cop's details again. He must have an update on the car that shunted Tugga. I'll let you know as soon as I hear anything.'

Mac nodded. 'Anyone seen Hackett around this week, or did the killer slip past the SAS during the holidays?'

That brought a round of laughter and suggestions on how the killer might have dispatched him.

'Was he drowned in the spa pool?' asked Dugal Cameron.

'Nah, probably spit roasted on that ginormous barbecue,' Ken Withers offered. 'You should've seen that thing – big enough to cook a herd of steaks.'

Templeton brought them down to earth. 'Sorry folks. He's alive and still counting his pennies. He's been sunning himself at Portsea and is expected back next week. I think he's currently in Sydney for a few days on some private business with his mate, Ferdy.'

That brought a groan: newsroom emotions can fluctuate wildly. Ken's mood was tougher to flatten. 'Damn, I thought that big target we left on his roof after the interview would have worked by now.'

Mac laughed and was about to call a halt to the mid-week meeting when Curly raised a finger.

'By the way, I'll be out of the office for an hour or so from one o'clock. Doctor's appointment.'

Mac glanced sharply at Curly, who seemed engrossed in his mobile phone contacts.

Appointment? We need a private chat about that!

Mac let it slide as the production crew drifted towards the door, most in search of caffeine. However, they found the way blocked by Jo and her chair. She rattled the kitty that held a solitary coin.

'Right, none of you leaves here until the kitty gets a fiver for coffee and biscuits. My espresso machine's stuffed again and I haven't had caffeine for 12 hours. That gives me a licence to kill cheap bastards.'

Dugal and Ken considered themselves masters at dodging kitty collection. They separated as they approached Jo's chair, giving themselves a 50:50 chance of escape. Jo dumped the kitty in her lap and latched onto their belts as they tried to slip past.

The *Spotlight* crew howled with delight as the camera operators dragged Jo through the office and out the door.

Pete Benson voiced the obvious. 'She'll be back in five minutes with $10; guaranteed.'

Mac was oblivious to the commotion as he watched Curly return to his desk. He walked into Templeton's office and shut the door.

'Boss, we've got a major problem.'

'Already? We've only been back for three days. What's up?'

'It's Curly – I think he's about to be poached by the opposition.'

'Bugger, we can't afford to lose him. Whose shopping list is he on?'

'There's gossip that Nine and Seven are sniffing around for new current affairs staff. And you heard Curly say he's got a doctor's appointment?'

'Yes.'

'The man's fitter than a Mallee bull. A doctor's appointment is the oldest trick in the book – a chance for a lunch meeting with another channel.'

Templeton stood. 'Okay, let's go chat to him. If we can find out what he's been offered, I'll talk to Reg to see if we can match it. Most of the executives and board members love us – might be time to cash in some chips to keep Curly.'

Mac saw that Kim Prescott was at her desk across from Curly as they approached their corner. She wore headphones and Mac presumed she was logging field footage on her terminal. He turned his back to Kim and perched his butt on the edge of Curly's desk.

'Curly, mate, about this doctor's appointment. Is there anything you want to tell us?'

Curly rolled his chair a few centimetres away from the desk. 'Not really guys. Just my annual check-up. He'll tell me to lose a couple of kilos, lay off the late-night tawny ports and get more exercise. Same as the past five years.'

Mac nodded and turned to let Templeton take over. But Curly hadn't finished.

'The good news is they don't have to stick a finger up your bum for the prostate exam any more – all done with blood tests now.'

Both men winced, being of an age to appreciate the advances in modern medicine. Curly saw Kim smirk behind their backs.

'That's good to hear you're keeping an eye on your health, Curly,' Templeton said. 'Would you by chance be looking at improving other areas of your life?'

'Not really, boss. Everything's hunky dory with me.'

Mac twigged that Curly was toying with them.

'So, this doctor's appointment isn't with anyone at Channel 9?'

'What makes you say that, Mac?'

'Apparently, the grapevine has those guys cock-a-hoop about securing the *hottest* producer in Melbourne. That wouldn't be you by any chance?'

Curly didn't say anything.

Mac knew the reality of television – there's always someone with a bigger cheque book. But he wasn't going to let Curly go without a fight.

'Have you signed anything yet, mate?' Mac glanced at Templeton. 'Look, I know we can't compete with the money they offer, but maybe we can work something out?'

Mac looked at Templeton again for reassurance. The Boss nodded. 'You know how important you are to this place – even before Tugga's Week. You've always been our backbone, you love the people around here. You'd hate to leave them for those wankers in suits.'

Curly responded with a wry grin which encouraged Mac to up the ante.

'Look, how about the boss gets on the phone to Reg. You write down what Nine, or Seven, has offered you and we'll see how close we can get. Is that enough to cancel the appointment?'

Curly considered Mac's offer for 10 seconds and then shook his head. 'I can't do that, it would be rude. But it would be good to look at something in writing before that appointment.'

Templeton was delighted. 'No problems, Curly. Give me that figure and I'll go call Reg now.'

Mac beamed. 'Is there anything else I can do to help clinch matters?'

Curly leaned back in his chair and put his hands behind his head. 'There is something, Mac.'

'Anything, mate, within reason – but you know I can't sign the cheques.'

'You could start by repaying me that Kit Kat you stole during Tugga Week.'

Mac's eyes narrowed as he checked his pockets for coins. 'You drive a hard bargain. *Mate.*'

Curly laughed. But Mac wasn't going to be denied. He saw a triumphant Jo peddle her chair back into the office, holding the coffee kitty aloft like a victorious gladiator. Mac dashed across the room and plucked the can from Jo's hand. Jo's howls of outrage were ignored as Mac ran towards the vending machine.

Kim removed her headphones and laughed as Jo did a u-turn to chase Mac. She didn't need to pause the footage on her terminal – it hadn't been playing.

'Well done, Curly. But is it too little too late?'

Curly rolled back to his desk to keep the conversation private. 'The media grapevine must be getting mouldy. I was approached about a job before Christmas.'

Kim nodded, fully understanding Curly's ploy. He explained how the interested channel monitored *Spotlight's* performance throughout November and December, wondering if they could sustain the production standards displayed during Tugga Week. They decided Curly wasn't a flash-in-the pan and offered him a job that involved a $50,000 pay increase.

'It was a great job, Kim, I have to admit that. I would've been their co-ordinating producer for current affairs on the network. Responsible for Sydney, Melbourne, Brisbane and Adelaide.'

'Wow. How could you pass that up – or have you?'

'I thought about it for a few days before saying no. The job's in Sydney. Janine and the kids don't want to move, not after all those renovations we've done in Middle Park. The pay increase would have been swallowed up in the higher cost of living up north. I would have had to commute from bloody Newcastle or Wollongong.'

'I guess that makes sense on a domestic front but, professionally, it's a massive career boost. That wouldn't have been easy to pass up.'

'I'm comfortable with my decision,' Curly grinned. 'Plus, I didn't want to wear a suit to work.'

Kim laughed, knowing there was probably another reason Curly decided to stay – he loved working with the people at *Spotlight*.

She saw Mac return with half a dozen Kit Kats, followed in by Jo who was still ranting about the kitty. Kim mentally filed Curly's bluff for her own contract negotiations in the future and went to work on the field footage.

Chapter 72

Curly devoured the last Kit Kat – which Mac treated as consummation of the deal to stay at *Spotlight* – as Andrew Hackett drove home from the airport. He was alone, as Mitch Stevens, the final bodyguard, was paid off after Christmas when the Hacketts went to their beach house at Portsea. Marianne was angry at the decision to cut Mitch loose as it put more stress on a marriage that had been off-kilter since November. But Hackett refused to let the bodyguard trail them around the trendy summer township. He argued it would remind their beach companions of his recent humiliation. Besides, the threat had passed, Hackett reasoned. There had been no sign of trouble or danger since the killer's frenzied attack on Eddie Malone.

Hackett parked the Beemer in the driveway as the stop-off at home was temporary. Susie, the office temp who covered Zara's holiday, had arranged to deliver important financial documents that needed his approval. Hackett refused to visit South Melbourne. He wanted to drop his suits in South Yarra and return to Portsea for the last days of his holiday. Hackett told the temp that if she wasn't at his home with the paperwork by one o'clock it would have to wait until Monday.

Hackett was peeved about the delay, but he wasn't particularly looking forward to the reunion with Marianne at the beach house. For 15 years it only took a few days in the sun and surf to wash away any lingering stresses of the previous year. Hackett and Marianne would regularly entertain friends with barbecues, or join them for boisterous dinners at Portsea restaurants. But not this season. There were few invites to accompany regular dining companions. Their own invitations to dinner either clashed with other engagements, or were ignored.

Marianne blamed Hackett for their loss of social status and that placed more tension on the relationship.

The trip to Sydney had come as a saviour for both. Ferdy wanted to buy a new business in Bondi and he begged Hackett to help with due diligence on the company's books. The work was expected to take until Friday. It took Hackett a day to work out the business was a dog and he advised Ferdy to put away his cheque book. Ferdy agreed and turned his attention to the surf and topless ladies at the beach.

Consequently, Hackett found himself back in Melbourne two days earlier than expected. He didn't call Marianne as he believed the news would be met with indifference. The call to the office was a check for anything urgent as he knew Reg Bradley had returned on January 16.

Hackett was being more conciliatory to the CEO and fellow executives since his Tugga's Mob problems. The financial statements showed the station was doing well and Hackett couldn't claim the credit. The current affairs and news departments were leading the revival.

Hackett was removing his bags from the back of the car when a rusty utility drove into the cul-de sac and parked outside his property. He saw it was driven by a blonde woman. She called through the open passenger window.

'Mr Hackett?'

'Yes, are you Susie?'

'Yes, sorry about this rust bucket. My boyfriend took my car this morning because it was first in the driveway.'

Susie was attractive, and vaguely familiar, but flirting with her wasn't on Hackett's mind. He wanted to complete the company business and get back to Portsea.

'Follow me and we'll get those documents signed.'

Susie nodded, slammed the driver's door and reached into the back of the ute as Hackett fumbled with his keys.

He unlocked the door and raised his hand to the alarm panel – it wasn't on. Hackett was sure he set it on Monday. He dropped his bag and walked into the living room. Nothing was out of place or obviously missing. There had been no communication between husband and wife since the weekend. He assumed Marianne might have made a fleeting visit to home to collect a dress, or have lunch with a girlfriend.

The cleaner was told to take a break; but maybe she'd come back for something. He didn't even know her name.

Hackett crossed to the French doors that led to the courtyard and discovered they were unlocked. That was weird.

Marianne could be lax with the security alarm, but leaving doors unlocked was careless. He pushed them open and walked out, hoping to find the cleaner or at least a logical explanation for the house being unlocked.

He glanced back at Susie, still standing with a box in her arms, then checked there was no one in the courtyard.

Stuff it. Let's sign these bloody documents.

Hackett turned to the living room to speak to–.

He froze.

Susie stood five metres away with a crossbow aimed at his chest.

Chapter 73

Amy was ready to shed the Susie persona. She needed Hackett to know she was Judy William's daughter and his executioner.

The rage coursed through her body again. It was a familiar, comfortable feeling by now and she welcomed the steely resolve it provided.

Hackett was the last vile member of Tugga's Mob. In seconds she would fire a crossbow bolt through his heart – and her mother would be avenged.

Everything had fallen into place from the moment Jason suggested a crossbow would be the best weapon to kill Hackett. It was silent, deadly at close range, and relatively easy to learn. Amy couldn't buy one at a sports store in Victoria without a licence. Jason's solution was to steal one from a farming colleague with poor security. It took him five minutes and a bolt cutter at the Ballarat property to obtain the perfect weapon.

Amy pointed the 16-inch bolt at Hackett's chest and watched him squirm and sweat. His underarms were already saturated, his eye brows and forehead glistened.

Hackett's terror was a joy to behold.

Hackett's gatekeeper, Zara, had also inadvertently set up her boss. Amy befriended Zara at a South Melbourne café in early December. The plan had been to get inside knowledge of Hackett's habits. But

Zara delivered more than Amy expected a few days before Christmas: when she asked the likeable and unemployed Kiwi to cover her absence from the office during the holidays.

'There won't be much to do – answer the phone and check the mail,' Zara assured.

Hackett's call on the way from the airport today had sealed his fate. The ute with the crossbow was in Zara's space in the station's underground car park.

And Hackett was now a few steps away – Amy couldn't miss.

Hackett fought the urge to pee as he stared at the crossbow. His life couldn't end like this.

'Why do you want to kill me? I've never hurt you – I don't even know you.'

But Tugga's Mob and Eddie really were killed by a woman!

The woman stood rock still.

Should he run? But where? The maniac blocked the only escape through the living room. Hackett was sure she would fire if he moved. 'Who the fuck are you?'

'Remember Judy Williams – your girlfriend from the trip?'

'She wasn't my girlfriend. Judy knew that. We were what you'd call friends with benefits these days. That's the way things happened then.'

'Those *things* have consequences – and I'm one of them.'

Hackett stared for a few more seconds. 'Judy had a baby?'

'Yes.'

'From the trip?

'Yes.'

'And the father?'

'No bloody idea,' Amy shouted and stepped towards Hackett.

He backed up, into the courtyard.

'I don't know.' she said. 'And I don't want to know. The possibility that you're my father isn't going to save you.'

'But why kill me?' Hackett pleaded. 'I had nothing to do with what happened in Amsterdam. I was too drunk and stoned to even stand up. I wasn't with Tugga's Mob at the campsite. You must have seen me on the TV – I told everyone I wasn't part of it.'

'You could have stopped it,' Amy screamed. 'You and Eddie are just as evil as Tugga because you knew – and did nothing. Judy told you that Tugga was stalking her, sexually harassing her, yet you and Eddie did nothing.

'I read her diary. She described every disgusting thing that Tugga did. He and his mates were animals, yet you treated them as your best mates. You could've prevented my mother from being gang-raped, but you ignored her. You're as guilty as the rest of them.'

Hackett saw a look in her eyes; he was about to be killed.

With a bloody crossbow?

He retreated another step but found he was trapped against a boundary fence. Amy stood in the middle of the courtyard. She sighted the bolt that couldn't miss Hackett's heart.

'No! Don't kill me – please, don't kill me.'

Hackett heard a blast and was slammed against the fence. A numbing sensation in his upper left chest was followed by excruciating pain.

I've been shot! Fuck. I've been bloody shot.

Hackett's right hand moved to cover the wound, to prevent his life draining away on his own courtyard. But instead of an open wound, his hand found the bolt below his collar bone.

And yet, Hackett couldn't match the blast sound with the aluminium shaft protruding from his shoulder. He was still alive.

But where was–?

The blonde was face down in the courtyard, her white blouse covered in blood.

Oddly, the sound of a sobbing woman drew Hackett's attention to the upper level of the house. He raised his eyes to the master suite. Mitch Stevens stood at Hackett's bedroom window with a black pistol pointed at the woman on the ground. The former bodyguard was naked. Beside him was Marianne, her nakedness covered by a bed sheet.

Hackett screamed as the pain radiated through his body.

Chapter 74

Jockey Graham nursed his pint in the bar of his favourite pub in Te Awamutu in February as he watched the six o'clock news. There were 23 drinkers in the bar, yet conversation and beer consumption were on hold as all eyes were glued to the television. It showed Heather and Jason Langer entering the Hamilton police station in handcuffs. They were accused of being accessories in the murders of Drew Harvey and Gerry Daly, the men from Tugga's Mob.

Heads shook with incomprehension; Heather and Jason were part of the fabric of the district. Surely this couldn't be true.

Jockey was the only person with an inkling the police were on the money. He listened as a TVNZ reporter outlined the police case against the Waikato family.

Their connection to the pre-Christmas murders was through Amy Stewart: the woman shot in the back by a bodyguard while trying to execute the final member of Tugga's Mob.

Everyone knew the story – and the climax in January. Andrew Hackett was shot with a crossbow while his wife bonked the former bodyguard in their bedroom upstairs. That tryst is what saved Hackett as the bodyguard fired his 9mm pistol a millisecond before Amy released the bolt.

The bullet struck Amy in the back and deflected her aim: the bolt slammed into Hackett's left shoulder. It missed his heart and lungs and penetrated the clavicular portion of the pectoralis major muscle. Hackett survived because of the bodyguard's combat medical training. Victorian Police searched the vehicle Amy drove to Hackett's home and found a hunting knife. Forensic tests confirmed it was used to murder former tour bus driver, Eddie Malone.

The TV reporter said police investigations revealed Amy's family connection with the Langers. New Zealand detectives interviewed them again and Heather tearfully disclosed Amy's vendetta for her dead birth mother.

Jockey sipped his beer as the news story finished.

They finally got justice for Judy, but they're going to prison.

He felt sorry for the Langers, but was more concerned for his own future. Would the Langers' arrest bring repercussions? Jockey believed he caused the trail of revenge with his drunken confession to Jason. Did that make him legally culpable in some way? Would Jason dob him in to the cops?

He saw Tugga drown Judy and did nothing to save her. Would the cops find a way to punish his cowardice?

Jockey mentally prepared himself in case the detectives called him to the station.

Admit nothing. I never spoke to Jason.

Jockey had stuck to the same story about finding Judy's body for 30 years – except for one drunken night, and there were no witnesses to that conversation.

Imagine what Jason and his kin might have done if I told him what really happened at the river!

Jockey saw and heard everything from his camouflaged hide.

Judy was outraged the giant, Tugga, had followed her home from London. When Judy said Tugga would never get anything from her the big fella laughed so hard tears rolled down his cheeks.

Jockey recalled Judy was puzzled by Tugga's mirth and demanded to know what the joke was. Tugga then showed Judy something from his shirt pocket.

That's when she became hysterical and lashed out at Tugga, 'you animals made me pregnant.'

Jockey held his breath as Tugga gripped Judy by her blonde ponytail and demanded an explanation.

'Where's the baby?'

Judy said, 'you'll never know because I aborted it'.

Tugga threw Judy into the river. Then he followed her in and held her head under the water, calling her a bitch for killing his baby.

Judy struggled, real hard, but Jockey couldn't muster the courage to save her, especially when another life – his own – was at risk.

Tugga was too big and too strong. He'd kill him too.

Judy soon stopped thrashing.

Jockey remembered Tugga waded to the bank where he sat for a few minutes with a horrified look on his face. He finally stumbled away.

Those few minutes haunted Jockey for half his life.

He only told one person about that day and it led to more death and misery.

No one else should ever know about Judy's final moments at the river.

Jockey lifted his pint of beer and sipped as he waited for the sports segment on the television news.

Epilogue

Curly Rogers sat at his work computer in March to write a submission to station management about their coverage of Heather and Jason Langer's trial in New Zealand. No date had been set, but Curly was being proactive.

It was *Spotlight's* story from the start and they should be there at the end when the co-conspirators faced justice.

Curly was going through the motions with the memo, as he expected The Hatchet to say no.

He also expected the station CEO would veto Hackett's decision, as *Spotlight's* audience ratings were so high. The scuttlebutt on the media grapevine had Andrew Hackett looking for a new job, probably in Sydney.

Curly suggested Kim Prescott should go to New Zealand as she was already regarded as one of *Spotlight's* best reporters, only four months since her on-air debut at the Eddie Malone murder scene. Curly was about to tackle the tougher issue of calculating trip costs when his mobile phone rang. The number was familiar.

'Hello Jim, how goes life on the coast at Lorne? You finally got your investigation into Tugga's crash completed?'

'I have, Curly,' responded Constable Jim Laidlaw. 'And reasonably quick by our standards if I don't mind saying. With so many bodies involved here and in NZ, the bosses are keen to tidy up all the loose ends.'

'I take it that your inquiry confirmed Tugga was shunted off the Great Ocean Road by Amy? But with her being dead, it leaves Heather and Jason Langer to take the blame. If only they weren't facing a million charges in New Zealand?'

'Right on all counts. We could charge Jason with conspiracy to murder, but I don't think we'll ever see him extradited to face charges.'

Curly assumed that was frustrating; Laidlaw's inspired detective work would never be presented to a court.

'I appreciate the heads-up, Jim. When do the Melbourne spin doctors release their statement on Tugga's crash – this afternoon or tomorrow?'

'First thing tomorrow, but there's some new information which won't be included in their Tugga's Mob update.'

'Oh?' Curly reached for a pen. Could Laidlaw point him in the direction of another exclusive?

'It turns out a couple of the participants in this sorry saga shared a rare blood group – AB.'

Curly was excited. 'I'm listening, Jim,'

'It prompted a detective to waste money on a DNA test. No need for it really – apart from curiosity.'

Curly laughed. 'Damn, Jim, you know how to tease. Come on, spit it out. Whose blood was it and what did the DNA results show?'

'They tested the killer and Hackett – Amy was *his* daughter.'

About the Author

Stephen Johnson is an Australian-born television news and sports producer who has swapped the TV studio for a writer's garret overlooking the Tamaki Estuary in Auckland.

Stephen's journalism career started with a cadetship at the Geelong News in 1978. It progressed to the ABC as a reporter, producer and director before an early midlife crisis prompted him to head overseas.

He returned to the news desk at Channel 7 in Melbourne, then TVNZ, TV 3, Touchdown Productions, Sky Sport and the New Zealand Racing Board. His inductee videos for the New Zealand Racing Hall of Fame were displayed at the Museum of New Zealand Te Papa Tongarewa.

Stephen's debut novel, *Tugga's Mob,* was inspired by his three seasons working as a tour guide on double-decker buses around Europe in the '80s; but written after he convinced his wife to sell their empty nest in 2016 to buy 'Kwozzimoto', a seven-metre motorhome.

Tugga's Mob was her annoying companion on a 33,000km tour of Europe, through a dozen countries, and a hundred campsites.